Ruth Rendell

THE BRIDESMAID

TO FEAR A
PAINTED DEVIL

ARROW

This edition published by Arrow in 1998
an imprint of The Ranodom House Group
20 Vauxhall Bridge Road, London SW1V 2SA

Papers used by Random House UK Ltd are
natural recyclable products made from wood
grown in sustainable forests. The manufacturing
process conform to the environment regulations
of the country of origin.

A catalogue record for this book is available from
the British Library

Printed in Australia by McPherson's Printing Pty Ltd

ISBN 0 099 27944 4

THE BRIDESMAID

For Don

1

Violent death fascinates people. It upset Philip. He had a phobia about it. Or that was what he called it to himself sometimes, a phobia for murder and all forms of killing, the wanton destruction of life in war and its senseless destruction in accidents. Violence was repellent, in reality, on the screen, in books. He had felt like this for years, since he was a small child and other children pointed toy guns and played at death. When it had begun or what began it he didn't know. A curious thing was that he wasn't cowardly or squeamish, he was no more nor less frightened by it than anyone else. It was rather that unnatural death neither entertained him nor exercised a ghoulish attraction. His reaction was to shy away from it in whatever form it might be presented to him. He knew this was unusual. He hid his phobia, or tried to hide it.

When the others watched television he watched it with them and he didn't close his eyes. He had never got into the way of denouncing newspapers or novels. But the others knew and had no particular respect for his feelings. It didn't stop them talking about Rebecca Neave.

Left to himself, Philip would have taken no interest in her disappearance, still less speculated about her. He would have turned off the set. Of course he would probably have turned it off ten minutes before and avoided Northern Ireland, Iran, Angola, and a train crash in France as well as a missing girl. He would never have looked at the photograph of her pretty face, the smiling mouth and eyes screwed up against the sun, the hair blown by the wind.

*

Rebecca disappeared at about three on an autumn afternoon. Her sister spoke to her on the phone on Wednesday morning and a man who was a friend of hers, a new friend who had been out with her just four times, phoned her at lunchtime on that day. That was the last time her voice was heard. A neighbour saw her leave the block of flats where she lived. She was wearing a bright green velvet tracksuit and white trainers. That was the last anyone saw of her.

Fee said, when the girl's face appeared on screen, 'I was at school with her. I thought I knew the name. Rebecca Neave. I thought I'd heard it before.'

'I've never heard it. You've never said you had a friend called Rebecca.'

'She wasn't a friend, Cheryl. There were three thousand of us at that school. I don't suppose I even spoke to her.' Fee was staring intently at the screen while her brother made as conscious an effort not to look. He had picked up the newspaper and turned to an inside page where the Rebecca Neave story had not penetrated. 'They must think she's been murdered,' Fee said.

Rebecca's mother appeared and made an appeal for news of her missing daughter. Rebecca was twenty-three. Her job was teaching ceramics to adult classes but needing to supplement her income, she advertised her services as a baby-sitter and house-sitter. It seemed possible that someone had phoned in answer to her advertisement. Rebecca had made an appointment for that evening – and kept it. Or that was what her mother believed.

'Oh, the poor woman,' said Christine, coming in with coffee on a tray. 'What she must be going through. I can just imagine how I'd feel if it was one of you.'

'Well, it's not likely to be me,' said Philip who was well-built though thin, and six feet two. He looked at his sisters. 'Can I turn this off now?'

'You can't stand anything like that, can you?' Cheryl had a ferocious scowl she seldom bothered to restrain.

'She may not have been murdered. Hundreds of people go missing every year.'

'There'll be more to it than we know,' Fee said. 'They wouldn't make all this fuss if she'd just gone off. It's funny, I remember her being in the same crafts group as I was for O Levels. They said she wanted to go on and be a teacher and the rest of them thought it was funny because all they wanted was to get married. Go on, turn it off, Phil, if you want. There isn't going to be any more about Rebecca anyway.'

'Why can't they put nice things on the news?' said Christine. 'You'd think they would be just as sensational. It can't be that there aren't any nice things, can it?'

'Disasters are news,' said Philip. 'but it might be an idea to try your kind for a change. They could have a list of today's rescues, all the people saved from drowning, all those who'd been in car crashes and didn't get killed.' He added on a more sombre note, 'A list of kids who haven't been abused and girls who've got away from attackers.'

He switched off the set. There was a positive pleasure in seeing the picture dwindle and swiftly vanish. Fee hadn't gloated over Rebecca Neave's disappearance but speculation about it obviously interested her far more than discussing one of Christine's 'nice things' would have. He made a rather artificial effort to talk about something else.

'What time are we all supposed to be going out tomorrow?'

'That's right, change the subject. That's so like you, Phil.'

'He said to be there by about six.' Christine looked rather shyly at the girls and then back to Philip. 'I want you all to come out into the garden a minute. Will you? I want to ask your advice.'

It was a small bleak garden, best at this time of the day when the sun was setting and the shadows were long.

9

A row of Leyland cypresses prevented the neighbours from seeing over the fence at the end. In the middle of the grass was a circular slab of concrete and on the concrete stood a birdbath and a statue, side by side. There was no moss growing on the concrete but weeds pushed their way through a split under the birdbath. Christine laid her hand on the statue's head and gave it a little stroke in the way she might have caressed a child. She looked at her children in that apprehensive way she had, half-diffident, half-daring.

'What would you say if I said I'd like to give Flora to him for a present?'

Fee seldom hesitated, was invariably strong. 'You can't give people statues as presents.'

'Why not, if they like them?' Christine had said. 'He said he liked her and she'd look nice in his garden. He said she reminded him of me.'

Fee said as if their mother hadn't spoken, 'You give people chocolates or a bottle of wine.'

'He brought me wine.' Christine said this in a wondering and gratified tone, as if taking a bottle of wine to the house of a woman you were having dinner with, was exceptionally thoughtful and generous. She moved her hand along Flora's marble shoulder. 'She's always reminded me of a bridesmaid. It's the flowers, I expect.'

Philip had never looked closely at the marble girl before. Flora was just the statue which had stood by the pond in their garden at home ever since he could remember. His father, he had been told, had bought her while he and Christine were on their honeymoon. She stood about three feet high and was a copy in miniature of a Roman statue. In her left hand she held a sheaf of flowers, with the other she reached for the hem of her robe, lifting it away from her right ankle. Both her feet were on the ground yet she seemed to be walking or dancing some sedate measure. But it was her face which was particularly beautiful. Looking at her, Philip realised that generally he didn't find the faces of ancient Greek or Roman statues attractive. Their heavy jaws and long bridgeless noses gave them a forbidding look. Standards of beauty had changed perhaps. Or else it was something more delicate that appealed to him. But Flora's face was how a beautiful living girl's might be today, the cheekbones high, the chin round, the upper lip short and the mouth the loveliest conjunction of tenderly folded lips. It was like a living girl's but for the eyes. Flora's eyes, extremely wide apart, seemed to gaze at far horizons with an expression remote and pagan.

'I've thought for ages she was wasted here,' said Christine. 'She looks *silly*. Well, what I really mean is, she makes the rest of it look silly.'

It was true. The statue was too good for her surroundings. 'Like putting champagne in a plastic cup,' said Philip.

'That's it exactly.'

'You can give her away if you want to,' Cheryl said. 'She's yours. She's not ours. Dad gave her to you.'

'I think of all the things as being ours,' said Christine.

'He's got a lovely garden, he says. I think I'd feel better about Flora if I knew she was in her proper setting. Do you know what I mean?'

She looked at Philip. No amount of proselytising on the part of her daughters could persuade her of the equality of the sexes, no pressure from newspapers, magazines or television convince her. Her husband was dead so she looked to her son, not her eldest child, for decisions, rulings, counsel.

'We'll take her with us tomorrow,' Philip said.

It didn't seem so very important at the time. Why should it? It didn't seem one of those life or death decisions like whether or not to marry, have a child, change a career, have or not have the vital surgery. Yet it was as significant as any of those.

Of course it was to be a long time before he thought

of it in those terms. He tested Flora's weight, lifting her up an inch or two. She was as heavy as he had expected. He suddenly found himself thinking of Flora as a symbol of his mother, who had come to his father on his marriage and was now to be passed on to Gerard Arnham. Did that mean Christine was contemplating marrying him? They had met the previous Christmas at Philip's uncle's office party and it had been a slow courtship, if courtship it was. That might in part have been due to the fact that Arnham was always going abroad for his company. Arnham had only once been to this house, as far as Philip knew. Now they were going to meet him. That made it seem as if things were taking a more serious turn.

His mother said, 'I don't think we'd better take Hardy.' The little dog, the Jack Russell Christine had named after Hardy Amies because she liked the clothes he designed, had come into the garden and stood close beside her. She bent down and patted his head. 'He doesn't like dogs. I don't mean he'd be cruel to them or anything.' She spoke as if an antipathy to dogs often implied a willingness to torture them. 'He just doesn't care for them much. I could tell he didn't like Hardy that evening he was here.'

Philip went back into the house and Fee said, 'Seeing Flora reminded me Rebecca Neave once made a girl's head.'

'What do you mean, made a girl's head?'

'At school. In pottery. She made it in clay. It was lifesize. The teacher made her break it up, she wouldn't have it put in the kiln, because we were supposed to be making pots. And, just imagine, she may be lying dead somewhere now.'

'I'd rather not imagine, thanks. I'm not fascinated by these things the way you are.'

Fee took Hardy on to her lap. He always came wooing people at this hour, hoping for a walk. 'It's not that I'm fascinated, Phil. We're all interested in murder and violence and crime. They say it's because we've got elements of it in ourselves. We're all capable of murder, we all sometimes want to attack people, strike them, hurt them.'

'I don't.'

'He really doesn't, Fee,' said Cheryl. 'You know he doesn't. And he doesn't like talking about it, so shut up.'

He was carrying Flora because he was the only male among them and therefore presumably the strongest. Without a car it was a terrible journey from Cricklewood to Buckhurst Hill. They had got the bus down to Kilburn station, the tube from Kilburn to Bond Street and there waited ages for a Central Line train. It had been just before four when they left the house and it was ten to six now.

Philip had never been to this part of metropolitan Essex before. It reminded him a little of Barnet where living had been gracious and the sun seemed always to shine. There were houses in the street they were walking up but they were hidden by hedges and trees and it might have ben a country lane. His mother and sisters were all ahead of him now and he hurried up, shifting Flora on to the other side. Cheryl, who had nothing to carry but was wearing high heels with her very tight jeans, said in a moaning way, 'Is it much further, Mum?'

'I don't know, dear. I only know what Gerard told me, up the hill and the fourth turning on the right.' Christine was always saying things were nice. 'Nice' was her favourite word. 'It's a very nice part, isn't it?'

She was wearing a pink linen dress with a white jacket. She had white beads and pink lipstick and looked the sort of woman who would scarcely stay single for long. Her hair was soft and fluffy and the sunglasses hid the lines under her eyes. Philip had noticed that though she had her wedding ring on – he had never seen her without it – she had left off her engagement ring. Christine prob-

13

ably had some unexpressed dotty reason for doing this, such as that engagement rings represented the love of a living husband while wedding rings were a social requirement for widows as well as wives. Fee, of course, was wearing her own engagement ring. The better to show it off, Philip conjectured, she carried something she called a clutch bag in her left hand. The formal dark blue suit with a too-long skirt made her look older than she was, too old, Arnham might think, to be Christine's daughter.

He hadn't taken any particular pains over his appearance. His efforts had been concentrated on getting Flora ready. Christine had said to try and get that green stain off the marble and he had had a go with soap and water but unsuccessfully. She had provided tissue paper to wrap the statue in. Philip had wrapped her in a second layer of newspaper, that morning's paper, which had the Rebecca Neave story spread all over the front page. There was another photograph of Rebecca and an account of how a man, unnamed, but aged twenty-four, had spent all the previous day with the police 'helping them with their enquiries'. Philip had quickly rolled the statue up in this paper and then bundled it into the plastic bag that Christine's raincoat had been in when it came back from the cleaners.

This hadn't perhaps been a good idea, for it made a slippery package. Flora kept slipping and having to be hoisted up again. His arms ached from shoulder to wrist. The four of them had turned, at last, into the road where Arnham lived. The houses weren't detached as theirs in Barnet had been but terraced in curving rows, 'town houses' with gardens full of shrubs and autumn flowers. Philip could see already that one of these gardens would be a more suitable setting for Flora. Arnham's house was three-storeyed, with Roman blinds at the windows and a brass lion's head knocker on the dark green Georgian front door. Christine paused at the gate with a look of wonder.

'What a pity he's got to sell it! But it can't be helped, I suppose. He has to share the proceeds with his ex-wife.'

It was unfortunate, Philip thought later, that Arnham opened the front door just at the moment when Cheryl said loudly, 'I thought his wife was dead! I didn't know he was divorced. Isn't that yucky!'

Philip would never forget his first sight of Gerard Arnham. His first impression was that the man they were visiting was far from pleased to see them. He was of medium height, strongly built but not fat. His hair was grey but thick and sleek and he was good-looking in what Philip thought of, without being able to explain why, as a sort of Italian or Greek way. His handsome features were fleshy and his lips full. He wore cream-coloured slacks, a white shirt with an open neck and a lightweight jacket in a large but not over-bold check of dark blue and cream and brown. The look on his face changed from dismay to an appalled disbelief that made him briefly close his eyes.

He opened them again very quickly and came down the steps and hid whatever it was that was upsetting him under hearty politeness. Philip expected him to kiss Christine, and perhaps Christine expected this too for she went to him with her face held up, but he didn't kiss her. He shook hands with everyone. Philip put Flora down on the step while he shook hands.

Christine said, 'This is Fiona, my eldest. She's the one I told you is getting married next year. And this is Philip who's just got his degree and is training to be an interior designer and this is Cheryl – she's just left school.'

'And who's this?' Arnham said.

The way Philip had set Flora down she did look like a fifth member of their party. Her wrappings were coming off. Head and one arm poked out of the hole in the cleaning bag. Her serene face whose eyes seemed always to be looking beyond you and into the distance, was now entirely uncovered as was her right hand in which she held the sheaf of marble flowers. The green stain on her neck and bosom had suddenly become very noticeable as had the chip out of one of her ears.

'You remember her, Gerard. She's Flora who was in my garden and you said you liked her so much. We've brought her for you. She's yours now.' When Arnham didn't say anything, Christine persisted, 'For a present. We've brought her for you because you said you liked her.'

Arnham was obliged to make a show of enthusiasm but he didn't do it very well. They left Flora out there and went into the house. Necessarily, because there were four of them and the hallway was narrow so that they had to proceed singly, they seemed to *troop* into the house. Philip felt glad they at least hadn't brought Hardy. This was no place for a dog.

It was very beautifully decorated and furnished. Philip always noticed these things. If he hadn't he probably wouldn't have been taking the training course at Roseberry Lawn Interiors. One day, a day that was necessarily far off, he would like a living room in his house like this one with ivy-green walls and drawings in narrow gilt frames and a carpet whose glorious deep soft yellow reminded him of Chinese porcelain seen in museums.

Through an archway he could see into the dining room. A small table was laid for two. There were two pink table napkins in two tall pink glasses and a single pink carnation in a fluted vase. Before he could fully realise what this meant Arnham was ushering them all into the garden by a back way. He had picked up Flora, very much as if, Philip thought, he feared she might dirty his carpet, and was swinging her along like a bag of shopping.

Once outside he dumped her in the flowerbed that was the border of a small rockery and making an excuse, disappeared into the house. The Wardmans stood on the lawn. Fee looked at Philip behind Christine's back and behind Cheryl's back, put up her eyebrows and gave the kind of satisfied nod that is the equivalent of a thumbs-up sign. She was indicating that she approved of Arnham, that Arnham would do. Philip shrugged his shoulders. He turned to look at Flora once more, at the marble face which certainly wasn't Christine's face or that of any real woman he had ever known. The nose was classical, the eyes rather too wide apart, the soft lips too indented, and there was a curiously glazed look on the face as if she were untroubled by normal human fears and doubts and inhibitions.

Arnham came back apologising and they set Flora up in a position where she could contemplate her own reflection in the waters of a very small pond. They wedged her in place between two grey stones over which a golden-leaved plant had spread its tendrils.

'She looks just right there,' said Christine. 'It seems a shame she can't stay there for ever. You'll just have to take her with you when you move.'

'Yes.'

'I expect you'll have another nice garden wherever it is.'

Arnham didn't say anything. There was a chance, Philip thought, for he knew his mother, that Christine would say a formal farewell to Flora. It would be like her. He wouldn't have been surprised to hear her say goodbye and bid Flora be a good girl. Her silence gratified him, the dignified way she preceded Arnham back into the house. He understood. There was no need to say goodbye to someone you would soon be living with for the rest of your life. Had anyone else seen or was he alone in noticing that the little table in the dining room had been stripped of cloth, silver, glass and pink carnation? That was why Arnham had come back into the house, to clear this table. Much was made plain to Philip. Christine had been expected on her own.

His mother and sisters seemed not to understand that

any social solecism had been committed. Cheryl sprawled on the settee, her legs apart and stuck out on the rug. She was obliged to sit like that, of course, because her jeans were too tight and her heels too high to permit of bending her knees and setting the soles of her feet on the floor. Fee had lit a cigarette without asking Arnham if he minded. As she looked round for an ashtray, conspicuously absent among all the variety of ornaments, little cups and saucers, china animals, miniature vases, and while she waited for Arnham to come back with one from the kitchen the inch of ash fell off the end of her cigarette on to the yellow carpet.

Arnham didn't say anything. Fee began talking of the missing girl. She was sure the man who had been helping police with their enquiries must be this Martin Hunt, the one the papers and television said had phoned on the day of her disappearance. It was what they always said, the terminology always used, when they meant they had caught a murderer but couldn't yet prove he had done it. If the papers said any more, gave the man's name for instance, or said he was suspected of murder, they might risk a libel action. Or be breaking the law.

'I bet the police grilled him unmercifully. I expect they beat him up. All sorts of things go on we don't suspect, don't they? They wanted a confession from him because they're too thick often to actually get evidence like detectives in books do. I don't suppose they believed he'd only been out with her four times. And it's hard for them because they haven't got a body. They don't even know for certain she's been murdered. That's why they have to get a confession. They have to *extort* a confession.'

'We have the most restrained and civilised police force in the world,' Arnham said stiffly.

Instead of denying this, Fee smiled a little and lifted her shoulders. 'They take it for granted when a person gets murdered it's her husband if she's got one or her boy friend. Don't you think that's awful?'

18

'Why do we have to think about it?' Cheryl asked. 'I don't know why we have to talk about it. Who cares about those revolting things, anyway?'

Fee took no notice. 'Personally, I think it was the person who phoned in answer to her advertisement. It was some mad person who phoned and enticed her to their house and killed her. I expect the police think it was Martin Hunt putting on a false voice.'

Philip thought he could see disgust and perhaps boredom on Arnham's face, but perhaps this was only a projection of his own feelings. He risked Fee's telling him he was changing the subject and said quickly, 'I was admiring that picture,' he began, pointing to the rather strange landscape over the fireplace. 'Is it a Samuel Palmer?'

Of course he meant a print. Anyone would have known he meant that but Arnham, looking incredulous, said, 'I shouldn't think so for one moment if Samuel Palmer is who I think he is. My ex-wife bought it in a garage sale.'

Philip blushed. His efforts anyway had done nothing to stem the tide of Fee's forensic narrative. 'She's probably dead already and they've found the body and are keeping it dark. For their own reason. To trap someone.'

'If that's true,' Arnham said, 'it will come out at the inquest. In this country the police don't keep things dark.'

It was Cheryl who spoke, who hadn't uttered a word since they came back from the garden. 'Who are you trying to kid?'

Arnham made no reply to that. He said very stiffly, 'Would you like a drink?' His eyes ranged over them as if they were a dozen people instead of four. 'Any of you?'

'What have you got?' This was Fee. Philip had a very good idea this wasn't a question you asked people like Arnham, though it might have gone down perfectly well in the circles Fee and Darren moved in.

'Anything you will be able to think of.'

'Then can I have a bacardi and coke?'

Of course that was something he didn't have. He dispensed second choices, sherry, gin and tonic. To Philip's astonishment, though he knew she could be strangely insensitive, Christine seemed unaware of how frigid the atmosphere had grown. With a glass of Bristol Cream in her hand, she continued along the lines Philip himself had set and made admiring comments on various items of Arnham's furniture and ornaments. Such and such a thing was nice, everything was very nice, the carpets were particularly nice and of such good quality. Philip marvelled at her transparency. She spoke as one humbly grateful for an unexpected munificent gift.

Arnham said harshly, smashing all that, 'Everything will have to be sold. There's a court order that everything has to be sold and the proceeds divided between myself and my ex-wife.' He drew a long breath that sounded stoical. 'And now I suggest you let me take you all out for a meal somewhere. I don't think we can quite manage anything here. The local steakhouse — how will that suit?'

He took them in the Jaguar. It was a big car so there was no difficulty about their all getting into it. Philip thought he ought to feel grateful to Arnham for taking them all out and paying for their dinner but he didn't. He felt it would have been better for him to have come out with the truth, said he had only been expecting Christine and then entertained Christine on her own as he had originally planned to do. He and Fee and Cheryl wouldn't have minded, they would have preferred it — at any rate he would — to sitting here in the glowing dimness, the pseudo country manor decor, of a second-rate restaurant above a supermarket, trying to make conversation with someone who was obviously longing for them to leave.

People of Arnham's generation lacked openness, Philip thought. They weren't honest. They were devious. Christine was the same, she wouldn't speak her mind, she would think it rude. He hated the way she praised every dish that came as if Arnham had cooked it himself. Away from his own home Arnham had become much more expansive, talking pleasantly, drawing Cheryl out as to what she meant to do now she had left school, asking Fee about her fiancé and what he did for a living. He seemed to have got over his initial disappointment or anger. The interest he showed in her started Cheryl talking about their father, the least suitable of all possible subjects, Philip thought. But Cheryl had been closer to Stephen than any of his children, hadn't, even now, begun the process of recovering from his death.

'Oh yes, it's quite true, he was like that,' Christine said with a shade of embarrassment after Cheryl had spoken of their father's love of gambling. 'Mind you, no one suffered. He would never have had his family go without. Really, we benefited, didn't we? A lot of the nice things we've got came from his gambling.'

'Mum got her honeymoon paid for out of Dad's Derby win,' said Cheryl. 'But it wasn't only horses with Dad, was it, Mum? He'd bet on anything. If you were with him waiting for a bus he'd bet on which would come first, the 16 or the 32. If the phone rang he'd say, "Fifty pee it's a man's voice, Cheryl, or fifty pee it's a woman's." I used to go to the dogs with him, I loved that, it was so exciting sitting there drinking a coke and maybe eating a meal and watching the dogs go round. He never got cross, my Dad. When he felt one of his bad moods coming on he'd say, "OK, what'll we have a bet on? There are two birds on the lawn, a blackbird and a sparrow, I bet you a pound the sparrow flies away first." '

'His whole life was gambling,' said Christine with a sigh.

'And us.' Cheryl uttered it fiercely. She had had two glasses of wine which had gone to her head. 'We were first, then the gambling.'

It was true. Even his work had been gambling, so to speak, speculation on the Stock Exchange, until one day,

21

the result perhaps of a lifetime of anxieties and stress, chain-smoking, long days and short nights, sitting with the phone in one hand and a cigarette in the other, his heart ruptured and stopped. The heart disease, of long standing but concealed from his wife and children, had meant there was no life assurance, very little provision of any kind and a mortgage on the Barnet house which was covered by no insurance policy. With no reason to expect it, he had planned to live for years, to amass in that time by speculation among other forms of gambling, a fortune to maintain his family after he was gone.

'We even got Flora through a bet,' Christine was saying. 'We were on our honeymoon in Florence, walking along a street that's full of antique shops, and I saw Flora in the window and said wasn't she lovely? The house we'd had built had a little garden, not the big garden we had in Barnet, but a nice little garden, and I could just imagine Flora standing by our pond. You tell him what happened, Cheryl, the way Dad told you.'

Philip could see Arnham was quite interested. He was smiling. After all, he had spoken about his ex-wife, so why shouldn't Christine talk of her dead husband?

'Mum said she'd be terribly expensive, but Dad was never one to care about things costing a lot. He said her face was like Mum's - but I don't really think it is, do you?'

'Perhaps a bit,' Arnham said.

'Anyway, he said he liked her because she looked like Mum. He said, "I'll tell you what, we'll have a bet on it. I bet she's Venus, I bet she's the goddess Venus. If she's not I'll buy her for you." '

'I thought Venus was a star,' said Christine. 'Stephen said not, she was a goddess. Cheryl knows, she's done all that at school.'

'So they went into the shop and the man in there spoke English and he told Dad she wasn't Venus, Venus is nearly always bare above the waist, sort of topless. . . .'

'You needn't tell him that, Cheryl!'

'Dad didn't mind telling me – it's art, isn't it? The man in the shop said she was a copy of the Farnese Flora. She was the goddess of spring and flowers and her own flowers were may blossom. That's what she's holding in her hand. Anyway, Dad had to buy her after that and she cost a lot, hundreds of thousands of whatever their money's called, and they had to have her sent home because they couldn't carry her in the aircraft.'

The conversation had come round to its starting point in Arnham's house when the statue had first been presented to him. It was this which was perhaps the signal for him to call for the bill. When Cheryl had finished he said, 'You make me feel I shouldn't have accepted her.' He seemed to be doing sums in his head, converting lire perhaps. 'No, I really can't accept her. She's much too valuable a gift.'

'Yes, Gerard, I want you to have her.' They were outside the restaurant by the time Christine said this. It was dark. Philip heard the words, though Arnham and Christine were walking a little apart from them and Christine had taken his hand. Or he had taken Christine's. 'It means a lot to me for you to have her. Please. It makes me happy to think of her there.'

Why had he got the idea into his head that Arnham meant only to drive them as far as Buckhurst Hill station? Nothing had been said. Perhaps he really was in love with Christine and put himself out for her as a matter of course. Or it might be that he felt under an obligation on account of Flora. Philip thought the earlier awkwardness had quite passed. Christine sat in the front and chatted to Arnham about the neighbourhood and where she used to live and where she now lived and about whether or not she should take up hairdressing again, which had been her job before she married. Because they needed 'a bit more coming in', which was all very artless but made Philip wince. It did seem as if she were throwing herself at him. She was really 'waiting to see what happened' before she definitely made up her mind to start a hairdressing business from home.

Arnham talked pleasantly enough about his own plans. The house had to be sold and all the furniture. He and his ex-wife had agreed it should be auctioned with all its contents and he hoped this might happen while he was out of the country on business. A flat wouldn't suit him, he would have to buy himself another house, but in the same district or not far away. What did Christine think of Epping?

'I used to go to Epping Forest on picnics when I was a child.'

'You've been very near Epping Forest today,' Arnham said, 'but I meant Epping itself. Or Chigwell even. I might stand a chance of finding a smaller place in Chigwell Row.'

'You could always come up our way,' said Christine.

Cricklewood, that was, and Glenallan Close where Christine, newly widowed, had been obliged to move. The most optimistic of estate agents would hardly have called it desirable. Philip reminded himself that Arnham had been there before, the clumps of red-brick houses with their flat metal-framed windows, pantiled roofs, wire fences and skimpy gardens, would come as no shock to him. Darkness and the shining mist from street lamps shrouded in leaves concealed the worst. It was no slum. It was only poor and barren and shabby. Philip and Fee and Cheryl, as if by mutual understanding, hurried into the house, leaving Christine and Arnham to make their farewells. But Christine was very quick about it, running up the path just as the front door came open and Hardy rushed out, hurtling himself at her with yelps of joy.

'What did you think of him? Did you like him?' The car had scarcely gone. Christine stood watching it depart, Hardy in her arms.

'Yes, he's OK.' Fee, on the settee, was hunting for

the latest on the Rebecca Neave affair in the *Evening Standard*.

'Did you like him, Cheryl? Gerard, I mean.'

'Me? Sure, yeah. I liked him. I mean, he's OK. He's a lot older than Dad, isn't he? I mean, he looks older.'

'I put my foot in it, though, didn't I? I realised as soon as we were in the door. I'd said to him, you must meet my children sometime, and he sort of smiled and said he'd like to and the next thing he said was to come over to his house next Saturday, and I don't know why, I took it he meant all of us. But of course he didn't, he meant me alone. I felt awful. Did you see that little table laid for just two with the flower and everything?'

Philip took Hardy round the grid of streets before going to bed. He came in the back way and stood there for a moment, looking at the empty space by the birdbath on which light from the kitchen window was shed, where Flora had stood. By then it was too late to undo what had been done. Returning to Buckhurst Hill on the following day, for instance, and retrieving Flora – that would have been too late.

In any case, he had no feelings of that sort then, only a sense that things had been mismanaged and the day wasted.

2

A postcard came with a picture on it of the White House. This was less than two weeks after the visit to Buckhurst Hill and Arnham was in Washington. Christine had been typically vague about what job he did but Philip found out that he was export manager for a British company in a building near the head office of Roseberry Lawn. Fee brought in the post on Saturday morning, noting the name of the addressee and the stamp but honourably not reading the message. Christine read it to herself and then read it aloud.

'Have come on here from New York and next week shall be in California or "The Coast" as they call it over here. The weather is a lot better than at home. I have left Flora to look after the house! Love, Gerry.'

She put the card on the mantelpiece between the clock and the photograph of Cheryl holding Hardy as a puppy. Later in the day Philip saw her reading it again, with her glasses on this time, then turning it over to look closely at the picture as if in the hope of seeing some mark or cross Arnham might have made there, indicative of personal occupancy or viewing point. A letter came in the following week, not an air letter but several sheets of paper in an airmail envelope. Christine didn't open this in company, still less read it aloud.

'I think that was him on the phone last night,' Fee said to Philip. 'You know when the phone went at — oh, it must have been all of eleven-thirty. I thought who's ringing us at this hour? Mum jumped up as if she'd been expecting it. But she went straight to bed afterwards and she never said a word.'

'It would have been half-past six in Washington. He'd

have finished his day's work and be ready to go out for the evening.'

'No, he'll be in California by this time. I worked it all out, it would have been early afternoon in California, he'd just have had his lunch. He was on the phone for ages, it was obvious he didn't care what it cost.'

Philip thought, though he didn't say so, that Arnham would have put the cost of phone calls to London on his expense account. The fact that he had had plenty to talk to Christine about was more significant.

'Now Darren and I have fixed on next May for getting married,' Fee said, 'if he and Mum got engaged at Christmas, why shouldn't we be married at the same time? I don't see why you shouldn't have this house, Phil. Mum won't want it, you can tell he's rich. You and Jenny could take over this house. I mean, I suppose you and Jenny will get married one day, won't you?'

Philip only smiled. The idea of the house was inviting and something he had never thought about before. He wouldn't have chosen it but it was a house, it was somewhere to live. That this was a real possibility he came to see more and more. His fears that their unexpected invasion of his house might have changed Arnham's feelings for Christine or at least made him proceed with caution seemed unfounded. No more postcards arrived and if there were letters Philip didn't see them, but another late phone call came and a few days later Christine confided in him that she had had a long conversation with Arnham during the afternoon.

'He has to stay on a bit longer. He's going to Chicago next.' She spoke on a note of awe as if Arnham were contemplating a space tour to Mars or as if the Valentine's Day massacre had taken place quite recently. 'I hope he'll be all right.'

Philip was never indiscreet enough to say anything about the house to Jenny. He managed to contain himself even when one evening, as they were walking back from the cinema along an unfamiliar street, she pointed out a block of flats where several were advertised to let.

'When you've finished your training . . .'

It was a flat ugly building, about sixty years old, with peeling art deco adornments over the front entrance. He shook his head, said something about an exorbitant rent.

She held on to his arm. 'Is it because of Rebecca Neave?'

He looked at her in astonishment. A month and more had passed since the girl's disappearance. Theories, whole articles of speculation, appeared from time to time in newspapers outlining their authors' ideas of what had become of her. There was no real news, there had been no leads that could be called firm. She had vanished as surely as if she had been made invisible and spirited away. The name for a second meant nothing to Philip, so securely had he banished it from his mind, hating to dwell on these things. The identity of its possessor came back to him uneasily.

'Rebecca Neave?'

'She lived there, didn't she?' Jenny said.

'I had no idea.'

He must have spoken very coldly, for he could sense her looking at him as if she thought he was pretending to something he didn't truly feel. But this phobia of his was real enough and sometimes it extended to the human beings who allowed violence to occupy their minds. He didn't want to seem smug or prudish. Because she expected him to do so, he looked up at the building, bathed in the orangeade sticky light of stilt-borne street lamps. Not a window was open on the facade. The front doors swung apart and a woman came out briskly and got into a car. Jenny was unable to say exactly which flat had been Rebecca's but she guessed its windows were the two in the very top right-hand corner.

'I thought that was why you didn't fancy it.'

'I don't fancy living all the way up here.' North of the

North Circular Road, he meant. He thought of the surprise it would be telling her of his acquisition of a house rent-free, but something stayed him, some inner prudence held him back. It might be only a matter of weeks before he knew – until then he could refrain. 'Anyway, I ought to wait till I've got a proper job,' he said.

The last time he knew Arnham had phoned Christine was at the end of November. He heard her speaking to someone quite late at night and call him Gerry. Soon after that he expected Arnham home - or Fee did. Fee watched their mother as once a mother might have watched her daughter, looking for an air of excitement, for changes in her appearance. They wouldn't ask. Christine never questioned them about their private affairs. Fee said she seemed depressed but Philip couldn't see it, she was just the same as far as he knew.

Christmas passed and his training course came to an end. He was on the Roseberry Lawn staff now, a very junior surveyor-planner, on a salary of which he was obliged to part with a third to Christine. When Fee went it would be more than a third and he must learn not to mind that either. Christine, quite quietly and not making any fuss about it, began earning a little by doing the neighbours' hair at home. If his father had been alive, Philip thought, he would have stopped Cheryl working at Tesco on the checkout. Not that this endured for long. She only lasted there three weeks and afterwards, instead of trying to get another job, went on the dole with indifferent acceptance.

In the living room in Glenallan Close, a room which had once been two – very tiny poky rooms they must have been, for combined they measured not much more than six metres – the postcard with the White House on it remained on the mantelpiece. All the Christmas cards had been taken down but Arnham's card remained. Philip would have liked to take it down and throw it away but he had an uneasy feeling Christine treasured it. Once, looking at it sideways in sunlight, he saw that its glossy surface was covered with her fingermarks.

'Perhaps he just hasn't come back yet,' Fee said.

'He wouldn't be away on a business trip for four months.'

Cheryl said unexpectedly, 'She's tried to phone him herself but the number's unobtainable. She told me so, she said his phone was out of order.'

'He was going to move,' Philip said slowly. 'He told us – don't you remember? He's moved without telling her.'

At work, when he wasn't out visiting clients and prospective clients, he divided his time between the show-rooms in Brompton Road and head office which was near Baker Street. Often, after parking his car or on his way out to lunch, he wondered if he might run into Arnham. For a while he hoped this might happen, perhaps only because the sight of her son might remind Arnham of Christine, but as he began to lose hope he shied away from a meeting. It had begun to be embarrassing.

'Hasn't Mum aged?' Fee said to him. Christine was out walking Hardy. In front of Fee on the table was a pile of wedding invitations. She was addressing envelopes. 'She looks years older, don't you think?'

He nodded, hardly knowing what answer to make. And yet six months before he would have said their mother looked younger than at any time since Stephen Wardman's death. He had concluded that she was a woman with the type of looks which only youth suited, as Fee herself would be. That white and pink skin with its velvety texture was the first kind to fade. Like rose petals it seemed to turn brown at the edges. Pale blue eyes lost their brightness sooner than the dark sort. Golden hair turned to straw, to ash - particularly if you reserved none of the bleach you put on your customers' hair for yourself. Fee didn't pursue it. She said instead, 'I take it you've split up with Jenny? I mean I was going to ask her to be one of my bridesmaids but I won't if you've split up.'

'It looks like it,' he said, and then, 'Yes, we have. You can take it that's all over.'

He didn't want to explain to her. This was something he felt he wasn't obliged to explain to anyone. There was no need for solemn announcements as if he had been in a permanent relationship and his marriage or even his engagement had broken up. In fact, it wasn't that Jenny had tried to pressurise him into marriage. She wasn't like that. But they had been going out together for a year and more. It was natural that she wanted him to move in with her, or rather, for the two of them to find a place where they could live together, as on the evening when she had shown him the block where Rebecca Neave had lived. He had to refuse, he couldn't leave Christine. Come to that, he couldn't *afford* to leave Christine.

'You and Mum both,' said Fee with a sigh. 'It's a good thing Darren and me are solid as a rock.'

It was an expression that applied rather too accurately to Fee's future husband, Philip thought. Even Darren's undeniably handsome face had something rock-like about it. He hadn't tried very hard to imagine why Fee could possibly want to marry him. The subject was one he shied away from. It might be that she would do anything to get away from the responsibilities of Glenallan Close and all they involved.

'Then I expect I'll have to ask Senta,' Fee said. 'She's Darren's cousin and Darren's mother wants me to ask her, says she'll be hurt if I don't. And then there'll be Cheryl and Janice and another cousin of his called Stephanie. I'm longing for you to meet Stephanie, she's absolutely your type.'

Philip didn't think he had a type. His girl friends had been tall and short, dark and fair. He found it hard to keep up with the ramifications of Darren's large extended family. So many of its members had been married two or three times, producing children each time and gathering in stepchildren. His father and his mother each had an ex-wife and an ex-husband. They made the Wardmans look rather sparse and isolated. His eyes went back to the card on the mantelpiece and without actually reading it again, he recalled the line about leaving Flora to look after the house, repeating it over and over to himself until it became meaningless. He began to notice too the empty space in the garden where Flora had formerly stood.

One day, in his lunch hour, he found the building where the company Arnham worked for had its headquarters. He passed its doors as he was walking back to head office, by a slightly different route than usual, from the café where he had his sandwich and cup of coffee. For some reason he was sure he would meet Arnham, that Arnham too, at this hour, would be coming back from lunch, but although he didn't meet him, he came, in a way, near to doing so. He saw his car, the Jaguar, parked in one of the marked slots in a small parking area designated for employees of the company whose building abutted on to it. Philip would have said, if asked, that he didn't remember the index number of Arnham's car but as soon as he saw it he knew it was the number.

His mother was in the kitchen doing a client's hair. Philip thought this was one of the things he most disliked about living at home, to come in and find the kitchen turned into a hairdresser's salon. And he always knew from the moment he let himself into the house. The smell of shampoo was rich and almondy in the air, or a worse smell if, as occasionally happened, she had been doing a perm. Then it was rotten eggs. He had remonstrated with her and asked what was wrong with the bathroom. Of course there was nothing wrong with the bathroom but it had to be heated and why go to the extra expense when the kitchen, with the Rayburn going, was warm anyway?

As he hung his jacket up he heard a woman's voice say, 'Ooh, Christine, you've taken a nick out of my ear!'

She wasn't a good hairdresser, she was always having little mishaps of that sort. It gave Philip nightmares sometimes when he imagined a customer suing her over a burnt scalp or bald patch suddenly manifesting itself or, as in this present case, a mutilated ear. No one ever had so far. She was so cheap, undercutting the salons in the High Road. That was why they came, these Gladstone Park housewives and shop assistants and part-time secretaries, as pinching and scraping and saving as she, as on the look-out for new ways to skimp. What with the cost of the hot water and the electricity, lighting the Rayburn when they needn't have, not to mention all those mousses and gels and moisturising sprays, he doubted if his mother was much better off than if she had stayed what she said she was not long ago, a lady of leisure.

He gave them five minutes. That was enough to get his mother used to the fact that he was in. Fee was out somewhere, round at Darren's place probably, but Cheryl was at home and in the bathroom. He could hear her transistor and then the water glugging out. He opened the kitchen door, making a throat-clearing sound first. Not that they could have heard him. His mother had the hand drier on. Philip's eyes went straight to the client's ear, to the lobe of which adhered a lump of bloody cotton wool.

'I expect Mrs Moorehead would like a cup of tea,' Christine said.

This, with the sugar she would ladle in and the cake she would eat, was another source of erosion into the four pounds fifty Christine got for a shampoo, trim and blow dry. But it was hateful thinking like this, despicable having to think like it. He was as bad as his mother and,

33

if he wasn't watchful, it would drive him to the extreme of offering the bloody woman a glass from their hoarded sherry stock. He could have done with one himself but had to be content with tea.

'Did you have a good day, dear? What did you do?' She had a quality of a kind of tactlessness, of saying, with the best intentions, the wrong thing. 'It's a treat for us two old women to have a man to talk to, isn't it, Mrs Moorehead? It makes such a nice change.'

He could see the client, blonded, painted, fancying herself young still, draw herself up, her mouth pinch in. Quickly he began telling them about the house he had visited that day, the proposed conversion of a bedroom into a bathroom, the colour scheme. The kettle came to the boil, spluttered and bounced. He put an extra teabag in, though he knew the waste troubled Christine.

'Where was that, Philip? In a nice part, was it?'

'Oh, Chigwell way,' he said.

'This is a second bathroom, is it, dear?'

He nodded, passed the client her cup, set Christine's down between the Elnett spray and a can of baked beans.

'We should be so lucky, shouldn't we, Mrs Moorehead? I'm afraid that's beyond our wildest dreams.' Another wince, the Moorhead woman's scalp knocking against the nozzle of the drier. 'Still, we must be thankful for what we do have, I know that, and Philip's promised me a new bathroom here one day, a really luxurious one, and quite a cut above what we're used to in this street.'

Mrs Moorehead probably lived a couple of houses down. She had an angry aggressive look, but that was very likely habitual with her. He talked about bathrooms and traffic, about the springlike weather. Mrs Moorehead departed, off to some Rotarians' function, saying unnecessarily, Philip thought, that she wouldn't give Christine anything over the odds because 'you don't tip the boss'. Christine started tidying up the kitchen, stuffing wet towels into the washing machine. He guessed there were potatoes baking inside the Rayburn and with a sinking feeling knew they would once more be having her favourite standby, a can of beans emptied over a split-open jacket potato.

Cheryl came in, dressed for going out. She sniffed, shivered. 'I don't want anything to eat.'

'I hope you're not getting to be anorexic,' Christine said worriedly. She peered at her daughter in that way she had. It was as if by extending her neck and bringing her face within inches of the other person, symptoms disguised by distance would startlingly manifest themselves. 'Will he buy you a meal?'

'Who's "he"? There's a crowd of us going bowling.'

Cheryl was nervous and very thin, her wispy fair hair touched here and there with green and standing up like a bottle brush. She wore skin-tight jeans and a bulky black leather jacket. If she wasn't his sister, if he didn't know her and what she was really like, if he had met her in the street, Philip thought, he would have taken her for a tart, a slag. She looked horrible, her face gleaming with gel, the lips almost black, her fingernails quite black like attachments of patent leather.

She was on something, he thought, but he didn't want to think of it. He almost trembled when he wondered if it might be hard drugs. How could she afford it? What did she do to be able to afford it? She hadn't a job. He watched her standing by the counter, investigating Christine's bottles and jars, notably a new type of foamy stuff for 'sculpturing', dipping in a black nail and sniffing it. If anything at all interested her it was cosmetics, what she called the 'beauty scene' but still she wouldn't apply for the beautician's course Fee had suggested. Over her shoulder hung a scuffed black leather handbag. Once, a week or two ago, he had seen it lying about open and notes spilling out, tenners and twenty-pound notes. He had forced himself next day to ask her where the money came from and she didn't flare at him or get on the

35

defensive. She just opened the bag and showed him its emptiness, the purse with fifty pee in it in loose change.

Philip was jerked from this reverie by Cheryl's slamming the front door. He wandered into the living room, carrying his refilled teacup. In this room he never specially noticed the furniture but he noticed it now. It was recalled to him, as it were, by the reversion of his mind to the past, by the shock of the re-encounter with Arnham's world. The furniture was too good for the room which held it – well, all but the rented television set. Christine had been obliged to sell the house and most of what she had, but not her living-room furniture, the settee and armchairs covered in hide, the mahogany dining table and chairs, the three or four antique pieces. It all looked incongruous in here, oversized, contrasting curiously with the tiles of the thirties' fireplace, biscuit-like in shape and colour, the unpanelled doors, the wall lights of pink glass platelets. Curled up in the armchair where he wasn't supposed to be, Hardy lay asleep.

Seeing Arnham's car had at last shown him what he avoided facing. The man was home, had very likely been home for months. He had moved house without giving Christine his new phone number. He had ditched her – 'jilted' her would probably be the term Christine's own generation would use. The evenings were beginning to grow light and it was possible to see from the french windows the birdbath and the patch of concrete where Flora had stood. Philip stood at the window, remembering Christine's enthusiasm at the idea of bringing the statue to Arnham as a gift.

She came into the room with the plates of potatoes and beans. Water had slopped on to the tray from overfilled glasses. He quickly took it from her. His mother did her best. It was only – dreadful accusation! – that she did nothing well except emotional things. She was good at loving a man and good at making children feel safe and happy. Those functions came naturally to her.

She couldn't help being expensive to keep, a waste-maker, one of those people who cost more by earning than they would by doing nothing.

They watched television. This obviated for a while the need to talk. It was still only seven. He looked unseeing at the screen where a dancer in lamé and feathers capered about. Christine, he noticed, her tray balanced on her lap, had surreptitiously opened her *Brides* magazine again and was looking longingly at ridiculous photographs of girls in white satin crinolines. Even Fee herself didn't want that, was resigned to a home-made wedding dress, and what the caterers called a 'finger buffet'. They would all share the cost but even so . . . And there was Christine still hankering after a thousand quid's worth of bridal gown, a sit-down dinner and a disco.

She was looking at him. It occurred to him that in the whole of his twenty-two years of life he had never known her to be angry. And when she anticipated anger from others her face wore that particular expression it wore now, the eyes afraid, the lips parted in the beginnings of a hopeful, mollifying smile. He said to her, 'Is there any point in leaving that card there any longer?' It was a roundabout way of asking what he didn't want to ask and knew the answer to, anyway.

She turned pink, looked away. 'You can take it down if you want to.'

Would she have given him that terrrible yet naïve reason for her continued hope if Fee hadn't come in at that moment? But Fee did come in, sweeping in swiftly like a human breeze, the front door banging first, then the living room one behind her. She looked at their trays, turned up the television, then turned it off, dropped into an armchair, her arms hanging down over its sides.

'Have you had anything to eat, dear?' Christine said.

If Fee had said no and what was there, Christine would have been hard put to it to produce even a sandwich.

37

But she routinely enquired and Fee almost always gave an impatient shake of the head.

'I can't understand why people don't do things. Why don't they do what they say they'll do? Can you believe it, Stephanie hasn't even started on her dress yet and she's supposed to be making Senta's as well.'

'Why can't Senta make her own?' Philip asked, though he wasn't much interested in the activities of his sister's bridesmaids.

'If you knew Senta you wouldn't have to ask that. It's quite funny actually, the idea of her sewing anything.'

'Is that the one that's Darren's cousin?'

Fee nodded in the way she had that made you think your enquiry irritated her. And then she grinned, wrinkling up her nose, looking at him as if they were conspirators. He realised quite suddenly how much he dreaded her departure from this house. There were only three weeks to go to her wedding and then she would be gone, never to return. Cheryl was useless, Cheryl was never at home. He would be alone with the responsibility of Christine and what guarantee had he now that this state of affairs would ever end, that he would ever be free?

He kept seeing Arnham's car, parked there at the foot of the windowless, ivy-clad wall. Perhaps, like Christine, he had believed, or half-believed, that Arnham had never come back, that he was unaccountably still in America. Or ill. Ill in hospital somewhere for months and unable to get in touch. Or even that he had died. He jumped up and said he was going to take Hardy out, take him a bit further than the usual evening ambulation round the block. Would Fee come too? It was a fine mild evening, very warm for April.

They walked along the pavements between the grassy patches with budding trees growing in them and the boundary walls of little square gardens. The grid of streets extended half a mile this way and half a mile that and then merged into Victorian sprawl. At one of the crossroads, waiting while Hardy investigated with exploratory sniffs a pair of gateposts and ceremoniously lifted his leg against them, Philip began to talk about Arnham, about seeing his car that day and therefore knowing now that he had simply deserted Christine. He had become indifferent to her. Unexpectedly, Fee said, 'He really ought to give Flora back.'

'*Flora?*'

'Well, don't you think he ought? Like giving back an engagement ring when you break things off, or returning letters.' Fee was an ardent reader of romantic fiction. She would need to be, marrying Darren, Philip sometimes thought. 'She's valuable, she's not a plastic garden gnome. If he doesn't want to face Mum, he ought to send her back.'

This seemed ridiculous to Philip. He wished Christine had been less impetuous in the first place and never decided to present Arnham with this unsuitable gift. They crossed the road, the dog obediently by their side until they reached the opposite pavement where he began to run on ahead, but decorously, his tail maintaining a constant cheerful wagging. Philip thought how strange it was, the different lights in which people saw things, even a brother and sister as close as he and Fee. He saw Arnham's offence in his encouraging Christine to love him and his abandonment of her. Then Fee surprised him by showing how nearly they did see eye to eye. She also shocked him.

'She thought he'd marry her, she thought that for ages,' Fee said. 'And do you know why? I don't suppose you do, but you know Mum, how sort of strange she is, like a child sometimes. I may as well tell you. You could say she confided in me but she didn't say I wasn't to tell you.'

'Tell me what?'

'You won't let on to her I told you, will you? I mean,

I think she told me because of being her daughter. It's sort of different, a son, isn't it? She just came out with it, out of the blue. It's why she was certain he'd marry her.' Fee's eyes returned to his face. They were almost tragic. 'I mean, any other woman wouldn't feel that way or she'd think just the reverse, especially someone her age, but you know Mum.'

Philip really didn't have to be told any more. He felt a flush spread up his neck across his face. His face was burning and he put his cold hand up to touch the skin. If Fee noticed she gave no sign of it.

'That time he came here and she cooked a meal for them or got takeaway or something and we were all out somewhere, well, he – they – had sex, made love, whatever you call it. In her bedroom. Suppose one of us had come in? It would have been very embarrasssing.'

He thrust his hands into his pockets and walked, looking down. 'I wish you hadn't told me.' The turmoil inside him frightened him. It was as if he were jealous as well as angry. 'Why did she tell you?'

Fee had put her arm through his. He gave her no answering pressure, he was suddenly upset by physical contact. The dog ran on ahead. It was the hour of dusk when, briefly, everything appears clear and defined but with an unearthly, very chilly pale light.

'I don't know really. I reckon it was on account of Senta. Her mother's ten years older than Mum but she's always having affairs. She's got this new lover, Darren was telling me, and he's not thirty, and I told Mum, and that's when she came out with it. "I had an affair with Gerard," she said. "Well, just the once." You know how she gets expressions just that little bit wrong. "We had an affair that evening he came round with the wine and said he liked Flora." '

He said nothing. Fee lifted her shoulders. He felt movement against his own but he didn't look at her. Without saying a word to each other, the idea came to them simultaneously to turn back. Fee called to Hardy and put him on the lead. After a little while she began talking about her wedding, the arrangements at the church, the times the various cars would come to the house. Philip felt confused and angry and inexplicably terribly upset. When they returned to the house he knew he would be incapable of facing Christine again that night and he went straight upstairs to his room.

3

As a place to sleep in it was rather small, but it would make a spacious bathroom. It wasn't for him to ask why Mrs Ripple should wish to sacrifice her third bedroom in order to have a second bathroom, though he tended to wonder about these things. In other people's homes as he so often was these days, Philip found himself speculating about all sorts of oddities and incongruities. Why, for instance, did she keep a pair of binoculars on the windowsill in here? To watch birds? To observe the behaviour of neighbours?

The dressing-table was very low and there was no stool. If a woman wanted to do her hair or put make-up on in front of the mirror, she would have to sit on the floor. In the small bookcase were nothing but cookery books. Why didn't she keep her cookery books in the kitchen? He took his tape measure from his pocket and began measuring the room. Four metres thirty by three metres fifteen, and the ceiling height two metres fifty-two. He wouldn't be doing the design himself, he hadn't progressed so far yet. In any case, there would be nothing inspired or ambitous about it. Champagne bath and basin, she had chosen, a vanity unit with black marble top, and milk-colour tiles with a black and gold floral pattern.

The window was to be double-glazed. He took his measurements with concentrated care. Roy would want to know widths and lengths to the nearest millimetre. The figures written down in his neat small hand in the Roseberry Lawn Interiors notebook, Philip leaned on the windowsill and looked outside.

A collage of gardens lay below him, all the same size,

each one separated from its neighbours by fencing with trellis on it. It was the most beautiful time of the year and the ornamental trees were in fresh new leaf, many of them in blossom, pink or white. Tulips were in bloom. These were among the few flowers he knew by name. The velvety brown and gold things which filled the end of Mrs Ripple's garden he thought might be wallflowers. Beyond the gardens which backed on to those on this side was a row of houses, their rear aspects facing him. No doubt they had started off all the same but various additions, a loft made into a bedroom, a conservatory built on, an extra garage, now differentiated them and made each an individual. Only one seemed still as the builder had built it but it had the best garden, with a pink may tree halfway down where the lawn was broken into by a rock garden. Over this spilled and sprawled a carpet of purple and yellow alpine plants.

Surveying this tumbled spread of flowers, sheltered to some extent by the branches of the tree with its rose-coloured blossom, stood a small statue in marble. Philip couldn't see it very clearly, it was too far away, but something in its attitude seemed familiar, the angle of its slightly upraised face, the outstretched right hand holding a bunch of flowers, the feet that though planted firmly on the ground yet seemed to be dancing.

He wished very much that he could get a closer look at it. Then he realised that he could. The binoculars were here on the windowsill. He took them out of their case and raised them to his eyes. A certain amount of adjustment was needed before he could see clearly – and then, suddenly, the vision they afforded him was amazing. They were excellent glasses. He could see the little statue as if it were no more than a metre away from him. He could see her eyes and her lovely mouth and the waves in her hair, the diagonal weave in the fillet which bound it, the almond curves of her fingernails and the details of the flowers, their stamens and petals, in the sheaf she carried.

And he could see too the green stain that travelled from the side of her neck to where her robe covered her breasts, and the tiny chip out of her left ear lobe. He had made that chip himself when he was ten and a stone fired from his catapult had clipped the side of her head. His father had been angry, taken away the catapult and docked his pocket money for three weeks. It was Flora. Not a look-alike or a copy, but Flora herself. As Fee had pointed out, she wasn't one of those mass-produced plaster ornaments to be seen in their dozens at every motorway junction garden centre. She was unique. He remembered, rather incongruously, what Cheryl had said of her while talking to Arnham about their father. She was the Farnese Flora who was traditionally associated with may blossom.

Philip replaced the binoculars in their case, put away his measure and his notebook and went downstairs. Some clients you had to search for, cough, knock on doors to summon them. Mrs Ripple wasn't of that sort but alert, spry, hawk-eyed. She was a middle-aged woman of great spirit and vigour, very sharp-tongued and, he suspected, critical. She had a shiny, sore-looking face and a lot of dark hair with threads of grey in it like fuse wire.

'I'll be in touch when the lay-out is completed,' he said to her, 'and then you'll see me again when work commences.'

It was the way they were taught to speak to customers at Roseberry Lawn. Philip had never actually heard a human being snort but that was the kind of sound Mrs Ripple made. 'When's that going to be?' she said. 'Some time next year?'

There had been a delay about sending her their brochures, Roy said, adding that he didn't think she was likely to forget it. Philip assured her, with as radiant a smile as he could manage, that he hoped it would be no more than four weeks at the outside. She said nothing in reply, left him to open the front door and close it after him. Philip got into his car, a three-month-old blue Opel Kadett, thinking as he sometimes did that it was the only nice thing he possessed, and he didn't really possess it, it belonged to Roseberry Lawn.

Instead of driving back the way he had come, he took the first left-hand turning and then turned left again. This brought him out into the street where the row of houses whose rears the back of Mrs Ripple's faced must be. They looked very different from this aspect. He hadn't counted precisely where in the row the house with the statue in its garden came but he knew it must be fourth or fifth from the block of flats with green pantiled roof. It was also the only one without additions. And here it was, this must be it, between the house with the window in its roof and the house with two garages. Philip drove past slowly. It was gone five, his day was over, so he wasn't wasting the firm's time, something he was still conscientious about.

At the end of the road, at a T-junction, he turned round and drove back. Opposite the house he parked the car by the kerb and switched off the engine. The front garden was small with a rosebed in which the roses were not yet out. Three steps led up to one of those Georgian front doors with a sunburst fanlight. A feature of the house — Philip was sure it would be called a feature — was a small circular stained-glass window a little way above the front door.

Through one of the panes of clear glass in that window, a lozenge shape in the pretentious coat of arms which formed the design, a woman's face could be seen, looking out. She wasn't looking at Philip, who in any case was invisible inside his car. She moved away and he was about to start the engine when her face reappeared, and the upper part of her body, at a casement of leaded lights which she opened.

She wasn't all that young by his standards but still he could see she was young. The afternoon sun shone full on her face and it was handsome in a bold aggressive sort of way, the mass of dark frizzy hair springing back from a broad white brow. She was a good distance from him but he saw the sun catch and flash fire from a diamond on her left hand and that told him she was Gerard Arnham's wife. Arnham had married and this was whom he had married. Anger bubbled up in Philip the way blood bubbles up through a sharp cut in skin. Like that blood flow he couldn't immediately control it, there was no cold tap to hold his rage under, and he cursed silently in the closed car.

Philip's anger made his hands tremble on the wheel. He wished he hadn't come, he wished he had driven back from Mrs Ripple's the way he had come, through Hainault and Barkingside. If things had gone differently, his mother might have been living there, surveying the street from that stained-glass shield, opening that casement to feel the sun.

He couldn't meet Christine's eyes. He was uneasy when he was alone with her. Sometimes he could hardly frame the words of some simple routine sentence, something about the dog or had she paid this or that bill. This was the first time he had experienced a mental preoccupation which had become obsessive. In the past there had been his grief at his father's death. He had worried a bit about exams, then been in suspense while waiting to hear if he was to be offered a place in the Roseberry Lawn training scheme. Another cause for anxiety had been his doubt that permanent employment would follow when his training was complete. But none of those invasions of his equilibrium had overwhelmed his waking thoughts as this knowledge did. It frightened him too because he couldn't understand what was happening to him.

Why did he care so much that his mother had slept with a man? He knew she had slept with his father. He knew that if she had married Arnham they would have slept together. Why did he have to think about it so much, torment himself with pictures of the two of them together, repeat in his mind over and over Fee's words, Fee's awful revelations? The postcard was still on the living-room mantelpiece, he had never carried out his threat of throwing it away, and it was always the first thing he saw when he went into the room. It was as if, instead of a small piece of card with a commonplace photograph on it, it had become a huge picture in violent oils depicting some scene of sadism and sexual depravity; the kind of thing you don't want to look at but which compels your eyes and stretches them from their sockets.

Somehow their roles had been reversed. He had become her father and she his child. He was the father who wants revenge on his daughter's seducer or for her seducer to marry her. Pity for her wrenched at him when he looked at her sitting there quietly, stitching away at Cheryl's bridesmaid's dress. If she had gone alone to Arnham's house that day they took Flora, would she be Mrs Arnham now? Philip couldn't help thinking that the arrival of all of them on that autumn evening instead of Christine on her own, had been a decisive factor in Arnham's marriage plans. The other woman, the one with the dark hair and the diamond ring, might also have been a candidate at that time, and he had chosen her because she wasn't accompanied by a bevy of children and a marble statue.

She asked him if he minded her putting the television on. She always asked. He tried to remember if she had done that while his father was alive and he didn't think she had. One of the items on the nine o'clock news was a sighting of Rebecca Neave by someone in Spain. It was nearly eight months since her disappearance but reminders of her came into the papers and on television from time to time. A man who sounded responsible and honest claimed to have seen her in her green velvet tracksuit in a resort on the Costa del Sol. It was a place where, according to her parents, Rebecca had twice spent holidays. The man had probably imagined it, Philip thought, or was one of those who will say and do anything to get publicity.

He hadn't meant to return to Mrs Ripple's house, had felt strongly that Chigwell was a corner of the outskirts of London he would be happy never to see again. But in the middle of the week before Fee's wedding, Roy who was designing the new bathroom, came up with a problem about the tiling. He needed Mrs Ripple's consent to certain changes he proposed in the design as well as further wall measurements, notably distances between window frames and door architraves and the ends of walls. Philip found himself saying that he could make a very good guess at those measurements and the householder's consent could be obtained by phone.

'That's the sort of reply I expect of certain other newly graduated trainees,' said Roy, 'but not of you.' His hard dark eyes swam behind the thick glasses he wore. When he wasn't making cynical unfunny jokes, Roy talked like a brochure. 'It's thoroughness and attention to the smallest detail which has established Roseberry Lawn's distinguished reputation.'

Philip realised there was no escape from going to Chigwell but he told himself that he need not drive along the street where Arnham lived or even, come to that, take a second look at Flora through the binoculars in Mrs Ripple's back bedroom. When he left home Christine's first client of the day had already arrived, a woman who was having copper-coloured low lights put into her hair. For once Philip was glad his mother wouldn't be carrying out this project in the bathroom. As it was he would come home to find the kitchen floor covered with orange splash marks.

'I want to make enough money to pay for Fee's flowers myself,' Christine whispered as she saw him off at the front door. She pulled on the rubber gloves that were to keep her hands stain-free for Saturday and stuck her thumbnail through the left-hand one.

Customers of Roseberry Lawn often behaved as if visits from employees of the company they had engaged to renovate their homes were a gross intrusion of privacy. Philip had been told of one householder who had taped up the doors on the kitchen he was having converted and obliged the fitters to climb in and out through the window. It was commonplace to be refused the use of lavatory or phone. Mrs Ripple, alerted to his coming, though not by him, opened her front door with alacrity. It was as if she had been waiting just inside it. He had scarcely set foot inside the hall when she said to him in a savage tone, 'What right do you think you had to use my husband's field glasses?'

Philip was briefly dumbstruck. Had she tested them for fingerprints? Had some neighbour reported seeing them in his hands?

'Caught you there, haven't I?' she said. 'You thought you'd got away with that one.'

Philip said he was sorry. What else could he say?

'I expect you're wondering how I found you out.'

This was uttered the reverse of roguishly, Mrs Ripple's thick brown eyebrows drawing together like a pair of furry caterpillars meeting, but Philip nevertheless hazarded a smile.

'I place them on that windowsill just so,' she said, 'in the corner and with the long side precisely parallel to the wall.' The caterpillars leapt apart and sprang towards her hairline. 'I've my own reasons for doing that which I shan't go into. But that's how I knew. They had been replaced out of alignment.'

'I won't touch them,' Philip said, making for the stairs. 'You won't get the chance.'

She had removed the binoculars. Philip felt quite shaken by this encounter. Like most people, he was frightened by madness even when manifested in its milder forms. Did she perhaps suspect her husband of using the glasses to watch women undressing or something like that? And if so, what good did having her suspicions repeatedly proved sound do her? At least temptation had been removed from him. He wouldn't be able to take a close look at Flora without them.

The guesses he had made at the measurements were so nearly accurate as to confirm his opinion that he was wasting time coming here. But denied the use of the binoculars, he perversely found himself longing to look at Flora again. He opened the window and leaned out. The may tree had bloomed and shed most of its blossoms. The grass and paving stones were pink with fallen petals, the purple rock garden sprinkled with pink as if covered by a rosy veil. Petals lay on Flora's shoulders and on her outstretched arm and the flowers she carried were no longer stone but a bouquet of may.

But she seemed very far away from him. The distance rendered her features and the details of sculpture invisible. He retreated, closing the window, wondering as he did so if Mrs Ripple had placed a hair across the catch. Perhaps she would come up after he had gone and sprinkle the window frame with fingerprint powder. Then woe betide him when he came to inspect the work in progress as he might easily have to do.

She was waiting for him at the foot of the stairs. She said nothing and her silence and long cold basilisk stare had the effect of making him speak in a nervous hearty way.

'Well, thank you very much, Mrs Ripple. That's done. You'll be hearing from us in due course. We'll keep you up to date with progress.'

He passed her, left her behind his line of vision, felt her eyes following him. Half-way down the path he saw Arnham's car go by. Not the Jaguar but a second car, he would have a second car. The Jaguar probably belonged to his company the way the Kadett belonged to Roseberry Lawn. The woman in the passenger seat, the nearside which was nearest to him, was the woman he had seen at the window. It was a warm day and the car window was open on her side. Her arm rested along the rim of the glass panel. On the hand was the diamond ring and on the wrist the diamond watch. Arnham he could see only as a dark heavy silhouette.

The direction they were going in was away from their house. It was this which made up Philip's mind for him – if his mind could be said to be made up, if his mind entered into it. The Kadett even seemed to drive itself. Caution and reason returned sufficiently to make him park it a little way down the road.

There was no one about. There never was, in suburbs in the afternoons. Philip could remember his father telling him of the time when he was a child and there had been people about in streets like this one, quite a lot of them, people on foot because cars were few. These houses might have been uninhabited, their garages closed, their front gardens empty. All down the road the green of foliage and grass, the whiteness of buildings, was patched with laburnums in full bloom, a pure glistening yellow. The sun shone on to stillness and silence.

Philip went into Arnham's garden by the gates to the garage drive and made his way to the wooden door that evidently led to a passageway between garage and house. If it was locked that would be the end of the enterprise, but it wasn't locked. Once inside, in a narrow defile with brick walls on either side, he realised he had brought neither container nor covering with him. And he knew that if he went back to the car to find something suitable he would never return, he would give up and drive away.

At the end of the passage was a yard or terrace of concrete slabs. A very commonplace coal bunker on one side, a pair of dustbins on the other. Arnham had changed the Buckhurst Hill house for something distinctly inferior. Of course he had had to divide the sale price with his former wife. Protruding over the rim of one of the dustbins was a blue plastic bag, provided no doubt by the local authority's refuse collection service. Philip helped himself to that bag.

He crossed the lawn to where she was. Close to, the fallen may blossom on her shoulders and the crown of her head gave her a neglected look. He brushed them off, lightly blew away a petal from her ear, the same ear that once, long ago, he had chipped with a stone from his catapult. Squatting down close in front of her, he observed as he had never quite done before, the remoteness of her gaze, the way her eyes seemed to stare past those who looked at her, to fix themselves on some distant and perhaps glorious horizon. Of course she was a goddess, she was above earthly things and human needs.

His thoughts surprised him. They were as fanciful as if he were dreaming or in a fever. This was the way he had thought and imagined things while in the throes of that bad bout of flu he had had in the winter. But why on earth had Arnham told Christine Flora looked like her? Or had that perhaps been wishful thinking on her part? She looked like no real woman Philip had ever seen, though he thought quite suddenly — and rather madly — that if he ever saw a real woman with that face he would at once fall in love with her.

He reached for Flora and lifted her up. Some of the pink petals fell off the bunch of marble flowers. She seemed even heavier than when he had carried her up the hill from Buckhurst Hill station. He drew the blue plastic bag over her head, laid her on the grass and tied a knot in the top of the bag. Carrying the bundle in his arms, he might have been holding a length of piping or some garden tool.

It was when he was half-way across the grass towards the passageway and the wooden door that he saw he was watched. A man in a window next door was watching him. Philip told himself he was doing nothing wrong. Flora didn't belong to Gerard Arnham. Or, rather, he thought somewhat obscurely, she might have belonged to him if Arnham had done the right thing by Christine, loved her and married her, but she certainly didn't in the present circumstances. Arnham, by his behaviour, had forfeited the right to own her. Philip had read somewhere that if you borrow an object and hold on to it the only person who has a right to take it from you is the true owner. That was the law. Well, he was the true owner. Flora had been lent to Arnham. She was his conditionally only on his marrying Christine, that surely was an understood thing. Nevertheless, he quickened his pace. In spite of the weight of her, he ran down the path to the garage gates.

His arms full, it took him a moment or two to get them open. A voice behind him, from the other side of the fence, said, 'I say, excuse me, what exactly do you think you're doing with that?'

The words were very similar to Mrs Ripple's. Philip didn't even turn his head to take a look at the enquirer. He ran. Gasping because Flora was so heavy, he ran down the street to where his car was parked. He heaved her into the back seat and struggled into his safety belt. The man hadn't followed him. Philip was certain he had done the more sensible thing and gone back into the house to phone the police.

He saw his job lost, a conviction recorded against him for a criminal offence. But be reasonable, keep your head, the man hadn't seen his car, hadn't taken a note of the number. Philip's hands shook on the wheel but he made a mammoth effort and steadied them. He began to drive, took the left-hand turn, then a right. There was no one behind him and no one ahead. Out on the big road, heading for Barkingside, he heard the siren of a police car. But why assume it was for him, that it had anything to do with him? A police car with a howling siren wouldn't turn out because a man had been seen coming out of a garden with something in a plastic bag. They would be more likely to send an officer round on a bike.

Perhaps because his mother was so helpless and his sisters often liable to irrational fears, Philip had grown up a cool-headed person. He was like his father, who had been a practical man, and though endowed with plenty of imagination, he had learned to keep it in check. Therefore, he didn't let himself become a prey to all kinds of unreal speculations, and by the time he reached Gants Hill and the big roundabout on the A12 he was quite calm again.

Flora had bounced about a bit on the back seat. When he reached the Ilford showroom where he was due to call on his way back to the office, he transferred Flora from the back of the car to the boot, wedging her comfortably between the spare wheel and a cardboard crate of wallpaper sample books he was carrying with him. There in the car park at the back of the showroom he was unable to prevent himself taking a look at her. He pierced the plastic with the tip of his pen, his finger-nails having failed to do it, and made a split long enough to reveal her face. She still gazed into Olympian distances, still maintained that grave but serene expression. Well, it would be something to get steamed up about if she didn't, thought Philip.

Driving home rather later than usual – Roy had handed him a list of customers, some of them angry or indignant, to telephone and placate – Philip reflected on his act of the morning. Why had he taken the marble girl? Supposedly, because he felt she was rightly his or his family's. It was as if Arnham had perpetrated some kind of con trick in order to gain possession of her. People shouldn't be allowed to profit from their deceit.

But having taken her, what was he going to do with her now? Not replace her in the garden at Glenallan Close. Too many explanations would be required if he were to do that. And there was Christine to consider. He would have to tell Christine where Arnham now lived and how he had seen Flora there. It was dangerous ground this, an area he continuously shied away from. Could he perhaps say she wasn't Flora but a Flora look-alike he had happened to see in a shop or garden centre and had bought? Hopeless, with that chip out of her ear and that green stain.

Even getting her into the house without being seen and questioned would be a problem. They weren't one of those families whose individual members led their own private secret lives, unnoticed by and of little interest to the others. They were a close-knit family, each concerned about the others, prepared to enquire into any oddity of behaviour, each knowing pretty well where the others were at any given time and what they were likely to be doing. He imagined himself encountering Cheryl on the stairs with his arms full of Flora and her amazement and her questions.

As he thought that, while waiting in a queue of cars in the Edgware Road, watching the red light, he glanced to the right side of the street and saw Cheryl. Her name and a kind of vague picture of her had been in his mind, and then he saw her. She was coming out of what looked to him – he couldn't see very clearly, only a crowded glittering conglomeration of colours and shapes – like a video shop or music centre. So much for always knowing where the others were and what they were doing. Cheryl was dressed in her customary jeans and black leather and she had a cowgirl's hat on, broad-brimmed, steep-crowned, with a fringed leather band.

There was no reason why she shouldn't be there. She was free, she wasn't doing anything she shouldn't be, or as far as he could see she wasn't. Philip had to drive on, he had to take his eyes from her, as the lights went to red and amber and a moment's delay would set the drivers behind him all braying on their horns. There was nothing to trouble him in her presence here, but in her appearance and stance there was.

She had moved out of that doorway like a girl drugged or drunk — or exhausted or driven out against her will. The cause of her exit might have been any of those. And she was crying, the tears were running down her face. He saw her bow her head and put her fists in her eyes, and then he had to turn his eyes back to the road and put the car into gear and move fast away from her.

4

The five girls took up their pose against the drawn curtains at Christine's french windows. These curtains had come from her old home and they were of rich dark brown velvet, lined and interlined, light-excluding. The May sunshine showed itself only as a single thin bright line on the right-hand edge of the window, and this vanished when the photographer fastened the curtain to the window frame with a piece of scotch tape.

Philip, a little uneasy in his Moss Bros morning coat and striped trousers, first put his head round the door, then came in and stood at the opposite end of the room. The photographer's lights made it very hot. The photographer was an oldish man, his clothes reeking of cigarette smoke. At first the appearance of the girls dismayed Philip. He knew he had good taste, an eye for the stylish and elegant colour combinations. If he hadn't he probably wouldn't have been in his present job or have wanted it. Who had so badly advised Fee that she had got herself up in white satin, a bluish, Arctic white, stiff and gleaming as a sheet of ice? But perhaps it was all her own choice. Couldn't she see that this patrician dress with its high throat and lean arum lily sleeves, its narrow bell skirt, was designed for a tall thin woman with a flat chest?

Her hat was the sort of thing lead actresses wore in period films of the forties. Philip had seen plenty of them on television. A kind of bowler sported by ladies side-saddle on horseback, only this one was white with the wrong length of veil. And it was arum lilies she carried. Funeral flowers, he thought, remembering a wreath on his father's coffin. As to the bridesmaids, being commanded to smile now, to look, not at the camera, but all adoringly at Fee, he would have laughed at their costumes — what other word for them was there? — if he had seen them in a magazine.

A kind of tunic, each in a different colour, rose, coral, lemon, apricot, great puffy sleeves of some net stuff with orange spots, and bursting from tunic hem at hip level, puffball skirts of the same spotty net. Pink and orange circlets of some unidentifiable flowers on their heads. They were grotesque. Well, he thought, surprising himself, they were all grotesque but one. Cheryl, Stephanie and Fee's old school friend Janice were absurd figures of fun but the other one, she was different. She was — words failed Philip as he stared at her.

This must be Senta. She didn't look as if connected with that family, she didn't look as if related to anyone of their sort. She was extraordinary. This wasn't in her height or something startling about the shape of her, for she was shorter than the other girls and very slender. Her skin was white but not what people mean when they talk about white skin, very fair or pale or creamy but whiter than milk, white as the inner side of some deep sea shell. Her lips were scarcely less pale. He couldn't tell the colour of her eyes but her hair, which was very long, nearly waist-length, straight and smooth, was silver. Not blonde, not grey, but silver with here and there streaks of tarnish on it.

But perhaps the most remarkable thing about her to him, the most exciting thing, was her resemblance to Flora. Her face was Flora's, the perfect oval contour, the straight, rather long nose which described an unbroken line from its tip to the top of her forehead, the widely separated calm eyes, the short upper lip, the lovely mouth that was neither full-lipped nor narrow. If that silver hair had been piled on to the back of her head and bound with ribbons she would have been Flora's image.

She carried herself with patient confidence. While the

others fidgeted, patting their hair between camera shots, adjusting bra straps, resettling bouquets, Senta stood as still as a statue. She was as calm and unruffled as the marble girl, thought Philip, whom three days before he had managed to sneak into the house and up the stairs while Christine finished off a trim in the kitchen. Her figure alone was not like Flora's, her body's bone structure delicate, her waist capable of being clasped in a pair of hands.

Then, as the photographer commanded them all to look at the camera and smile for the last time, she turned fully to face him and gave him an unwelcome shock. Her smile was horribly forced and unnatural, a grimace rather. It was almost as if she were deliberately mocking or sending up this whole rite. But surely she couldn't be, surely that wasn't a purposely ugly sneering grin? If it was, no one but he seemed to notice. The photographer called out, 'Lovely! Hold it, girls, this is positively the last one. ' The picture was taken, the record made. It would have its place no doubt along with the rest in Fee's wedding album. Now Fee only was left to pose for what the photographer called 'two exclusive portraits of the lovely bride'. She had scarcely settled herself into position and allowed Stephanie to arrange the folds of her train, when the door was pushed open and Hardy came in.

'Oh, I must have one shot with him,' Fee exclaimed. 'Look at him, he's so sweet. It'll be quite all right to hold him, he's just been shampooed.'

Two of the bridesmaids had seated themselves on the settee which was pushed back against the wall, but white-faced Senta, her strange metallic hair now cloaking her shoulders, hesitated only for a moment and then walked slowly across the room to Philip. She walked as if she were a much taller woman, up straight with her head held high, but at the same time very gracefully. Before she spoke to him he looked at her mouth and thought it was the most beautiful mouth he had ever seen in a girl's face. What could the voice that came from that mouth be like?

The lips parted. She spoke. 'What a peculiar dog,' she said. 'He has orange spots. He looks like a mini-Dalmatian.'

Philip said slowly, smiling at her, noticing something for the first time, 'He matches your dresses.'

'Did you do it on purpose?'

That made him laugh, her seriousness. 'What happened was my mother splashed him a bit while she was tinting someone's hair. It wouldn't come out when she washed him.'

'I thought he must be some rare breed.'

He had expected a low voice but hers was rather high-pitched, the vowels rounded and pure, the tone cool. She sounded as if she had been taught to speak instead of picking speech up. He noticed that the hands which held her absurd Victorian posy of orange tulip heads and pink carnations, were very small and blunt-nailed, like a child's. She had turned upon him almost colourless eyes, clear as water in which a single drop of dye is spreading in streaks and whorls its dark greenness.

'Are you Philip? Are you Fee's brother?'

'That's right.' He hesitated. 'I'm got up in all this gear because I'm giving her away.'

She said, speaking very precisely as if someone were writing her name down, 'Senta Pelham.'

'I've never met anyone called Senta before. It sounds foreign.'

Her voice took on a cool edge. 'Senta is the name of the girl in *The Flying Dutchman*.'

Philip wasn't sure what or who the Flying Dutchman was – something musical, an opera? – and he was glad of Christine's voice urgently calling his name, 'Philip, Philip, where are you?'

'Excuse me.'

She said nothing. He was unused to people who looked

you straight in the eye without smiling. He closed the living-room door behind him, found Christine in the kitchen, panicky, fraught with anxieties, but looking prettier than she had done for months. Her sudden resurgence of good looks embarrassed him and he would have liked to close his eyes tightly. She was in blue, always her best colour, with a small round hat made of swathed silk in peacock's feather turquoises and lavenders.

'The car is here for me and your aunties and the one for the bridesmaids!'

'That's all right. Everyone's ready.'

She is nicer than Arnham's wife, he thought, she is more of a woman, sweeter and gentler – and surprised himself by his thoughts. Her sisters came down the stairs, one mushroom hat, one parrot's wing, stilt heels, twenty-denier nylons, every ring and bracelet and necklace to be found in their jewel boxes, accompanying clouds of Tweed and Fidji.

'You won't forget to shut Hardy up in the kitchen before you leave, will you?' Christine said to him. 'Otherwise he'll go and do a wee-wee on the white rug. You know how he always does that when he's excited.'

He was alone with Fee. If only she had looked romantic, beautiful! There was nothing in her appearance to inspire a brother's emotion, to raise a lump in the throat, call forth memories of a shared childhood. Her face was creased up, petulant with a myriad small anxieties. She stood in front of a mirror, seeing or imagining she saw, dots of mascara adhering to the skin under her left eye, rubbing with a finger whose cuticle she had bitten in stressful moments before the photographer turned up.

'Don't forget to put your engagement ring on your other hand.'

She pulled it off impatiently. 'I look awful, don't I?'

'You look fine.'

'If it doesn't work out we can get divorced. Most people do.'

I wouldn't get married if I thought like that. He didn't say it aloud. It seemed to him that he had begun keeping everything from her, his views, opinions, feelings. She neither knew that Flora was upstairs in his wardrobe nor that he had seen Cheryl come weeping out of a shop in the Edgware Road. Soon she would have someone else to confide in, tell her innermost thoughts to, but who would he have?

She stepped back from the glass and turned to pick up her sheaf of arums from the table. But instead of doing this she stopped in mid-act, as it were, and threw herself upon him and into his arms. Tense currents seemed to vibrate through her body. It was as if she were full of wires that thrilled with electricity.

'Come on,' he said. 'Come on. Calm down.' He held her in a hug that wasn't tight enough to crush the icy satin. 'You've known him for years, he's the one for you.' What else could he say? 'The original childhood sweethearts.'

He heard the car coming, the brakes, a door close slickly, then footsteps on the front path. 'D'you know what I keep thinking?' she said, disengaging herself, drawing herself up, smoothing her waistline, 'I keep thinking if only that bloody Arnham had done right by Mum we could have been having a double wedding.'

He had made his speech, conscious while he brought out the stiff phrases of praise for Fee and Darren, of Senta Pelham's eyes resting on him. They seemed to rest there in a cold and speculative manner. Every time he looked in her direction, which was often, he found she was looking at him. He asked himself why this should be. Did he truly, as he feared, look ridiculous or unsightly in the grey morningcoat, white shirt and silvery tie? It seemed to him, for all his fears, that the coat in fact fitted rather well. He knew – he couldn't help knowing – that he was good-looking and attractive to girls. Luckily, wherever that gene of shortness and dumpiness came from in his family, it had passed him and Cheryl by. He looked rather the way Paul McCartney had done when young. An old record sleeve of one of the Beatles albums showed him his own face smiling.

The party would break up soon. They only had St Mary's Church hall, an ancient hut smelling of stewed tea and hymn books, until six. The guests, uncles and aunts and cousins and school friends and workmates past and present, would leave as soon as Fee and Darren had gone. Christine was talking to a rather good-looking middle-aged man, another of Darren's innumerable relatives. Giggling, behaving naturally for once, Cheryl stood eating wedding cake with two boys whose shoulder-length hair looked odd with their formal clothes. He accepted a piece of cake handed him by Stephanie and raising his eyes, met those of Senta, of Flora's double.

They seemed to have darkened, the green staining that drifted through their watery depths having curiously intensified. Somewhere during the course of the afternoon she had shed the wreath of flowers which had encircled her head and her hair, unconfined, hung in two gleaming curtains between which the soft seductive features were enclosed. Her eyes widened as they held his and, still gazing at him, she parted her lips and ran her tongue slowly and deliberately over the upper lip and then the lower. The lovely mouth was the pale pink of fruit blossom but her tongue was red. He turned sharply away, convinced she was mocking him.

Fee and Darren came back dressed as no one had ever seen them dressed before, each in a suit, his dark grey, hers white. It would be impossible for anyone they encountered on their journey tonight to an hotel, tomorrow to Guernsey, to mistake them for other than a honeymoon couple. This had been the first wedding Philip had been to since he was a child and he was unprepared for the feeling of anti-climax he experienced as he got into the car. Once the bride and groom were gone, their trim suits smothered in confetti, their car decorated with slogans and a tin can tied on behind, came an immediate sense of let-down. Everyone was going. The evening yawned emptily ahead. Christine would be spending it with one of her sisters. It was left to Philip to drive the bridesmaids back to Glenallan Close where their everyday clothes were.

All but Senta who, standing by the bar in conversation with a man Philip didn't know, sent him a peremptory message by Janice that she would find her own way back to the house, she would get a lift. She would need to, Philip thought aggrievedly, for after the bright start to the day and sunny afternoon, a heavy rain had begun to fall. It made returning home and entering the empty house an even more gloomy business. The three girls went up to the room that Cheryl and Fee had shared and now was Cheryl's alone, while Philip let Hardy out of the kitchen. He changed into jeans and a sweater and, as the rain seemed briefly to have lessened, took the little dog round the block, passing the departing Stephanie and Janice on his way back.

Now was his chance to try and talk to Cheryl. She must still be upstairs. Half-way up he heard music coming from behind her closed door and he went into his own room. He would give her ten minutes or so. Philip's room was very small, too small to hold more than a single bed, a clothes cupboard, desk and narrow upright chair. And although he worked for a firm which specialised among other things in making the most of tiny boxrooms like this one with space-saving fitments and built-in furniture, he had never felt inspired to do something of that kind here. This was partly because he didn't want Glenallan Close improved. Make it more attractive and Christine

– and therefore himself – might be tempted to remain there for ever. On the other hand, it would have been a different story if Christine was Mrs Arnham living in Chigwell and this house had been made over to him. He would have smartened it up then all right.

He opened the clothes cupboard and lifted Flora out. She was still wrapped in the blue plastic bag with the split in it for her face to show through. Philip untied the knot in the bag and pulled it off over her head. He stood her in the corner by the window. It was interesting that just having her there immediately improved the look of the room. Her white marble skin seemed to gleam in the grey, rain-filtered light. He wondered if it would be possible to remove the green stain which mantled her neck and breast. Her eyes looked beyond him and her face seemed alight with pagan wisdom.

Arnham and his wife would have missed her as soon as they looked out into their garden. Probably the neighbour would have told them as soon as they returned about the thief he had seen carrying a log-shaped bundle and they would have put two and two together. But Philip didn't think they would connect the removal of Flora with him. If Arnham remembered him at all it would be as he then was, a recent student, a newly recruited Roseberry Lawn trainee, who had presented a very different appearance from the man the neighbour would have described as short-haired and wearing a suit. Arnham might even be relieved at the loss of Flora, while perhaps superstitiously unwilling to get rid of her himself. He was wondering whether to try working on that stain with paint stripping fluid or to talk to Cheryl first when she spoke to him from outside on the landing. They never knocked at each other's doors but they didn't walk into rooms uninvited either.

'Phil? Are you in there?'

He hung his Moss Bros clothes over the chair and pushed it in front of Flora to hide her. Opening the door, he found no one there and then Cheryl came out of her room, dressed to go out in her usual uniform, the cowgirl hat in her hand. Her hair, done that morning in soft loose curls falling from a centre parting, bridesmaid's coiffure, looked incongruous with the heavy black eye make-up and the green star she had drawn on one cheekbone.

'Will you do me a favour?' she said.

The inevitable reply to that one: 'Depends what it is.'

'Would you lend me five pounds?'

'Cheryl,' he said, 'I have to tell you I saw you in the Edgware Road on Wednesday. It was around six or six-thirty. You were crying and you were sort of staggering around.'

She stared at him, her underlip protruding.

'I couldn't stop, I was stuck in the traffic. You looked like you were drunk. I've been thinking lately you might be on drugs but you looked more as if you were drunk.'

'I don't drink,' she said. 'Don't you notice anything about people? Couldn't you see I didn't even drink that fizzy stuff at the wedding? A glass of wine is enough to knock me sideways.' She laid her hand on his arm. 'Will you lend me five pounds? I'll give it back to you tomorrow.'

'It's not the money,' he said, though of course up to a point it was. He had very little spare cash. 'It's not the money that's the trouble. But what do you mean, I can have it back tomorrow? Tomorrow's Sunday. How are you going to get money on a Sunday?' She was gazing at him, her eyes glaring with a kind of desperate intensity. 'Cheryl, how *do* you get money? Where does it come from?'

'You sound like a policeman,' she said. 'Just like a policeman would question a person.'

He said unhappily, 'I think I've got a sort of right to ask you.'

'I don't. I'm over eighteen. I'm as much an adult as you are. I can vote.'

'That's got nothing to do with it.'

'Please,' she said, '*please* just lend me five pounds. You'll get it back tomorrow.'

'When you get your dole on Wednesday will do.' He went back into his room and took the last five-pound note he had from his wallet in the pocket of the Moss Bros trousers. That left him with three pound coins and some odd pence.

She snatched it from him. Once she held it crushed in her hand up against the lapels of the leather jacket, she managed a smile, she managed a, 'Thanks very much, Phil.'

He could find nothing to say to her. He went back into his room and sat down on the bed. Her feet went fast down the stairs and he waited for the front door to slam. Instead he heard her speaking to someone, a brief exchange of indecipherable words. Their mother perhaps had come back for something she had forgotten. Forgetting things, money, keys, a coat, suitable shoes, was a commonplace with Christine.

The door slammed rather less violently than usual. The house didn't shake from foundations to roof. He took the hired clothes off the chair, emptied the pockets, placed them on hangers and hung them inside the cupboard. The rain had begun again, buffeted against the glass by the rising wind. Someone knocked at the bedroom door.

But no one in the household ever did. He thought, supposing it is the police, sent after me for taking Flora, just suppose it is. A cold thrill went down his spine. But he didn't cover her up or put her away. He opened the door.

It was Senta Pelham.

*

He had forgotten she was coming back.

She was still in her bridesmaid's dress and she was very wet. Her hair was wet, water dripping from it, and the spotted net, intended to be puffed and stiff, drooped like the petals of a rain-soaked flower. The coral satin clung to her thin, fragile-looking ribcage and to the large round breasts, incongruously big for so slight a girl. Her nipples stuck out erect at the touch of the cold wet stuff.

'Is there a towel somewhere?'

'In the bathroom,' he said. Didn't she know that? Hadn't she got herself up in that absurd garment in this house?

'I couldn't get a lift after all,' she said, and he noticed she was out of breath. 'I had to walk,' though it was more as if she had been running.

'Dressed like that?'

She laughed in a throaty gasping way. She seemed tremendously nervous. She went into the bathroom and came out, rubbing her hair dry with one bath towel and with another slung over her shoulder. Philip expected her to go into Cheryl's room but instead she came into his and shut the door behind her.

'There's a hairdryer somewhere.'

She shook her head, took off the towel and really shook it. The gleaming hair flew out and she ran her fingers through it. He had hardly realised what she was doing, he had hardly taken in that she was kicking off shoes, stripping off pale, wet, mud-splashed tights, before she stood up and peeled the dress over her head. She stood there looking at him, her arms hanging by her sides.

The room was too small for two people in it ever to be separated by more than a few feet. As it was he found himself at no more than arm's length from this naked girl whose strange thin big-breasted body was marble-white with at the base of her flat belly a triangle, not of silver or blonde but of flame red. Philip was in no doubt, whatever he may have felt thirty seconds before, of what was going on and what she intended. She was eyeing him with that intense yet mysterious gaze with which she had so frequently favoured him at the wedding. He took a step towards her, put out his arms and held her shoulders with his hands. The coldness of marble was what he had strangely expected, but she was warm, hot even, her skin silky and dry.

Philip folded her slowly in his arms, savouring the slippery soft full and slender nakedness against his own body. As she moved her head to bring her mouth against his, the long wet hair slapped at his hands, making him shiver. She whispered to him as her tongue flickered, her hands unbuttoning his shirt, 'Into bed. I'm cold, I'm cold.' But she felt as hot as a body on a tropical beach, the heat shimmered from her.

It warmed the cold sheets. Philip pulled the duvet over them and they lay pressed into each other's bodies in the narrow little bed. The rain began crashing against the window. Suddenly she started to make love to him with a greedy passion. Her fingers dug into his neck, his shoulders, she moved down his body, kissing his flesh, licking him with a curious gasping savour. Bowed over him, arching up the quilt, she swept him with her curtain of hair, teased him with her tongue. Her lips felt tender and rapturous and gentle.

He gasped, 'No!' and then, 'No!' because it was too much, it stretched him to explosion point. Behind his head and inside his eyes was a red rolling light. Groaning, he pulled her on to him and entered her, her white body, now streaming with sweat, sinking on to his with a strange quivering rhythm. She held him in a total clutch, holding her breath, then relaxing as she expelled it, drawing breath again, gripping him, releasing himself and her with a final expulsion and a little thin scream.

*

Her silver hair which draped his shoulders, hung like the rain he could see falling straight and glittering beyond the glass. He felt a deep extraordinary profound satisfaction, as if he had found something he had always been searching for and found it finer than he expected. There were things he thought he ought to say but all that came to mind was 'thank you, thank you,' and he sensed that to utter this aloud would be wrong. Instead he took her face in his hand and turned it to his and kissed her mouth long and very gently.

She hadn't spoken a word since saying she was cold and they should go to bed. But now she raised her head and laid it on the arm which held her. She took his right hand in her left one, interlocking their fingers. In that high pure tone of hers she said,

'Philip . . .' She uttered his name reflectively and as if she were listening to the sound of it, as if she were putting it to the test to see if she liked it. 'Philip.'

He smiled at her. Her eyes were close to his, her mouth as close to his face as it could be without their lips touching. He saw every detail of its soft and tender curves, the sweetly tucked-in corners of it.

'Say my name,' she said.

'Senta. It's a beautiful name, Senta.'

'Listen to me, Philip. When I saw you this morning I knew at once that you were the one. I knew you were the only one.' Her tone was deeply solemn. She had raised herself on one elbow. She was looking deeply into his eyes. 'I saw you across the room and I knew you were the one for me for always.'

He was astonished. This was not at all what he had expected from her.

'I've been looking for you for a long long time,' she said, 'and now I've found you and it's wonderful.'

Her intensity had begun, slightly, to embarrass him. He could only handle this awkwardness by speaking lightly, almost facetiously. 'It can't be all that long. How old are you, Senta? Not more than twenty, are you?'

'I'm twenty-four. You see? I'm going to tell you everything, I'll keep nothing from you. You can ask me anything.' He didn't particularly want to ask her things, just to hold her and feel her and have this glorious pleasure. 'I've been looking for you since I was sixteen. You see, I've always known there was just one man in the world for me and I knew that when I saw him I'd know.'

Her lips brushed his shoulder. She turned her face and printed a kiss where the muscle swelled beyond the collarbone. 'I believe that souls come in pairs, Philip, but when we're born they are split in two and we spend all our lives trying to find our other half. But sometimes people make a mistake and get the wrong one.'

'This isn't a mistake, is it? It wasn't for me.'

'This,' she said, 'is for ever. Don't you feel that? I saw you across the room and I knew you were the twin to my soul, the other half. That's why the first thing I ever said to you, the first word I spoke, was your name.'

Philip thought he remembered the first word she had spoken was to say Hardy was a peculiar dog but he must be mistaken. What did it matter anyway? She was in his bed, had made love with him more gloriously than any girl ever before, and would do so, almost certainly, again.

'For ever,' she whispered, a slow hieratic smile spreading across her face. He was glad of that smile, for he didn't want her becoming too serious. 'Philip, I don't want you to say you love me. Not yet. I shan't tell you I love you, though I do. Those words are so commonplace, everyone uses them, they're not for us. What we have and are going to have is too deep for that, our feelings are too deep.' She turned her face into the hollow of his shoulder and ran her fingers lightly down the length of his body, quickly exciting him again. 'Philip, shall I stay the night here with you?'

He hated having to refuse that. Christine wouldn't come into his room that night but she would in the morning, she always did, bearing with her the cup of tea slopped into its saucer, the encrusted sugar bowl with the damp spoon stuck in it. She wouldn't criticise him, she might not even mention that she had found him with a girl in his bed, she might only look dismayed and terribly embarrassed, her eyes wide and her hand going up to her pursed lips, but he wouldn't be able to bear it. It would be too much for him.

'I'd love you to, more than anything, but I don't really think it's on.' Without yet knowing her very well he anticipated an immediate scene, fury perhaps or tears.

She surprised him by her radiant smile, the way she took his face in her hands and planted a tiny light kiss on his mouth. In a moment she was out of bed, shaking her hair, drawing her fingers through it. 'It doesn't matter. We can go to my place.'

'You've a place of your own?'

'Of course. It's yours as well now, Philip. You understand that, don't you? It's yours as well.'

In Cheryl's room, absent for an instant, she changed into the clothes she must have arrived in that morning, a long full black skirt, a long loose sweater of silvery knitted stuff the colour of her hair. These garments hid the shape of her as nearly as the burka hides the contours of the Islamic woman. Her slender legs, tiny ankles, were in black tights, her feet in flat black pumps. She came back into his room and saw Flora in the corner for the first time.

'She looks like me!'

He remembered what he had thought in Arnham's garden before he stole her, if he ever met a girl like her he would fall at once in love. His eyes went from Senta to the statue and he saw the resemblance. So often when you thought someone looked like someone else or like a picture, say, the likeness disappeared when they were together. This didn't happen. They were twins, in stone and flesh. It made him shiver a little as if something solemn had happened. 'Yes, she looked like you.' He realised he had spoken quite gravely. 'I'll tell you about her sometime,' he said.

'Yes, you must. I want to know all about you, Philip. I want to know everything. We must have no secrets from each other. Get dressed and come with me now. I'm scared of seeing other people – oh, your mother, your sister, I don't know. I just don't want to meet anyone else. I think our first evening should be sacred somehow, don't you?'

The rain lifted for them just before they left and when they came out into the streaming street, the setting sun showed. The sun made all the puddles and sheets of water shine like a paving of gold. She had hesitated a little before leaving the house, as if to go out was to take some kind of plunge. Perhaps it was, for the street was like a shallow river bed. Once inside the car, she drew in her breath and sighed as if with relief or perhaps just with happiness. He sat beside her and they kissed.

5

This was a part of London he hardly knew, lying in westernmost West Kilburn and north of the Harrow Road. It was growing dark and after the rain the streets were empty of people. Opposite a huge sprawling school building, dating from the beginning of the century, surrounded by a high brick wall, was a food supply centre for down-and-outs, a soup kitchen. On its steps a queue of men waited and one old woman with a basket on wheels in which a dog sat. Philip drove past a church set in a churchyard dark and dense as a wood and turned into Tarsus Street.

Only the plane trees, breaking into leaf, soon to be abundant, concealing and overshadowing fissures in the pavement and broken fences, saved it from being a slum. Their tender unfolding leaves caught the light from street lamps as a gilding and shed vine-like sharp-edged shadows. The house where Senta lived was in a terrace of plum-coloured brick. All the windows were flat and rectangular and recessed in the facade. A flight of ten steps led to the front door, a heavy panelled wooden door, once, many years past, painted dark green, and now so pitted with chips and actual holes that it seemed as if someone had used it for target practice. From these steps it was possible to look over the plastered wall which served them as a balustrade and into the area, clogged with rubbish, tin cans, paper, orange peel, that fronted the basement window.

Senta unlocked the front door. The house was large, with three floors above the basement, but as soon as he was inside Philip sensed, without knowing how, that they were alone in it. This didn't mean, of course, that Senta had sole possession of the house. The two bicycles leaning up against the wall, the pile of junk mail lying on a dilapidated mahogany table, made this improbable. All the doors were closed. She led him along the hall and down the basement stairs. The smell of the place was new to Philip. He couldn't have defined it except to say it smelt very subtly of an accumulation of various kinds of ancient dirt, dirt that was never removed, never even shifted from one surface to another, one level to another, of food crumbs years old, fibres of unwanted clothes, dead insects, cobwebs, grains of mud and shreds of excrement, spilt liquids long dried, the hair of animals and their droppings, of dust and soot. It smelt of disintegration.

The basement had once been a self-contained flat. Or so it seemed. Its rooms, all but one, were used to store things, the objects that were perhaps partly responsible for the smell. Old furniture and crates of bottles and jars and heaps of old newspapers and piles of folded darkish woollen things that had once been blankets but which moths were reducing to a crumbling grey flocculent mass. An ancient lavatory with an overhead cistern which could be made private by drawing a sketchily rigged-up shower curtain. There was a clawfooted bath and a single cold tap of brass coated with a green crust and bandaged in rags.

Senta's was the only inhabitable room. It was at the front of the house, the room whose window could be seen beyond the area. It contained primarily a large bed. This bed was six feet wide with a sagging mattress and made up with purple sheets and pillowcases that smelt as if they hadn't been changed for rather a long time. There was also an enormous mirror, its frame adorned with plaster cherubs and fruit and flowers, from which much of the gilding as well as the occasional limb, twig and petal, had been chipped or had disappeared altogether.

On a low table stood a burnt-out candle in a saucer full of wax with an empty wine bottle beside it. There was a wicker chair draped with discarded clothes and a dying plant growing out of a brass pot full of dust. No curtains hung at the window but it could be covered by a pair of wooden shutters. A greyish watery light was shed into the room between these shutters but it was insufficient to see by. Senta had lit the lamp which had a bulb of low wattage under a parchment shade. That first evening, having looked wonderingly at the room, shocked by it and therefore feeling unsure of himself, he had asked her what she did.

'I'm an actor.'

'You mean an actress.'

'No, I don't, Philip. You wouldn't talk about a doctoress or a lawyeress, would you?'

He conceded that. 'Have you been on television?' he asked. 'Would I have seen you in anything?'

She laughed but in a kindly way, an indulgent way. 'I was at RADA. Now I'm waiting for the kind of part someone of my sort needs to make the best beginning. It would be letting myself down to take just anything, don't you think?'

'I don't know,' he said. 'I don't know anything about it.'

'But you will. You'll learn from me. I want you to have opinions about me, Philip, that's going to be the most important thing in my world, our world, what we think about each other. A spiritual interchange is going to be the essence of our life together.'

But there had been nothing very spiritual that evening. Soon after that they had got into her bed. When you were lying in her bed you could see the legs of people walking along the pavement outside the window. That meant that if they bent down they could see you. She laughed at him when he got up to close the shutters but he closed them just the same. The lamp with its fringed

76

shade gave a brownish dim light that laid a mysterious glaze on their love-making, a coat of gold to their moving limbs. She seemed to have an inexhaustible ardour, an inventiveness she pursued with a frown of concentration until she broke into high breathless laughter. She laughed a lot, he already loved her laughter. He already loved her extraordinary voice, high without shrillness, smooth and pure and cool.

He had meant to get up and go home at midnight but used and repeatedly ridden by her, devoured and chewed and grasped and drawn in, expelled only with desperate reluctance, excavated with a child's little strong fingers and excoriated with a tongue as coarse as a cat's, he had whimpered and sighed and slept. The last thing he remembered hearing her say before that deathlike sleep came was, 'I don't just want to have you, Philip, I want to *be* you.'

Next morning, Sunday, he had walked in at ten – he hadn't awakened till past nine – to find Christine and Cheryl on the point of calling the police. 'I thought,' his mother said, 'how awful it was going to be if I'd lost a son as well as a daughter.' She didn't ask him where he had been and that wasn't tactfulness or discretion. Now she had him back she simply didn't think of where he might have been or what he was doing.

He walked into the living room and the postcard was gone. Because he had spoken about it to her or Fee had? On the rug in front of the fireplace lay a tiny bruised pink rosebud. It must have come from one of the bridesmaids' wreaths or bouquets, perhaps from Senta's. It was a funny thing, though, that you couldn't think of Senta in the sort of way, a sentimental or romantic way. You wouldn't think of needing a flower that had been hers to remember her by. He picked it up and smelt it and it said nothing to him. But why should it? He had Senta and would have her again tonight, he had the real woman herself with her tarnished silver hair.

Cheryl came into the room and handed him a five-pound note. He felt differently from yesterday, fourteen or fifteen hours ago only, an entirely different person, and Cheryl's troubles if such existed, were remote from him, not his business.

'Thanks,' he said, and in such a preoccupied way as to make her stare at him. He would have liked best to tell her about Senta. Well, he would have liked best of all to tell Fee if Fee hadn't been on her way to St Peter Port. Senta, in any case, had said no.

'I don't want anyone knowing about us yet, Philip. Not yet. For a little while it must be our sacred secret.'

That had been a week ago. And since then he had seen her every day. By Tuesday he was telling Christine he would be staying away for the night, at least for tonight and maybe the next one, because Roseberry Lawn were involving him in a project of theirs at Winchester and were putting him up in an hotel. Now, for the first time, he understood the value of having a mother like Christine. That vagueness and unworldliness which had formerly irritated him, and worse, troubled him as to what this would mean for her future welfare, that apparent lack of knowledge of any sort of conventional response, now appeared a godsend.

Senta had no phone. There was a phone on that table in the hall half-hidden among the litter of junk mail but seldom anyone at home to answer it. Other people must live in the house but Philip had never seen them, though one night, awakened by it, he had heard dance music above his head and the sound of waltzing feet. He went home to eat the meal Christine had prepared for him, took Hardy for a walk round the block, then drove to Kilburn. It was a relief one morning when Christine said she thought of spending the evening with her friend but she would leave him a meal and would that be all right?

The friend was someone she had met at Fee's wedding. What a lot of significant things had happened at Fee's wedding!

Philip told her not to bother with a meal, he would eat out. He went to Senta's straight from work and for the first time they ate out together. It was a change, it was more like reality. Up till then he had been parking the car in the street at eight-thirty or nine, worrying a bit about it because this was a rough area. He would run down the basement stairs, his heartbeat racing. The smell was strongest here, in the well of the staircase. But inside Senta's door it faded. There the damp sour smell of decay was overcome by the perfume of incense sticks, one of which was usually smoking in her room. She would be waiting for him, sitting in the window or cross-legged on the floor. Once she was reclining naked on the bed, reminding him of a picture someone had once sent Fee on a postcard, the *Olympe* of Manet.

To go out with her to a restaurant was a new experience. He discovered her to be not merely a vegetarian but a vegan. It was fortunate he had chosen to eat at an Indian place. She wore a strange old dress that might have belonged to her grandmother, grey with silver threads woven into it, the belt missing, though you could see there should have been a belt, and a crumpled rose of grey silk on the bosom. Her silver hair hung like a veil bought to match it. She had painted her eyes green and her mouth dark purple. He didn't know whether he liked this kind of dressing but it disturbed him, it excited him, to look at her thus caparisoned. In the cheap Indian restaurant where a tape played sitar music and the walls were papered with a design of turbanned men and elephants, where the lights were dim, she looked like a goddess of mystery and the arcane. The mouth though – he hated to see it concealed under that layer of greasy purple. Tentatively he had asked her to wipe it off, her mouth was so beautiful. Why had he expected defiance? She wiped her lips clean with a piece of toilet paper, said to him in a tone that was humble, 'I'll do whatever you want. Whatever you like is right.'

'Tell me about yourself,' he said. 'I don't know anything about you, Senta, except that you're an actress – sorry, actor – and you're Darren's cousin. Though I find that hard to believe,'

She smiled a little, then began laughing. She could be intensely serious, in a way he would have found embarrassing if he had tried to copy it, and she could laugh more freely and gaily than anyone he had ever known. He could understand she might not want to be too closely associated with the Collier family, a beefy-faced jolly crowd of sport-mad men and bingo-addicted women. 'My mother was an Icelandic woman,' she said. 'My father was in the Navy, you see, and he met her when they put in at Reykjavik.'

'What do you mean 'was', Senta. Your mother's still alive, isn't she?' She had told him her parents were separated, each now living with a new partner. 'You said your mother had a boyfriend you don't much like.'

'My mother died when I was born.'

He stared at her, it seemed so strange. He had never heard of anyone dying in childbirth except in old books.

'It was in Reykjavik, I was born there. My father was away at sea.' Her expression had grown suspicious, slightly displeased. 'Why do you look like that? What are you thinking? They were married, if that's what you're thinking.'

'Senta, I didn't mean . . .'

'He brought me back here and soon after that he married Rita, she's the woman I call my mother. My real mother's name was Reidun, Reidun Knudsdatter. It means Canute's daughter. Don't you think that's amazing? Not 'son' but 'daughter'. It's an ancient matrilinear system.'

That evening too she told him how she had won a

scholarship to drama school and come out top student of her year. During the holidays, in her second year, she had gone to Morocco and taken a room for two months in the Medina of Marrakesh. Because it was difficult to be a western woman alone there she had worn Moslem women's dress, the veil which allowed only her eyes and forehead to show, and a floor-length black dress. Another time she had gone with friends to Mexico City and been there during the earthquake. She had been to India. Philip felt he had little to tell her about himself in return for these accounts of remarkable or exotic experiences. The death of a father, responsibility for a mother, worries over Cheryl, were a poor exchange.

But once back in the basement room, sharing a bottle of wine he had bought, he did tell her about Christine and Gerard Arnham and Flora. He gave her a detailed account of what had happened after he saw the marble girl from Mrs Ripple's bedroom window. She laughed when he described how he had stolen the statue and been seen by one of Arnham's neighbours, and even asked exactly where this was, what was the name of the street and so on, but still he had a feeling she hadn't listened as closely to his narrations as he had to hers. Reclining on the big bed, she seemed preoccupied with her own image in the mirror. This relic of some vanished once-elegant drawing room, its gilded cherubs missing a leg or arm, its swags of flowers denuded of their leaves, reflected her mistily, as if she were suspended in cloudy greenish water, her marble-white body spotted by the flaws in the glass.

If she hadn't concentrated on what he said, he soon thought, this was due only to her desire for him which seemed as great as his for her. He wasn't used to this with girls who, in the past, when his need was insistent, were tired or 'not feeling like it' or having periods or peeved by something he had said. Senta's sexual impulses were as urgent as his. And, blessed relief from those girls

81

of the past, she was as quickly and easily satisfied as he. Uniquely, no long-drawn out patient attention to a partner's needs were here required. His needs were hers and hers his.

On the last night of the week, the night before Fee and Darren were due home from their honeymoon, he began to get to know her. It was a breakthrough, that evening, and he was glad of it.

They had made love and rolled apart from each other on the bed. He lay spent and happy, the only alloy to his contentment being the niggling concern which now wormed back into his mind: how could he broach the subject of getting her to change the sheets? How could he do this without offence or seeming to criticise? It was such a silly small thing, yet the smell of the sheets upset him.

Her silver hair covered the pillow. Tresses of it here and there she had made into little plaits. She lay on her back. The hair in her crotch was a bright fiery unnatural colour and he could see that vivid red patch twice, both on her white body and reflected in the mirror, which hung at a wide angle, its top jutting at least a foot from the wall. Almost without thinking, on an impulse, taking her hand in his and laying it on the bright fuzzy triangle, he said with laughter in his voice, idly, 'why do you dye your pubic hair?'

She sprang up. She flung his hand from her, and because that hand had been relaxed and her movement utterly unexpected, it struck his chest a blow. Her face was contorted with rage. She trembled with anger, her fists clenched as she knelt up over him. 'What do you mean, dye it? Fuck you, Philip Wardman! You've got a fucking nerve talking to me like that!'

For a second or two he could scarcely believe what he was hearing, those words uttered in that pure musical voice. He sat up, tried to catch her hands in his, ducked to avoid the blow she aimed at him instead.

82

'Senta, Senta, what's the matter with you?'

'You, you're the matter. How dare you say that to me about dyeing my pubic hair?'

He was nearly a foot taller than she and twice as powerful. This time he did get hold of her arms, did subdue her. She breathed in gasps, wriggling in his hold. Her face was twisted with the effort to escape. He laughed at her.

'Well, don't you? You're a blonde, you can't be that colour down there.'

She spat the words at him. 'I dye the hair of my head, you fool!'

Laughter made him relax his hold on her. As he did so he expected an onslaught, put up his hands to cover his face, simultaneously thinking, how awful, we're quarrelling, what now, what now? She took his hands away gently, held his face, brought soft warm lips on to his, kissing him more sweetly and lengthily than she ever had, stroking his face, his chest. Then the hand she had let fall to slap him with its knuckle bones, she took in her own and laid it delicately on the region of her body that had caused their strife, on the red hair and the thin white silky skin of her inner thighs.

Half an hour later she got up, said, 'These sheets do niff a bit. Go and sit in the chair for a minute and I'll change them.'

And she had, purple to emerald green, the soiled ones stuffed into her carpet bag for carrying to the launderette. He thought to himself, we are getting close, she read my mind, I like that, I love her, temperamental little spitfire that she is. But some time after midnight, leaving her asleep and covered by the quilt in its clean green cotton cover, climbing the dark smelly stairs, it came to him that he hadn't believed what she said about dyeing the hair of her head. She must be making that up. Of course she bleached it and put something on it to make it silvery, you could see that, but no one with red hair would dye it metal colour. Why would they?

He experienced a pang of something he quickly recognised as fear. It frightened him that she might tell him lies. But it was after all a very small lie, a matter of no importance, the sort of thing all girls perhaps failed to tell the strict truth about, and he remembered Jenny saying her tan was natural when in fact she had been having daily sessions on a sunbed.

Jenny - it was a long time since he had given her much thought. He hadn't seen her or heard her voice since they had quarrelled back in January. She had wanted them to be engaged, had started on about it while they were away on holiday in Majorca together the previous October. I can't get married, he had said to her, I can't think about getting married for years. Where would we live? Here with my mother? If we were engaged, she had said, I'd feel I meant something to you, I'd feel we were together, a couple. And then of course it had come out, the true reason behind it: I don't think I should sleep with you if it's just casual, I don't think it's right, if we aren't going steady.

She had nagged him to make her a promise he couldn't, then wouldn't, make. Parting from her had been a far greater wrench than he expected but now it seemed the wisest thing he could have done. Strange comparing, or rather contrasting, her with Senta. Driving home, he found himself laughing aloud at the thought of Senta asking to go steady, to get engaged. Her idea of permanency was something Jenny in her mousey little suburban way had never dreamed of, total commitment, utter exclusivity, the perfect unparalleled union of two human beings embarking on life's adventure.

The return of Fee and her husband served to show Philip something amazing, that he had known Senta only a fortnight. Fee and Darren had been absent for two weeks and when they were last here Senta was virtually a stranger to him, a girl in an absurd orange-spotted dress who looked at him across a crowded room in certain mysterious ways which he, fool that he was, had been unable to interpret.

Her daily society since then had made him believe, all experience to the contrary, that Darren, being her cousin, must be a far more interesting and clever person than he remembered. He must have been wrong about Darren. Perhaps it was natural to feel no man was really good enough for one's sister. But now he was in the company of his new brother-in-law he realised he hadn't been mistaken. Thickset and at twenty-four with a fat belly already developing, Darren sat guffawing at some television serial which it seemed imperative for him to see, never to miss, even though he might be in someone else's house. He had insisted on watching it the two Sundays they were away, Fee said in the proud tone of a mother talking of her baby's feeding requirements.

Returned home the day before, they had come to tea, though tea as such wasn't a meal ever eaten in the Glenallan Close household. Christine had supplied one of her culinary masterpieces in the shape of sliced ham sausage and canned spaghetti rings. Afterwards she was going to do Fee's hair, was childishly delighted because Fee, for once, was permitting this. Philip thought she was looking rather nice. There was no doubt she had looked better, younger and somehow happier, since the wedding. It couldn't be relief at getting the wedding over and Fee married, for she had once or twice suggested – she never did more than suggest – that Fee, at her age, could easily afford to wait a couple of years before settling down. It must be the new friend, having the companionship of someone her own age. She had pink lipstick on, rather well-applied and not muzzy at the edges, and had given her hair one of those golden rinses that had hitherto been reserved for clients.

They disappeared to the kitchen. Philip heard his mother compliment Fee on the navy-blue jumper she was wearing and say wasn't it funny to buy a guernsey actually in Guernsey. Fee's patient explanation that the garment took its name from the island, as jersey did, gave rise to cries of wonderment.

Cheryl, as usual, was out somewhere. Philip was left alone with his brother-in-law. Denied further television, Darren was talkative on the subjects of international sport, the new Fiat and congestion on the roads, and expansive on his honeymoon location. The cliffs of Guernsey were the highest he had ever seen, they must surely be the highest in the British Isles, he couldn't begin to estimate their height. And the currents in the Channel were particularly treacherous. He wondered how many swimmers had come to grief through those currents. Philip, who had been abroad on several package tours, thought Darren would be one of those tourists who are always asking the guide how old or new something is, how deep this water, how high this mountain, how many bricks did it take to build this cathedral, how many men to paint this ceiling.

Photographs were produced, though no colour slides yet, thank God. Philip longed to speak to Darren about Senta. Here, he had thought, while the women were absent, was his opportunity. Of course, he didn't intend to break his word to Senta and reveal their relationship. In a way there would be something delightful in speaking of her while concealing that she was any more than an acquaintance. But so far Darren, talking non-stop, entranced by his chosen subject of conversation, gave him no chance. Philip had to bide his time. He had already discovered the joys of speaking her name to others and had mentioned her, in a light-hearted indifferent sort of way, to his mother and Cheryl.

'Senta, that girl with the sort of silvery-blonde hair, who was Fee's bridesmaid, I bet she'll come out well in the photographs,' and, rather more daringly, 'You wouldn't think that girl Senta who was Fee's bridesmaid was related to Darren, would you?'

Her father was his mother's brother. It was hard to believe. They had no feature, no shade of skin, hair or eye in common. They were of totally different build and might have belonged to different races. Darren's hair was yellow and thick and rather rough, like new thatch. He had blue eyes and strong handsome features and ruddy skin. One day wine-coloured jowls would hang over his shirt collar and his nose would become an outsize strawberry. He was a square man, the jack on a playing card.

Philip said suddenly, filling the brief silence which fell while Darren was putting all his photographs back into the yellow envelope, 'I'd never met your cousin Senta till the wedding.'

Darren looked up. For a moment he didn't say anything and it seemed to Philip that he was staring in astonishment. Philip had the extraordinary notion, coupled with the start of panic, that he was going to deny having a cousin or even say, 'Who? You mean Jane, don't you? She only says she's called that.'

But it wasn't astonishment. It wasn't wonder or indignation or anything like that, just Darren's habitual slowness at comprehension. Gradually a sly smile spread across his face.

'You fancy her then, do you, Phil?'

'I don't know her,' Philip said. 'I've only met her once.' He realised he had told his first lie for Senta and he wondered why he had done it. But he plunged on. 'She's your first cousin?'

This was too much for Darren who said with some bewilderment, 'First, second, I don't reckon I've been into all that. All I know is my mum is her auntie and her dad is my uncle and that makes us cousins in my book.

Right?' He returned to safer and better-known ground. 'Come on now, Phil, you do fancy her.'

The knowing look and sophisticated smile were all Darren required and these Philip, without too much strain, supplied. Darren responded with a wink. 'She's a funny piece, Senta. You should see the place she lives in, a real rat-hole, a dump. Fee wouldn't set foot there when they were fixing up about the dresses and whatnot and I don't know as I blame her. And she could have a nice home with Uncle Tom in Finchley, she must want her head tested.'

Although he felt he was betraying himself with every word, Philip couldn't stop yet. 'Fee doesn't know her very well then?'

'Don't let that worry you, old lad. I know her. I can get you in there if that's what you're after.'

He wasted no more words on Senta but reverted to Guernsey and his passion for heights, depths, weights, measures and extremes of temperature. Philip let him run on, then excused himself. He was due at Senta's at nine. Before leaving the house he had something to see to upstairs. It had occurred to him that Fee might go into his room if she was still in the house after he had gone out. She never had gone in there during the days when she lived in Glenallan Close and there was no reason for her to do so now. But he had been struck by some kind of premonition or simple apprehensiveness. The marble girl still stood, uncovered, in the corner between clothes cupboard and window wall.

It was ten to nine but not dark yet and the glimmering light made her marble skin very radiant, pearl-like yet human too, as if she lived. She was Senta to the life. Was not that calm yet starry gaze at distant horizons hers alone? Those folded lips set in exquisite proportion to the straight delicate nose? She had even done her hair like that when they went out together, bound closely around her head in little waves from where the plaits had crimped it. He had a sudden desire, which he recognised as absurd and to be quickly suppressed, to kiss that marble mouth, to press his own lips against the lips that looked so soft. He wrapped the statue up again, not in the cold slippery plastic, but in an old Aran sweater and thrust her into the back of the cupboard.

Talking of Senta, hearing her declarations confirmed – he felt treacherous there, but it was true, he had doubted and feared – tasting her euphonious name on his lips and hearing it spoken so idly by another, somehow fired him with a newer, fiercer ardour. He could hardly wait to be with her and he was breathless in the car, cursing at the red traffic lights. Down the dirty stairs he ran, his body taut and tense with longing for her, his fingers fumbling the key in the lock, the scent of smoking joss stick coming to him as the door slid open and admitted him to her pungent, dusty, mysterious domain.

6

Under the may tree from which all the flowers had long fallen, which was now just an ordinary green tree, stood a figure of Cupid with his bow and quiver of arrows. Philip couldn't see it very clearly, for the binoculars were still missing from the room. Everything else was missing too. Mrs Ripple had carried out Roseberry Lawn's requirements and had the interior stripped of cookery books, fireplace, extraneous woodwork and floor covering. It was now a shell.

The Cupid amused Philip. He knew this was the god of love and he wondered if Arnham had chosen it for this reason or simply because he liked it. A month ago he would have been affronted, incensed by the presence of this substitute for Flora. But in those intervening weeks he had changed a lot. He could hardly remember why he had stolen Flora. He found he no longer minded about Arnham, he had become indifferent to him, even felt friendly towards him. His anger was all gone. Why, if he were to meet the man now, he would say hallo to him and ask him how he was.

His mission on this Saturday, generally accepted as a day off, had simply been to come here and inspect Mrs Ripple's house, to check if what she had said on the phone about the room being ready – you couldn't trust these customers – was accurate. The Roseberry Lawn fitters would be coming in on Monday. Philip closed the door behind him and went downstairs. Mrs Ripple was waiting for him at the foot.

'I shan't be able to make tea for them.'

'That's quite all right, Mrs Ripple, they won't expect it.' They would, but what was the use of arguing? There seemed no point either in anticipating trouble by telling her that if she didn't give them a mid-morning and mid-afternoon drink the fitters would take half an hour off at eleven and half an hour off at three to go down the café. 'You'll find them very easy and I think you'll be pleased by the way they clear up after themselves.'

'I won't tolerate smoking or transistors.'

'Of course not,' said Philip, thinking she could argue it out with the workmen. He knew who would win that battle.

The door slammed behind him. No wonder she had cracks in her ceilings. He went down the path to the car where Senta sat waiting for him in the passenger seat.

This was the first time she had been out with him since that Indian meal, which had never been repeated, though with the exception of an evening a week unwillingly spent at home with Christine, he had been with her every night. There was no point in eating out, she said, and he could tell food didn't mean much to her, though she liked chocolates and she liked wine. Nor had she ever cooked for him. He often remembered Fee's remark when, before he knew her, he had asked why Senta couldn't make her own dress. Fee had said he wouldn't have asked that if he had known Senta. Well, he knew her now and he wouldn't ask. The same applied to cooking or any domestic task. She lay in bed most mornings, she had told him, until noon or later. Her life apart from him was a mystery. If she was in on the few occasions he had tried to phone her, she hadn't answered the phone, though he had let it ring and ring to allow time for her to get upstairs.

Their cloistral life together, half of every night spent in her bed, was wonderful, the most marvellous experience of his life, but he sensed somehow that it wasn't right, it wasn't *real*. They should be together for talk and companionship, not just for sex. Yet when he invited her to come out with him on this trip to Chigwell, get the call on Mrs Ripple over and then have lunch somewhere, maybe drive out into the country, he had anticipated refusal. He was surprised and pleased when she said yes. He was even more delighted to hear her echo his own thoughts and tell him they should be spending all their spare time together, all the time they weren't working.

'But you never do work, Senta,' he had said to her, his tone half-teasing.

'I went for an audition yesterday,' she said. 'It's for quite a good part in a feature film. I didn't get it, Miranda Richardson got it, but the director liked me, he said I was remarkable.'

'Miranda Richardson!'

Philip had been impressed. Even for Senta to be considered in the same breath, so to speak, as Miranda Richardson said a lot for her ability. He had found out a bit about RADA too since she told him she had been there. It was *the* drama school, it was like saying you'd been to Oxford.

But since then he had doubted. It was awful to think like that when you felt about someone the way he felt about Senta, but nevertheless, deep in his own mind, he doubted. It was her telling him that to keep herself fit and at the ready she went down to a place in Floral Street most afternoons, worked out and did ballet, which sparked off his doubts. She met all sorts of famous people there, actors and actresses and dancers. One afternoon, she told him, she and a couple of people she knew had had a cup of tea with Wayne Sleep.

He couldn't quite believe it. She was embroidering the truth, that was all. Probably she had walked through Covent Garden and seen Wayne Sleep across the street. Once perhaps she had been to a health club and tried out the aerobic dance class. There were people like that, people for whom the truth was too stark and bare, who needed to pretty it up. It wasn't lying, you couldn't call it lying. Very likely she told her friends, whoever they might be, about him. But you could bet your life she didn't say he was a junior surveyor with a company that built new bathrooms and kitchens and who lived at home with his mother in Cricklewood. In her account he would be transformed into an interior designer from Hampstead.

Thinking this made him smile, and she, turning her head towards him as he got into the car, asked him what amused him.

'I'm just feeling happy. It's great being out with you like this.'

For answer she leant sinuously towards him and pressed her soft warm pink lips against his. He wondered if Mrs Ripple were watching from the window.

'We'll soon be always together, Philip,' she said. 'I'm sure of it. I believe it's our hidden karmic destiny.'

A few days before she had drawn his horoscope and this morning she had told him the single key number of his name was eight. Now she began talking of numerology, telling him how his number vibrated to the planet Saturn and represented wisdom, learning through experience, stability, patience and responsibility. Philip turned the corner into the street where Arnham's house was and pointed it out to her.

She didn't pay it much attention but turned to him with a displeased look. He felt guilty, for it was true what she said, that he hadn't been listening very closely to her.

'You eight people,' she said, 'often appear cold and undemonstrative with those you ought to love and trust.'

'Cold?' he said. 'Undemonstrative? You must be joking. You are joking, aren't you, Senta?'

'It's because you're afraid of being considered weak. To be considered weak is the very last thing you eight people want to happen.'

They had lunch in a country pub and forgot what Senta called the secret codes of the universe. Afterwards they parked the car somewhere out in a part of Essex where the lanes were narrow and few tourists came, and Senta led him in between the trees and they made love on the grass.

He asked himself if he loved her, if he was in love with her. She had told him that first time not to say he loved her, not to talk in that way. They were to be together always, they were to be one, they had found each other. But was he in love? Did he even know what that expression, so widely and constantly used, so trite and stale, really meant?

Desire, lust if you liked, passion, an absolute over-powering need to possess and re-possess her, he had all that all right. And he thought of her all the time. She occupied his thoughts on his long drives, on his visits to houses Roseberry Lawn was converting, when he was with Roy, at home with Christine and Cheryl, even in his own bed in Glenallan Close, though by that time, having come back from Kilburn in the small hours, he was usually too tired for anything but heavy sleep. Sometimes, inside his head, he talked to her. He told her his thoughts and fears as, for some reason, he couldn't tell the real woman. The real Senta, though silent while he spoke, seemed not to listen. And when some rejoinder was due from her, as likely as not it would be a remark about mystical meanings of polarity points or some strange affirmation that he and she were united souls with no need of words for communication.

How could he be the other half of her, a twin soul, if he wasn't sure that he loved her?

At the end of June Christine and Cheryl went away on holiday together. Philip was glad now that when he broke up with Jenny and cancelled the package tour to Greece they had arranged to take together, he hadn't arranged to go away with his mother and sister. He would have two weeks alone with Senta.

In a way it was unfortunate he had to stay in Glenallan Close. But someone had to be there to take charge of Hardy. And Philip admitted to himself that although he went there every night, loved going there because Senta was there, longed for the place with a breath-catching excitement, he had never really got used to the house in Tarsus Street, had never accepted it. The filth and the smell continued to bother him. There was something sinister about the place too, the way you never saw anyone else, heard no sound ever but occasionally that music and those dancing feet. He ought really to have become apprehensive about her living there. If he was truly one of those wise responsible 'eight' people – and it made him smile to think of it – surely it should worry him to think of his girl friend, his twin soul as she would say, having her home in that part of London, in that sordid house. There were drunks on Tarsus Street at night and gangs of boys loitering on the corners, derelicts lying on the pavement or crouched in doorways. Why didn't it worry him? Was it because – awful thought – she seemed to belong there, to be as suited to the place as they?

Once, going to her at nine at night, as he drove into her turning, he had seen a strange girl coming towards him along the pavement, gliding along in a black dress that touched the ground, her head wrapped in a red striped cloth like an African woman's. She had touched his arm as he got out of the car and smiled into his face before he knew it was Senta. For an awful moment he had thought it was some prostitute soliciting him.

Christine and Cheryl were going to Cornwall. Philip hadn't given much thought to Cheryl lately – so much for being wise and responsible! – but now he wondered how she would handle this habit of hers, whatever it might be, while she and Christine were in Newquay. Drink or drugs – well, they were available anywhere, he thought. Remembering his experience in that squalid street with the disguised Senta, he wondered if his unexpressed fears were after all justified, and Cheryl raised the money for her habit by prostitution. Uneasily, he recalled the fiver she had returned to him so promptly, no more than a night and a morning after she had borrowed it.

He drove them to Paddington Station. Christine wore a dress of floral cotton with a white cardigan she had knitted herself during the long winter evenings. From a distance you couldn't see the mistakes in the pattern. He told her she looked nice (her word) and it was true that the contrast between her and Cheryl in jeans, Mickey Mouse tee shirt and black leather, was almost laughable. Cheryl no longer looked young or much like a girl or even very human. The skin of her face looked stretched and rough, her eyes were bitter. She had had her hair shorn off close to the crown.

'You've had a crew cut,' was all Christine said.

'I don't know what a crew cut is. This is a suede head.'

'I expect it's very nice if you like it,' – the nearest Christine would ever get to criticism.

Leaving them there on the ramp with their suitcases, it was hopeless to think of finding a place to park, he drove back up to Cricklewood wondering what would become of his sister. She was trained for nothing, had no job or prospect of one, was terrifyingly ignorant, had no boy friend or any other kind of friend, and appeared hooked on some habit whose nature he was afraid to discover. But, as was always the case now, these thoughts were soon replaced by Senta. As soon as he had taken Hardy out for a walk he would be off to Kilburn to spend the rest of the day with her. He wanted to persuade her to return to Glenallan Close with him for the night.

Hardy got a proper walk for a change, he deserved it.

The poor dog had been obliged to put up with too many quick traversings of the block lately. Philip drove him to Hampstead Heath and walked through the woodland between the Spaniards Road and the Vale of Health towards Highgate. June was being a cool month, dry and grey. The bright green of the grass, the darker richer colour of the foliage were soothing to the eyes, curiously pacifying. Ahead of him the little dog ran along, stopping sometimes to push an excited snout into rabbit holes. Philip thought about Senta, her body as white as marble, those over-large breasts, nipples that were neither brown nor rosy but the palest pearl-pink, and that rosy-bronze cluster under her belly like red flowers . . .

He switched his mind and its image-making on to her face with Flora's pagan eyes. On to her voice and the things she said. Now he could think quite tenderly of the silly little untruths she had told him, about dyeing her hair, for instance, about being auditioned for that film and meeting Wayne Sleep. That stuff about her mother being Icelandic and dying when she was born, that too was probably made up. Hadn't Fee said something once about Senta's mother having this young lover? So much for dying in childbirth.

She had fantasies, that was the truth of it. No harm in that. Some of the things she told him had been invented to impress him and that was very very flattering. That a girl like Senta should want to impress him was an enormous compliment. Fantasies, he had read somewhere, were what people had whose lives were rather empty, for whom reality was inadequate. He felt protective towards her when he thought like that and tenderly loving. Considering her like this, he had no doubt he loved her.

Reaching these conclusions in a very level-headed way made Philip feel comfortably sophisticated. It almost seemed that this numerology stuff might have something in it, for perhaps he was one of those who learned by experience and grew wise. He would not care to have been taken in for long by fantasising, but as things were, he was neither duped nor disillusioned and that was fine. She wasn't deceiving him and, to be fair, perhaps that wasn't her intention, but only to appear to him more glamorous and exciting than she really was. It was impossible, he thought, for her to *be* more exciting, and as for the glamour – he liked best to think of her as the little girl with a sweet loving nature which she truly was underneath all that, the passionate lover who was at the same time an ordinary woman with an ordinary woman's doubts and uncertainties.

On the way to Tarsus Street he went shopping. He bought a Chinese takeaway. If she wouldn't eat it, he would. He bought biscuits and fruit and two bottles of wine and a big box of Terry's Moonlight chocolates. Senta didn't cost him as much as Jenny had because they so seldom went out. He liked to splash out on the things he brought her.

Outside her house an old man wearing what looked like a woman's raincoat tied round his middle with string was rooting through one of the plastic bags piled on the pavement. Despite notices on lampposts informing them that littering the street constituted an environmental hazard, the people down here piled their rubbish bags outside the broken railings in ill-smelling mounds. The old man had retrieved half a sliced loaf in cellophane wrapping and, thrusting his hand back in again, was perhaps in search of a lump of green cheese or the leftovers from a joint. Philip saw him fumbling with the crimson sticky bones of what had once been a wing of Tandoori chicken. The luxury foods he was carrying made him feel even worse about the old man than he normally would have done. He felt in his pocket for a pound coin and held it out.

'Thanks very much, governor. God bless.'

The possession of the coin did nothing to prevent further excavations in the stack of rubbish bags. Should he have made it a fiver? Philip ran up the steps and let himself into the house. As usual it was silent, dirty. During the previous night it had rained heavily and someone, it was plain to see, had walked across the tiled floor toward the stairs in wet shoes whose deeply indented soles made a pattern in the dust.

The scent of her joss stick was powerful today. He could smell it on the basement stairs where it fought with the permanent all-pervading sour reek of that dark well. She was waiting for him just inside. Sometimes, and today was one of those times, she wore an old Japanese kimono in faded blues and pinks on the back of which was embroidered a rose-coloured bird with a long curving tail. Her hair was looped up and fastened on top of her head with a silver comb. She put out her arms to him and held him in her slow, soft, all-the-time-in-the-world sensuous embrace, kissing his lips lightly, daintily, then drawing his mouth into a deep, devouring, enduring kiss.

The original painted shutters were still attached to the window frame and these she had folded across the glass. The uneasy light of the June day, the watery sun, was excluded. Her lamp was on, the shade tilted, to shed yellow light on to the bed that was as rumpled as if she had just got out of it. A candle was burning too beside the sandalwood incense stick smouldering in its saucer. In the mirror the whole room was reflected, a frosty dusty purple and gold, and it might have been midnight, it might have been any time. Traffic grumbled out there and sometimes there came the clack-clack of a woman's heels on the pavement, the trundling sound of pram or bicycle wheels.

He opened the wine. She didn't want to eat, she wouldn't eat meat. She sat cross-legged on the bed, picking out of the box the chocolates she liked best, and drinking the wine out of one of a pair of cloudy bottle-green glasses she had. Philip wasn't a wine drinker. He didn't like the taste of it nor the effect which left him with a swimming head and a bad taste in his mouth. Alcohol in any form he found rather distasteful with the exception of an occasional half of bitter. But Senta liked him to share the wine and he sensed she would have felt guilty if allowed to drink alone. It was easy, though, with coloured glass. You couldn't see if there was wine in there or water. And if it was inescapable that he pour himself a measure he could usually manage to get rid of it into the pot which held her only houseplant, a kind of imperishable aspidistra. This plant, having long survived darkness, drought and neglect, was beginning to flourish on its wine diet.

She consented to go out to eat with him, though as always she seemed reluctant to leave her room. It was about ten when they got back to Tarsus Street. They hadn't taken the car to the restaurant, an Italian place in Fernhead Road, but had walked there and back, their arms round each other's waists. On the way back Senta became very loving, stopping sometimes to hold him and to kiss. He could feel the urgency of her desire, like rays, like trembling vibrations. In the past Philip had often seen couples who embraced in the street, oblivious apparently of those around them, mutually absorbed, kissing, fondling, seemingly gloating over each other with an intense exclusivity. He had never done that himself and had sometimes felt a kind of prudish disapproval of it. But now he found himself a willing, an ardent, partner in one of those couples, glorying in the pleasures of kissing in the street, in the lamplight, the dusk, against a wall, in the shadowy embrasure of a doorway.

Back there in her basement room, she couldn't wait. She was greedy for him and for love, sweat gleaming on her upper lip, her forehead, her white marble skin bearing a hectic flush. Yet when they were in bed together she was sweeter and more generous than she had ever been, yielding instead of overwhelming, giving rather than taking. Her movements seemed all for his delight, her

100

hands and lips and tongue for him, her pleasure held and delayed until his came. A slow tide of joy, lapping in tender tiny waves, increasing, crashing like falling towers, broke upon him and the room, making the mirror shudder, the floor move. He groaned with the glory of it, a groan that became a cry of triumph as she held him and pressed and undulated swiftly and drew from him at last her own success.

He lay thinking, next time I will give her what she has given me, she shall be first, I will do for her from the fullness of my happiness what she has done for me. There was no way he could have known that in a moment or two, by a tiny action, an ill-coloured word, he was to destroy the chance of this.

Her hair spread out on the pillow beside his face in silvery points. It glittered like long brittle slivers of glass. The flush had faded from her face and it was white again, pure, lineless, the skin as smooth as the inner side of an ivory waxen petal. Her wide open eyes were crystals with the green fluidity tinting them like weeds in water. He ran his fingers through her hair, holding the tresses of it in his fingers, feeling the sharp healthy harshness of the strands.

The lamp he had turned round and tilted the shade so that the light should fall on their faces, their passion-expressing eyes. That light was now shed on to the crown of her head. He peered more closely, lifted a silver gleaming lock, and exclaimed without thought, without pause,

'Your hair's red at the roots!'

'Of course it is. I told you I bleached it. Well, I have it bleached.' Her voice wasn't angry, only faintly impatient. 'It needs redoing. I should have had it done last week.'

'You actually have it bleached? You have it made that silver colour?'

'I told you, Philip. Don't you remember I told you?'

He laughed a little, relaxed, easy, happy. He laughed, shaking his head. 'I didn't believe you, I honestly didn't believe a word of it.'

What happened next was very quick.

Senta sprang up. She crouched on the bed on all-fours. She was like an animal, her lips drawn back, her hair hanging. There should have been a long feline tail swinging. Her eyes were round and glittering and a hissing sound came from her between clenched teeth. He had sat up and drawn back, away from her.

'What on earth's the matter?'

It was a different voice, low, coarse, vibrating with rage. 'You don't trust me! You don't believe me!'

'Senta . . .'

'You don't trust me. How can we be one, how can we be joined together, one soul, when you've no trust in me? When you've no faith?' Her voice rose and it was like a siren howling. 'I've given you my soul, I've told you the deep things in my soul, I've exposed the wholeness of my spirit, and you – you've just shat on it, you've fucked it over, you've destroyed me!'

Then she came at him with pounding fists, aiming for his face, his eyes. He was a man and he had a foot of height advantage over her and weighed half as much again as she. But for all that it took him a while to subdue her. She writhed in his grip, tossing herself this way and that, hissing, twisting to bite his hand. He felt sharp teeth break the skin and the blood come. He was surprised she was so fit. Her strength was wiry, like electrically charged wire. And like wire when the current is switched off, it suddenly died.

She weakened and collapsed like something dying, like

102

an animal whose neck has been wrung. And as she shuddered and yielded so she began to weep, great sobs tearing through her, roaring out of her, as she caught her breath on gasps like an asthmatic, breaking afresh into sobs of passionate misery. He held her in his arms, horribly distressed.

7

He couldn't leave her. He stayed the night. There was some wine left and he gave her the rest of it in one of the green glasses. She hardly spoke, only cried and clung to him. But she surprised him by falling immediately asleep once the wine had been drunk and the duvet pulled over her.

Sleep came less easily to him. He lay awake hearing the feet begin their dancing above his head. One two three, one two three, and the tune throbbed, the 'Tennessee Waltz', something of - Léhar, was it? – he seldom knew the names but Christine had records. The room always grew cold at night. It was summer and outside had felt like a warm muggy night but in here a dank chill crept from the walls. Of course it was below ground. After a while he got up, folded back the shutters and opened the window at the top. With the extinguishing of the incense stick the sour smell of the house always returned.

Their faces and curled bodies, their shapes under the lumpy bundled purple cotton, showed in the dimness of the mirror so that it appeared not like a reflecting glass but an old, soiled, dark oil painting. Overhead the feet danced on, one two three, one two three, pim-pom-pom, pim-pom-pom, from the window wall across the floor to make the mirror tremble, then over to the door, back to the window. Their rhythm and the music sent him, at last, to sleep.

In the morning he had to go home to see to the dog. Things were always so different in the morning. A fresh-ness had come in through the open window, a light green scent perhaps from one of the back gardens that weren't filled with dismembered motor vehicles and builders' junk. Philip made instant coffee, set out bread and butter and oranges. She was sullen and quiet. Her eyes were heavy with a swollen look. He feared he had a black eye where one of her flying fists had got him and the cloudy spotted mirror showed him a bloodshot white and a blue bruise starting. His wrist was swollen where she had bitten him and the teeth marks had turned purple.

'I'll be back in a couple of hours.'

'Are you sure you want to come back?'

'Senta, of course I want to. You know I want to. Look, I'm sorry I said that about not believing you. It was tactless and stupid.'

'It wasn't tactless. It showed me you don't understand me at all. You don't feel at one with me. I searched all my life for you and when I found you I knew it was my karma. But it isn't for you, I'm just a girl friend to you.'

'I'll convince you if it takes me all day. Why don't you come back with me? That's a better idea. We don't want to stay in this room all day. Come back with me.'

She wouldn't. He thought resentfully as he climbed the stairs that he was the injured party, not she. A dentist had once told him, while filling one of his molars, that a human bite is more dangerous than an animal's. Of course it was ridiculous thinking like that, he wouldn't come to any harm from the bite. He just wondered how he could hide it from view until it healed.

Hardy got his walk and, because Philip felt guilty about him, rather more Kennomeat than was strictly correct for a dog of his size. He had a bath, put a piece of sticking plaster on the bite and then took it off again. If Senta saw that she would think he was making an unnecessary fuss or trying to draw attention to what she had done. Anyway, he couldn't put a plaster on his eye. Roy would have some comments to make in the morning but he couldn't think about that now.

Philip considered buying more wine. It might please

Senta but, on the other hand, if he took nothing with him they would have a reason for going out. It was a beautiful day, the sky cloudless, the sun already hot. He contemplated spending the whole day in that underground room with dismay. For the first time since they had been together he was without desire for her, could think of her without that image being accompanied by a need to make love to her. Perhaps that was natural after the excesses of the day before.

Arriving at the house, he paused before climbing the steps to look down at the basement window. She had closed the shutters once more. He let himself in and went down the basement stairs. Inside her room there was no joss stick burning today. She was back in bed, deeply asleep. He felt disappointed and rather impatient. If he had known he could have stayed longer, done some 'Sunday thing', played tennis with Geoff and Ted as he sometimes did or gone for a swim at Swiss Cottage. At any rate he could have brought a Sunday paper back with him.

He sat on the single chair the room boasted and watched her. Gradually a tenderness for her, a kind of pity, brought a yearning to touch her. He took off his clothes and lay down beside her, holding one arm round her curled body.

It was past one when she woke up. They dressed and went out to a wine bar. Senta was calm and quiet, preoccupied by something and inattentive to the things he said. His desire for her was still in abeyance but his enjoyment in being with her seemed to have increased. He continually surprised himself that there had been a time when he hadn't thought her beautiful. There was no other woman they saw while they were out to touch her. She had put on the silvery grey dress with the drooping rose at the bosom and silver shoes with enormously high heels that made her suddenly tall. Her hair was pushed behind her ears from which hung long pendant earrings of crystal drops like chandeliers. Men turned to stare covertly at her bare white legs and thin waist and large breasts in the clinging stuff. Philip felt proud to be with her and, for no known reason, rather nervous.

On their way back she talked of the curious occult and astrological things that interested her, of harmonics and multiple-layered vibrational frequencies, of the beautiful synchronicity of the universe and of discordant patterns. He listened to the sound of her voice rather than to what she said. It must have been at drama school that she had learned to speak in that accent and with that timbre, the voice that spoke like a soprano singing. Then he remembered he couldn't really credit her having been at drama school. How hard it all was, how complicated when you didn't know what to believe and what not to!

A little fear came to him as they went into the house as to how they would pass the rest of the day. Could you be ordinary with her, could you just sit and be together and do things, not love-making, with her as his mother and father, for example, had been together? She would want to make love and he thought, fearfully, that he might be incapable. It was almost a relief when she sat down on the bed and motioned him to the old wicker chair and said she wanted to talk, she had something to say to him.

'What do I mean to you, Philip?'

He said simply, truthfully, 'Everything.'

'I love you,' she said.

It was so simple and gentle the way she said it, so natural and childlike, that it went to his heart. She had told him not to say it, said she would not, so he knew that now the time had come when saying it was right. He leant towards her and put out his arms. She shook her head, seeming to look past him and beyond, with Flora's gaze. She touched his hand, moved her finger softly to the injured wrist.

'I said we mustn't say that till we were sure. Well, I'm sure now. I love you. You are the other half of me, I was incomplete till I found you. I'm sorry I hurt you last night, I was mad with misery, I just struck you and bit you because it was a way of releasing my misery, my unhappiness. Can you understand that, Philip?'

'Of course I can.'

'And do you love me like I love you?'

It seemed a solemn occasion. Gravity and an intense seriousness were called for. He said in a steady deliberate way, as if making a vow, 'I love you, Senta.'

'I wish it were enough, saying it. But it isn't enough, Philip. You have to prove your love for me and I have to prove mine for you. I thought about that all the time you were away this morning. I lay here thinking about it, how we each have to do some tremendous thing to prove our love for each other.'

'That's all right,' he said. 'I'll do that. What would you like me to do?'

She was silent. Her crystalline greenish eyes had shifted their gaze from some unknown horizon and returned to meet his. It won't be Jenny's thing of getting engaged, he thought, that's not Senta's style. And it won't be buying her something. Squeamishly he hoped she wasn't going to ask him to cut a vein and mingle his blood with hers. It would be like her and he would do it but he felt distaste for it.

'I believe life is a great adventure, don't you?' she said. 'We feel the same about these things, so I know you do. Life is terrible and beautiful and tragic but most people make it just ordinary. When you and I make love we have a moment of heightened consciousness, a moment when everything looks clear and brilliant, we have such an intensity of feeling that it's as if we experience everything fresh and new and perfect. Well, it ought to be like that all the time, we can learn the power of making it that way, not by wine or drugs but by living to the limit

108

of our consciousness, by living every day with every fibre of our awareness.'

He nodded. She had been saying something like that on the way back here. The awful thing was he had begun to feel sleepy. He had eaten a heavy lunch and drunk a pint of beer. What he would best have liked would have been to lie down on the bed with her and cuddle her until they fell asleep. Her telling him she loved him had made him very happy and with that knowledge a sleepy desire was returning, the kind of mild lust which can be pleasantly delayed until sleep has come and gone and the body lies warm and easy. He smiled at her and reached for her hand.

She withdrew her hand and held the index finger up at him. 'Some say that to live fully you have to have done four things. Do you know what they are? I'll tell you. Plant a tree, write a poem, make love with your own sex, and kill someone.'

'The first two — well, the first three really — don't seem to have much in common with the last.

'Please don't laugh, Philip. You laugh too much. There are things that shouldn't be laughed at.'

'I wasn't laughing. I don't suppose I'll ever do any of those things you said, so I hope that won't mean I haven't lived.' He looked at her, taking a deep pleasure in her face, her large clear eyes, the mouth that he could never tire of gazing at. 'When I'm with you I think I'm really living, Senta.'

It was an invitation to love but she ignored it. She said very quietly, with an intense dramatic concentration. 'I shall prove I love you by killing someone for you and you must kill someone for me.'

He was aware for the first time since they got back of the stuffiness of the room, the close raunchy smell of the bed and the bag overflowing with dirty washing, and he

109

got up to unfold the shutters and open the window. Standing there with his hands on the sash bar, breathing such fresh air as penetrated Tarsus Street, he said to her over his shoulder, 'Oh, sure. Who have you got in mind?'

'It doesn't have to be anyone in particular. In fact, it'd be better if it's not. Someone in the street at night. She'd do.' She pointed past Philip out of the window to where one of the street people, an elderly bag woman, had seated herself on the pavement with her back to the railings above the basement area. 'Someone like that, anyone. It's not who it is that matters, it's doing it, it's doing this terrible deed that puts you outside ordinary society.'

'I see.'

The old woman's back looked like a sack of rags someone had dropped there to be collected by the council refuse men. It was hard to grasp that there was a human being inside there, a person with feelings, who could experience joy and suffer pain. Philip turned slowly from the window but he didn't sit down. He leaned against the mirror's bruised and broken frame. Senta's face wore its intense expression, blank yet concentrated. He thought she spoke like someone – and someone not very talented – uttering lines learned for a play.

'I would know what you'd done for me and you would know what I'd done for you but no one else would. We should share these terrible secrets. We should really know each of us meant more than all the world besides to the other, if you could do that for me and I could do it for you.'

'Senta,' he said, trying to keep his patience, 'I know you aren't serious. I know these things are fantasies with you. You may think you're deceiving me but you're not.'

Her face changed. Her eyes shifted and returned to look into both of his. She spoke in a still cold voice, but warily. 'What things?'

'Oh, never mind. I know and you know.'

110

'I don't know. What things?'

He hadn't wanted to say it, he didn't want a confrontation, but perhaps there was no help for it. 'Well, if you must have it, about your mother and going to all those foreign places and going to auditions for parts with Miranda Richardson. I know they're daydreams. I didn't want to say it but what else can I do when you talk about killing people to prove we love each other?'

All the time he was speaking he was bracing himself to repel the same sort of attack as she had made on him the night before. But she was calm, statue-like, her hands folded and her eyes fixed on them in hieratic pose. She raised her eyes to his face. 'You don't believe what I say, Philip?'

'How can I when you say things like that? I believe some things.'

'All right. What don't you believe?'

He didn't quite answer her. 'Look, Senta, I don't *mind* you having fantasies, lots of people do, it's just a way of making life more interesting. I don't mind you inventing things about your family and about your acting, but when you get to talk about killing people — it's so ugly and pointless and it's a waste of time too. It's the weekend, it's Sunday, we could be having a nice time, out somewhere, it's a lovely day, and here we are sitting in this — well, frankly, disgusting hole, while you talk about killing that poor old creature sitting out there.'

She became a muse of tragedy, sombre, grave. She might have been imparting terrible news of his family to him or telling him all those she loved were dead. 'I am absolutely, utterly, profoundly serious,' she said.

He felt he was contorting his face, screwing up his eyes and frowning in an effort to understand her. 'You *can't* be.'

'Are you serious about loving me, about doing anything for me?'

'Within reason, yes.' He said it sulkily.

111

'Within reason! How sick that makes me! Don't you see that what we have has to be without reason, beyond reason? And to prove it we have to do the thing that is outside the law and beyond reason.'

'You really are serious,' he said bitterly. 'Or you think you are, which in your present mood comes to the same thing.'

'I am willing to kill someone to prove my love for you and you must do the same for me.'

'You're mad, Senta, that's what you are.'

Her voice was stony now, remote. 'Don't ever say that.'

'I won't say it, I don't really mean it. O God, Senta, let's talk about something else, *please*. Let's do something. Can't we forget all this? I don't even know how we got into it.'

She got up, approached him. He found himself, to his own humiliation, shielding his face. 'I won't hurt you.' She spoke with contempt. With her little hands, her child's hands, she took him by the upper arms. She looked into his face. The stilt heels had elevated her so that she had only a little way to look up. 'Are you refusing to do this, Philip? Are you?'

'Of course I am. You may not know it, you don't really know me yet, but I hate the whole notion of killing and any sort of violence, come to that. It doesn't just make me feel sick, it *bores* me. I can't even watch a violent film on TV, and I don't want to either, it doesn't interest me. And now you say you want me to kill someone. What kind of a criminal do you think I am?'

'I thought you were the other half of our united souls.'

'Oh, don't talk such rubbish! It's such a load of shit, all this balls about souls and karmas and destinies and rubbish. Why don't you grow up and live in the real world? You talk about living – do you think you're living stuck in this filthy dump sleeping half the day? Making up tales to convince people how clever and amazing you are? I thought I'd heard it all, all that about going to

112

Mexico and India and wherever and your Icelandic mother and the Flying Dutchman, but now I get told I've got to kill some poor old bloody vagrant to prove I love you.'

She made that hissing cat's sound and with both hands shoved him so hard that he staggered. He grabbed the edge of the gilded frame to steady himself, thought for a moment the whole great swinging dangerous sheet of mirror would come crashing down. But it was only shivering on the chain which fastened it to the wall and it stilled as he leaned against it, grasping it with both hands. When he turned round she had flung herself face-downwards on the bed, where she lay making curious convulsive jerks down the length of her body. As he touched her tentatively, she rolled on to her back, sat up and began to scream. The sounds were terrible, mechanical seemingly, short staccato shrieks tearing out of her wide open mouth from which the lips curled back in a snarl like a tigress.

He did what he had heard and read about and slapped her face. It had an instant silencing effect. She went white as paper, gagged, gasped, put her hands up to cover both cheeks. Her whole body trembled. After a moment she spoke to him through her fingers, whispered, 'Get me some water.'

She sounded weak and breathless as if she were ill. For a moment he was afraid for her. He went out of the room and along the passage past the other basement rooms to where the lavatory was and next to it the relic and ruin of a bathroom. Here the single brass tap, wrapped in rags, stuck out of the green and fungus-coated wall over the bathtub. He filled the mug, drank it down himself and refilled it. The water had a dead metallic taste. He made his way back to where she was. She was sitting on the bed with the purple duvet wrapped round her as if it were a winter's day. Behind and above her, outside the window, the old woman's back, covered now by some sort of khaki-coloured jacket, could still be seen beyond the railing. She had given no sign of having heard the screams from below, having perhaps heard so much of life that she had become detached.

Philip held the mug to Senta's lips and helped her drink as if she really was ill. He put his other arm round her and rested his hand tenderly on her neck. He could feel tremors passing through her body and a feverish heat on her skin. She sipped the water quietly until she had finished it to the dregs. Her neck extricated itself from his fondling hand, her head ducked away from him and she took from him the mug the water had been in. It was all done very quietly and gently which made the next thing she did shocking because it was so unexpected. She hurled the mug across the room where it crashed against the wall.

'Get out of here!' she screamed at him. 'Get out of my life! You've ruined my life, I hate you, I never want to see you again.'

8

Darren's car, an ancient banger just this side of vintage value, was parked by the kerb and the front door was open. On the step, in the sunshine, Hardy lay asleep, but he woke up when Philip appeared and ran to make a fuss of him. Now Philip remembered that Fee had said she would come on Sunday afternoon to take away the rest of her things, and as he entered the house she came downstairs with a pile of clothes over one arm and a teddy bear clutched in the other.

'Whatever's happened to your eye? Have you been in a fight?'

'Someone hit me,' he said, trying to be truthful; then, untruthfully, 'They mistook me for someone else.'

'I've phoned about fifty times since yesterday morning.'

'I've been out,' he said. 'I've been out quite a bit.'

'I realise that. I thought you must have gone away. That looks awful, that eye. Was it in a pub it happened?'

His mother didn't question and check up on him, so he didn't see why he should put up with it from a sister. She went out to the car, came back rather shrilly, 'How long's that poor dog been on his own?'

He didn't answer. 'Shall I give you a hand with that stuff?'

'All right. I mean, thanks. I thought you'd *be* here, Phil.'

She preceded him up the stairs. In the room that was now Cheryl's alone the doors of a clothes cupboard were open, one of the twin beds piled with dresses and coats and skirts. But the first thing he saw, the first thing he really took in, was the garment that lay in a heap on the floor of the cupboard. It was the bridesmaid's dress which Senta had stripped off that day they first made love.

'She must really have liked that dress, mustn't she?' said Fee. 'She must really have appreciated it. You can see she just took it off and dumped it there. By the look of it, it somehow got soaking wet first.'

He said nothing. He was remembering. Fee picked up the ruined dress, the satin stained with water spots, the net creased and the skirt torn at the hem. 'I mean, I can understand if she didn't like it. It was my taste, not hers. But you'd think she'd think of my feelings, wouldn't you? I mean, finding it there sort of just discarded. And poor old Stephanie. She sat up nights to finish making that.'

'I suppose she just didn't think.'

Fee pulled a suitcase down from the top of the cupboard. She began folding things up and putting them in the case. 'Mind you, she's very peculiar. I only asked her to be my bridesmaid because Darren's mother specially asked me to. She said Senta would feel left out. I'm sure she *wouldn't* have. They've really split off from the rest of the family, that lot. I mean, we asked Senta's father and her mother but they didn't come, they didn't even answer the invitations.'

With seeming indifference, he said, 'Someone said Senta had a foreign mother but that she was dead. I suppose they'd got hold of the wrong end of the stick.'

It gave him an odd little thrill to speak her name so casually. He waited for Fee's denial, watched her, expecting her to turn round to him, her upper lip raised, her nose wrinkled up, the face she made when something she found incredible was said to her. She folded the bridesmaid's dress up, said, 'I may as well take it with me. I suppose I can have it cleaned, someone might want it. It's miles too small for me.' She closed the lid of the case, fastened it. 'Yes, there was something like that,' she said. 'Her mother died when she was born. She came from some funny place. Greenland? No, Iceland. Darren's

116

uncle was in the Merchant Navy and they put in there or whatever the expression is, and he met her but her family were funny about it because he wasn't an officer or anything. Anyway they did get married and he had to go back to sea and she had this baby – I mean, Senta – and died of some awful complications or whatever.'

It was all true then. He felt both aghast and terribly pleased, relieved and appalled. There were more questions to be asked but before he could ask them, Fee said, 'Uncle Tom – I mean I'm supposed to call him uncle now – he went back and fetched the baby. Her people were mad, Darren's mother says, because they thought they'd get to keep her. Uncle Tom brought her home and very soon after he married Auntie Rita. She's the one that lives with the young guy. Would you carry the case, Phil? And I'll bring my winter coat and the two dolls.'

They loaded up the car. Philip made a cup of tea. It was so warm and sunny that they sat in the garden and drank it. Fee said, 'I wish Mum hadn't given Flora away. I expect it sounds silly to you but I thought she gave the place a touch of class.'

'That's something it needs,' said Philip.

He toyed with the idea of setting Flora up out here somewhere. Why shouldn't he build a rockery for her? No one had done anything to the garden except mow the grass since they moved here. And that was all it was, grass with fences round it on three sides and bang in the middle the concrete birdbath. He tried to imagine Flora standing on rocks with flowers at her feet and a couple of little cypress trees behind her, but how could he explain to Christine?

'Come over and have a meal with us one night,' said Fee. 'I mean, I won't say you must miss Mum's home cooking but at least you don't normally have to get it for yourself.'

He said he would and fixed on Thursday. By that time he would have seen Senta three times, so it would be reasonable to have an evening away from her the way he did when Christine was at home. After Fee had gone he took Hardy for a long walk up to Brent Reservoir, leaving by the back door and with the back door key in his pocket.

Senta's telling him to get out, he had ruined her life, he took rather less than seriously. Certainly, he now saw, he had been at fault. She had naturally been furious at being disbelieved when she told the truth. For it *was* the truth, that was the amazing thing. All that must be true, for if the account of her mother's nationality and her own birth was not fantasy neither would her travels be nor her drama school training nor her meetings with the famous. Of course she was hurt and upset when he doubted her, when he told her so in that blatant way.

It was rather an awkward situation. He couldn't exactly tell her he now believed her because he had questioned his sister about her. It needed some thinking out. In the light of what Fee had said, Senta's rage was easy to understand. He had behaved like a narrow-minded clod, living up to her estimate of people as ordinary and bent on living in an ordinary world. Was it perhaps hysteria, a kind of uncontrollable angry misery at her word being disbelieved, that had led her to all that talk about proving his love for her? The difficulty was he couldn't now remember what had come first, his declaration or disbelief or her demand that he kill someone for her. He would set it right, waste no more time. Take Hardy home and go straight back to Tarsus Street.

Falling asleep and staying asleep quite a long way into the night was something he wouldn't have expected to happen to him. But he had had almost no sleep the night before and no more than two or three hours on Friday night. Returned from their walk, he had fed the dog, eaten a hunk of bread and some cheese, gone upstairs to change and there lain down on the bed for what was to be a ten-minute nap. It was dark when he awoke, long dark. The illuminated green numerals on his digital clock told him it was twelve thirty-one.

Their confrontation, his deep apology and request for forgiveness must wait until tomorrow. Well, tonight really, he thought as he drifted off once more into sleep. Hardy, for once not shut up in the kitchen for the night, lay curled up on the end of the bed by his feet.

It was the little dog coming close up to his face, licking his ear, which awoke him. He had forgotten to set the alarm but it was only seven. Soft hazy sunshine filled the room. Already, at this hour, you could feel in the air the promise of a hot and perfect day, that kind of expectant smiling serenity that breathes from a sky that is cloudless but veiled in a fine mist. It was what the older people called 'settled'. Rain and cold seemed something that happened in another country.

He had a bath, shaved, put Hardy out into the garden which was going to have to suffice for him this morning. Yesterday's miles ought to last him a day or two. Philip put on a clean shirt and the suit which Roseberry Lawn expected its personnel to wear when visiting customers. He had a kitchen conversion to keep an eye on in Wembley and a projected bathroom installation to estimate in Croydon. Wembley wasn't far away but the fitters would start work at eight-thirty. He felt for his keys in the pocket of the jeans he had worn yesterday.

There were two sets, the keys to the Opel Kadett and a second ring on which he kept the key to this house, the key to the outer door of head office and, for the past month, the keys to the house in Tarsus Street. These last, he saw to his extreme dismay, were missing.

His own house key was there and the one to the office. The ring was a plain one without a fob. It was impossible for the keys to have slipped off. Could Senta have taken them off? He sat down on the bed. He felt rather cold in spite of the warmth of the day but his hands, which held the ring with two keys on it only, were damp. It was easy to see, when he thought about it, what had happened. She had asked him to fetch her a drink of water and while he was away she had abstracted her own keys from the ring.

At midday, while he was taking his lunch break, he tried to phone her from a call box. Never yet had he succeeded in getting a reply from that phone in the hall in Tarsus Street and he didn't now. He did something strictly against Roseberry Lawn rules and asked Mrs Finnegan, the Croydon householder, if he might use her phone. Someone of Mrs Ripple's sort would have made a thing out of it, refused and lectured him, but Mrs Finnegan only stipulated that he make his call through the exchange and pay the cost of it. It made no difference, anyway, for no one answered.

He had measured up the tiny area of bedroom she wanted transformed into a bathroom with full-size bath, lavatory, vanity unit and bidet, told her he doubted it would be a possibility, listened to her protests, argued very politely, smiled and agreed when she said he was very young, wasn't he, and would he get a second opinion? She kept staring speculatively at his eye. By then it was a quarter-past five. There was hardly a worse time for driving across London.

The time was twenty to seven when he got to the Harrow Road and turned off into the hinterland. In Cairo Street he stopped outside an off-licence and bought wine and crisps and after-dinner mints, the only chocolates they had. Now he was nearly there he was aware of a kind of sick excitement building up inside him.

The old man in the woman's raincoat was sitting on the pavement with his back to the railings above Senta's area. He was still wearing the raincoat, though it was very hot, the pavements white in the sun and the tar melting on the roadway. The old man whose face was

120

covered with a yellowish-white stubble had fallen asleep, his head lolling against a heap of rags he had used to cushion the railings. In his lap lay an assortment of food scraps, a piece of burnt toast, a croissant in cellophane, a jam jar with about an inch of marmalade in the bottom of it. Philip thought that if he woke up he would give him another pound coin. He didn't know why this old vagrant, wretched and destitute, moved him so much. After all, you saw plenty like him, men and women, he wasn't unique. They congregated here and in the neighbouring streets because of the proximity of the Mother Teresa Centre.

The front doors of houses like this one where there were many tenants were often left open. But he had never found this one open and he didn't now. There was no bell. This place was a far cry from the kind of house where there was a row of bells by the front door with the tenant's name on a neat card above each one. The door knocker was of brass long turned quite black. Something sticky came off it on to his fingers. He banged and banged.

She had taken the keys off the ring because she didn't want to see him. She didn't want him to come back. That must be the truth but it was something he didn't want to face. He bent down and looked through the letter box. All he could see was the phone on the table and the shadowy passage leading away to the basement stairs. He went back down the steps and looked over into the area. The shutters were folded across her window, and this in spite of the heat. It made him feel she must be out. Those auditions she went to, those famous people she knew, that was all true.

He stepped back across the pavement and looked up at the house. There were three floors above the basement. It was the first time he had ever looked up at it like this. In the past he had always been in too much of a hurry to pause, too eager to get into the house and find her.

The roof was shallow, of grey slates with a kind of little railing round. This was the only ornamental thing on the forbidding facade, liver-coloured bricks punctured by three rows of windows, each on a plain flat oblong, deeply recessed. On one of the windowsills on the middle floor was a broken window box that had once been gilded and flakes of gilt still adhered to it. In it were some dead plants tied up to sticks.

Philip was aware that the old man had woken up and was watching him. He had a strange superstitious feeling about the old man. If he ignored him, repudiated him, he would never see Senta again. But if he gave him something substantial it would count in his favour in that mystical hand-out centre, where people received benefits according to the measure of their charity. Someone, whose opinion he had privately derided at the time, had once said to him that what we give to the poor, that is what we take with us when we die. Although he could ill afford it, he took a five-pound note out of his wallet and put it into the hand that was already stretched out to receive it.

'Get yourself a good meal,' he said, by now embarrassed.

'You're a nobleman, governor. God bless you and your loved ones.'

It was a strange one, that term 'governor', Philip thought, getting back into his car. Where did it come from? Did it originate with the governor of a prison — or a workhouse? He shuddered a little, though the car was hot and stuffy. The old man was still sitting on the pavement, contemplating the fiver with great complacency and satisfaction. Philip drove home, made himself coffee, baked beans on toast, ate an apple, took Hardy round the block. Much later, at about nine-thirty, he tried that phone number again but there was no reply.

A postcard came from Christine next morning. It showed St Michael's Mount off the southern coast of

Cornwall. Christine wrote: 'We haven't been to this place and don't suppose we shall as the coach trip doesn't go there. But it was the prettiest card in the shop. Wish you were here enjoying this heatwave with us. Much love Mum and Cheryl.' Cheryl hadn't signed it though. It was all in Christine's writing. Philip suddenly remembered who it was that had said that about the money we give to the poor being all we take with us when we die. It was Gerard Arnham. The only time Philip had met him Arnham had said that. When they went down to the steakhouse perhaps it had been and Christine had talked of Stephen, quoted him as saying, 'Oh, well, you can't take it with you . . .'

When she stopped hearing from Arnham had Christine felt the way he did now? But that was nonsense. Senta was only peeved, sulking, punishing him. She would keep it up for a few days maybe, he must be prepared for a few days. It might be the best thing not to attempt to get into the house again, to leave it for today. But when he was driving home that evening from a call he had made in Uxbridge, he found the pull of Tarsus Street impossible to resist. The heat was greater than on the previous evening and more humid, sultrier. He left the car windows open. He left them open, thinking sod's law will operate, if I close the windows and lock up the car she won't let me in but if I leave the windows open she will let me in and I shall have to come back to close them.

The old man was gone, all that remained of him a rag tied round one of the railings at ground level. Philip went up to the front door, banged on the knocker, banged a dozen times. As he retreated he looked down into the area and fancied he saw the shutters move. He thought for a moment that the shutters had been open and she, or someone in there, had closed them at the sound of his feet on the stone steps. He had probably imagined it, he

123

was probably deluding himself. At any rate, they were closed now.

On Wednesday he kept away. It was the hardest thing he had ever done. He had begun to long for her. The longing wasn't only sexual but it was sexual. The continuing heat made it worse. He lay on his bed naked with the sheet half over him and thought of that first time when she had come to him here in this bed. He rolled over on to his face and clutched the pillow and groaned. When he went to sleep he had the first wet dream he had for years. He was making love to her in the basement bed in Tarsus Street, and unlike most dreams of this kind, he was really making love to her, was deep inside her, moving towards one of their triumphant shared climaxes, experiencing it and shouting out with happiness and pleasure. He woke up at once, making noises, whimpering, turning over to feel sticky wetness against his thigh.

That wasn't the worst thing. The worst was having had the joy of it and knowing it wasn't real, it hadn't happened. He got up very early and changed the sheets. He thought, I've got to see her, I can't go on like this, I can't imagine another day of this. She has punished me enough, I know I was wrong, I know it was unkind of me and insensitive and cruel even, but she can't want to go on punishing me, she has to give me the chance to explain, to apologise.

It was a joke, wasn't it, an ordinary house in an ordinary slummy London street, that no one could get into? The place wasn't boarded up, it had ordinary doors and windows. Driving across London to another encounter with Mrs Finnegan in Croydon, he had the strangely unwelcome idea no one else lived there but Senta. That whole great barrack of a place was empty but for Senta living in one room in the basement. I could get in, he thought, I could break the basement window.

Tentative plans for Mrs Finnegan, sketched by Roy,

were for a shower room the area of a medium-size cupboard.

'I want a bath,' Mrs Finnegan said.

'Then you'll have to sacrifice half the bedroom area, not a quarter.'

'I have to have a bedroom big enough to get twin beds in or at least a double bed.'

'Have you considered bunks?' said Philip.

'That's all very well at your age. Most of my friends are over sixty.'

Philip asked if he could use her phone. She agreed if he would reverse the charges. He phoned Roy for advice. Roy, who was being unusually happy and expansive these days, said to tell the silly old fart to move to a bigger house.

'No, better not do that. Suggest a hip bath. Actually, they're good, a great way to have a bath, especially if you've got one foot in the grave and another — ' he laughed a lot at his own joke '- on a bar of soap.'

Through the exchange Philip tried to put a call through to the house in Tarsus Street. She must answer sometimes, she had to. What if her agent wanted her? What if one of those auditions was successful? She didn't answer. He suggested the hip bath to Mrs Finnegan who said she would have to think it over. There must be ways of getting into a house. Didn't she ever answer the door? What about the gasman, the man who read the electricity meter, the postman with a parcel? Or was she only failing to answer because she knew it was the time he was likely to come?

He got off early. It was too late to go back to the office but too early really to stop work. He stopped work. What about all the times he had worked Saturdays without overtime? It was twenty to five and he was in West Hampstead, ten minutes drive away even at a bad time for traffic. She wouldn't expect him at ten to five.

Thunder was rumbling from over the Hampstead

125

Heath direction. Mrs Finnegan had said to him there would have to be a storm soon to clear the air. A bright tree of lightning grew out of the roof of the Tricycle Theatre and threw branches across the purple sky. Raindrops as big as old pennies he could just remember lay black on the white pavements in Tarsus Street. The old man was back but busy in a dustbin from which red Tesco bags bulged, stuffed with rubbish. Philip stood and looked up at the house. He noticed this time that there were no curtains at any of the windows but at the window behind the box of dead plants a pair of shutters like Senta's had been folded across.

It was possible that they had been like that last time he looked. He didn't think so but he couldn't really remember. Did she really live alone there? Was she perhaps a squatter? He wasn't going to bang on that knocker today. He leaned over into the area and tapped on the glass of her window. The shutters, of course, were closed. He banged harder and shook the sash bar. A man and a woman walked by along the pavement. They took no notice of him. He might have been a real burglar, breaking in to steal or do damage, but they were indifferent, they ignored him.

Philip mounted the steps and, forgetting his resolve, knocked at the front door. He stood there, knocking and knocking. A tremendous clap of thunder seemed to shake the whole terrace of which this house was a part. Someone in the house next door closed a downstairs window. The rain came down in a sudden cascade of straight glittering silver rods of water. He stood well back under the porch, little splashes of rain hitting him with sharp cold stings. Mechanically, he went on knocking, but by now he was sure no one was in there. Because he couldn't have done so himself he was sure no one could have stood being in there and hearing this racket on the door knocker without doing something about it.

When the rain let up a little, he made a run for it to

the car. He could see the old man sitting at the top of an even longer flight of steps than Senta's and, sheltered by a porch with pitched roof and wooden pillars, begin gnawing on chicken bones. Senta was never out for long. He thought he would wait there till she came back. It amazed him that only last week he had asked himself if he was in love with her. Had he been totally blind, totally out of touch with his own deepest feelings? In love with her! If she came along the street now he wondered how he would keep from casting himself at her feet. How would he keep from lying at her feet and embracing her legs and kissing her feet, from weeping with joy at just seeing her, at being with her again, even if she refused to speak to him?

After two hours had passed and he had just sat there thinking of her, imagining her appearing, picturing her appearing in the far distance and gradually approaching, after two hours of that he got out of the car and went back up the steps and knocked on the door again. While at Mrs Finnegan's he had considered breaking her window. There was a loose brick lying on the concrete ridge between railings and the dip down into the area. Philip climbed over on to this concrete and picked up the brick. He happened to look back along the street at that point, he was looking to see if the old bag man was watching, and that was how he saw the policeman in uniform strolling along. He dropped the brick down into the area, went back to the car and drove up to Kilburn High Road.

There he had a hamburger in McDonald's and afterwards two pints of bitter in Biddy Mulligan's. It was getting on for half-past eight but still broad daylight. The rain had stopped, though the thunder still rolled. Mrs Finnegan had been wrong and it hadn't cleared the air. Back in Tarsus Street he knocked on the front door again and hammered on the basement window. Looking up at the house, this time from the opposite pavement, he saw that the shutters at the window on the middle floor were still closed. Perhaps they always had been and it was an illusion of his that they had been open until that afternoon. He had begun to feel a little mad, that maybe it was all illusion, that she lived here, that anyone lived here, that he had ever met her and made love to her and loved her. Perhaps he was mad and it was all part of his delusion. It could be schizophrenia. After all, who knew what it was like to have schizophrenia until you had it yourself?

At home he found the poor dog hiding from the storm under the dining table, shivering and whimpering. His water bowl was empty. Philip filled the bowl and put out Kennomeat and when Hardy didn't want to eat it, took him on his lap and tried to comfort him. It was plain that Hardy only wanted Christine. When the thunder growled in the distance he trembled till his skin shook. Philip thought, I can't go on like this. I can't face life without her. What shall I do if I never see her again, if I never touch her, hear her voice? Carrying the dog under one arm, he went out to the phone and dialled her number.

The line was engaged.

That had never happened before. The phone was answered, then. Someone answered it. At worst, someone took the receiver off so that when people tried to get through they heard the engaged signal. He felt a great absurd surge of hope. The last thunder clap had been at least ten minutes ago. In the darkening sky, clear areas were opening between the rolling hills of cloud. He carried Hardy into the kitchen and set him down in front of his food dish. As the little dog began cautiously to eat, the phone rang.

Philip went to the phone, closed his eyes, held his fists clenched, prayed, let it be her, let it be her. He picked up the phone, said hallo, heard Fee's voice. Immediately, before she had said two words he remembered.

'Oh, God, I was supposed to be coming to have a meal with you and Darren.'

'What happened to you?'

'We've been run off our feet at work. I was late home.' How well lately he had learned to lie! 'I forgot. I'm sorry, Fee.'

'So you bloody should be. I have to work too, you know. I went shopping in my lunch hour for you and I made a pie.'

'Let me come tomorrow. I can eat it tomorrow.'

'Darren and I are going to his mum tomorrow. Where were you anyway? What's happening to you? You were funny on Sunday, and that eye and everything. What have you been doing the minute Mum goes away? I've nearly gone mad sitting here waiting.'

You and me both, Fee. 'I said I'm sorry. I really am. Can I come on Saturday?'

'I suppose so.'

It was his first experience of expecting, when the phone rang, to hear one special loved longed-for voice, and hearing another. He found it very bitter. To his shame, though there was no one there but Hardy, he felt his eyes fill with tears. Suppose she wasn't holding out on him, though, suppose something had happened to her. Unwillingly, he remembered Rebecca Neave who had disappeared, who had not been there to answer phone calls when needed. Tarsus Street was a slum compared to where Rebecca had lived. He thought of the street by night and of the big empty house.

But the line *had* been engaged. He would try again and if the signal he had heard before still obtained, would ask the exchange if the line was engaged speaking. The idea that in a moment or two he might actually hear her voice was almost too much for him. He sat down crouched over the phone and expelled his breath in a long sigh. Suppose he spoke to her and in five minutes, less than five minutes, he were to be back in the car, driving down to Cricklewood, down Shoot-up Hill, bound for Tarsus Street. He dialled the number.

It was no longer engaged. He heard the familiar ringing tone as he had heard it at Mrs Finnegan's, as he had heard it thirty, forty times in the past days. It rang four times, stopped. A man's voice spoke.

'Hallo. This is Mike Jacopo. We are not available to speak to you right now but if you would like to leave a message and your name and phone number, we will get back to you as soon as possible. Please speak after the bleep.'

Philip had known from almost the first word, from the stilted manner and enunciation, that these sentences were recorded for an answering machine. The tone sounded on a single shrill beep. He replaced the receiver and wondered as he did so if the long indrawn gasp he had made was recorded for Jacopo to hear.

9

Fee and Darren were buying their flat on an enormous mortgage extending over forty years. They had been granted it only because they were so young. Philip, sitting in their small bright living room with its view of the entrance to a new shopping mall, wondered how they could bear it, any of it, the prospect of those forty years, like forty links in an iron chain.

The flat was in West Hendon where there was a large Indian community and most of the grocer's shops sold poppadoms and Indian spices and gram flour. Most of the building was newish but it was also mean. If it had been anywhere else they wouldn't have been able to afford it, even paying back the loan over more than half a lifetime. For the first few years, Darren said, they wouldn't exactly be paying it back anyway, they would just be paying interest. There was this room and a bedroom and the kitchen where Fee ran around like a real housewife cooking potatoes and inspecting her pie through the glass door of the new oven, and a shower room about the size of the one he had suggested Mrs Finnegan should have. Darren said he hadn't had a bath for a month. He laughed when he said this and Philip could imagine him repeating it over and over to people at work, delighted by his joke.

'No, seriously, I'm hooked on showers. I wouldn't give you a thank-you for a bath now. Indians never have them, did you know that? What was it that chap in the shop told you, Fee, what's-his-name, one of those funny Indian names?'

'Jalal. His name's Jalal. He said his people laugh at us slurping around in our own dirty water.'

'When you come to think of it,' said Darren, 'that's just what we do. Those of us with baths, that is.' He reeled off statistics about the number of households in Britain with baths, the number with two and the number without any. 'You want a shower while you're here, Phil?'

Philip hadn't been back to Tarsus Street since he heard the voice on the answering machine. Thursday night had been sleepless. Mike Jacopo, he was convinced, must be Senta's lover. He and she lived there together, that was what that 'we' on the recording meant. Jacopo had gone away or they had quarrelled and to spite him or show she didn't care or something, she had turned to Philip and led him to that secret room down there in the basement. For three weeks. Then Jacopo came back and she staged a quarrel with Philip to be rid of him. There were holes in this theory but he held on to it with variations all through Friday and Saturday until, late on Saturday afternoon, it came to him that there was no reason why Jacopo shouldn't simply be another tenant, the tenant perhaps of the ground floor. 'We' didn't necessarily mean him and Senta. It could be him and anyone.

Now, at Darren and Fee's flat, he knew he could probably get answers to this by simply asking straight out. But if he asked any more questions about Senta, if he asked one more, they would guess. He thought, the truth is I don't want to know about Jacopo, I only want her back, I only want to see her and speak to her. Darren talked about the new Rover and football and football hooligans in Germany. They ate the pie and a very rich sweet trifle and then Darren got out his colour slides, at least a hundred of them, which Philip felt obliged to look at.

The wedding photographs had come, the ones taken by the elderly photographer who smelt of tobacco, and Philip found himself looking at Senta in her bridesmaid's dress. Was that the nearest he would ever get to her, a portrait she shared with four others and which he had to share with two? Darren sat beside him and Fee looked over his shoulder. He was aware of the thudding of his heart and wondered if they could hear it too.

'You can see she's done acting,' Darren said.

Philip's heart seemed to beat louder and faster. 'Has she?' he managed and his voice sounded hoarse.

'You can see that. When she left school she went to this acting college. She's a bit of a show-off, isn't she? Look at the way she's standing.'

Fee asked him to come back and have Sunday lunch with them, she was doing roast lamb. Philip didn't think he could face it. He said he had things to do at home, work to catch up on. In the morning he regretted his refusal, for the empty day stretched in loneliness before him, but he didn't phone Fee. He took Hardy up on the Heath and walked about trying to think of some way of getting into that house, short of breaking in. Later, during the long light evening, he phoned her number and once more heard Jacopo's recorded message. Philip replaced the receiver without saying anything and tried desperately to think. After a few moments he picked it up again, re-dialled and when the tone had sounded said, 'This is Philip Wardman. Will you please ask Senta to phone me? It's Senta Pelham who lives in the basement. Will you please ask her to phone me as a matter of urgency?'

Christine and Cheryl would be home on Wednesday. He couldn't face the thought of being with other people, having to talk to them, to hear about yet another holiday. Lying awake in the dark, listening to soft rain stroking the windowpanes, he thought of Senta's truthfulness and honesty and how he had ascribed her accounts of her experiences to fantasising. The rain fell more and more heavily throughout the night and in the morning it was still pouring. He drove along partly flooded roads to Chigwell to see if the fitters were having any problems with Mrs Ripple's bathroom.

This time he didn't even glance out of the window towards Arnham's garden. He had lost interest in Arnham. He had lost interest in everything and everybody but Senta. She occupied his mind, she had moved into his mind and lain down on the bed from where she stared into his inner eyes. He moved dully, he was like a zombie. Mrs Ripple's hard snapping voice uttering complaints was just a noise, a nuisance. She was complaining about the marble top of her vanity unit, there was a flaw in the veining, a tiny flaw, no more than a scratch and on the underside, but she wanted the whole slab of marble renewed. He shrugged, said he would see what he could do. The fitter winked at him and he managed a wink in return.

Last time he was here Senta had been with him. She had kissed him in the car outside Mrs Ripple's house and later, out in the country, they had made love on the grass, hidden by a ring of trees. He had to have her back, he was desperate. He thought once more of breaking that window, forcing those shutters apart, sawing through them if necessary. His imagination showed him himself thus breaking and entering and her waiting there for him, crouched on the end of the bed, reflected in the great mirror. And it showed him a similar entry to the room, through smashed glass and shattered wood, to find it empty.

Tarsus Street was bad enough in sunshine, horrible in the rain. One of the ever-present rubbish bags had burst and its contents, mostly paper, exploded across pavement and roadway, scraps alighting in surreal ways. The rain had pasted a biscuit-packet wrapper round the trunk of a lamp standard in the manner of some council notice. The railing spikes speared the separated leaves of a paperback book. Wet newspaper squelched in corners with matchboxes and juice cartons in its lap. Philip got out of the car and stepped across a puddle in which a yogurt pot floated. The façade of the house was unchanged

134

except that the window box had filled with water which overflowed in a stream down the dark wet bricks. The shutters upstairs and her shutters remained closed.

He stood in the rain staring up at the house. There was nothing else to do. He had begun to notice all kinds of things about it that at first he had missed. There was a Greenpeace sticker in the left corner of the top left-hand window. On the painted framework of the middle floor shutters something had been written in pencil beside a little pencil drawing. He was too far away to see what was written or drawn. Inside the middle window on the top floor a green glass wine bottle stood on the sill, a little way right of centre. The rain continued to fall steadily from a sky which was precisely the same shade as the grey slates on the roof. He noticed that from the pitched roof of the porch one tile was missing.

He went up the stairs and banged on the front door, avoiding the coiled pile of dog turd on the second step. After a while he looked through the letterbox. This time he saw the phone and the passage leading away to the basement stairs and something new. Two envelopes lay on the table beside the phone.

At home he changed out of his suit and hung it up to dry, dried his hair on a towel, remembering how, that first day, she had asked for a towel to dry her own. He cooked egg and bacon but when it was served up on a plate with a hunk of bread and butter, couldn't eat it. The phone rang and his heart hit his ribs. No voice would come when he lifted the receiver, he was sure of that. It was a kind of croak he gave.

'Are you OK?' Fee said. 'You sound peculiar.'

'I'm fine.'

'I rang to know if you wanted me to get anything in for Mum on Wednesday. You know, a loaf and some ham or something.'

The question he longed to ask, was dying to ask, was displaced by another, seemingly less significant. 'Was it

RADA Senta was at? Was it the Royal Academy of Dramatic Art?'

'*What?*'

He repeated the question. He was starting to feel sick. 'I wouldn't know,' she said. 'How should I know?'

'Would you ask Darren, please?'

'Why do you want to know?'

'Just ask him, please, Fee.'

He heard his question relayed to Darren in a tone stiff with sarcasm. They seemed to be arguing. Had it taken marriage to show Fee her childhood sweetheart was somewhat slow on the uptake? She came back to the phone.

'He says he went there once with his brother to see something she was in. It wasn't like a building, you know what I mean, it was just a big house. Out west somewhere, Ealing, Acton.'

'RADA is near the British Museum, it's in Bloomsbury. Is he sure it wasn't there?'

'He says Ealing definitely. What is all this, Phil? What's going on? You're always asking questions about Senta.'

'I'm sure I'm not.'

'Darren says do you want her phone number?'

The irony! He knew that phone number better than his own, better than his own birth date, his address. He said, 'No to that and yes to the first question. If you could get a loaf in and something for their supper, Fee.'

She was laughing as she said goodbye.

He sat there, pondering. It was new to him, this revelation that someone could both tell the truth and fantasise, for that was what it amounted to. She had told him true things and she had embroidered the truth. Where the truth was adequate she had offered it to him and where it fell short of glamour or drama, she had invented. Did he do that? Do we all? And where in this scheme of things did her request that he prove his love for her find its place? Was it a fantasy or a real demand for a real act?

Presently he dialled her number. This time the answering machine wasn't on and the phone rang and rang unanswered.

It was late at night. The sky was dull and without visible stars, moonless, faintly misty, a smoky red where a horizon of roofs could be seen. Dampness was palpable in the cool still air. On the corner where Tarsus Street met Caesarea Road stood three men about Philip's own age, one of them a Rastafarian, the others white, nondescript, one wearing several rings in the lobe of his right ear. Philip noticed the rings because they glinted in his car lights. The men turned to stare at him, watched the car, watched him get out of it. They did nothing.

The old bag man was nowhere to be seen. Philip hadn't seen him since the weather changed. The street was still littered with rags of paper, cardboard boxes, cuboid juice cartons with straws still sticking out of them. A greenish lamplight glazed the moist sticky pavements, the railings, the gleaming humpbacks of parked cars. A dog came along the pitted concrete from Samaria Street, busy in pursuit of some unknown goal, perhaps the same dog which had deposited the heap of turds on the step. It disappeared down into the area next door. An occasional drop of water trickled and fell from the leaves on the plane trees.

Philip, momentarily, had a strange feeling that came quite unbidden. It was as if a voice within him asked him what he was doing seeking love, passion, perhaps a life's partner, in this awful place. For what woman who had any choice about it, any alternative, would choose to live in this filthy sink of north-west London, this rancid hole? This unwelcome reflection fled as fast as it had come for, looking up wearily by now at the house he saw the shutters had been closed at the middle window on the ground floor and between their boards, where the wood had warped, light showed in bright lines.

He ran up the steps. The front door was open. That is, it was unlocked, on the latch. He could hardly believe it. From somewhere inside came the sound of music in waltz time, the same kind of music as he had sometimes heard late at night lying in bed beside Senta. The *Blue Danube*. As he stood there it stopped and he heard laughter and hands clapping. He pushed the door open and went in. The music, which was coming from inside the room on the left where the light showed through the shutters, began again, this time a tango, *Jealousy*. On all his visits to this house he had scarcely noticed that there were doors opening off this hallway, had never conjectured that there must be rooms behind. He had thought of nothing but going to Senta. This room, of course, would be directly above hers.

He must have made a sound, though he was unaware of it. Perhaps he had drawn in his breath sharply or his footsteps had made a floorboard creak, for the door was suddenly flung open and a man shouted, 'What the fuck do you think you're doing?'

Philip was silenced and in fact stricken statue-like as much by the sight of the two people who stood just inside the room as by the man's violent and abusive tone. The pair of them were in evening dress. They reminded him of Fred Astaire and Ginger Rogers in one of those thirties films you sometimes saw on television, and then he saw that they were not really like that at all. The woman was in her fifties, with a mane of long grey hair and a coarse, lined, though lively face and a sleek sinuous figure to which her shabby red silk dress clung. A bunch of bruised artificial flowers on the bodice, red and pink, trembled as she drew breath. Her partner was smart enough, though unshaven and with ragged hair. His face was white and thin, his hair yellow, and he was no more than four or five years older than Philip himself.

Finding a voice, Philip said, 'I'm sorry. I was looking for Senta - Senta Pelham, she lives downstairs. The front door was open.'

'Christ, she must have left it open again,' the woman said. 'She's always doing that, it's bloody careless.'

Her partner went over to the tape player and turned the sound down. 'She's gone to a party,' he said. 'Who are you anyway?'

'Philip Wardman. I'm a friend of hers.'

For some reason the woman laughed. 'You're the one who left a message on our answerphone.'

So this was Mike Jacopo. Philip said, stammering a bit. 'Are you - do you – do you live here?'

The woman said, 'I'm Rita Pelham and this is my house. We've been away a bit lately with the competitions up north.'

He had no idea what she meant but he understood this was Senta's mother, or the woman she called mother, and Jacopo the young lover Fee had talked about. Confusion robbed him of words. All that mattered anyway was that she wasn't here, she was out, she had gone to a party.

Jacopo had turned the sound up again. The tango played. They moved into each other's arms, hands stiff, heads erect. Rita swayed backwards, in the loop of Jacopo's arms, her grey hair sweeping the floorboards. Jacopo moved into the stylised steps of the dance. As they passed the door he kicked it shut. They had forgotten Philip. He went out through the front door, pushed up the latch, closed the door behind him.

Tarsus Street was empty. The Rastafarian and the two white men had gone. So had the radio from his car which he had left unlocked and the raincoat from the back seat.

It was only when he was home and in bed that he thought

how he should have stayed there. He should have sat in the car until she came back, all night if necessary. He hadn't thought of it because the theft of his radio and the raincoat, which was a Burberry, which he had bought with his Visa card and still hadn't finished paying for, had shaken him rather a lot. Perhaps he could have persuaded Rita Pelham or Jacopo to let him into Senta's room and stay the night there. Of course they wouldn't have agreed to that, of course not.

That Rita owned the house and lived there somehow changed the aspect of things. It meant that Senta, like him, lived at home with her mother. It wasn't quite like that, he could see it wasn't, but it was a similar state of affairs. Things somehow became less sordid when seen in that light. Senta lived with her mother, she wasn't responsible for the decay of the place and the dirt and the smell.

He slept and dreamed of her. In the dream he was in her room, or rather, he was inside the mirror, watching the room through the glass, the bed that was piled with purple pillows and quilt, the wicker chair with her discarded clothes on it, the shutters folded across the window, the door that led to those corridors and caverns of rubbish, closed and with a chair set against it. He sat inside the mirror and it was like sitting in a tank of greenish water in which tiny speck-like organisms swam, in which thin green fronds faintly swayed and a crawling snail left its silver trail on the other side of the glass. She came into the room, forcing the door open and knocking the chair over. She came close up to the glass and looked into the green speckled translucence without seeing him, she didn't even see him when their faces were pressed together with the wet glass between.

Out with Hardy in the morning, along Glenallan Close, round Kintail Way, and back by way of Lochleven Gardens, he met the postman who handed him his own mail. There was another postcard from Christine, though she was coming home today, and a letter for her from one of her sisters. The postcard was of a street in Newquay this time and said: 'I may be home before you get this so won't give you any news. The X is supposed to mark our room but Cheryl says it is wrong because we are on the third floor. Much love, Mum.'

Philip put Christine's letter on the mantelpiece. They seldom got letters, any of them. The people they knew and their relatives phoned if they wanted to communicate. But why shouldn't he write to Senta? He could type the envelope at work so that she wouldn't know who it was from. Yesterday morning he wouldn't even have considered this but things had changed. Rita and Jacopo were there and they got letters. He had seen two envelopes lying by the phone when he looked through the letter box. If a letter came for Senta one of them would probably take it down to her and she would at least open it. When she saw it was from him, would she throw it away?

Bereft of his radio, he was driven back to his own thoughts as he drove down to the West End to head office. The difficulty would be in knowing what to say to her that would stop her throwing it away.

Philip hardly ever wrote personal letters. He couldn't remember the last time he had and he had never written a love letter, which this must be. Normally, when he put pen to paper, or more often, dictated something to Lucy the typist he shared with Roy and two others, the result was on the lines of: 'Dear Mrs Finnegan, This is to confirm receipt of your cheque for a deposit on the agreed work in the sum of £1,000. If you have any queries please do not hesitate to contact me at the above showroom at any time . . .' Still, he could write a love letter, he knew he could, phrases from the fullness of his heart and his longing were already coming to him, and he could apologise and beg forgiveness. He wouldn't mind that, he wouldn't find it humiliating. But she had asked him to prove his love for her . . .

Roy, still in a good mood, caught him doing the envelope on Lucy's typewriter. 'Writing your love letters in the company's time now, I see.'

It was uncanny how near the bone people could get and all unwittingly. Philip pulled the envelope off the roller. No doubt Roy really thought it was to Mrs Ripple, for he said, 'The order for that new bit of marble's come through. Can you give the old bag a ring and tell her it'll be with her by midday?'

He tried to do so on Lucy's phone. The line was engaged for the first couple of attempts. While he waited he had a look at Lucy's *Daily Mail*, read a story about the IRA, one about a dog rescuing its owner from drowning in the Grand Union Canal, another which was an account of the murder of an old woman in Southall. He picked up the phone again and dialled Mrs Ripple's number.

'Hallo, who is it?'

Her voice came out of the receiver in a sharp blast, the sentence as if one polysyllabic word, not four. He told her who it was and passed on Roy's message.

'About time too,' she said, then, 'I shan't be here. I'm going out.'

He said he would get back to her. An idea had come to him out of the air, out of nothing, an idea of stupendous magnitude, a total solution. It felled him so that he spoke to her in a tone of vagueness, hesitantly, unable to find the ordinary simple words.

'What did you say?'

He pulled himself together, said, 'I have to talk to my colleague, Mrs Ripple. With your permission, I'll come back to you within five minutes.'

As if an observer or listener could read his thoughts, he shut the door. He picked up the newspaper again and looked once more at the account of the murder of the

142

Southall woman. Why hadn't he thought of this way out before? It was so simple, it was only another move in the game. For that was all it was to Senta, a game, but one that he also had to play. He even liked the idea of that, of a private secret game they both played, even when neither quite knew the truth of the other's strategy. That only made it more exciting.

She was a fantasist who also told the truth about her own history. He still found that hard to get used to, but he knew it was an accurate analysis of her. Another aspect of her character was now revealed to him. She would want a lover – *a husband*? – to have an equally fantastic dream life. Even in the short time they had known each other he might already have disappointed her by his failure to relate adventures and exploits of his own past. The point was *that she would know he was inventing and expect him to do this*. She did it herself, it was a way of life with her. He saw himself suddenly as stupid and insensitive. Because he had been too thick to respond to her invitation, a simple and innocent invitation to a shared fantasy, he had caused them all this misery, the worst ten days of his life.

The door opened and Lucy came in. It was she who picked up the receiver when the phone rang and held it at arm's length to defend herself from Mrs Ripple's ear-shattering blast.

The letter he composed sitting at the table in the living room, where he was subject to a series of interruptions. First Hardy wanted a walk. Philip took him as far as the end of Kintail Way and began again: 'Dear Senta . . .'

It looked cold. He wrote 'Darling Senta,' and though he had never in his life called anyone darling, liked it better. 'Darling Senta, I have missed you so terribly, I didn't know what it was to miss anyone before. Please don't let us ever be apart again like that.' He would have liked to write about the sex they had, about making love to her, and the terrible deprivation not making love to her had been, but some deep inner shyness held him back. The act was lovely and open and free but the words embarrassed him.

The sound of a key in the lock made him think it must be Christine, though it was early for her. He had forgotten Fee was coming round with the loaf and the ham. She had also bought Danish pastries, a basket of strawberries, a carton of double cream.

'Who are you writing to?'

He had quickly covered the letter with the *TV Times* on which he had been resting the paper, but a corner showed. The truth would never be believed, so he told her the truth in an airy tone.

'Senta Pelham, of course.'

'You should co-co. Chance'd be a fine thing. That reminds me, I had that bridesmaid's dress cleaned, the one she kindly dumped on the floor, and it's come up looking super. Will you tell Mum I picked up her winter coat at the same time and I've put it up in her wardrobe?'

He waited until the front door had closed behind her.

'Darling Senta, I have tried to see you, I ..on't know how many times I have been to your house. Of course I can understand now why you wouldn't let me in and didn't want to see me. But please don't ever do that again, it hurts too much.

'I have thought a lot about what you asked me. All this time I have been thinking of you, I don't think I have had a thought for anything or anyone else, and of course I have naturally thought about what you said I should do to prove I love you. Personally, I think the proof is in what I've been through since I left you that day and you took the keys to your house away from me. . . .'

Perhaps he shouldn't put that bit in. It sounded too much like a reproach, it sounded like whining. The throbbing of a diesel engine outside told him Christine had

144

arrived. He put the *TV Times* over his letter again and went to the door. She was alone, without Cheryl. Her skin was tanned, her face golden with pink cheeks, her hair bleached by the sun. She looked young and pretty and he hadn't seen the dress she had on before, a natural-coloured linen coat-dress that was plainer and more sophisticated than what she usually wore. Hardy rushed past him and hurled himself at Christine, yelping with joy.

She came up the step with the dog in her arms and kissed Philip. 'You said to have a taxi so I did, and it was ever so nice, but he charged me over five pounds. I said to him I didn't think it was fair that clock or meter or whatever it is still ticking the price up even when you're stuck in a traffic jam. It ought to stop when the taxi isn't moving, I said, but he just laughed.'

'What happened to Cheryl?'

'It's funny you should ask that because she was with me right up until we'd been in the taxi for ten minutes. We were going along this street with lots of quite nice shops and she suddenly said to the driver to stop and let her out and he did and she said, "Good-bye, see you later", and got out, and I must say I did think it was funny because all the shops were closed.'

The Edgware Road, he thought. 'Did you have a good time in Cornwall?'

'Quiet,' she said. 'It was very quiet.' This was what she said when people asked her if she had enjoyed Christmas. 'I was on my own a lot.' She wasn't complaining, just stating a fact. 'Cheryl wanted to be off by herself. Well, a young girl, you know, she doesn't want an old bat flapping after her. Isn't Hardy pleased to see me? He does look well, dear, you've been taking good care of him.' She peered into the dog's adoring face and then into Philip's in her gentle rather apprehensive way. 'I can't say the same for you, Phil, you're looking quite peaky.'

'I'm OK.'

Thanks to Cheryl's defection, he would have to stay with her now instead of finishing the letter. He couldn't go upstairs and desert her on her first evening at home. Looking back over those terrible ten days he thought, what a waste, what a waste! We could have been together every night, all night, if I hadn't been such a fool . . .

It was gone ten-thirty when he got back to his letter. Christine wanted an early night. A quick scan of her appointments book had shown her she was doing a shampoo, trim and blow-dry at nine next morning. Philip sat on his bed, rested letter paper on the *TV Times* and the *TV Times* on his old school atlas on his knees.

'Darling Senta, I have missed you so terribly . . .' He read over what he had written, felt fairly satisfied. At any rate he knew he couldn't do better. 'I don't know why I made such a fuss when you suggested what we should do to prove our love for each other. You know I would do anything for you. Of course I will do it. I would do fifty times that for you, just to see you again I would do it. I love you. You must know that by now but I will tell you again because this is what I want you to know and what I will prove to you. I love you. With all my love for ever and ever, Philip.'

10

She didn't reply.

He knew she must have got his letter. Unwilling to
entrust it to the post, he had taken it to Tarsus Street
himself on his way to work and put it through the letter
box. Then he had looked through and seen it lying there,
not on the doormat for there was no doormat, but on
the dirty red and black tiles. The house had been quite
silent, the shutters closed at the basement window and
the two windows above it. The phone on the table was
hidden behind a pile of leaflets, freebie magazines and
junk mail.

Once the idea of writing to her had come to him, or,
rather, once the idea of what he should write had come,
his unhappiness had gone and he had been filled with
hope. This euphoria was quite baseless. Simply writing a
letter and delivering it wouldn't bring her back. He knew
that this was true on one level of consciousness, but on
another which seemed most to affect his emotions, he
had solved his problems, put an end to misery, won her.
At work he was happy, he was almost as he had been
before that Sunday when he had said those things to her
and she had turned him out.

What form her return to him would take he hadn't
considered. A phone call, surely. Yet she had never
phoned him in the past, not once. He couldn't imagine
her writing a letter in return. Should he go to her house
as in the old days? It was less than a fortnight ago but just
the same it was the old days. Thursday passed without his
going back to Tarsus Street. On Friday he phoned her
number from work and got Jacopo on his answering
machine. He left the same message as he had last time,

to ask Senta to phone him. But this time he stipulated that it should be that evening and added his phone number. It occurred to him, strange though this seemed, that Senta might not know his phone number. There were unlikely to be phone directories in that house.

Christine took Hardy out for his evening walk. Philip wouldn't leave the house. He told her he was expecting the art director to call from head office. Christine believed anything he told her, even that a company like Roseberry Lawn had an art director and that this mythical personage might work late on Friday evenings and need to consult very junior executives like Philip. While she was out with the dog, he experienced one of the worst things that can happen to you on an emotional level: to wait by the telephone for long hours for someone you are desperately in love with to phone, get a call at last and have it turn out to be your sister.

Fee wanted to know whether Christine would do her hair if they came round for supper on Sunday. She had a fancy for ash-blonde highlights. Usually Philip wouldn't have known anything about Christine's appointments and engagements but he had overheard her telling her friend on the phone that she was going out at six on Sunday to do a perm for an old lady who was housebound with arthritis. Fee said, OK, she'd call back a bit later when Christine was in and Philip had to say that was all right, though he thought that if Senta hadn't phoned by then he wouldn't be able to help hoping it was she when the phone rang. He wouldn't be able to keep himself from rushing to it and seizing the receiver.

And this in fact happened, for Senta didn't phone but Fee did and he suffered the same hope and destruction of hope all over again. She hadn't phoned by midnight when at last he went to bed.

On Saturday afternoon he drove to Tarsus Street. The old man in the woman's raincoat had obtained from somewhere a wooden trolley or barrow on which were piled his possessions stowed into plastic carriers. These were arranged like cushions and were in gaudy cushion colours: Tesco red, Marks and Spencer's green, Selfridge's yellow and the blue and white of Boots the Chemist. The old man reclined on top of them, like an emperor in a chariot, eating a sandwich of something greasy in white bread on which his fingers made black prints.

He waved the sandwich at Philip. He had never looked so cheerful. His open-mouthed grin showed greenish carious teeth. 'See what I got meself with your more than generous gift, governor.' He kicked the wooden side of the barrow. 'I've got me own transport now and what's more, it runs on shanks's pony.'

After that Philip could hardly avoid giving him a pound coin. He was entitled perhaps to something in return. 'What's your name?'

The reply came a little cagily and it was indirect. 'They call me Joley.'

'Are you always about here?'

'Here and Caesarea –' he pronounced it Si-saria '– and over to Ilbert.'

'Do you ever see a girl come out of that house?'

'Kid with grey hair?'

Philip thought it a bizarre way to describe Senta but he nodded.

The old man stopped eating. 'Not the fuzz, are you?'

'Me? Of course I'm not.'

'I'll tell you one thing, governor, she's in there now. She come home and went in there ten minutes back.'

Without shame, he held out his hand. Philip didn't know whether to believe him or not but he gave him another pound coin. A flicker of hope that the front door might have been left open once more was soon dispelled, but when he looked down into the area he saw that the shutters had been folded back a little way. By climbing over the low plaster wall of the steps and squatting down on the concrete it was possible to see into her room. Looking into it after two weeks deprivation – except for dreams, except for those – hastened his heartbeat, he could feel the blood drumming. The room was empty. Over the wicker chair hung her silver dress and a pair of lilac-coloured tights, worn and discarded, for they still held, faintly, the contour of her legs and feet. The bed was still made up with purple cover and pillowcases.

This time he didn't knock on the door. The old man was watching him, grinning, though not unsympathetically. Philip said goodbye to him and 'See you' though he now doubted whether he would ever see him again. He drove home, telling himself not to return, to bear it, to contemplate life without her, to soldier on without her. But, although he didn't mean to do this, he made his way up to his bedroom on dragging feet and there, having pushed the chair against the door, lifted Flora out from the cupboard. Her face, her neat crimped hair, her remote smile and mesmerised eyes no longer recalled Senta to him. For all that, he had a feeling new and alien to him. He wanted to smash her, break her to pieces with a hammer, and stamp on those pieces, grinding them to dust. For someone who hated violence in all its forms, these were unwelcome shameful desires. He simply put Flora back in her hiding place. Then he lay face-downwards on the bed and, to his own surprise and shame, found himself beginning a dry-eyed painful sobbing. He wept without tears into the pillow, wadding the linen against his mouth in case Christine should come upstairs and hear him.

It was half-way through Sunday when he gave up hope. Fee was there, having arranged for Christine to do her highlights in the afternoon. And Cheryl was at home, affording Philip his first sight of her since her return from Cornwall. But she wasn't there for long. Having eaten or picked at the rather better than usual lunch Christine had provided, roast chicken with Paxo stuffing, reconstituted

150

potato and real fresh runner beans, she got up from the table and five minutes later left the house. Philip she had asked, when she was briefly alone with him, to lend her five pounds. He had to say no, he hadn't got five pounds, adding, perhaps pointlessly, that she couldn't want money on Sunday. He sat at the table, with two halves of tinned peaches in a glass dish in front of him, and thought, I will never see Senta again, this is it, all over, the end, it is over. The frightening thing was that he couldn't imagine how he was ever going to get through another week of it. Would next Sunday come and would he be here alive and surviving? Would he actually survive the torture of another week of this?

When the dishes were done Christine and Fee took over the kitchen. Christine never charged her daughters for doing their hair but she did allow them to pay for the cost of the preparations she used. Now she and Fee engaged in an argument as to how great a proportion of this cost Fee should be allowed to pay.

'Yes, but, dear, you got us all that nice ham and the strawberries and cream and I've only paid you for the loaf,' Christine was saying.

'The strawberries were a present, Mum, my pleasure, you know that.'

'And doing your highlights is my pleasure, dear.'

'I'll tell you what then, you tell me the price of the ash-blonde tint and I'll want conditioner so you can count that in, and the bit of mousse you use, and take away whatever the ham was, one twenty-two it was, and I'll give you the difference.'

Philip was sitting in the living room, looking at the *Sunday Express*, not reading it but pretending to, with Hardy on his lap. Christine came in with the PG Tips tin she kept small change in.

'Do you know, I could have sworn there was a good seven pounds fifty in here before I went away and now it's down to thirty pee.'

'I haven't been making raids on it,' he said.

'I wish I'd looked in it on Wednesday. I keep wondering if it happened yesterday afternoon while you were out and I popped round the block with Hardy and didn't lock up. I know I should have locked up but I still think of this as a nice neighbourhood. I was only gone ten minutes but you know that's quite long enough for someone to come in and take a quick look round and help themselves to what's going. Some poor person down on their uppers and desperate, I expect. I can sympathise, there but for the grace of God, I always say.'

Philip thought he knew very well who the poor person, down on her uppers and desperate would be. The theft had happened just before lunch, not yesterday. Once he would have cared, would have known he must do something, at least would have communicated what he knew to Christine. Now he was concerned for no one but himself. But he emptied his pockets, giving what change he had to his mother. Briefly he wondered where Cheryl was now, what dealing she was involved in with the seven pounds fifty. What could you buy with such a miserable sum? Not smack, not grass, not crack. A bottle of whisky? That, certainly. Some sort of solvent? He couldn't see his sister as hooked on glue sniffing.

Fee's hair, when finished, was a helmet of puffed-out glinting honey and cream stripes. Even Philip, who understood very little about these things, knew Christine continued to do hair in styles fashionable in her own early youth. She even referred to them by name sometimes, the Italian and the Beehive, as if these titles were eternal and understood by all subsequent generations, not just those who had been young in 1960. Fee seemed satisfied. If she too suspected Cheryl of stealing the contents of the PG Tips tin she said nothing about it to Philip.

After Fee had gone, Christine began packing into her holdall the things she needed for perming the housebound old lady's hair. She kept up a commentary to

Philip while she did this, describing her own mother's experience of having a perm in the twenties when you had your hair strung up to an electric machine and baked into curl, how you sat there all day attached to this curious instrument of cookery. He wished she wasn't going out, he didn't want to be left alone with himself and his own thoughts. It was absurd, it was like when he was a little boy and never wanted his mother to leave the house even though there was always someone there to look after him.

Yet a month ago he heaved a sigh of relief when she said she was going out. Less than a year ago he was longing for her to marry Arnham. He said, surprising himself, using a phrase she with her curious occasional tact never used to him, 'What time will you be back?'

She looked at him in astonishment, as well she might. 'I don't know, Philip. It'll take three hours. I try to make a nice job of it for the old dear.'

He said no more. He went upstairs. The doorbell rang as he was entering his own bedroom. Christine opened the door almost immediately. She must have been standing just inside it, preparing to leave. He heard her say, 'Oh, hallo, dear. How are you? Have you come to see Cheryl?'

There must have been some reply but it was inaudible. Since he heard nothing, saw nothing, how did he know? How did he know enough to come back to the head of the stairs, hold his breath, clench his hands?

His mother said, 'Cheryl's out but she's sure to be back soon. I have to go out myself and, oh dear, I *am* late. Did you want to come in and wait for Cheryl?'

Philip came down the stairs. By then Senta had entered the house and was standing in the hall, looking up. Neither of them spoke and neither had eyes for anything or anyone but each other. If Christine thought this odd she gave no sign of it, she gave no sign of having noticed but went out of the front door, closing it behind her. Still

153

in silence, Philip approached Senta and Senta took a step towards him and they fell into each other's arms.

Holding her, smelling her and tasting her soft, curved, moist and salty lips, feeling the pressure of her breasts against his chest, he thought for a moment he would faint with the ecstasy of it. Instead there came to him a surge of strength and power, of sudden enormous well-being, and he lifted her off the ground up into his arms. But half-way up the stairs she struggled and jumped down and ran on ahead up to his bedroom.

They lay on his bed as they had that first time. Love-making had never been so glorious, so infinitely rewarding, not that first time certainly, not even those repeated luxurious indulgent times in her basement bed. Now, as they lay side by side, his arm slack under her shoulders, he felt as if bathed in a warm and deep tender-ness for her. To have reproached her for anything would have been unthinkable. Those dreadful visits to Tarsus Street, the hammering on the door, peering through the windows, attempts at phoning, all took on the character of a dream; the kind of dream which while taking place was very vivid and real, which lingered in a troubling way for a little while on waking, then receded rapidly into oblivion.

'I love you, Senta,' he said. 'I love you, oh, I do love you.'

She turned her head towards him and smiled. She drew one small milk-coloured fingernail down the side of his cheek to the corner of his mouth. 'I love you, Philip.'

'It was wonderful of you to come here like that. It was the most wonderful thing you could have done.'

'It was the only thing to do.'

'I met Rita and Mike Jacopo, you know.'

She was unperturbed. 'They gave me your letter.' She curled herself into his body in the way she had of making

154

as much of her flesh touch as much of his as possible. It was in itself another kind of sexual act and as if she was using this means to make herself one with him. 'I haven't told them anything. Why should I? They're nothing. They've gone away again anyway.'

'Gone away?'

'They go to these ballroom-dancing contests. That's how they met. They've won silver cups.' Her soft giggle called laughter from him.

'Oh, Senta, oh, Senta. I just want to say your name over and over. Senta, Senta. It's funny, it's as if you've never been away and at the same time it's as if I'm just realising you're back, I've got you back, and I want to laugh and shout and yell with happiness.'

When she spoke he felt the movement of her lips against his skin. 'I'm sorry, Philip. Can you forgive me?'

'There's nothing to forgive.'

Her head lay nestling into his chest. He looked down on to the crown of her head and saw that the red roots of hair had been bleached silver. For a moment a cold finger touched his happiness and the thought came unbidden and most unwelcome, she was all right without me, she was doing her own thing, she had her hair done. She went to a party . . .

She lifted her head and looked at him. 'We won't talk about what we're going to do for each other tonight. We won't spoil it. We'll talk about all that tomorrow.'

Fantasising had no part in Philip's emotional make-up. He had never, while making love to one girl imagined another, more beautiful or more sexy, or lain in bed at night conjuring up visions of women in fantastic undress lounging in invented pornographic situations. He had never day-dreamed of himself as successful, rich and powerful, the possessor of some lavish home, large fast car, or as a sophisticated world traveller or financier or tycoon. His imagination never even took him as far as the carpet in front of the Roseberry Lawn's managing director's desk, the recipient of congratulations and swift promotion. He had a strong sense of the present and of reality.

To create a fantasy for Senta's satisfaction, for that was what it amounted to, would be a daunting task for him. That first week after their reunion, the necessity of this creation rather loomed over him. He felt its dark pressure even when he was most happy, when he was with her in Tarsus Street, for instance, and into the deep peace of the aftermath of love-making, when he should have been most free of care, intruded this silent staring threat. For it did seem to stare at him, it did seem almost a living thing, which entered his consciousness when least welcome and stood there, arms folded, exercising its menace.

The act he must perform, albeit only a verbal act, he couldn't put off much longer. It must be confronted and a form found for it, a scenario constructed with actors – or two actors, himself and his victim. More than once Senta reminded him of it.

'We do need proof of each other's love, Philip. It's not enough that we were unhappy when we were apart. That happens to anyone, to ordinary people.' She always insisted that he and she were not ordinary, were more like gods. 'We have to prove that for each other we're prepared to transcend ordinary human laws. More than that, to set them at nothing, show they simply aren't important to us.'

She had decided, thinking much about this while they were apart, that he and she were reincarnations of some famous pair of lovers of the past. The precise identity of these historic personages she hadn't yet decided on, or, as she put it herself, this truth hadn't yet been revealed to her. Also while they were separated she had auditioned for and got a part in a fringe theatre production. It was a minor part with less than twenty lines to speak, but not all that minor really, since the woman she played turned out in the end to be the secret agent the entire cast had been seeking through fifteen surrealistic scenes.

All this brought Philip an uneasiness that was undesired at this phase in their relationship. He would have liked simply to exult in her renewed love, perhaps make reasonable and sensible plans for the future, thinking ahead to eventual marriage. Whether he actually wanted to get married for quite a long while he was less sure, but he knew there was no other woman he would ever be able to dream of marrying. Instead he was made to feel very awkward by being asked to try to recall whether in a previous life he had been Alexander or Antony or Dante. He had, too, the problem of deciding if the fringe theatre part was a fantasy or actual fact.

A fantasy, he was pretty sure. That she had frequently told him the truth about her past didn't mean she was invariably truthful, he had already persuaded himself of that. Her biggest fantasy was what he now had to cope with and he put off his own moves in this rather unpleasant and absurd game from day to day. The more he did so the more he thought about it and the more distasteful it became to him. Killing someone was such a monstrous thing, the worst thing one could do surely – which was why, of course, she talked about their doing it – so that even to have claimed to have done it when you hadn't would be somehow wrong and even corrupting. Philip hardly knew what he meant by this term but of the feeling he was certain.

Would a truly sane and normal man tell a woman he had killed someone, lay claim to murder, when he was actually quite innocent? And, come to that, could a person who said that *be* innocent? He knew he ought to be able to persuade her that this particular fantasy of hers was folly, wasn't even very good for them to think about. If they loved each other as fully as he knew they did they ought to be able to talk about anything to each other, explain everything. The fault, he thought, was as much his as hers. He knew he wasn't a god but when he protested she merely told him he wouldn't know if he was or not but in time the truth of it would be declared to him.

'We are Ares and Aphrodite,' she told him. 'Those old gods didn't die when Christianity came. They just hid themselves and from time to time are reborn in certain specially selected individuals. You and I are two of those individuals, Philip. I had a dream last night in which all that was revealed to me. We stood there on the curve of the earth's globe in blinding light and we were dressed in white robes.'

He was by no means sure who Ares and Aphrodite had been, though with a good idea that they had existed only in the minds of men. In the minds perhaps of women like Senta? She told him that this pair of gods (they were called Mars and Venus too which made better sense to him) had had many mortals killed, thought little of striking with death anyone who had offended them or even obstructed them by their very existence. Philip could scarcely think of anyone who had offended him, still less been a nuisance to him by existing. Once, not long ago, Gerard Arnham would have come into this category. Now it was unreal even to consider doing him harm.

On the Monday, which was more than a week after Senta had come back to him, he made up his mind that whatever the consequences to his own moral assessment of himself, he could put off this significant move no longer. Once done, it would be the end of his problems. Senta would see his love as proved, would play some similar game to prove her own, and with that behind them they could settle into their joyous relationship which must reach the point of living together, becoming engaged, even marrying. He conforted himself with the notion – a brilliant one that had come to him unsought

– that the reality of their love would before long cure her of this need to fantasise.

For once, it wasn't a very busy day. He bought several morning papers on his way to work. Returning from an inspection of the refitted flats in Wembley, he bought an evening paper. The first batch hadn't been rewarding. They had reverted, after nearly a year, to the case of the missing Rebecca Neave. Her body had never been found. Now her father and her sister were jointly setting up something called the Rebecca Neave Foundation. They were appealing for donations. These would fund a centre offering classes to women in self-defence and martial arts. A photograph showed Rebecca in the green velvet tracksuit she had worn when she disappeared. They would use a stylised representation of this for the foundation's logo.

The *Evening Standard* had a follow-on story about Rebecca and two other girls who had gone missing in the past year. It also offered Philip a paragraph which seemed the very thing he was looking for. He read it sitting in the car in one of the parking areas at Brent Cross Shopping Centre where he had called to buy wine and strawberries and chocolates for Senta.

> The body of a man found on a demolition site in Kensal Rise, north-west London, has been identified as that of John Sidney Crucifer, 62, described as a vagrant and of no fixed address. Police are treating the case as murder.

Senta herself had suggested to him that someone like that would do, pointing out the elderly bag woman who had sat with her back to the railings. The only difficulty would be if the police found the murderer of John Crucifer and it appeared in the papers. He didn't like to think that Senta might not care if someone else were sent to prison for a crime he, Philip, had committed. But he was being stupid, wasn't he? What did he mean, she wouldn't care? It was all fantasy with her. She might not actually say she knew he hadn't really killed anyone, but she knew he hadn't. She knew already, she must know, that his undertaking to her was one of the moves in the game. Anyway, she never read newspapers, he had never seen her handle or even glance at a newspaper.

This John Crucifer would do. He needn't worry about details, he needn't worry even about the unlikely event of the case being blown up into something important, becoming of nationwide interest, because the truth was that Senta didn't want the daylight of reality let in on to it. She wanted dreams and, for once anyway, she should have them. A certain shame afflicted him as he sat there in the shopping centre car park. This was really caused by the idea of the conversation with Senta ahead of him in which he would have to tell her all this and witness her satisfaction. He would be lying and she would be accepting his lie as truth and they would both know it.

In the event it was rather worse than he had imagined.

He went home first for his evening meal and got to Tarsus Street at about half-past seven. For by no means the first time that day, he found himself on the way carefully rehearsing the story he had prepared for Senta. He also had the piece from the *Standard* which he had snipped out with Christine's hair-cutting scissors and a pound coin in his pocket for the old man called Joley.

His feelings about Joley remained superstitious. It was as if he had been appointed both the guardian of Senta and of their love, and yet it was not that in any real sense but more as if the old man had to be placated with gifts to keep his, Philip's, relationship with Senta secure. Some sort of malevolence would make itself felt if these pound coins were not forthcoming, a malice that might positively harm him and Senta. He had tentatively said something of this to her the night before — he was trying to supply flights of fancy of his own to match hers – and she had talked of fees for a ferryman and sops for a dog that guarded the entrance to the underworld. This was mostly incomprehensible to Philip but he was glad to see Senta pleased.

Joley wasn't there this evening. There was no sign of him or his trolley laden with coloured cushions. It seemed somehow a bad omen. A terrible temptation visited Philip to put off for another day the story he had to tell Senta. But when would the opportunity come again? There might not be another chance of this kind for weeks. He would have to do it, to stop thinking of it in this self-examining, excruciatingly analytical way, but just do it.

In a cold tone, quite unlike the usual way he spoke to her, he said abruptly that he had done what she wanted. Her face became alive with expectancy. The sea-wave eyes, green and water-white, flashed. She took hold of his wrists. He found it impossible to say the words baldly. He gave her the cutting.

'What's this?'

He spoke as if testing his knowledge of a foreign language, listening to each word. 'It will tell you what I did.'

'Aaah!' It was a long satisfied indrawing of breath. She read the paragraph two or three times, gradually smiling. 'When did you do it?'

He hadn't supposed too many details would be required. 'Last night.'

'After you left me?'

'Yes.'

It reminded him of an amateur production of *Macbeth* he had seen while still at school.

'You took up my suggestion, I see,' she said. 'What happened? You left here and drove to the Harrow Road, did you? I suppose you had a piece of luck and just found him there hanging about?'

He experienced a tremendous feeling of revulsion, not

from her but from the subject itself, a physical distaste as strong as the recoil would be from the dog's turds on the step, from a seething mass of maggots. 'Let's just take it that I did it,' he managed to say. His throat was constricted.

'How did you do it?'

He would have shunned the idea if he could. He would have escaped from the knowledge, absolute and indisputable, that she was excited, was revelling in a kind of lustful pleasurable prurient interest. She moistened her lips, parted them as if a little breathless. The hands that held his wrists moved up his arms drawing him to her. 'How did you kill him?'

'I don't want to talk about it, Senta, I can't.' And he shuddered as if he had actually committed some terrible act of violence, as if he remembered a knife going in, a gush of blood, a scream of agony, a struggle and a final helpless yielding to death. He hated these things and other people's gloating fascination with them. 'Don't ask me, I can't.'

She took his hands and held them out, palm-upwards. 'I know. You strangled him with these!'

It was no better than contemplating the knife and the blood. He fancied he could feel his hands tremble in hers. He forced himself to nod, to answer. 'I strangled him, yes.'

'It was dark, was it?'

'Of course. It was one in the morning. Don't ask me any more about it.'

He could see she didn't understand why he refused to give details. She expected him to furnish her with a description of the night, the empty silent street, the victim's helpless trust – and his own predatory seizing of opportunity. Her face blanked as it sometimes did when she was disappointed. All animation departed, all feeling, and it was as if those eyes turned inwards to contemplate the workings of her mind. With her little girl's hands she

162

took hold of two thick locks of her silver hair and drew them down across her shoulders. Her eyes seemed to turn outwards and fill with light.

'You did it for me?'

'You know it. That's what we agreed.'

A long shudder, that might have been real or equally might have been contrived, shook her body from head to foot. He reminded himself that she was an actress. This kind of thing was necessary to her and he would have to live with it. She laid her head against his chest as if to listen to his heartbeat and she whispered, 'Now I shall do the same for you.'

11

To follow Cheryl had been far from his intention when
they set out. It was the first time he had actually been
out with his sister since the day they had all gone to
Arnham's house, and Christine and Fee had been with
them then. Not since before his father's death had he and
Cheryl gone out alone.

It was Saturday evening and he was on his way to
Tarsus Street. It was somehow harder to tell a mother
who never asked questions that you wouldn't be back
till the following evening than if she probed and pried.
But he had told her, in a casual way, and she had given
him her innocent unsuspecting smile.

'Have a nice time, dear.'

Soon it would all be out in the open. Once he was
engaged there would be no problem about saying he
would be staying overnight at Senta's. He was getting
into the car when Cheryl came running out and asked
for a lift.

'I'm going down the Edgware Road, that way.'

'Go on, make a detour and take me to Golders Green.'

It would be a hefty detour but he agreed, he was
curious. There was something disquieting in the idea that
while she had a secret from him he also had one from
her. No sooner had they turned the corner into Lochleven
Gardens than she was asking him for a loan.

'Just a fiver, Phil, then you could take me straight down
the Edgware Road.'

'I'm not lending you money, Cheryl, not any more.'
He waited a moment and when she didn't say anything,
'So what's going to happen in Golders Green? What's
the big deal there?'

'A friend I can borrow it from.' She said it airily enough.

'Cheryl, what's going on? I've got to ask. I know you're into something. You're never home except at night, you don't have any friends, you're always alone and you're always trying to get money. You're in some kind of bad trouble, aren't you?'

'It's nothing to do with you.' The old brooding sulky note was back in her tone but there was indifference too, a edge of don't-care to it that told him questioning didn't bother her, interference amounted to nothing when she could parry it by admitting nothing.

'It's to do with me if I lend you money, you must see that.'

'Well, you're not going to, are you? You've said you're not, so you might as well shut up.'

'You can at least tell me what you're going to do this evening.'

'OK, you tell me what you're doing first. Only don't bother. I know. You're seeing that Stephanie, aren't you?'

Her conviction, quite erroneous, as to what he had been and would be doing made him wonder fleetingly if his own certainty that she was addicted to drugs or drink might be equally mistaken. If she could be wrong, and she *was* wrong, so could he. He didn't even bother to deny what she had said and he was aware of her triumphant nodding. At Golders Green, by the station where the buses turned round, he dropped her. It was his intention to drive down the Finchley Road, but as he watched Cheryl move off in the direction of the High Road the idea came to him to follow her and watch what she did. It struck him as very odd that she was carrying an umbrella.

It had been raining and looked as if it would rain again. The few people he saw about were carrying umbrellas but for Cheryl to do so seemed to him unprecedented. What could she want to protect from the rain? Not her short spiky hair surely. Not her jeans or the shiny plastic jacket. It was as incongruous seeing her with an umbrella as it would be if Christine were to put on jeans. He parked the car in a side turning. When he emerged into the main street again he thought he had lost her and then he spotted her quite a long way away in the curve of the High Road, walking along the rather wide pavement.

When the green figure of the marching pedestrian lit up he ran across the Finchley Road. It was midsummer light and would be for two hours yet but the light was gloomy from rain and a threatening dark overcast. This place would be crowded when the shops were open, cars double parked on the roadway and the passage of buses between them slow. It was a shopping centre only and now, without cinemas or pubs, with scarcely a wine bar, the street was deserted but for Cheryl walking along close to the windows. Not quite deserted. Philip realised rather unhappily that what he meant was it was empty of responsible conventional orderly sort of people. There were three punk boys looking into the window of a motor-cycle accessories store. A man walked alone on the other side, Cheryl's side, a tall thin man in leather and with his hair in a pigtail.

For a moment Philip thought Cheryl was going to accost this man. He was walking towards her but much nearer the kerb and as he approached she seemed to veer out from the shelter of the shop windows. By this time Philip had stationed himself in the doorway of a building society's office on the same side as the punk boys. He had wondered from time to time if it were some kind of prostitution Cheryl engaged in. The idea was extraordinarily distressingly distasteful. It would account for her sudden accessions of money but not for her desperate need of small temporary loans. And now he saw that he had been wrong — at least in this instance — for Cheryl walked past the leather-clad man with head averted. She had let him pass by and now she stood, looking warily about her. There was no doubt she was looking to see if the street was as empty as it appeared to be.

Him she couldn't detect, he was sure of that. She stared directly at the punk boys who had come away from the window and looked across the street at her, but without interest, without thought of involvement. And Philip realised something. Before Cheryl performed the act that was to overthrow all his guesses as to what she had come here for, he realised that she didn't care if she was observed by the punk boys, for they and she were of a kind, not only heedless of the law but joined in a silent pactless conspiracy against it. They were the last people who would tell on her.

Tell on her for what misdeed?

Satisfied that she was unobserved, she slipped into the entry of one of the shops. It was a clothes boutique with a plate glass door. Philip saw her crouch down in front of this door and apparently insert something through the large letterbox of silver-coloured metal. Was she breaking in? A cry of protest sprang up in him and he suppressed it, hand over his mouth.

It was impossible for him to see from this distance and in this light what she was doing. He could only see her back and bent head and the action she performed which was that of a person spearing something. The street remained empty, though a car passed in the direction of the station. Philip was aware of a purring silence, the purr being the distant, eternal, regular throb of traffic. Suddenly Cheryl gave a sharp tug with her right arm, backed, still on her haunches, sprang to her feet and drew something out through the letterbox. Then Philip saw it all, understood it all.

The umbrella, used as a hook, had withdrawn a garment from some rack or counter inside the shop. It might have been a sweater or a blouse or a skirt. He couldn't tell. She gave him no chance to see but rolled whatever it was up and thrust it inside her jacket. He

167

was stunned by what he had seen, his feelings temporarily deadened, but he was also fascinated. It wouldn't be true that he wanted her to do it again but he wanted to see it done again.

For a moment he thought this would happen, for she approached another boutique a few shops along and stood there with her nose pressed to the glass. But then, shocking him once more with the suddenness of it, she spun round and began to run. She ran, not in the direction he expected, that is back to the Finchley Road, but the opposite way, crossed the road and plunged down a side street near a railway bridge. Philip considered following her but very quickly dismissed this idea and returned to his car.

Was that what it was about? Was that all it was about, a kind of crazy addiction to stealing things from shops? He had read somewhere that kleptomania was nonsense, it didn't really happen. What did she do, anyway, with the things she stole?

When he first considered telling Senta about it he dismissed the idea almost at once. Second thoughts, surfacing as he drove across North London and down West End Lane, made him confront this propositionagain. Wasn't that what a relationship like theirs ought to be about, confiding in each other, telling each other their doubts and fears? If they were going to be together always, in a life-long partnership, they must unburden themselves to each other, they must share their troubles.

He drove to Senta's by way of Caesarea Grove, passing the big gloomy church of rough-hewn grey stone in whose west porch Joley sometimes encamped himself for the night. But the porch was empty and the iron gates into the graveyard fastened with chains and a padlock. When he was a child Philip had been afraid to pass places of this sort, churches or houses built to look like some grim edifice of the Middle Ages, and would have made a detour or gone by at a run with eyes averted. He remembered this now, the memory of his fear strongly felt, though not the fear itself. A dozen gravestones, no more, remained under the trees with their black trunks and pointed leathery leaves. He had slowed for some reason to look in there but now he accelerated, turned the corner and parked outside Senta's house.

More shutters were closed at the upper windows than he had ever seen before. The only light came from the basement and the sight of that light alone was enough to make his heart beat faster. The breathless feeling was back. He ran up the stairs and let himself in. Music drifted to him but not the kind of music Rita and Jacopo danced to. It was coming up the basement stairs. This was so unusual that he had a momentary fear she might have someone with her and he hesitated outside her door for a moment, listening to the bouzouki music, wondering. She must have heard his feet on the stairs, for she opened the door to him herself and came immediately into his arms.

Of course there was no one else there. He was moved with love for her by what she had done, what she seemed so proud of: food and wine set out on the bamboo table, the tape playing, the room somehow cleaner and fresher, the purple sheets on the bed changed for brown ones. She was wearing a dress he had never seen before, black, short, thin and clinging, with a low oval neck that showed her white breasts. He held her in his arms, kissing her softly, slowly. Her little hands, warm with cold rings on them, stroked his hair, his neck.

He whispered, 'Are we alone in the house?'

'They've gone away up north somewhere.'

'I like it better when we're alone,' he said.

She poured glasses of wine for them and he told her about Cheryl. It was a strange treachery in him, he sometimes thought, a mistrust without foundation, that he expected her not to be interested in the things he told her, in his family, his doings. He expected her to be preoccupied, anxious to return to her own concerns. In fact, she *was* interested, did like to hear, gave him all her attention, sitting there with hands clasped, looking into his eyes. When he got to the bit about Cheryl poking the umbrella through the letter box a smile dawned on her face, which, if you didn't know it couldn't be, you might have taken for admiration.

'What do you think I ought to do, Senta? I mean, should I tell anyone? Should I even tell *her*?'

'Do you really want to know what I think, Philip?'

'Of course I do. That's why I'm telling you. I want your opinion.'

'My opinion is that you worry too much about the law and society and things like that. People like you and me, exceptional people, are above the law, don't you think? Or let's say beyond it.'

All his life he had been taught to be law-abiding, to respect authority, man-made government. His father, gambler though he had been, was adamant about honesty and strict integrity in his dealings. Making one's own rules savoured to Philip of anarchy.

'Cheryl won't be beyond the law if she gets caught,' he said.

'We don't see the world in quite the same way, you and I, Philip. I know you're going to learn to see it as I do but that hasn't happened yet. I mean seeing it as a place of mysticism and magic, as if on a different plane from the dull practical things most people waste their lives on. When you come on to that plane with me you'll find a world of wonderful occult things where everything is possible, nothing is barred. There aren't any policemen there and there aren't any laws. You'll start seeing things you never saw before, shapes and wonders and visions and ghosts. You took one step towards that plane when you killed the old man for my sake. Did you know that?'

Philip returned her gaze, but puzzled, not as happy as he had been moments before. He was well aware that she hadn't given him any sort of opinion he might want to hear, hadn't really answered him. Her terms were vague, open to any sort of definition, they bore no relation to concrete things, to rules and restrictions, decency, socially acceptable behaviour, respect for the law. She talked well, he thought, she was beautifully articulate and the things she said, they couldn't be nonsense. That feeling came from his own inability, as yet, to understand. He learned something as she spoke, though not what she had meant him to learn. It was interesting but disquieting at the same time. What he learned was that if you have told a lie about something you have done, as in his case about the murder of the vagrant, you very quickly forget all about it, something inside your memory blots it out. He knew that if, instead of speaking as though she took this act of his for granted, she had asked him artlessly what he had been doing the previous Sunday night, he would have replied that after he left her he had driven home and gone to bed. He would have done the natural thing and told the truth.

The sun crept through the splits in the old shutters, making gold bars on the ceiling and laying rods of gold on the brown quilt. That was the first thing Philip saw when he woke up very late on Sunday morning, a string of sunlight drawn across his hand which lay limply outside the covers. He withdrew the hand and, turning over, reached for Senta. She wasn't with him. She was gone.

Again she surprised him. He was sitting up, already full of fears that she had left him, he would never see her again, when he saw the note on her pillow: "Back soon. I had to go out, it was important. Wait for me, Senta." Why hadn't she written "love"? It didn't matter. She had left him the note. Wait for her? He would have waited for ever.

His watch told him it was past eleven. Most nights he simply didn't get enough sleep, he never seemed to get more than five or six hours. No wonder he had been tired, had slept on and on. Fully awake now but still relaxed, he lay thinking about Senta, relieved and happy because in the region of his mind which was the place for Senta and himself he had at this moment no worries and no fears. But as if his consciousness didn't want him to be without anxieties, it allowed Cheryl to creep into it. For the first time since he had witnessed that act of hers, the enormity of it struck him. He had been in a state of shock but now the shock had worn off. He knew at once that he couldn't just let it alone, pretend he hadn't seen what he had seen, he was going to have to confront Cheryl. The alternative would inevitably be the phone call from the police to say they had arrested Cheryl on a theft charge. Would it be worse or better to tell Christine first?

After that Philip couldn't just lie there, he had to get up. In the nasty corner where the lavatory was and the dripping, bandaged brass tap over the bath, he managed a wash of sorts. Back in her room he folded back the shutters and opened the window. Senta said opening the window let flies in, and as the sash went up a great blowfly sang past his cheek, but the room seemed sometimes to gasp for air. It was a bright shimmering summer's day, the last sort of weather you would have expected to follow the bleak grey week which had preceded it. The short shadows up there on the concrete were black and the sunlight a burning dazzling white.

Something happened then which had never happened before and which brought him an enormous exciting pleasure. He saw her come to the house. He saw her legs in jeans and feet in trainers – unprecedented, he had never before seen her in trousers. Would he even have known it was she if she hadn't bent down at the railings and looked at him through the bars? She put her head through the bars, then her arm, stretching it towards him in a yearning kind of way. Her hand was open, palm-upwards, as if she wanted to take his hand in hers. The hand was withdrawn and she came up the steps. Listening intently, he heard every step she took, along the hallway, down the passage, down the stairs.

It was a slow entry she made. She closed the door behind her with extravagant care, as if the house were full of sleeping people. He wondered how he could say of someone who was white-skinned, who never had colour in her cheeks, that she was very pale. Her skin had that greenish-silvery look. With the jeans and the trainers she was wearing a kind of loose tunic of dark red cotton with a black leather belt round her waist. Her hair was twisted up or tied up on top of her head under a flat cap of cotton cord like a boy's. She took this cap off, threw it on the bed and shook out her hair. Philip saw her looking at him, the beginnings of a smile on her lips, and saw the back of her in the misty spotted mirror, her hair spread over her shoulders in a great silver fan.

She extended her hand and he took it in his. He drew her towards him where he sat on the end of the bed. He smoothed her hair back from her face in both hands, turned her face and brought it to his, kissed the lips which felt cool for so warm a day.

'Where have you been, Senta?'

'You weren't worried, Philip? You had my note?'

'Of course I did, thank you for it. But you didn't say where you were, only that it was important.'

'Oh, it was. It was very important. Can't you guess?'

Why did he naturally think of Cheryl? Why did he assume she had been to Cheryl, had said something he would want unsaid? But he didn't answer her, he didn't put this into words. She spoke softly, her lips almost against his skin.

'I went to do for you what you did for me. I went to prove my love for you, Philip.'

It was strange how any mention of those reciprocal acts immediately made him uneasy. More than uneasy, causing a recoil, a reflex of shying away. In those few seconds he thought, she may be going to try and teach me her philosophy, but I'll also teach her mine, that fantasising has to stop. But all he could say was, 'Did you? You don't have to prove anything to me.'

She never heard what he said when she didn't want to. 'I did what you did. I killed someone. That's why I went out so early. I've trained myself to wake up when I want to, you know. I woke up at six and went out. I had to go so early because it was a long way. Philip will worry, I thought, so I'll leave him a note.'

In the midst of his growing exasperation, warmth touched him at her sweetness, her concern for him. He was aware of something wonderful, yet frightening. She loved him more now than before their separation, her love for him was always growing. He took her face gently in his hands to kiss her again but she broke away.

'No, Philip, you have to listen to me. It's very important what I'm telling you. I was going to Chigwell, you see, on the tube and it's a very long way.'

'Chigwell?'

'Well, a place called Grange Hill, it's the next station. It was the nearest one to where Gerard Arnham lived. You haven't guessed, have you? It's Gerard Arnham I killed for you. I killed him at eight o'clock this morning.'

12

For perhaps half a minute he actually believed her. It seemed infinitely longer, it seemed hours. The shock of it made something strange happen on his head, a kind of singing throbbing and a dark redness before his eyes, a sensation as of wheels turning and rolling behind his eyes. Then reason dispelled all that. You fool, he told himself, you fool. Don't you know by now she lives in a world of daydreams?

He dampened dry lips with a dry tongue, shook himself a little. His heart was thudding and shaking his ribs. Strangely, she seemed not to notice these earthquakes in him, these overturnings and attempts to grasp at reality, these splits in reassurance through which nightmares came grinning.

'I'd been observing him,' she said. 'I've been over to that house you showed me twice in the past week. I found out he takes his dog for a walk in these woods every morning before he goes to work. I calculated he'd still do it on Sunday but he'd be a bit later – and he was. I waited there, hiding in the trees, and saw him come with his dog.'

If any doubts about the falseness of what she said still lingered, this would have dispelled them. Gerard Arnham with a dog! Philip remembered how Christine had told him Arnham didn't care for dogs, had cited this as a reason for not taking him with them on that fateful day. It provided him with a question for Senta, a policeman's sort of question aimed at ferreting out the kind of information which the liar may have left unconsidered.

'What kind of dog?'

'Quite a little one, black.' She answered at once. She

was prepared with her circumstantial details. 'A Scottie, are they called? If it had been a big fierce Dobermann, Philip, I probably wouldn't have been able to do what I did. I chose Arnham, you know, because he was your enemy. You'd told me he was your enemy, so that's why I picked him.'

Philip wanted to ask her what Arnham looked like but he remembered what had happened the last time he seemed to doubt her stories. He tried to think of ways of rephrasing that question.

'It's an interesting thing that a girl will be quite frightened if she meets a man she doesn't know in a wood,' she said, 'but a man's not frightened if a girl comes up to him. I came up to him holding my eye. I said I'd got something in my eye and it was hurting and I couldn't see out of it and I was frightened. That was clever, don't you think?'

'He's a very tall man, isn't he?' Philip was proud of himself. This was the kind of thing he had come across in police procedural serials on television. 'He must have had to bend right over to look at your eye.'

'Oh, he did, he did. He bent right down and I held my face up for him to see my eye.' She nodded with a kind of pleased satisfaction. And Philip found himself smiling at this second and surely final confirmation, all that was needed. Arnham was no more than five feet eight, if that. 'He was as near to me as you are now. I knew where to strike. I stabbed him in the heart with a glass dagger.'

'You what?' said Philip, half-amused now by her inventiveness.

'Didn't I ever show you my Venetian dagger? They're made of Murano glass, those daggers, and they're as sharp as razors. When you plunge them in they break off at the handle and they only leave a scratch to show. The victim doesn't even bleed. I used to have two but I used the other one for something else and they're both gone now. I bought them in Venice when I was on my travels.

176

I did feel sorry for the poor little dog, though, Philip. It came running up to its dead master and it started this awful whimpering.'

He didn't know much about Venice, he had never been there, and less about Venetian glass. But he wanted to ask her, he had to stop himself from asking her, if she had worn one of those bird face masks and a black cloak.

'It will be in all the papers tomorrow,' she said. 'I don't usually see a paper but I shall buy one tomorrow to read about it. No, I know! I'll go upstairs later and see it on their TV.'

First, she would have a bath in their bathroom. She didn't think there was any blood on her but whether there was or not, she felt less than clean after what she had done. That was why she had worn the dark red tunic, so that blood wouldn't show if it splashed on to her. If there were any splashes they must be tiny ones. She had conducted a thorough search of her clothes while in the train.

Philip followed her upstairs, up on to the first, then to the second floor. He had never been into the upper regions of the house before. It was uniformly shabby, dusty and with a kind of dreary squalor. He glanced into a room where an unmade bed was piled with plastic sacks from whose open tops clothes spilt. Cardboard crates that had once contained tins of food were stacked against the walls. There were a lot of flies, buzzing about pendant light bulbs without shades. Senta went into a bathroom where the walls and ceilings were a shiny bright green, the floor composed of patches of variously coloured linoleum. She stripped off her clothes, leaving them in a heap on the floor.

An unexpected thing had happened. He felt no desire for her. He could look at her naked, undeniably beautiful, and feel nothing. She was less than a picture, far less than a photograph, as unerotic as stone Flora. He closed his eyes, rubbed his closed eyes with his fists, opened

177

them again and watched her step into the water – and felt nothing. From the bath she talked to him about coming back in the train, her initial fear that she was followed, her later obsessive search for a spot of blood somewhere, her examination of fingers and her nails. He felt afraid, out of control. It was the kind of thing he especially hated, crime, the stuff of thrillers, an absorption with hideous violent things.

He couldn't stay in the bathroom with her. He wandered aimlessly in and out of rooms. She called after him in that sweet, rather high-pitched tone of hers, as if nothing had happened, as if he were a casual visitor.

'Go and have a look at the top floor. I used to live up there.'

He went up. The rooms were smaller and narrower, the ceiling sloping under the roof. There were three rooms, no bathroom, but a lavatory and a small kitchen with a very old oven in one corner and a space where perhaps a refrigerator had once stood. All the windows were closed and on one of the sills stood the green wine bottle he had seen from the street. It felt and smelt as if no window had been opened for months, years. Outside the sun was shining but it seemed remote, barriers of dirty glass like a fog hanging between here and that distant sunlight. Through the grey encrusted panes the roofs of Queens Park and Kensal were a faded photograph or one over-exposed.

Philip had come up here for something to do. He had come to be alone with pain and with fear. But now he was distracted from those emotions. He walked about in a kind of wonderment. The rooms were dirty with the kind of dirt he was growing used to in this house and the smell was thick, like burning rubber in places, in others sweet and fishy, in the lavatory where the pan was dark brown, as sharp and yellow-sour as rotting onions. But these were rooms, this was *accommodation*. He found himself noting the kind of things it was his job to

178

note, the big cupboards with their panelled doors, the floorboards, the sink of stainless steel, the curtain rails, the few pieces of furniture.

She was calling him. He came down to her and said, 'Why did you move down to the basement?'

She burst out laughing, a long musical trill. 'Oh, Philip, your face! You look so disapproving.' He tried to smile. 'I didn't like climbing all those stairs.' she said. 'What did I want with all those rooms anyway?'

She dried herself and put on the silver dress with the grey flower and they went out to a pub for lunch. He drove her to Hampstead and they sat in a pub garden and ate bread rolls and cheese with salad and drank sparkling rosé Lambrusco. They went for a walk on the Heath, Philip spinning out the time, delaying their return to Tarsus Street. The way he felt, he thought it unlikely he would be able to make love to her. A terrible desolation had taken hold of him. What he thought of as his great love for her was all gone, vanished. The more she talked — and she talked of everything, of gods and men and magic, of murder, of what society calls crime, of herself and him and their future, of her past and her acting — the worse it became. She held his hand and his cold hand lay inert in her warm one.

He suggested they go to the cinema, the Everyman or the Screen on the Hill, but she wanted to go home. She always wanted to go home. She liked indoors, underground. It made him wonder if she had moved down from that top flat because it was too exposed and vulnerable for her, up there. They lay down side by side on the bed and to his relief — a very temporary unhappy relief — she fell asleep. He put his arm round her then and felt the warm aliveness of her, the rise and fall of her breath. But there was no more desire than if it were a stone girl that lay there, life-size in marble.

*

She had written him a note and now he would write her one. 'I'll see you tomorrow. Good night.' She hadn't written love but he would. 'All my love, Philip.' He got up carefully without disturbing her, closed the window and folded the shutters. She looked very beautiful lying there, her eyes shut, the long coppery lashes resting moth-like on the white skin. The closed lips were Flora's, sculpted in marble, indented at their corners. He kissed her lips and felt with a shudder that he was kissing a mortally sick woman or even a corpse.

Before he left he checked that the keys were safe in his pocket. For all that, there seemed something final about the hollow clang with which the front door closed behind him, though he knew of course it wasn't final, he was still only at the beginning.

Arnham wasn't really a short man. You couldn't call five feet eight short. It was only he who saw it this way because he was himself so tall. Arnham had been unfamiliar with dogs but Arnham was married now. Suppose it was his wife's dog? It might be that his wife was fond of dogs, already had a dog, this Scottie, before they were married. If Arnham had married Christine they would have kept Hardy, of course they would. Philip thought about this all the way home. He walked into the living room and found Fee and Darren there with Christine, watching television.

The news was just coming on, in shortened form for a Sunday evening. Philip felt a bit sick. He wouldn't have actually put the news on, he didn't want to know, but as it was on, had started, he had to stay and know. His suspense was made worse by Darren's constant interjections, urging the news reader to get on with it and come to the sport. But there was no item about a murder, a murder of any sort, and Philip felt better. He had begun asking himself how he could have been so stupid as even for a moment to think Senta could have killed someone, tiny, slight, child-fingered Senta.

180

'Cheryl says you've been taking Stephanie about,' said Fee, lighting a cigarette. The smoke brought him another flicker of nausea. 'Is that a fact?'

'That's all in Cheryl's head,' he said, and, 'You've seen Cheryl then?'

'Why shouldn't I have seen her? She lives here.'

He was going to have to talk to Fee about Cheryl. Fee would be the best person. But not now, not tonight. He got himself something to eat, a meat sandwich and a cup of instant coffee, and offered to take Hardy round the block. Walking along with Hardy on the lead made him think of Arnham again, of Arnham lying dead and his own little dog whimpering over his body. The trouble was that Senta had described it all too vividly, had gone on and on about it. It was he who was going on and on about it now, his consciousness dominated by it. He was unable to alter the trend of his thoughts and that night he dreamed of glass daggers. He was in Venice, or he was at any rate walking along by a canal in a city, when turning a corner he saw a man set upon by another in cloak and mask, a dagger of perfect and wicked transparency flash in the moonlight. The assassin fled, Philip rushed up to the victim who lay on his back with one pendant hand trailing in the dark water. He searched for the wound but found nothing where the dagger had gone in, only the kind of scratch a cat's claw might make. But the man was dead and the body fast cooling.

During the previous week Philip had avoided newspapers. He hadn't wanted to know if the police had found the murderer of the vagrant, John Sidney Crucifer. Blotting out the whole business from his mind, he had avoided everything that might be associated with it, every medium that might reveal more details of it. Television he had scarcely watched anyway since his reunion with Senta. Now he realised he had done nothing about replacing the radio in his car because he didn't want to have to hear its news broadcasts.

This ostrich-like behaviour was possible only when it was a minor matter which was at stake. Today he couldn't afford to ignore newspapers. He had to know for sure. On his way to Highgate, where Roseberry Lawn were putting two new bathrooms into an actress's house, he stopped off and bought three morning papers from a newsagent's. The car was parked on a double yellow line but he couldn't wait any longer before knowing. It was just a matter of keeping on the alert for an approaching traffic warden.

Two murders had taken place during Sunday, one in Wolverhampton, one in a place called Hainault Forest in Essex. All three newspapers had details, though none was leading on these stories. It would have been different had the victims been women, particularly young women, but both were men. Murdered men are less newsworthy. The Hainault Forest one wasn't named, was described as being in his fifties. A Forest Ranger had found the body. There was nothing in any of the papers about the cause of death or the murder method.

Philip drove on to the actress's house. She was a young woman called Olivia Brett who had had a phenomenal success in a television series. Now she was in constant demand. She was very thin, emaciated, and her hair was bleached to the same shade as Senta's but it was shorter than Senta's and much less thick and shiny. She was ten years older than Senta and the heavy pancake make-up she wore made her look older than that. She wanted to know Philip's first name and called him by it, called him darling too, and asked him to call her Ollie, which everyone did, she said. She adored Roseberry Lawn bathrooms, they were better than anything she had seen in Beverley Hills. She adored colour, colour was what made life worthwhile. Would he like a drink? She wouldn't have one, she would only have Perrier, because she was getting so enormously fat that soon the only parts open to her would be those of obese grandmothers.

Reeling somewhat under all this, refusing the drink, Philip made his way upstairs to look at the two rooms designated as bathrooms. This was to be simply a preliminary survey, too soon even for measuring up. Philip stood in the first of these rooms, already in use as a bathroom with very old-fashioned shabby fitments, and stared out of the window. London lay below him, spread out at the foot of the northern hills. Chigwell was London, wasn't it, not Essex? He was remembering now that there was a station on the Central Line called Hainault. In 'confessing' to him, she had spoken of woods. Was that what she had meant, Hainault Forest? Was that the open wooded countryside near where Arnham lived?

The man was the right sort of age. A man of five feet eight might seem tall to Senta who was so small. Oh, stop it, he said to himself, stop it. It's all fantasy with her, it's all invention. You might as well say that dream you had last night about the man stabbed with the glass dagger was real. Where could a girl like Senta get a glass dagger anyway? They're not the kind of thing that are going to be on open sale. A small voice whispered to him: Ah, but she makes some of it up and some of it is real, you know that. She did go to drama school. It just wasn't RADA she went to. She did travel, only not as far and widely as she said.

Olivia Brett had disappeared and a hard-faced housekeeper was waiting downstairs to show him, as she put it, off the premises. Philip said to himself, it's obviously not Arnham, you know it's not, you're becoming neurotic over nothing. The only thing to do now is to put it all out of your head the way you did Crucifer. Don't buy an evening paper, don't watch the news. If you're going to make a go of this, you have to show her fantasising isn't on, fantasising is childish, and you're not going to

183

do that by going along with her fantasies like this. You should never have let any of it get started.

But look what happened when he protested, when he resisted. She had refused to see him. But would he really mind now if she refused to see him? The idea turned him cold, the enormity of it. You couldn't love someone the way he had loved her and then be turned off them in five minutes by nothing more than lies and daydreams. Could you? Could you?

It didn't occur to him not to go to Tarsus Street that evening. He told himself as he drove down Shoot-up Hill that he knew now why lying and fantasising was wrong. Because it brought so much trouble and misery and pain. He bought wine and chocolates for her. They were bribes and he knew it.

Entering the street from Caesarea Grove, he was assailed by a sudden anxiety over Joley. This was the longest period since the first time he had seen him that Joley had been absent from his regular beat. Again the church gates had been locked and the church porch empty. This time a week ago nothing would have delayed Philip from rushing to Senta as soon as he could. Things had changed. He was quite prepared, even content, to put off seeing her for half an hour while he went in search of Joley.

Ilbert Street was his other haunt, he had told Philip. This long street linked Third Avenue with Kilburn Lane. He drove the length of it between the parked cars. It was a sultry still evening which certainly presaged a warm night, the sort of night on which Joley would contentedly sleep outdoors with no more than benefit of a doorway or patch of waste ground. Philip found it impossible to see much of the pavement because of the nose-to-tail parking. He managed to park his own car and then he set off to walk the street. Joley was nowhere. Philip left the main street and made a foray into the shabby dull little hinterland. By now the sun had set and feathers of red were uncurling all over the smoky grey sky. The feeling came back that his luck depended on Joley and now Joley was gone.

His reluctance to see Senta increased as he returned to Tarsus Street. Why had he ever told her he had killed someone? Why had he been such a fool? It was true that he had told her in a very perfunctory way, in such a casual dismissive way that almost anybody would know he was making it all up. Surely she hadn't really believed him. He let himself into the house slowly, almost wearily. He was like an unhappy husband coming home to noisy children and a quarrelsome wife.

Her burning joss stick scented the basement stairs. He let himself into the room. The shutters were closed, the bedlamp was on. It felt insufferably stuffy and the heady spicy smell was almost overpowering. She lay face-downwards on the bed, her head in her arms. As he came in she made a convulsive movement. He touched her shoulder, spoke her name. She turned slowly on to her back and looked up at him. Her face was crumpled and runnelled and squeezed with crying, pink and soggy and wet. The pillow into which her head had burrowed was actually wet, with tears or sweat.

'I thought you weren't coming. I thought you were never coming back.'

'Oh, Senta, of course I came back, of course I did.'

'I thought I was never going to see you again.'

He took her in his arms then and held her. It was like hugging a frightened weeping child. What has happened to us? he thought. What have we done? We were so happy. Why did we spoil it with all these lies, these games?

Philip went into the library and looked Gerard Arnham up in the telephone directory which covered Chigwell. His name wasn't there. The date on the directory was a year ago so naturally he wouldn't be there. It could be no more than six months since he had moved. An alternative would be to ask directory enquiries for the number but at this point Philip wondered what he would say if someone other than Arnhan answered, if for instance his wife answered. He could hardly ask her if her husband was still alive.

Three days had passed since Senta had told him she had killed Arnham. In that time she had been different and he had been different. The tables were turned. Now it was he who distanced himself from her and she who clung to him and wept. She said she had killed his enemy for him and instead of being grateful he hated her for what she had done. This was very nearly accurate except that he knew very well she hadn't killed Arnham, had only said she had. Examining his feelings, he discovered his antipathy came from Senta's pride in the idea of killing someone in a particularly brutal way. Or did it? Wasn't it rather that he wasn't sure she hadn't done it, that there still lingered somewhere the germ of a fear that she actually had done it?

By now he had seen in a newspaper that the murdered man in Hainault Forest had been identified as Harold Myerson, aged 58, an engineering consultant from Chigwell. That was coincidence that he came from Chigwell, for there was no possibility Myerson could be Gerard Arnham. He wouldn't have two names and Arnham wasn't as old as that. The only other murder which had taken place in the British Isles on the previous Sunday was the Wolverhampton one, a boy of twenty stabbed in a fight outside a pub. Philip knew that was true because he had been through three of Monday's morning papers and the evening paper and had bought and scrutinised three more on Tuesday. This meant that Senta had done nothing on that Sunday and Arnham must be alive and Philip was being stupid, imagining crazy things. People one knew didn't kill other people. It was outside one's knowledge, a different world.

To account for his attitude towards her he had tried to make her believe it stemmed from his anxiety. He made her tell him in precise detail the whole story over again, hoping to pick holes in it, to find discrepancies between the original account and this later one.

'Which morning did you go over there? You said you went over to Chigwell and watched the house in the mornings.'

'I went on the Tuesday and the Friday, Philip.'

He forced himself to say it, though he nearly gagged on the words. 'That Tuesday was only the day after I told you I'd killed John Crucifer. I came here on the Monday night and told you how I killed Crucifer the night before.'

'That's right,' she said. 'That's right. I knew I had to make a start. Once you'd done that for me I knew I had to lay my plans. I got up very early, I didn't get much sleep, and I got the tube out there and watched the house. I saw the woman open the door in her dressing gown and take a bottle of milk in. She's a woman with a big nose and mouth and lot of wild dark hair.'

Revelations like this made Philip shiver. He recalled the first time he had seen Arnham's wife through the panes of the window patterned like a shield. Senta, sitting on the bed beside him, her legs tucked under her, her arms loosely round his neck, snuggled up to him.

'I felt good when I saw her. I thought, she's the woman he married when he should have married Philip's mother, and I thought how it would serve her right when he was dead and she was a widow. It's wrong to steal other women's men. If some woman tried to steal you from me I'd kill her, I wouldn't hesitate. I'll tell you a secret about that but not now, later. I'm not going to have any secrets from you, Philip, and you're not going to have any from me — ever.

'It was eight o'clock when Arnham came out with the little dog. He walked him to this bit of green where the trees were and took him in under the trees and then he walked him back. It only took about twenty minutes. I didn't go away, though, I went on watching, and he came out again after a bit and he was dressed up in a suit and carrying a briefcase and she was with him still in her dressing gown. He gave her a kiss and she put her arms round his neck like this.'

'And you went back on the Friday,'

'I went back on the Friday, Philip, to check up that he always did it. I thought she might sometimes do it, the thief woman. I got to give them names in my mind. Do you think that's funny? I called him Gerry and her Thiefie and the little dog Ebony because he was black. I thought, suppose it turns out Thiefie takes Ebony out on Sundays. I'll have come all the way out here for nothing, but I'd just have had to come back on Monday, wouldn't I?'

Philip found he couldn't bear to hear about the stabbing again. When she reached the point where she had stepped up to Arnham under the trees and told him she had something in her eye, he stopped her by asking why she thought she might have been followed on her return journey to the tube station.

'It was just that there was this old woman on the station platform. I had ever such a long time to wait for a train and she kept looking at me. I thought, have I got blood on me? But I couldn't see any blood. And how could she have seen it when I was wearing the dark red tunic? And then when the train came I was sitting in the train and I took my cap off and my hair came down. The old woman wasn't there, she wasn't in the same bit of the train, but other people were, and since then, Philip, I've been thinking, suppose she thought I was a boy but they could tell I was a girl and all of them sort of made the connection and thought it was suspicious? Don't you think the police would have been here by now? They would, wouldn't they?'

'You needn't be afraid of the police, Senta.'

'Oh, I'm not *afraid*. I know the police are just agents of a society whose rules mean nothing to people like us. I'm not afraid but I have to be on the watch, I have to have my story ready.'

If it had not been so distasteful, there would have been something ludicrous about the police tracking down Senta who was so tiny and so innocent-looking, with her big soulful eyes and her soft unmarked skin, her child's hands and feet. Philip took her in his arms and began kissing her. He shut out the awful thoughts. He asked himself if it was not she but he who was mad, allowing himself to believe for an instant these elaborate inventions. Yet, within moments, opening their second bottle of wine, unwrapping for her a chocolate cherry encased in red silver paper, he was asking her for more details, to tell once again of following Arnham from his house to the open place where the grass and trees were.

In the underground room dusk came sooner than up above. It was gloomy and close down here where the smell of dust mingled with the scent of burning patchouli. At this hour, in the dimness, the big hanging mirror seemed like a sheet of greenish water in which their reflections could only vaguely be seen. It had a sheen on it like mother-of-pearl, thick and translucent. The bed, with its rumpled brown sheet and pillows and quilt rather resembled some terrain of folded hills and deep valleys. Philip stopped her when she reached out to put the bedlamp on. He pulled her to him, sliding his hands inside the thin black skirt, the loose top of cheesecloth. Her skin was like warm silk, slippery and yielding. In the dark, with the shutters half-closed and only a little greyish light showing above the pavement level, he could imagine her as she had been before she made these revelations to him, he imagined her as she had been on those two occasions in his own bed.

Then and only then, with his eyes closed, was it possible for him to make love to her. He was learning how to fantasise.

In the middle of the night he woke up. He had decided long before not to go home that night. Once at least in the week he didn't go home and the previous evening and night he had spent at home with Christine. What had happened was that he had got into the habit of waking up, dressing and silently letting himself out of the room and the house. He still woke up when he didn't need to.

She lay asleep beside him. Yellow lamplight from the street fell across her face and turned the silver hair to a brassy gold. The window was open a little at the top and the shutters were ajar. In the past, often at this hour, the music had played overhead and the two pairs of feet danced, but now Rita and Jacopo were away somewhere. The old house with its weight above them of dirty cluttered rooms, a repository of stored rubbish, slowly gradually decaying, was empty but for them. Senta breathed with a silent regular rhythm, her slightly parted lips as pale as a shell.

But when he came back from closing the shutters and then fetching himself a drink from the bandaged brass tap, she was awake and sitting up. A white shawl with a fringe was around her shoulders. The light was on now, bright and uncompromising. The holes in the parchment shade made a spotted pattern on the ceiling. She must have put a more powerful bulb in the lamp since it was last on, for the higher wattage revealed the room in every aspect of its squalor, the dust on the wooden floor that showed as a clotting of grey fluff round the skirting board, the spiders' webs and dark gritty deposits on the cornices, the chair whose wicker was coming unravelled, the dark old stains and spills on rug and cushions. He

190

thought, I must take her out of this, we can't live like this. Now that the light was on, a blowfly, awakened, zoomed round the sticky neck of one of the wine bottles.

Senta said, 'I'm wide awake now. I want to tell you something. Do you remember I said I'd a secret to tell you and I'd tell you it later? It's about women stealing men.'

He got back into bed beside her, wanting only sleep, aware that he had only five hours before he must get up, before he must get out of this bed and wash somehow, dress and go to work. It was ridiculous now to remember that he had forgotten to bring clean underpants and a clean shirt with him, such unimportant trivial things, doubly ridiculous in the light of what she said to him:

'You know you're not the first with me, don't you, Philip? I wish I'd saved myself for you but I didn't and nothing can change the past. Even God can't change history — did you know that? Even God can't. I was in love with someone else once — well, I thought I was. I know I wasn't really now I know what love really is.

'This man — well, he was a boy, he was just a boy, there was this girl set herself out to steal him away and she did for a bit. Perhaps he would have come back in the end, I wouldn't have wanted him then, not after her. Do you know what I did, Philip? I killed her. She was my first murder. I used the first Murano glass knife on her.'

He thought, is she mad? Or is she just mocking me? What went on in her mind that she had to invent these tales? What did she gain by it? He said, 'Put the light out now, Senta. I have to get some sleep.'

13

A smell of rotten eggs crept up the stairs. That meant Christine was making an early start on a perm. Dogs had a sense of smell a million times better than that of man, Philip had read somewhere, so if it stank like this in his nostrils, what must it be like for Hardy? The little dog lay on the landing and feebly wagged his tail as Philip passed on his way to the bathroom. Each sight of him reminded Philip of the dog Senta said was Arnham's, the dog she called Ebony.

He was tired. Given the chance, he could have gone back to bed and slept for hours. TGIF as his father used to say, Thank God It's Friday. Cheryl had already been in the bathroom and had used his towel as well as her own. His thoughts drifted in her direction, to the night he had seen her steal whatever it was from the shop in Golders Green. He had done nothing about that, taken no action. His mind had been too full of Senta. Senta obsessed him and exhausted him.

The night before he had played with the idea of not going to Tarsus Street, but in the end he had gone. He had put himself in her shoes, remembering what it was like for him when she deserted him. He couldn't bear her tears, her misery. Her room depressed him and he had taken her out, intending to kiss her and leave her to go back into the house alone. But the crying had begun and the pleading, so he had gone in with her and listened while she talked. It was the Ares and Aphrodite stuff again and about belonging to an élite, and power and disregarding man-made laws. They hadn't made love.

Now, when he was alone, he kept asking himself what he was going to do. He had to rid his mind of these several obsessions, these pegs from which terrors hung: the sight of a dog, a knife, a tube station even. He had to dispel all that and think of their future, his and hers. Had they a future together? It struck him painfully that he had never carried out his intention of telling Christine and the rest of his family about Senta. Yet, until she began damaging their relationship with all this pretence of killing, the need to tell had been urgent. He had longed for everyone to know. He had wanted his love to be public, his commitment known.

Philip went downstairs. The house reeked of the sulphurous stuff Christine was using, even though the kitchen door was shut. No one could imagine eating breakfast in this atmosphere. He opened the door, said hallo to an elderly woman whose snow-white hair Christine was engaged in winding round blue plastic rollers.

'It isn't a very nice smell, dear, I know that, but it'll be gone in ten minutes.'

'So will I,' said Philip.

He found the coffee jar stuck amidst giant cans of hair lacquer and two tubes of relaxing gel. What did she want relaxant for? She hadn't any black customers. It was made, he noticed – of course he noticed – by a company called Ebony. The old woman, who had been talking almost ceaselessly since he came in, now embarked on an anecdote about her granddaughter's exchange visit to a French family who couldn't speak. Neither the mother nor the father could speak. It was needless to say that the grandparents couldn't and even the children could manage only a few words.

'Were they deaf too, poor things?' said Christine.

'No, they weren't deaf, Christine, I never said they were deaf. I said they couldn't speak.'

Philip, who half an hour before had thought he would never laugh again, was choking over his scalding hot Nescafé. 'She means they couldn't speak English, Mother. Come on, get a grip on yourself.'

Christine began to giggle. She looked so pretty when she laughed that Philip couldn't help remembering Arnham and understood why he had been attracted to her. He finished his coffee, said goodbye and left the house. Recalling Arnham had plunged him back once more into the pit of anxiety and doubt. He hardly noticed the sunshine, the scent from a hundred little gardens in bloom, the relief from sulphur stench. He sat in the car, moving off, automatically going through the motions. Head office today for his first call which meant joining the sluggish queue of cars crawling down the hills to London.

How could you say people you knew didn't kill other people? Murderers were just ordinary, weren't they, till they murdered? They weren't all gangsters or mad. Or if they were their madness or indifference to society's rules was concealed under an exterior of normality. In company they were just like anyone else.

How many times had he read in books and newspapers of a murderer's wife or girl friend who said she'd had no idea what he was like, had never dreamed that he did those things while he was away from her? But Senta was so small, so sweet, so childish. Sometimes, when she wasn't lecturing him on power and magic, she talked like a child of seven or eight. Her hand nestled in his like a little girl's. He imagined her going up to a man, whimpering with pain and fear, lifting her face to his, asking him to see what was hurting her eye. It was a sight he saw when he closed his eyes. Opening a newspaper, that vision superimposed itself over the photographs and the print. He remembered her coming into that room in her cap and red tunic and now he thought he could also remember stains on that tunic. Surely there had been a bloodstain high up on the shoulder.

The man bent his kindly head, peered into her eye. Perhaps he asked Senta's permission to touch her face, to pull down the lower eyelid. As he came closer, looking for the speck of grit, she drew the dagger of glass from her tunic pocket and thrust it with all her childish force into his heart . . .

Had he cried out? Or had he only groaned and crumpled up, sagged at the knees, given her a last look of terrible bewilderment, of agonised enquiry, before he collapsed on to the grass? The blood had spurted on to her, splashing her shoulder. And then the little dog, the small black Scottie dog, had come running up, barking until its barks changed to whimpers.

Stop it, stop, Philip said to himself as he said unavailingly each time his imagination turned in this direction. Harold Myerson was his name, Harold Myerson. He was fifty-eight. He happened to live in Chigwell but that was coincidence. Thousands of people lived in Chigwell. Philip thought how it would be possible to go to the police and actually ask about Harold Myerson. Where he lived, for instance, his full address. Newspapers never gave that. It would look very strange going to the police, making an enquiry like that. They would want to know why he asked. They would take his name and they would remember him. And that might in the end lead them to Senta.

You do believe she killed him, his inner voice said. You do. You're just unable to face the fact. There is no rule that murderers have to be big and strong and tough. Murderers can be small and delicate, children have done murder. As in certain tactics of martial arts, the perpetrator's own weakness is made use of to take advantage of the victim's strength. Tenderness and pity deflect that victim from his guard when an appeal is made, a wounded place proffered, help asked.

There was something else that hadn't occurred to him till now. He got it out and confronted it, the traffic paused and the light red. Suppose Gerard Arnham hadn't been called that at all? Suppose his real name had been Harold Myerson but he had given Christine a false name the better to get away from her when he needed to? Unscrupulous people did that, and Arnham had been unscrupulous, telling Christine lies about the length of time he would be in America and then, on his return, abandoning her.

The more Philip considered this the more he believed it. After all, he had never put it to the test. He had never seen Arnham's name in any phone directory, had never heard anyone but Christine call him by it. Philip began to feel sick. He had an urge to jump out of the car, leaving it where it stood half-way down the Edgware Road, and run away. Run where? There was nowhere to go he wouldn't have to come back from. There was nowhere he could hide and dissociate himself from Senta.

Arnham might be fifty-eight. Some people looked young for their age and the fact that Arnham had told Christine he was fifty-one meant nothing. It was known that he had lied to her. He had lied when he said he would be in touch with her when he returned from America. A man of five feet eight would seem tall to tiny Senta. He Philip, at six feet and more, towered over her. And the dog? He had been through that one before. It was Mrs Arnham's dog. Mrs Myerson's dog.

It was Ebony, the property of Thiefie.

Roy was in another of his good moods. This seemed largely brought about by the fact that Olivia Brett had twice phoned and asked for Philip.

'Not by name, mark you,' said Roy. ' "The terribly sweet dishy boy with the fair curly hair" was what she said. Oh, chase me, Charlie, I should be so lucky.'

'What did she want?'

'Are you asking me? At your age you ought to know. I expect she'll show you if you pop up to Highgate when the sun's over the yard arm.'

Philip said patiently, 'What did she say she wanted?'

'In words of a few simple syllables, can she have you to keep an eye on things when the fitters start. Not me or some bloke less easy on the eye is what the little darling means.'

It was rare for Philip to involve himself in the crush which filled the pubs and cafés of this part of inner London at lunchtime. He usually stopped somewhere in a suburb on his way to a client call. But today, as a result of having had no breakfast, he was very hungry. Before starting on the long drive to Croydon he needed something solid inside him, a couple of hamburgers or a plate of sausages and chips. Two towel rails in cardboard crates, replacements for a damaged pair, were needed in Croydon. He might as well take them with him in the boot of the car.

This was an area of office blocks. Passages and alleys led between them into car parks and warehouses. Only one old street remained, much as it had always been, a relic of a Georgian terrace with three little shops tacked on to the end of it. The shops themselves were not old-fashioned but modern tourist traps aimed at those who might conceivably pass along here on their way to Baker Street station. Returning from the car park, making for a café where he thought the worst of the rush would now be over, Philip came out of one of the passages under an arch into the old street which seemed to go from nowhere to nowhere.

He had often been this way before but had never previously even glanced at the shops. It would have been impossible for him to say what wares were displayed in their windows. But now the gleam of red and blue glass attracted his attention and he paused to look at the glasses and jugs and vases ranged on the shelves.

Most of it was Venetian glass. In the very front were pairs of glass earrings and strings of glass beads, behind these glass animals, galloping horses and dancing dogs and long-necked cats. But what made him stare almost

197

incredulously — what had perhaps, unknown to his conscious mind, originally caught his eye? — was a glass dagger.

It was displayed on the left-hand side of the window and was contained, for safety's sake or out of prudence or possibly because the law required it, in a case not of glass but of some kind of glass-like plastic. The glass of which it was made was translucent, lightly frosted. Its blade was some ten inches long, the cross-piece of the handle three inches wide. Philip stared at it, incredulously at first, then with a kind of sick recognition. How could it be that he had never even heard of the existence of daggers made of glass until five days before but in the time since he had heard persistent talk of the things and now actually seen one in the shop window?

It was like the word you read in the paper that you've never heard before, he thought, and that same day someone speaks it to you and you read it in a book. These things couldn't be rationally accounted for. It couldn't be merely that you actually had seen the word many times before (known about glass daggers subconsciously for years) and that it was only some emotive force which now brought it sharply to your attention. Something occult must be at work, some force as yet beyond human knowledge. Senta would account for it like that and who could say she was wrong? Worse for him than the coincidence was the discovery that glass daggers actually existed. Senta hadn't lied. She hadn't lied about her mother being Icelandic and dying when she was born, or about going to drama school. Had he ever caught her out in a real lie?

That was a thought too appalling to linger over — that her lies might exist only in his imagination. He went into the shop. A girl came up to him and with a slight foreign accent, Italian perhaps, asked if she could help him.

'The glass dagger in the window,' he said, 'where does it come from?'

'Murano. It's Venetian glass. All our glass is Venetian made on Murano.'

That was the name Senta had told him. He had been trying to remember it. 'Isn't it rather dangerous?'

He hadn't meant to sound accusing but she was at once on the defensive. 'You couldn't hurt yourself with it. It is quite – what do you call it? – blunt. The glass is smooth – here, let me show you.'

She had dozens of the things in a drawer, all in Perspex cases. It was an effort for him to bring himself to touch it. He felt sweat break out on his upper lip. His finger just touched the edge of the blade. It was quite smooth. The tip ended in a small blob or bubble of glass.

'What's the point,' he said, almost as if she wasn't there, as if he were talking to himself, 'of a knife that won't cut?'

Her shoulders lifted. She said nothing, just looked at him in a way which was growing suspicious. He didn't ask the price but handed the box and knife back to her and left the shop. The answer to his question was simple enough – the glass would be ground, a not much harder task then sharpening metal. By now he thought he was beginning to understand Senta's way of mixing truth and fantasy. She might have bought the daggers but not in Venice. She could have bought them here in London.

He turned almost blindly out of the old street. No buses ran along here and there were no shops, only the rears of more office blocks. In front of an almost window-less concrete wall, four storeys high, was the area of car parking with a notice at the gate announcing that it was strictly reserved for the use of employees of the company who occupied the block.

A car had just turned in. Because it was a black Jaguar it caught Philip's attention, having the effect of just distracting him from these painful and terrifying ideas. Half-bemused, he watched the car move into the one vacant space and park there. The door opened and the driver got out.

It was Gerard Arnham.

14

In the past his feelings had alternated between never wanting to see Arnham again, then wanting to see him in order to have the whole thing out, and had finally faded into indifference. But he had for a long time been conscious of the fact that he might bump into Arnham on any occasion he went to head office. That, as much as the crowds, had made him avoid having lunch in any of the local eating places. Now he couldn't imagine anyone he would rather have seen. It was nearly as wonderful as being reunited with someone you loved after a separation. Philip could hardly restrain himself from shouting out an excited greeting to Arnham as the man came walking from the car park.

Arnham, seeing Philip some few seconds after Philip had seen him, hesitated on the opposite pavement. It was as if he were abashed. But he must almost immediately have sensed Philip's delight, for a smile, slowly dawning on his face, spread and widened as he raised one hand in a salute and, having allowed a couple of cars to pass, hastened across the street.

Philip advanced towards him with outstretched hand. 'How are you? It's good to see you.'

Afterwards, when some of the euphoria had passed, he thought how astonished Arnham must have been by this fulsome greeting. After all, he had only met Philip once before, hadn't treated him and his sisters very warmly, and had unmercifully thrown Philip's mother over. Perhaps the truth was he just felt relieved at Philip's ability to let bygones be bygones or else thought him insensitive. Whatever his feelings he didn't show them but shook hands heartily and asked Philip how life was treating him.

'I'd no idea you worked round here.'

'I didn't when we last met,' Philip said. 'I was still doing my training then.'

'It's a wonder we haven't come across each other before.'

Philip explained that his visits to head office were not very frequent but said nothing about his own knowledge of precisely where Arnham worked. Rather tentatively Arnham said, 'How's your mother?'

'She's well. Fine.' Why shouldn't he pile it on a bit? Delighted as he might be to see Arnham he needn't lose sight of the fact that this was the man who had jilted Christine, had slept with her – Philip could face this quite equably now – and deserted her. 'She's got quite a profitable business going, as a matter of fact,' he said and proceeded to glib invention, 'and a man who's very keen on her.'

Was he imagining it or did Arnham really look a bit upset? 'My sister Fee got married.' As he spoke the words he seemed to see Senta in her bridesmaid's dress, her silver hair spread across the coral satin, and a surge of love for her rose in him and choked the rest of what he meant to say.

Arnham didn't seem to notice. 'Have you got time for a quick drink? There's a pub I sometimes go to just round the corner.'

But for the drive ahead of him Philip might have said yes. Anyway, he didn't specially want to spend any more time with Arnham. The man had served his purpose, had proved his existence, had brought the total glorious peace of mind Philip thought he might never attain again.

'I'm afraid I'm in a bit of a rush.' It was funny how his appetite had entirely gone. Food would have choked him. Alcohol would have made him sick. 'I'm running late as it is.'

'Some other time then.' Arnham seemed disappointed. He hesitated, said almost shyly, 'It would be – would it be all right if I gave your mother a ring sometime? Just for old time's sake?'

Philip said, rather coldly now, 'She's still at the same place.'

'Yes, I've got her number. I've moved, of course.'

Philip didn't say he already knew that. 'Give her a ring if you want to.' He added, 'She's out a lot but you may catch her.' An urge to run seized him, to dance and shout proclamations of joy to the skies, to the world. He could have grabbed Arnham and danced him down the street, waltzing like Rita and Jacopo waltzed, singing with happiness the tra-la-las of *Merry Widows* and *Vienna Woods*. Instead he held out his hand to Arnham and said goodbye.

'Goodbye, Philip, it was good seeing you again.'

Keeping himself from running, marching like a soldier with a banner, like a trumpeter, he had a feeling the man still stood there on the pavement behind him, following with a long disappointed gaze the jaunty departing figure. But when at the corner he looked back to wave, Arnham was gone.

Philip got into his car and immediately drove to the garage Roseberry Lawn used to ask them about replacing the radio in his car.

To make things perfect Joley should have been there in Tarsus Street, seated on his barrow, munching his dustbin retrievings. Philip was sure he would be and even had a five-pound note ready to give him. But when he turned the corner out of Caesarea Grove he saw at once in the clear evening light, as bright as noon, that Joley hadn't returned. In spite of his need to see Senta, a longing which all afternoon he had believed couldn't be postponed for a second longer than was necessary, he parked the car

203

and walked back to look for Joley in the environs of the church.

The gates were unlocked and the church door itself stood half open. Philip walked round the back over bleached grass that was permanently deprived of light, between mossy half-buried gravestones, in the deep shade of an ilex and a pair of great ragged cypresses. The smell here was of mould, like stale damp mushrooms. It would have been easy, if you were fanciful, to imagine this was the smell of the dead. He could hear from the interior of the church an organ mournfully playing a hymn tune. There was no sign of Joley anywhere nor even of those remnants he sometimes left behind him as evidence of his sojourn in some sheltered corner, screwed-up bits of paper and a bone or two.

Philip came back and went into the church. It was empty but for the organist who was invisible. The windows were of stained glass, darker and heavier glass than that in the Venetian shop, and the only light was from an electric bulb in a kind of censer that hung in the apse. The summer evening was warm but the cold in here was bitter. It was a disproportionate relief to come out once more into the mild hazy sunshine. As he approached the house he saw Rita come down the steps from the front door. She was dressed very showily in a short dress of flowered silk. Her stockings were white lace and her shoes scarlet with high heels. Jacopo followed, slamming the front door behind him. He took her arm and they walked off in the opposite direction. Tonight, in the small hours, Philip thought, they would dance above his head, waltzing to *La Vie en Rose* and tangoing to *Jealousy*. He didn't care. He wouldn't have cared if two hundred people had come to a ball up there.

He let himself into the house and ran down the basement stairs. As she had done once or twice before, as she had done in the way that delighted him beyond expression, she opened the door to him before his key turned in the lock. She was dressed in something new — or new to him. It was a long dress, nearly ankle-length, of silky semi-transparent pleated stuff, sea-green with silvery-green beads sewn into it. The thin slippery material clung to the voluptuous curves of her breasts, seeming to drip from them like slowly cascading water and trickle over her hips to stroke her thighs in a wave's caress. Her bright silver hair was like needles, like the blades of knives. She put her mouth up to his, her little hands on his neck. Her tongue darted into his mouth, a little warm fish, withdrew itself with delicate slowness. He gasped with pleasure, with happiness.

How did she know there was nothing to say? Words were for later. But how did she know of the earthquake which had taken place, of his enormous change of feeling and of heart? She was naked under the green dress. She drew it over her head, pulled him gently on to the bed with her. The shutters were half-closed, the light that came in a distant dazzlement. In a saucer a joss stick of cinnamon and cardamom smouldered. Why had he ever thought he hated this room, found squalor in this house? He loved it, it was his home.

'Then you'll come and live here with me,' she said.

'I've been thinking about that, Senta. You once told me you used to live in the top flat.'

She sat on the bed, her arms clasped round her knees. Her face had become very thoughtful. It was as if she was calculating. If it had been anyone else, any other girl, Jenny say, he would have thought she was considering rates and service bills and furniture, but that wasn't Senta's way.

'I know it's a mess,' he said, 'but we could clean it up and paint it. We could get some furniture.'

'Isn't it good enough down here here for you, Philip?'

'Basically, it's too small. Doesn't it seem a bit silly for

two of us to try and live here when that top flat's going begging? Or is it that you think Rita wouldn't like it?'

She dismissed that with a wave of her hand. 'Rita wouldn't mind.' She seemed to hesitate. 'The thing is I *like* it down here.' Childishly diffident, her face took on its shy look. She said softly, 'I'm going to tell you something.'

Momentarily he felt a tautening, the bracing of nerves that was preparatory now to hearing her tell some new lie or make some grotesque confidence. She moved close up to him, held on to his arm with both her hands, snuggled her face into his shoulder. 'I do have a little bit of an agoraphobia problem, Philip. Do you know what that is?'

'Of course I do.' It rather irritated him, the way she had sometimes of treating him as if he were ignorant.

'Don't be cross. You must never be cross with me. It's why I don't go out very much, you know, and why I like living below ground. Psychiatrists say it goes with schizophrenia. Did you know that?'

He tried a light approach. 'I hope we're going to live together all our lives, Senta, and I can tell you I don't intend to spend fifty years in a burrow. I'm not a rabbit.'

It wasn't very funny but it made her laugh. She said, 'I'll think about the flat. I'll ask Rita. How will that do?'

It did wonderfully. Everything was at once made smooth. He marvelled, but in a calm and simply interested way, that things could have been tragic and terrible yesterday and today, only because he had seen and spoken to a man who was the merest acquaintance, restored to perfection. He took her in his arms and kissed her.

'I want everyone to know about us now.'

'Of course you can tell them, Philip. It's time to tell.'

As soon as he got Christine alone he told her about Senta.

She said, 'That's nice, dear.'

206

What response had he expected? While Christine pottered about the kitchen, getting their evening meal, he thought about that. The truth was that Senta was so beautiful in his eyes, so wonderful, so utterly different from any other girl he had ever known, that he expected awe first, then amazed congratulations. Christine had received his announcement in a rather preoccupied way or as if he had said he had been going about with some ordinary girl. He would have got more enthusiasm, he thought, if he had said he'd taken up with Jenny again. Doubtful if she had really taken it in, he said, 'You do know who I mean, don't you? Senta who was one of Fee's bridesmaids?'

'Yes, Philip, Tom's girl. I said it was nice. So long as you're fond of each other I think it's very nice.'

'Tom?' he said, surprised she could place Senta in this way as if her parentage were the most remarkable thing about her.

'Tom Pelham, Irene's other brother, the one with an ex-wife that dances and lives with a young boy.'

What did she mean, 'other' brother? He didn't ask. 'That's right. Senta's got a flat in their house.'

'Flat' was a bit over the top, he thought, but in a month or two it might be true. Should he also tell Christine about meeting Arnham?

No, it would only upset her. Somewhere, treasured among other mementoes, he had no doubt she still kept that postcard with the White House on it. Arnham would never phone, anyway, Arnham would have been put off by what he had told him of another man in Christine's life. Now his euphoria was past Philip wondered if he had spoiled his mother's chances by inventing that other man. Still, Arnham was married himself or at least living with a woman. It was all too late.

They sat down to one of Christine's specialities, rounds of toast topped with scrambled egg into which flakes of tuna and a spoonful of curry powder had been stirred.

Philip didn't want to have to think about the future, about how she was going to manage on her own and with no one but the ghostly flitting presence of Cheryl. But sooner or later he would have to think about it.

'I'm popping over to Audrey's for a couple of hours,' Christine said, reappearing in a floral cotton dress Philip couldn't remember having seen before but which she had probably resurrected from some summer wardrobe of the past. 'It's such a nice evening.'

She beamed at him. She looked happy. It was her innocence and her ignorance that made that sunny temperament, he thought. He would have to support her financially, emotionally, companionably, for the rest of her life. The world out there was no place for her, even its manifestation in the shape of a job in a hairdresser's salon would overwhelm her. It was as if his father had sheltered her under his great sweeping protective wings. A fledgling that never grew up, she peeped about her in amazement. He wondered sometimes how, on her own, she managed such ordinary things as paying her bus fare.

Cheryl, coming in, must have passed her on the doorstep. Philip would have been surprised if she had come into the living room. She didn't come in. He heard her feet dragging their way up the stairs. It was more than a week since he had spoken a word to her. Her reaction to any news he might give about himself and his future would be met, he knew, with blank indifference.

Her footsteps sounded above his head. She was in Christine's bedroom, walking about. He heard the creak the wardrobe door made when it was opened. No longer worrying about Cheryl's welfare, he found himself seeing her only as an added burden. As a minder for his mother she would be worse than useless. The bedroom door slammed and, standing just inside the living room, with the door open a crack, he listened to her descent of the stairs. She was indifferent, he realised, to whether he heard her or not, to whether he knew or not. Only a fool would fail to understand that she had been in Christine's bedroom to take whatever money was concealed there, to rob the handbag in whose zip pocket Christine kept her hairdresser's tips or open the china teddy bear with detachable head that usually contained ten and twenty pee pieces.

The front door closed. He waited a few moments for her to have disappeared and then he drove to Senta's.

'I don't believe it,' Fee said. 'You're kidding.' It was such a shock that she had to light a cigarette from the stub of the last one.

'He's pulling our legs, Fee,' said Darren.

Philip was very taken aback. He had expected his announcement to be greeted with rapturous pleasure. Senta was Darren's cousin and had been Fee's bridesmaid. You would have thought they would be overjoyed to welcome a member of Darren's extended family into their immediate circle.

'You were always teasing me about Senta,' he said. 'You must have realised how I felt about her.'

Darren started laughing. He was sitting, as usual, in an armchair in front of the television. Fee snapped at him.

'What's so funny?'

'I'll tell you later.'

It was rude and it was also disconcerting. Fee made things no better.

'Do you mean that all the time we were sort of making cracks about you fancying Senta and asking you if you wanted her phone number and all that, all the time you were actually meeting her and going about with her?'

'She didn't want people to know, not then.'

'Well, I must say I do think it's very underhand, Phil. I'm sorry but I do. It makes you feel such a fool when people deceive you like that.'

'I'm sorry, I didn't know you'd take it this way.'

'No good making a fuss now, I suppose. It's too late for that. And now you say she's supposed to be coming here to see us?'

He began to regret he had ever arranged it. 'We thought it would be best for me to tell you first and for her to come over after about half an hour. Fee, she *is* supposed to be a friend of yours, she *is* Darren's cousin.'

Darren, who had stopped laughing, put one hand up and snapped his thick fingers. 'Can we have a bit of hush while the snooker's on?'

Philip and Fee squeezed themselves into the kitchen which was the size of a moderately spacious cupboard.

'Are you engaged or something?'

'Not exactly but we will be.' He thought, I will propose to her. I will make her a formal proposal, I might even go down on my knees. 'When we are,' he said rather grandly, 'We'll put an announcement in the paper. In *The Times*.'

'No one ever does that sort of snobby stuff in our family. It's just showing off. Will she want things to eat? Will she want a drink? There isn't any drink in the place.'

'I brought a bottle of champagne.'

Fee, who necessarily stood very close to him, gave him a look of half-exasperation, half mischievous conspiracy. 'You're so daft, going on like that. Why didn't you tell us sooner?'

'The champagne's in the car, I'll go and get it.'

Having a rare few minutes alone with Fee should have allowed him to confide in her about Cheryl. The moment seemed particularly inappropriate. He imagined her saying in her sharp way that she supposed he was just shifting his problems on to her now he was leaving and getting married. Instead she put her arms round him and gave him a brief hug, laying her cheek against his, whispering, 'Well I'll have to congratulate you, won't I?'

Taking the champagne out of the car, he looked up

and saw Senta. She too held cradled in her arms a bottle of wine. It was the first time he had ever met her in the open street. There was a special breathless pleasure in going up to her and kissing her in public. Not that anyone was watching but they were there on view, on the pavement embracing, the two hard cold glass bottles pressed between their bodies and keeping them apart like chastity devices.

She was in black. It made her skin look shell-white and gave her hair a glassier steelier brightness. She had painted her nails the same colour and put silver on her eyelids. She walked lightly on her stilt heels up the stairs ahead of him. In spite of their height she was still a head's length shorter than he and when she was on the step in front he could look down on to the crown of her head. The red roots of her hair glowed with a curious pinkish luminosity under the silver strands and he was touched with feelings of an intense tenderness for her quirky ways and her harmless vanity.

He was aware too of something else: her nervousness when off her own home ground. He noticed it because of what she had told him about her agoraphobia. It was worse in the street, fading to something that seemed like shyness when she was inside the flat and in the presence of Darren and Fee. They both seemed embarrassed but Fee came out with it bluntly. 'I'm not saying it wasn't a surprise but we'll get used to it.'

Darren, the snooker concluded and a re-run of some golf tournament showing with the sound turned off, took this as an occasion for catching up on family news. 'What's Auntie Rita up to now then?'

In near-silence which was demure and diffident, Senta drank her champagne. She said a soft thank you when Fee proposed a toast to Senta and Philip - 'not engaged yet but soon will be.' This was her first time in the flat but when Fee asked if she would like to see over it — a necessarily brief exercise since there were only the small bedroom and tiny shower room left to see — she shook her head and said thanks, but she wouldn't, not this time. Darren, who worried at his joke like a dog with an old bone, said he hadn't had a bath since he came back from his honeymoon and would she like a shower?

In the car going back to Tarsus Street he felt as if he were bursting, choking, with his proposal. But he didn't want her to remember, in the years ahead, perhaps twenty years ahead when they celebrated some wedding anniversary, that he had proposed to her in a car in a north London suburb.

'Where are we going?' she said. 'This isn't the way? Are you kidnapping me, Philip?'

'For the rest of your life,' he said.

He drove up on to Hampstead Heath. It wasn't very far. There was a large round moon shining, the colour of her hair. Off the Spaniards Road where the path runs down into the back of the Vale of Health, he led her to the edge of the woodland. It amused him because she so plainly thought he had brought her there to make love in the open air on this mild dry summer night. Docilely, her little hand soft in his, she allowed him to lead her. The moonlight turned the grass white and the bare earth of the paths to chalk, while under the trees the shadows were black. There must have been other people about, it was impossible that they were alone there, but it was as quiet as in the country and as still as indoors.

When it came to it kneeling was an impossibility. She would have thought him mad. He held both her hands and drew them up to clasp closely in between their bodies. He looked into her greenish eyes which she had lifted to his and opened very wide. In each of them he could see a moon reflected. Formally, in the manner in which his great-grandfather might have spoken, in a way in which he knew he must have read of in the pages of a book, he said to her, 'Senta, I want to marry you. Will you be my wife?'

212

She smiled faintly. He knew she was thinking that this wasn't quite what she had expected. Her voice when she replied was soft and clear.

'Yes, Philip, I'll marry you. I want to marry you very much.' She put up her lips. He bent and kissed her full on the lips but very chastely. Her skin felt like marble. But she was a marble girl that some god was in the process of changing from a statue to a live woman. Philip could feel the warmth surging through the stone flesh. She said with gravity, drawing a little away, her eyes fixed on his, 'We were destined for each other from the beginning of time.'

Then her mouth was more ardently on his, her tongue stroking the inside of his lips. 'Not here,' he said. 'Senta, let's go home.'

It wasn't until the middle of the night, the deep dark early hours that he realised why, in the midst of that romantic scene which he had set up, at the moment when he asked her to marry him, unease had seemed to step between them, to mar everything. He understood now. It was because the scene, and even more the setting, seemed to mirror what she had described to him as happening between her and Gerard Arnham in another grassy place and under other trees. Just as he looked into her eyes, bent down and spoke gently to her, she had clutched the glass dagger and thrust it into his heart.

The yellow light from street lamps was shed in windowpane shapes across the brown bedcover. Above his head he could hear the *Skaters' Waltz* and the dancing feet of Rita and Jacopo circling the floor. He thought he must be neurotic, dwelling like this on the foolish past. Hadn't he seen Arnham and spoken to him? Didn't he know beyond a doubt the man was alive and well?

Up on the Heath, though he had felt her happiness and known she was glad to be there with him, he had sensed too her unease in the outdoors, the spacious night. How could he seriously have considered it possible for

213

someone like her to perform a violent act while out in the open? The outdoors was her dangerous place.

Senta's silver head lay on the pillow beside him. She was deeply asleep. The music and the dancing never disturbed her, safe down here under the ground. Philip heard the feet approach the window and as the waltz ended a thin little shriek of laughter as if Jacopo had taken Rita in his arms and whirled her round and round.

15

He brought Senta home to see Christine. She held out her left hand almost timidly, like a little dog lifting its paw, to display her engagement ring, a Victorian antique of silver with two moonstones. He had given it to her the day before when the announcement of their engagement appeared. In company Senta was very quiet, answering in monosyllables or sitting in a silence she broke only to say please and thank you. He tried to remember back to Fee's wedding, the only time he had seen her in a group of others. She had been talkative then, a different girl, going up to people and introducing herself. He could recall, just before he left to go home, how she had been talking and laughing with two or three men, all friends of Darren's. But he didn't mind this silent manner of hers, knowing as he did that her talk and her sweetness and all her animation were reserved for him when they got back to her room.

They stayed in Glenallan Close for about an hour. It was Sunday and Cheryl was also at home. Philip had glanced at the newspaper's colour supplement and seen an article in it on Murano glass daggers. There was a huge photograph of a dagger very like the ones he had seen in the shop and another picture of people at the Venice Carnival in the snow. He closed the magazine as quickly as he might have done if it was hard pornography which was displayed and which the women might have seen. Christine kissed Senta when they left. Philip hardly knew why it was that he was afraid Senta would draw back. She didn't. She pleased him tremendously by presenting her cheek to Christine, her head tilted a little to one side, a small sweet smile on her lips.

His suggestion that they should visit her father met with a stubborn refusal. She took the line that Tom Pelham was lucky to get his name in the paper in a respectable way without having to pay a penny for it. Rita had brought her up, not he. Often she hadn't seen him for months on end. It was Rita who gave her a home rent-free. Not that she wanted to impart the news to her stepmother either. Let her find out for herself. Rita had changed since she took up with Jacopo.

At the first wine shop which was open that they came to Senta wanted to get out of the car and go in and buy supplies. She had had enough of being out, she said. Philip had wanted to take her for a meal and then to meet Geoff and his girl friend in Jack Straw's Castle. He had it all planned, a further protracted celebration of their engagement with a meal in Hampstead, then the pub where he thought it likely some old college friends of his would be on a Sunday night.

'You're trying to cure me of my phobia by over-exposure,' she said to him, smiling. 'Haven't I been good? Haven't I really tried for you?'

He had to give in, only stipulating that they got hold of some proper food to take back with them. It worried him sometimes, the way she seemed to live on air and wine with the occasional chocolate. She waited in silence, standing with clasped hands, while he foraged in a Finchley Road supermarket, buying biscuits and bread and cheese and fruit. He had noticed how, out in the open, she mostly looked down at the ground or kept a kind of discreet custody of the eyes.

They approached Tarsus Street from the Kilburn end. There were rather a lot of people about, sitting on walls, lounging, standing, gossiping, leaning out of windows to talk to people leaning on windowsills, as there are on fine summer evenings in London streets such as this one. A strong odour of diesel, melted tar and cooking spices filled the air. Philip looked for Joley the way he always did and for a brief moment thought he had spotted him on the corner where the street met Caesarea Grove. But it was a different man, younger, thinner, who wandered aimlessly along the pavement with his possessions contained in carpet bags.

She asked him as they got out of the car with their load of food and heavier load of wine bottles, who he was looking for.

'Joley,' he said. 'The old man with the barrow. The tramp, I suppose you'd call him.'

She gave him a strange sidelong glance. Her eyelashes were very long and thick and they seemed to sweep the fine white skin under her eyes. The hand with the moonstone ring was lifted to hold back a long lock of silver hair which had fallen to cover her cheek.

'You can't mean the old man who used to sit on our steps? The one who was sometimes in the churchyard round the corner?'

'Why can't I? That's the one I do mean.'

They were in the house now, going down the basement stairs. She unlocked the door. That room only had to be shut up for a few hours for it to become intolerably close and stuffy. Senta took one of the bottles of wine out of the bag he had put down on the bed and reached for the corkscrew.

'But that was John Crucifer,' she said.

For a moment the name meant nothing to him. 'Who?'

She laughed. It was a light, rather musical laugh. 'You ought to know, Philip. You killed him.'

The room seemed to shift a little. The floor rose up the way it does when you feel faint. Philip put two fingers, which were surprisingly cold, up to touch his forehead. He sat down on the edge of the bed.

'Do you mean that the old man who said he was called Joley and used to have his beat down here was really the man who was murdered in Kensal Green?'

'That's right,' she said. 'I thought you knew.' She

poured a large measure of wine into a glass which hadn't been washed since the last Riesling had been drunk from it. 'You must have known it was Crucifer.'

'The man who was murdered . . .' He was speaking slowly, abstractedly, '. . . his name was John.'

She was impatient in a smiling way. 'John, Johnny, Joley – so what? It was a sort of nickname.' A bead of wine trembled on her lower lip like a diamond drop. 'I mean, didn't you pick on him because it was Crucifer?'

His own voice sounded feeble to him, as if he had suddenly become ill. 'Why would I?'

'Have some wine.' She passed him the bottle and another dirty glass. He took it mechanically and sat there holding glass in one hand and bottle in the other, staring at her. 'I thought you picked him because he was my enemy.'

A terrible thing happened. Her face was the same, white and soft, the pale lips slightly parted, but he saw madness staring out of her eyes. He couldn't have said how he knew, for he had never seen or known a person even slightly mentally disturbed, but this was madness, stark and real and awful. It was as if a demon sat inside there and looked out of her eyes. And at the same time it was Flora's look he saw, remote, pre-dating civilisation, heedless of morality.

He had to exercise all the control he could muster. He had to be calm, even maintain a light touch. 'What do you mean, Senta, your enemy?'

'He asked for money. I hadn't any money to give him. He started shouting out after me, making remarks about my clothes and my – my hair. I don't want to say what they were, but they were very insulting.'

'Why did you think I knew?'

She said softly, moving nearer to him, 'Because you know my thoughts, Philip, because we are so close now we can read each other's minds, can't we?'

He looked away, turned his eyes back reluctantly to

look at her. The madness was gone. He had imagined it. That was what it must have been, his imagination. He refilled her glass and filled his own. She started telling him about some audition she was going to in the coming week for a part in a television serial. More fantasy, but of a harmless kind, if any of it was harmless, if it could be. They sat side by side on the bed in the airless room that was full of dusty orange sunlight. For once, he didn't feel like opening the window. A superstitious fear had come to him that not a single word they spoke must be overheard.

'Senta, listen to me. We mustn't ever talk about killing again, not even as a joke or a fantasy. I mean killing isn't a joke, it never can be.'

'I didn't say it was a joke. I never said that.'

'No, but you made up stories about it and pretended about it. I'm just as bad. I did it too. You pretended to have killed someone and I pretended to have killed someone and it doesn't matter now because we didn't really do it or even believe the other one had. But it's bad for us to keep on talking about it as if it was real. Can't you see that? It's sort of bad for our characters.'

Just for an instant he saw the demon in there behind her eyes. The demon came and chuckled and vanished. She was silent. He prepared himself for an enraged onslaught such as had been made on him last time he questioned her word. But she was still and silent. She threw back her head and drank the wine down in one swallow, then held out the empty glass to him.

'I'll never mention it again,' she said slowly, and, 'I understand how it is with you, Philip. You're very conventional still. You were glad when you found out it was my mother I lived here with, weren't you? It made things seem respectable. You were pleased when I got a real job that paid. How could you be otherwise with that family? You were brought up to be very straight and rigid and you aren't going to change in a couple of months. But listen to me now. What we had to do for each other to prove our love was a terrible thing, I realise that, I realise it was terrible, and I do understand it makes it easier for you if we just bury it in the past. As long as you also know we can't change the past. We just don't have to talk about it.'

He said almost roughly, 'If you're going to drink so much wine we ought to eat something. Come on, let's eat.'

'Are you telling me I drink too much, Philip?'

The early warning signs were becoming familiar to him. He was beginning to know them and how to handle them. 'No, of course I'm not. But I think you don't eat enough. I'm trying to look after you, Senta.'

'Yes, look after me, Philip, take care of me.' She turned and clutched at him, holding on to his shoulders, her eyes suddenly wild and frightened. 'We don't want to eat yet. Please don't let's. I want you to love me.'

'I do love you,' he said, and he put his glass down and took the glass out of her hand and pulled her down with him in his arms on to the brown quilt.

It was another small hours return home for him that night. He had meant to discuss their future with her. Were they going to live together in the upstairs flat? Had she thought about that as she had promised? Were they going to set a wedding date for sometime next year? Could she come up with any ideas as to how the problem of Christine and, come to that Cheryl, could be dealt with? They had scarcely talked at all but made love all the evening. At one point he had got up and eaten something and washed himself under the tap.

Coming back to open the window and let some fresh air into the dusty staleness, he had found her sitting up starting on the second bottle of wine, and she had

220

welcomed him back into bed with outstretched yearning arms.

He slept soundly. He slept like the dead, exhausted and at peace. His future with Senta looked glorious to him, a series of days of dreaming of her and of nights of love. Their love-making got even better as time went on and she loved it as much as he did. It was hard to imagine that it could get better than it was now but that was something he had said three weeks ago and it had got better. When the alarm went off and he woke up he reached for her, but he was in his own bed and she wasn't there and he felt bereft.

On the way to work, a reluctant visit to Olivia Brett, Philip castigated himself for imagining he had seen signs of some kind of neurosis in Senta. It was the shock of course. It was caused by the shock of finding out that John Crucifer was Joley. Poor Senta had told him a simple fact which he might have gathered for himself by this time and he had been so upset by it that he had off-loaded his hysterical feelings on to her. Didn't the psychologists call that projection?

It was hardly surprising anyway that she believed he had killed Joley. After all, he had told her he had. He had actually told her, fantastic and unreal though this now seemed, that he had killed the old man. Of course she believed him. For a while, remember, he told himself, he had believed her story of killing Arnham. Well, off and on he had believed it. And all this really illustrated what he had said to her about this kind of talk harming them, damaging their characters. It was certainly damaging his character if it made him believe his Senta wasn't quite sane.

But Joley . . . Philip found he hated to think that it was Joley who had been murdered in Kensal Green, and hated it the more because he had told Senta he was responsible for that death. Now he found it hard to understand why he had ever done that. If she really loved him, and there was no doubt she did, she would have come to realise there was no need for fantasies about proofs of love. It would only have been a matter of sticking it out till she came round, maybe bearing the brunt of a few temper tantrums. Philip had a fleeting qualm at even using the expression in connection with Senta, having a very good idea of how she would react, but how else would you describe it?

In saying he had murdered Joley he had somehow involved himself in that death. Worse than that, he had in part made himself responsible for it, becoming a kind of accessory after the fact. He had aligned himself with Joley's killer, put himself into the same category. With these ideas unpleasantly occupying his mind, Philip went up the steps of Olivia Brett's house and was admitted by the actress herself. He couldn't help remembering the complimentary things she was supposed to have said about him and he felt awkward in her company.

Stories proliferated in his kind of job about women alone at home who were simply waiting to come across for men like himself, women who invited the surveyor or site manager or fitter into their bedrooms or suddenly appeared in front of them with no clothes on. Nothing like that had ever happened to him but it was early days yet. Olivia Brett wore a dressing gown which was white with a lot of frills on it but not see-through. She smelt like a bowl of tropical fruit that has been left out in the sun.

She insisted on walking upstairs behind Philip. He wondered what he would do if he felt her hand caress his neck or a fingertip run down his spine. But she didn't touch him. He didn't want to think about her at all, he wanted her to be an answering machine only or to make her requests in a neutral practical tone. She showed him into the recently gutted bathroom and stood behind him now while he made a draft chart of how he thought the electric wiring should be planned.

'Oh, darling,' she said, 'I don't know if they told you I changed my mind and I'm going to have one of those showers that squirt water out of the walls at you.'

'Yes, I've got a note of it.'

'I showed my friend the picture in your book and do you know what he said? He said it was a jacuzzi standing up to pee.'

Philip was a bit shocked. Not by what she said but because she had said it and to him. He didn't say anything, though he knew he ought to have laughed appreciatively. He got out his tape measure and pretended to measure something in the far corner. When he turned round he could see she was looking at him with calculation and he couldn't help contrasting her with Senta, her lined pinched greasy face with Senta's pure velvety skin and the mottled cleavage between the *broderie anglaise* lapels with Senta's white breasts. It made him smile quite pleasantly at her as he said, 'That seems to be that then. I shan't be troubling you again until the electrician has done his stuff.'

'Have you got a girl friend?' she said.

He was astonished. Her tone was harsh and direct. He felt a hot blush redden his face. She took a step nearer.

'What are you afraid of?'

It was a stroke of genius. For all the times Philip had thought of things he ought to have said, perfect rejoinders, when it was ten minutes too late to say them, this paid. He didn't know how he thought of it. It came to him on wings of serene appropriateness.

'I'm afraid,' he said, 'I got engaged to be married last week.'

With that he passed her, smiling politely, and descended the stairs, not hurrying. She came out on to the landing behind him. He had a momentary qualm. But prostituting oneself for Roseberry Lawn was surely way beyond the call of loyalty.

223

'Goodbye for now,' he called. 'I'll let myself out, shall I?'

The interlude made him feel rather jaunty. He had acquitted himself well. It had also served to distract him from the business of John Crucifer alias Joley. The real world, or at least a different one, had intruded. Philip could now see that Joley's death had absolutely nothing to do with him. In fact, his gifts to Joley had probably made the old man's last days brighter.

He put the car in the car park when he reached head office. It was ten past one. Just the sort of time when, if he went to find somewhere for lunch, he might bump into Arnham again. Philip told himself that was why he avoided the passage which led into the street of Georgian houses but he knew it wasn't really. The true reason was that he wanted to avoid passing the Venetian glass shop where he might see in the window the dagger of Murano glass.

All his life, probably, the name Murano or even the word dagger would evoke unpleasant memories. That was another good reason why he had to cure Senta of fantasising. There were whole areas of life he now found himself shying away from: the district of Kensal Green, the name Joley and the name John, Scottie dogs, Venice and glass daggers, little grassy glades. Of course time would change it, time would wipe the past clean of all this.

He took the other direction and came out into a busy thoroughfare where street vendors sold souvenirs to tourists. Philip wouldn't have dreamt of buying anything from one of these stalls, he would have passed them without a glance, but as he came close to one on which tee shirts with the Tower of London printed on them were displayed, and teddy bears in Union Jack aprons and tea towels with pictures of the Prince and Princess of Wales, the press of the crowd slowed his pace. He was forced to stand almost still and for a moment he thought he was going to witness some sort of assault or raid on stall and vendor.

A car had pulled into the kerb, on the double yellow line, and two men jumped out. They were young and they looked thuggish, heavy-set with cropped hair and wearing studded leather jackets like Cheryl's. Both of them came up to the stall, one standing at either end. The bigger and older one said to the vendor, 'Got a licence somewhere about then, have you?'

At once Philip knew they were not thieves or thugs but policemen.

Never before had he looked at the police with fear. And it wasn't quite fear that he felt now, more a cautious defensiveness. As he watched them standing over the vendor of souvenirs while the man fumbled through the pockets of a coat hanging up on a pole, he thought about Joley and his death. He thought how he had actually said he had killed Joley. Of course he had only said this to Senta, who in this respect didn't count, but he had uttered an admission of murder aloud. It might be that these very police officers, one of whom was now scrutinising the vendor's licence with a deep frown, were part of the team working on the case of Joley's murder. Why had he allowed himself to be drawn into this game of Senta's? Why had he ever played it?

Philip had a sandwich and a cup of coffee. While he ate he kept trying to travel those few weeks back in time. He remembered how Senta had withdrawn her love from him and how, to regain it, he had confessed to a murder he hadn't committed, wouldn't even in his wildest nightmares have committed, he who hated these things. It was far worse than what she had done. She had simply invented a killing. He couldn't understand now why he hadn't done a similar thing, why he hadn't appreciated that almost any preposterous tale would have done for her. What had made him think it necessary to claim responsibility for a real murder? He felt soiled by it, he

225

felt that his hands were actually dirtied, and he looked down at them, spread them out in front of him on the yellow formica of the café table, as if he might see graveyard earth in their lines and blood under the nails.

The way Joley had called him governor came back to him as he went up in the lift to Roy's room. Philip had liked him, had liked the humour Joley still retained in spite of the dreadful life he led. Of course it wasn't so good thinking of him insulting a young girl just because she wouldn't give him money. Philip wondered why Joley had ever gone to Kensal Green. Perhaps there was a soup kitchen up there.

Roy was working on his design for the complete remodelling of a flat. It was clear that he was in one of his bad moods.

'What the hell are you doing here?'

'Coming to see you, of course. You said to come in around two.'

'I said to get over to Chigwell *by* two and find out just why La Ripple is still dissatisfied with her marble whatsit. No wonder this company's fast going down the plughole when even a little squirt on the bottom rung of the ladder can't get to an appointment on time.'

Roy hadn't said anything about going to Mrs Ripple's, Philip was sure of that. But there was no arguing. He wasn't hurt by being called a little squirt. What went sharply home was the bit about the bottom of the ladder.

The drive to Chigwell took a long time. It had begun to pour with rain. Heavy rain always slowed up the traffic. The cars and trucks crawled along through Wanstead and by the time he was on the doorstep ringing Mrs Ripple's bell it was five to three. She had a friend with her, a woman she called Pearl. The two of them somehow managed to open the front door together, as if they had simultaneously and ritually put hands to latch. He had the impression they were waiting just inside it, and had been waiting there for some time.

'We'd just about given you up, hadn't we, Pearl?' said Mrs Ripple. 'I suppose we're behind the times. We're naïve. We've just got this old-fashioned idea in our heads that when someone says two o'clock he means two o'clock.'

'I'm very sorry, Mrs Ripple. There was a misunderstanding about that, nobody's fault, but I didn't actually know I was supposed to be here until an hour ago.'

She said very sourly, 'Now you are here at last you'd better come straight up. You'd better see if you can explain why I have to put up with the shoddy rubbish you've seen fit to instal in my bathroom.'

Pearl came up too. She looked enough like Mrs Ripple to be her sister but somehow a more richly furnished, more ornate version. It was as if Mrs Ripple were the standard model and Pearl the de luxe. She had black curly hair like an uncut poodle's and her tight-fitting silk dress was shiny peacock blue. She stopped on the threshold and said in a theatrical way, 'How much did you say you had to pay for this job, dear?'

Mrs Ripple didn't hesitate. The little scene had probably been rehearsed while they waited for him. 'Six thousand, five hundred and forty-two pounds, ninety-five.'

'Highway robbery,' said Pearl.

Mrs Ripple pointed with a quivering finger at the marble top of the vanity unit. She looked like a character in an amateur dramatic production indicating the presence of a ghost offstage. Philip examined the marble, the minute fissure in one of the white veins of the marbling. To his alarm and intense displeasure, Pearl took hold of his wrist and moved his hand so that the tip of his forefinger just touched the fissure.

'But that isn't a fault or damage, Mrs Ripple,' he said, doing his best to disengage his hand without giving offence. 'That's the character of the stone. This is a natural substance. It isn't as if it's plastic which could be made with a perfectly smooth surface.'

227

'I should just hope it isn't plastic,' said Mrs Ripple, 'considering what I paid for it.'

Philip would have liked to tell her that she had not only chosen the vanity unit from a selection of illustrated brochures but had actually examined samples of the marble they proposed to use. That would only have caused more trouble and in any case have been ineffective. Instead he tried to convince her that any visitor would at once appreciate the quality and taste of her bathroom from the undeniable evidence of that tiny flaw in the marble which would never have occured in a synthetic material. Mrs Ripple wasn't having any of that. She wanted marble, of course she did, she had always known what she wanted and that was marble, but she wanted a piece which had all the veining and the proper look of marble without any flaws.

Not daring to promise that they could get it for her, still less instal it free of extra charge, Philip said he had the matter in hand and she would hear from him personally in a day or two.

'Or a week or two,' said Pearl nastily.

The rain had stopped. Water lay in pools across the roadway which the sun turned into blazing mirrors. You could see the steam rising. Philip drove down the road and round the corner, heading for where Arnham lived. His wheels made fountains of water splash up, the sun was in his eyes and if he hadn't slowed to pull the visor down, he might have killed the running cat or the little dog which came rushing across the road in pursuit of it. As it was, swerving, braking as hard as he could with his foot slammed on to the floor of the car, skidding on the wet surface, his nearside wing must have struck the dog a glancing blow. It yelped and rolled over.

It was a Sealyham, white and fluffy. Philip picked it up. He didn't think it was hurt, for now that he held it, feeling its body for broken bones or painful area, it reacted by a rapturous licking of his face. Arnham's wife or girl friend had come down the steps and was standing at the gate. She looked older than when he had last seen her and thinner, but on previous occasions he had only seen her through glass. Out here in the sunshine she looked thin and ugly and middle-aged.

'He ran straight out in front of me,' Philip said. 'I don't think he's come to any harm.'

She said coldly, 'I suppose you were going too fast.'

'I don't think so.' He was getting rather tired of being accused of things of which he wasn't guilty. 'I was driving at about twenty miles an hour because of the wet road. Here, you'd better take him.'

'He's not my dog. What made you think he was mine?'

What had? the fact that she and she alone had come out? or because he somehow connected Arnham with a dog? That had been a Scottie, he remembered, *that had been Senta's invention*. Arnham disliked dogs, had never had a dog.

'I heard your brakes,' she said. 'I came out to see what was going on.' She went back up the steps and into the house and closed the door.

Philip, in whose arms the Sealyham was now comfortably snuggled, read the tag on its collar which proclaimed it to be Whisky, the property of H. Spicer, who lived three houses down from Mrs Ripple. He carried the dog home and was offered a five-pound note as a reward, which he refused.

But returning to his car, he thought what confusion deception causes, what a muddle in the mind, so that facts are mixed up with truth and truth distorted. Because of what Sehta had said he had made certain assumptions based on her story. The story was proved false but the assumptions still held.

He got into the car and glanced up at the house again as he switched on the ignition. All you have to hang on to, he told himself, is that Arnham lives there and Arnham is alive. Now forget everything else and be happy.

16

'I just wonder if maybe she's only been getting money together and saving it up. What do you think? I mean she's unemployed and likely to go on being and she's no skills, poor little love, and maybe she thought if she got a nice bit of money behind her . . . ? I don't know. Am I being silly?'

Philip had brought himself to tell his mother what had happened on the evening he had followed Cheryl, only to find his story not believed. Christine was aware that Cheryl pilfered from the members of her own family and had learned not to leave sums of money about the house unless she expected to lose them. But that she would steal from a shop was too much for her mother to digest. Philip only thought he had witnessed a theft. What he had really seen was Cheryl's retrieval of her own property that she had somehow left behind there earlier that day.

'It wasn't very nice of you to suspect your own sister of something like that.' This was the nearest she would ever get to a reproach and her tone was gentle rather than reproving.

Philip could tell there was no point in arguing. 'All right. Perhaps it wasn't. But if you know she steals from you, why does she?'

But Cheryl's purpose in stealing was beyond her. It was as if Christine's mind stopped short at the stealing itself, giving no thought to what Cheryl stole *for*. Philip's suggestion that it might be for drink or drugs made her stare. Drugs were something that happened to other people's children. Besides, she had seen Cheryl in the bath only two days before and there had been no needle marks on her thighs or upper arms.

'Are you sure you'd have noticed if there had been?'

Christine thought she would have. She would have known if Cheryl drank. While they were away on holiday other guests in the small private hotel they had stayed in had missed sums of money. The police had been called in but Cheryl hadn't even been questioned. Christine seemed to think this must imply her innocence. Stealing from one's own mother was different, hardly stealing at all really, one had a sort of half-right to it already.

'The unemployment benefit she gets doesn't amount to much, you know, Phil.' She was pleading for her duaghter with a kind of wide-eyed piteousness, as if Philip were determined on condemning her. 'I'll tell you what,' she said, 'I'll speak to my friend that's the social worker, the one who works with teenagers.'

That would be this Audrey. Inwardly Philip reproached himself for finding it hard to believe his mother could know anyone with that sort of job, counted among her friends someone in a responsible caring position. He said firmly. 'That might be a very good idea. And you can explain what I saw. I did see it and it *was* stealing. It isn't going to help anyone to pretend otherwise.'

That evening he had resolved to stay at home with her but Christine seemed anxious for him to go out. He could tell it wasn't just selflessness. She really wanted the house to herself. It made him wonder if Arnham had fulfilled his promise to phone her, if he had made a reappearance in her life and was due this evening. Philip smiled to himself when he thought of Arnham in this house, talking to Christine, perhaps telling her of his loss of Flora, while all the time the statue was upstairs, no more than a few feet above their heads.

Thinking like this made him look at Flora, standing there in the recesses of the cupboard. Senta's face looked out at him from the shadows and the way the soft vague evening sunlight fell on it gave the illusion of a smile. Philip couldn't resist putting out a finger to touch one cool marble cheek and then stroking it lightly with the back of his hand. Had he stolen Flora? Was he then as much a thief as Cheryl? Something, some unlooked-for intuition, brought him to Cheryl's bedroom door. He hadn't been into the room or even seen inside it since the day Fee had found the crumpled bridesmaid's dress lying on the wardrobe floor. Now he opened the door, surprised to find it unlocked, and stepped inside.

Three transistor radios, a portable television with a screen the size of a playing card, a tape player, two hairdryers, some kitchen thing, a food processor probably, other electrical equipment — it was all stacked on top of a chest of drawers and Philip knew at once it had been stolen. One of the radios still had a scarlet band of some sort of sticky tape round it. He wondered how she had managed to take these large bulky objects without being detected. Ingenuity born of despair and desperation, he thought. This store of stolen goods was like someone else's savings or investment, waiting to be turned into cash — for what?

His sister was a criminal but he couldn't see what there was to be done about it. A fatalistic acceptance was all that was possible now. Appealing to the police or the social services must lead to Cheryl's being charged with theft and because she was his sister, he couldn't give her away to some outside authority. He could only hope for the best, pin his faith to some help or advice coming from the social worker friend of Christine's. He closed the bedroom door behind him, somehow knowing he would never go in there again.

As soon as he got to Tarsus Street that evening he told Senta what he had seen. She looked at him. Most people, when they say they look into the eyes of another, in fact look into only one eye. Senta actually looked into both his eyes and because this always made her squint, gave her an expression of concentrated intensity. Her lips were parted a little, her clear green-flecked eyes very wide open with the pupils turned towards one another.

'It doesn't matter so long as she's not found out, does it?'

He tried laughing at her. 'That's not a very moral way of looking at things.'

She was deadly serious. She spoke pedantically. 'But we don't subscribe to conventional morality, Philip. After all, in that sort of morality the very worst thing anyone can do is kill someone. Don't you think you're being a hypocrite condemning poor Cheryl for a very trifling thing when you've done murder yourself?'

'I'm not condemning her,' he said for something to say, something to express because his thoughts were inexpressible: did she really believe he had killed John Crucifer while knowing her own confession was a fantasy? 'I only want to know what to do. What shall I do?'

He meant what should he do about Cheryl. Senta was indifferent, he could tell that, absorbed with herself and him. She was smiling.

'Come and live here with me.'

It had the effect she must have wanted and brought temporary forgetfulness of Cheryl. 'Do you mean that, Senta? In the top flat? Can we?'

'I thought you'd be pleased.'

'Of course I'm pleased. But you – you don't feel comfortable up there. I don't want you making yourself miserable for me.'

'Philip, I have to tell you something.' Again the bracing of his nerves, the tensing of muscles, as he awaited revelations. But quite suddenly he knew it would be all right, what she was going to say. And it was all right, it was more than that. 'I love you so much,' she said. 'I love you far far more than I ever thought I would when we first met. Isn't that funny? I knew I'd been looking for you and I'd found you but I didn't know I was capable of loving anyone the way I love you.'

He took her in his arms and held her close against him. 'Senta, you're my love, you're my angel.'

'So you see I couldn't feel uncomfortable anywhere with you. I couldn't be miserable when I'm with you. Wherever I am with you I'd be happy. I'm happy all the time I know you love me.' She put up her face and kissed him. 'I asked Rita about the flat and she said she didn't see why not. She says she wouldn't want rent. Of course that means she could throw us out when she wanted, we wouldn't have a proper tenancy.'

He was surprised at Senta's unusual practicality, her actually knowing about things like that. Then he understood what it also meant, that he would be able to go on paying Christine without continuing to live in her house. This might be his release from Christine and Cheryl and Glenallan Close, and an honourable release.

It was a long time now since he had even glanced at a newspaper. Newspapers he had avoided along with television and the radio, but had he avoided them because he was afraid of what he might see? He hardly knew what he meant by that himself. Surely not that if he knew a hunt was mounted for Joley's killer it would make him afraid?

Sometimes he imagined that his confession to Senta had been overheard, that there were people walking about the streets who had heard him admit to killing John Crucifer. He half-expected Christine to tell him the police had called or that they had been enquiring for him at head office. These things worried him for moments at a time and then he would come to himself and see what folly all this was, the stuff of nightmares and fantasies. But when he went to the warehouse at Uxbridge to search through the marble tops they had in stock in the hope of finding one which had no fissures anywhere in its veining, a motor-cycle policeman was outside. This man was only taking the name and particulars of some traffic offender but for a moment Philip experienced a gut fear that had nothing to do with reason.

The first thing he heard when he got in was that Roy was off sick 'with a bug' and that Mr Aldridge wanted to see him 'the minute he arrived if not sooner.' Mr Aldridge was the managing director of Roseberry Lawn.

Philip didn't feel nervous about it. He was sure he hadn't stepped out of line. He went up in the lift and Mr Aldridge's secretary, who sat by herself in the outer office, said to go straight in. He expected to be asked to sit down. By now he had some optimistic ideas that he might have been called there to be congratulated or even that promotion was coming.

Aldridge was seated but he let Philip stand on the other side of the desk. His glasses had slipped half-way down his nose and he looked rather sour. What he wanted to tell Philip was that Olivia Brett had complained about his behaviour, had described him as insufferably rude and insulting, and would Philip like to explain?

'What does she say I said?'

'You're getting this first hand, I hope you realise that. She phoned and spoke to me personally. Apparently, you made a disgusting remark, something lavatorial, about the shower she's having installed, and when she didn't laugh at this famous joke of yours you told her you were afraid you couldn't waste any more time on her, you had more important things to do.'

'It isn't true,' Philip said hotly. 'I thought, she led me to think – well, it doesn't matter what I thought. But she was the one who made the remark about the shower, not me.'

Aldridge said, 'I've always admired her. When I've seen her on TV I've always thought her one of our loveliest actresses, a real English lady. If you imagine I could for a moment credit that a beautiful and refined woman like her would make a cheap joke of that sort – and she brought herself to tell me explicitly exactly what was said, though I needn't repeat it – you're thicker than I take you for. Frankly, I don't think you're thick, I think you're devious and underhand. I don't think you've begun to understand the kind of unwavering courtesy and consideration to our customers which is the highest aim of Roseberry Lawn. Now you can go away and never, repeat never, give any lady or gentleman cause to make a complaint like that again.'

It upset him because he hadn't known that people can be as bad as that. He had never supposed that a successful, good-looking, famous and rich woman, with everything going for her, would take such a mean revenge on a man simply because that man had backed out of making love to her. It made him feel sick and sore. But there was no use in giving in to it. He got back into the car and drove to Uxbridge where, searching through twenty marble vanity unit tops encased in flat cardboard cartons, he at last found one that was free of fissures.

On his way back to London he bought an evening paper. He hadn't expected there to be anything in it about Joley's death and he was surprised to see a photograph of frogmen searching the Regent's Canal for the weapon police believed might have been used to kill John Crucifer.

'I've got the part, I've got the part,' she sang to him, rushing into his arms. 'I'm so happy, I've got the part!'

'What part is that?'

'I heard this morning. My agent phoned me. It's the part of the mad girl in *Impatience*.'

'You've got a part in a TV serial, Senta?'

'It's not the lead but it's more interesting than the lead. This is my really big chance. It's going to be in six episodes and I'm to be in every episode except the first one. The casting director said I'd got a fascinating face. Aren't you pleased for me, Philip, aren't you pleased?'

He simply didn't believe her. It was impossible for him to force a smile, simulate pleasure. For a while she didn't seem to notice. Upstairs in Rita's fridge she had a bottle of pink champagne.

'I'll fetch it,' he said.

Going up the stairs, making his way into Rita's dirty kitchen that smelt of sour dairy foods, he wondered what to do. Take a stand now, confront her, challenge her with her lies, or else live in her fantasy world, never deceived but playing up to the deceiver, for the rest of his life? He walked back into her room, set the bottle down and began the work of carefully freeing the wires from the cork. She held a glass out to catch the first gush of foam, exclaimed with delight as the cork popped.

'What toast shall we say? I know, we'll say: "To Senta Pelham, a great actor of the future!" '

He raised his glass. He had no choice but to repeat her words. 'To Senta Pelham, a great actor of the future!' In his own ears his voice rang very coldly.

'I'll be doing the read-through next Wednesday.'

'What's a read-through?'

'All the cast sits round a table and reads through the script. I mean you all read your own parts but without actually acting.'

'What's the name of the company that's making it?'

Her hesitation was brief but there was hesitation. 'Wardville Pictures.' She looked down at her hands and the glass of champagne held in both her hands on her lap. Her head fell forward like a flower on a stalk and the silver hair fell across her cheeks. 'The casting director's called Tina Wendover and their address is Berwick Street in Soho.'

She spoke calmly, coolly, as if replying somewhat defiantly to precise questions. It was as though he had challenged her. He was uncomfortably aware that she was able to read, at least up to a certain point, what went on in his mind. In saying they could read each other's thoughts she had been right in respect of herself. He looked at her and found that her eyes were on his. Once again she was playing that disconcerting trick of looking into both his eyes.

Was she inviting him to check up on her? Because she knew he wouldn't? Her fantasising would have been easier to accept, he thought, if she deceived herself, if she believed these tales of hers. The disquieting thing was that she didn't believe them and often didn't expect others to believe them either. She refilled their glasses. She said to him, still fixing him with her eyes, 'The police aren't very clever, are they? It's a dangerous world where a young girl can go up to someone in daylight, in the open, and kill him and no one know.'

Was she doing this to him because he so plainly disbelieved her first story? When she talked like this he had a sensation of a kind of internal falling, a dropping of the heart. He could find no words.

'I've wondered sometimes if Thiefie might have noticed me outside their house on those other mornings. I was careful but some people are very observant, aren't they? Suppose I went there again and Ebony knew me? He might smell me and start howling and then everyone would guess.'

Still he said nothing. She persisted.

'It was very early,' she said, 'but a lot of people did see me, a boy delivering newspapers and a woman with a baby in a buggy. And when I was in the train again I saw someone staring really hard at me. I think it was because the blood stains showed, though I was wearing red. I took my tunic to the launderette and washed it, so I don't know if there were any stains or not.'

He turned away from her and contemplated them both in the mirror. The only colour in the picture they made, subdued in the dim subfusc light, their clothes shadowy, their skin pallid and shimmering, was that of the wine, the pale bright rose pink that the green glass turned to blood red. His love for her, in spite of the things she said, in spite of everything, caught at him and seemed to wrench at the inside of his body. He could have groaned aloud for what they might have had if she hadn't persisted in flawing it.

'I'm not afraid of the police. It's not the first time anyway. I know I'm cleverer than they are. I know we're both too clever for them. But I have wondered. We both did those tremendous things and no one even suspected. I thought they might come and ask me about you and I suppose they might yet. You mustn't worry, Philip. You're quite safe with me, they'll never learn anything about your movements from me.'

He said, 'Let's not talk about it,' and put his arms round her.

The night was gloomy and overcast. To Philip it seemed curiously quiet, the traffic rumble very distant, the street empty. Perhaps that was only because he was later than usual in leaving Senta. It was past one.

He looked over the low wall as he came down the steps and saw that her shutters were open a crack. He had meant to close them before he left. But no one in the street could have seen her, sleeping naked on the big mirrored bed. Her self-appointed guardian, he put it to the test and satisfied himself, peering over railings into the gloom. What had she meant, 'not the first time'? He hadn't asked her because what she said had taken a while to sink in. It surfaced starkly now. Had she meant there had been a previous occasion when the police had reason to suspect her of some terrible thing?

The lamplight, dim and greenish, and the thin hanging mist created an underwater look as of a drowned town, the houses reef-like, the trees branched seaweed stret-ching upwards through the cloudy darkness to some invisible light. Philip found himself walking carefully to the car, keeping his footfalls soft, so as not to disturb the heavy unusual silence. It was not until he had started the car – a shockingly loud noise, the engine springing into life with a lion's roar – and turned the corner into Caesarea Grove, that he noticed the leaflet someone had stuck under his windscreen wipers while he was in Senta's house. The wipers, switched on to clear the mist, dragged shreds of paper across the wet screen. Philip pulled in, stopped and got out.

He crushed the wet paper into a ball. It had been an advertisement for a carpet sale. A droplet of icy water from one of the churchyard trees fell on to his neck and made him jump. It was dark in there with a kind of cold clammy steaminess. Philip put his hand on the gate. The rusty ironwork was wet to the touch. He felt a colder trickle on the back of his neck than the drop of water had made, a shiver that fingered all the way down his spine.

A single candle was burning on one of the steps that led up to the porch on the side of the church. He drew a long breath. The gate opened with a creak that was like a human groan. He took a few steps on the stones, the drenched grass, led by the bluish aureole, the yellow ring, that encircled the flame.

There was someone lying on a bed of blankets and rags inside the porch. Joley's face reared up like a ghost's and revealed itself in the candlelight.

17

He hated doing it. Deviousness was alien to his nature. The idea of pretending to be someone else, of telling a false story to gain information, all that was so distasteful as to make him feel an actual physical sickness at the thought of it. He had postponed doing it for four days. Now, alone in Roy's room with Roy out at lunch and the secretary doing Mr Aldridge's letters because his secretary was off sick, an opportunity presented itself which he would be cowardly to refuse.

Encountering Joley was the event which made this act imperative. For some reason, though now he could hardly imagine what reason, he had utterly believed Senta when she told him Joley and the murdered man John Crucifer were one. He had believed her and been brought to feel terrible things, almost that Joley's death was somehow his fault; if not quite that he had murdered him, that but for his own existence and presence there, Joley would still be alive.

Joley was alive. His month-long absence was due to his having been in hospital. Philip had never considered vagrants leading lives which in any way approximated to those led by more conventional humanity, that they might have doctors, for instance, that they might sometimes penetrate when in need the world of the respectable house-dwelling classes.

'I been having me prostrate done,' Joley had said, welcoming him round the hearth the candle made and offering him a cushion of a scarlet Tesco bag stuffed with newspapers. 'In my mode of living, as you might say, it's not desirable having an urgent need to pee every ten minutes. Mind you, I was going bonkers in that hospital.'

'Always washing you, were they?'

'It wasn't that, governor. It wasn't so much that as the doors. It's doors being shut what I can't stomach. We was six in this room like, five others and me, and it's OK by day but come the night they shuts the door. I sweat like a pig when the door's shut. Then I had to go convalescent. I had to, they forced me. You're not going straight out of here back on the streets, they said. Made me sound like a whore, I should be so lucky.'

Philip gave him a five-pound note.

'Many thanks, governor. You're a gentleman.'

Since then he had seen Joley twice more. He had said nothing about any of this to Senta. What was there to say? All he could have done was reproach her once more for lying to him. Besides, she might genuinely have believed John Crucifer was Joley. Now, in the office, he gave directory enquiries the address of Wardville Pictures and was surprised when they came up with an actual phone number. Bracing himself, taking a deep breath, he dialled.

'May I speak to Tina Wendover?'

The voice said, 'She's at a read-through. Who is it speaking?'

Philip was very taken aback. Senta had said there would be a read-through of *Impatience* on Wednesday and today was Wednesday. He gave his own name.

'Would you like to speak to her assistant?'

He said he would and when he was put through said, in a reluctant mumble, that he was speaking on behalf of Senta Pelham's agent. He understood that Senta had been offered a part in *Impatience*.

'Yes, that's right.' She sounded astonished at his enquiry, surprised that he was in doubt, said suspiciously, 'Who exactly is that?'

Feeling guilty at once because he had doubted her, he was astonished just the same. This confirmation of what she had told him restored her to him in a new light. Not

242

as a new person, but as a fuller, rarer Senta, cleverer, more sophisticated and accomplished than he had ever supposed. Even at this moment she would be at the read-through. He hardly knew what would be happening at this preliminary gathering of the cast of a television serial, but he imagined actors and actresses, some of them famous faces, sitting round a long table with their scripts in front of them, reading their parts. And Senta was among them, one of them, knowing the correct way to behave, the proper procedures to follow. He imagined her in her long black skirt perhaps and the silvery-grey top, the silver hair spread over her shoulders, with Donald Sinden on one side of her and Miranda Richardson on the other. Philip had no idea if this actor and actress had parts in the serial but theirs were the faces which came into his mind.

She was suddenly more real to him, more of an active responsible human being who lived in the world, than she had ever been before. He understood that because of this, he loved her more. His fears receded. They seemed neurotic suspicions, borne of his ignorance of people like her and the world of dreams and imagination they must necessarily inhabit because of their art. So much that made up their lives was unreal, or unreal to ordinary people like himself. Was it any wonder they saw the truth, not as the cut-and-dried thing which was how it presented itself to him, but vague and blurred at the edges, open to numberless imaginative interpretations?

When he reached home that evening he heard voices from the living room, Christine's and a man's. He opened the door and saw that the visitor was Gerard Arnham.

Arnham, apparently, had phoned Christine on the very day he and Philip had encountered each other. Christine had said nothing about it. His mother could also be secretive, Philip was beginning to discover. She was looking pretty and young and might easily have been taken for Fee's elder sister. Her hair was newly blonded and newly set and Philip had to admit that she wasn't, after all, a bad hairdresser. She had a pale blue dress on with white spots, a dress of the kind, he somehow recognised, that men always like and women often don't, with a full skirt and a tight waist and a low-cut square neck.

Arnham jumped up. 'How are you, Philip? We're on our way out to dinner. I just thought I'd like to wait and see you.'

Shaking hands, Philip thought immediately about the woman who had come out of their house and accused him of driving too fast. He would have to warn Christine of the existence of this woman and he disliked the prospect. It need not, however, indeed could not, be undertaken at this moment. He thought too of the presence upstairs, inside his wardrobe, of Flora.

'We could all have a glass of sherry, Phil,' Christine said, as if this were a very daring thing to do.

Philip fetched the sherry and the glasses and they made conversation rather uneasily, talking of nothing much. Before Philip came in Arnham had apparently been giving Christine some sort of account of his move from his former home and the circumstances in which he had found his present house. He reverted to this, going into close details, while Christine listened avidly. Philip didn't pay this much attention. He found himself speculating once again as to the prospect of Arnham as a husband for Christine. It occurred to him that the woman who had come running out at the sound of his brakes had looked unhappy. Hadn't they been getting on, he and she? Were they on the point of parting?

He watched them go down the path, giving Christine a little wave from the window in response to her own. Arnham's car was parked on the other side of the street, which was why he hadn't noticed it when he came in.

He handed Christine into it in a courtly old-fashioned way, making Philip feel that if it hadn't been a warm sultry summer evening he would have tucked a rug round her knees. Impossible now to keep from imagining Christine as Mrs Arnham and living in the house in Chigwell with the may tree in the garden. Perhaps the woman he had seen was Arnham's sister or his housekeeper.

He would be free to go. There would be no bar to his moving into the top flat in Tarsus Street with Senta. He thought about this as a likelihood, not an impossible dream, as he drove down Shoot-up Hill. Cheryl would naturally go with Christine, it would be the best thing that could happen to Cheryl, to have two parents again, to have a more attractive place to live in. He was aware that he had thought along these lines before, when Christine had first known Arnham, but things had been different then, that had been before Senta.

Joley was outside on the pavement, resting on his barrow in the warm sunshine like an old dog. Philip raised his arm to him in a salute and Joley made the thumbs-up sign. A heat wave was coming, you could feel it in the air, in the calmness of the evening, the steady dark gold of the sunset light. And Philip felt, as he let himself into the house and heard from the front room the sound of a waltz, that things had returned to what they once were, had come full circle, been restored to an earlier perfection. No, more than that – a new perfection that was the result of trial and error and subsequent full knowledge. Down there Senta awaited him, his honourable truthful day-dreaming love. Christine had got Arnham back. Joley was at his post. The weather would once more be glorious.

The heat was terrible and wonderful. It would have been desirable at the seaside where Philip wished again and again he and Senta might be. In London it brought with it drought and smells and sweat. But Senta's basement room grew cool. In the ordinary warm weather it had been stuffy, in the cold very cold. Now she opened windows he hardly knew existed at the back of the house and let a draught blow through the cluttered subterranean rooms.

It was an outdoor time when London briefly became a European city with pavement cafés. Philip wanted to spend their evenings in the open air. As much as anything he liked being seen with her, he liked the envy of other men. To walk about Hampstead or Highgate holding hands with Senta among the crowds of other young people seemed to him the most inviting way to pass their evenings - with of course the prospect of an early return to Tarsus Street. And although perhaps it was true that she preferred to stay in, she consented.

On the fourth day of the heat wave, when the weather showed no signs of breaking, he drove to Chigwell in the afternoon. Mrs Ripple's new marble slab had arrived, a perfect one as far as Philip could see, too smooth and flawless to seem like the real thing. He decided to take it to her himself, ask for her approval and give her his personal undertaking that a fitter would come in to instal it that same week. It was Monday.

He and Senta had been tremendously happy during the weekend. Without of course telling her he had checked up on her, he congratulated her on her part in *Impatience* and he could tell how much she loved his praise and how happy she was to answer his rather naïve questions. She showed him how she meant to act her part, altering her voice quite subtly and changing her facial expression so that she became, briefly and alarmingly, a different person. She seemed to know most of her lines already. He anticipated the pride he was going to feel when he actually saw her on screen. His emotion was powerful and he felt almost choked by it.

They were together from the Friday night until this

morning. On Saturday there had been some talk of going up to the top floor and making a start on cleaning the flat, preparing it for their occupancy which now might not be long delayed. But it was too hot. Both agreed there would be time enough for that when the weather got cool again. Their work on the flat could wait until the following Friday.

There must have been thousands of other people about in that heat, in those sunlit streets, but he hardly saw them. They were shadows or ghosts, scarcely real. They were there only to make Senta, by contrast, more real, more beautiful, more his own. Any misunderstandings were over, arguments past, quarrels forgotten, talk of death and violence melted away by the sun and the leisurely sensuous pace of life. They ate their meals in pub gardens or on the grass of the Heath, they drank a lot of wine. Hand in hand, they meandered back to the car, back to Tarsus Street, white and dusty and brittle with heat, and to bed in the underground cool. He had begun to feel he was curing her of her agoraphobia. Very little persuasion had been needed to get her out into the open air, the sunny noons and the sweet warm night-times.

'Just think,' she had said to him, 'in a week's time we may be together all the time.'

'Well, perhaps not a week, but very soon.'

'We won't put it off, we'll get started on Friday. Maybe we could move the bed up, that would be a start. I'll ask Rita to make that horrible Mike help us, shall I? There's just one thing I want you to help me with first but it won't take long and then we'll really begin thinking how we're going to arrange our flat. I'm so happy, Philip, I've never been so happy in all my life!'

Throughout that weekend she had never once fantasised. Not a tall story of the past or present had been offered him. A kind of exorcism had taken place, he thought. She was purged of the need to alter truth. How could he avoid the perhaps conceited belief that it was her love for him and his for her that had changed her? Reality had become adequate.

Grounded in a traffic jam on the way to Chigwell, he thought tenderly of Senta. He had left her lying in bed, the shutters half-closed, a breeze of early morning that would later die, airing the room, blowing from open window to open window. Sunlight fell across the bedlinen in bands but avoided her face, her eyes. He had seen to that. She had awakened for a little while and put up her arms to him. It had been more of a wrench even than usual to leave her and she knowing it, had held on to him, kissing him, whispering to him not to go yet, not yet.

There was such a long tail-back of cars on the approaches to the A12 that Philip briefly thought it might be wiser to turn back when the opportunity of doing so came. Afterwards he was to wonder what sort of a difference to his life it would have made had he done so. Not much probably. Happiness would have endured for a few more days, along with the heat and the sunshine, but it would soon have passed. In the nature of things there could be no escape for him and her, not now. If he had turned back all that would have happened was that the bubble of illusion and self-deception and mysterious false assumptions would have been broken later and not that afternoon.

He didn't turn back. His shirt was wet with sweat and sticking to the back of the seat. A car somewhere ahead of him, half a mile ahead for all he knew, had overheated and its radiator boiled. It was this breakdown which was causing the delay. He was glad he hadn't given Mrs Ripple a definite time, only said something about the middle of the afternoon, which by its vagueness had raised another of her reprimands.

Twenty minutes later he was past the stranded car with steam coming from its raised bonnet that blocked the inside lane. The marble slab fell off the back seat as he turned the corner into Mrs Ripple's road and he had a momentary panic lest it was cracked. Finding it intact when he was finally parked outside the house made a fresh surge of sweat break over him. The tar was melting on the roadway and on the camber, in the hard bright light, mirages of sheets of water danced. Lawns were yellowing, drying up. He hauled the marble slab in its cardboard container out of the back of the car.

Mrs Ripple's front door opened as he came up to the gate and a woman came out with a black Scottie dog on a lead. She paused on the step as people do who spin out their leave-taking. It was Gerard Arnham's woman, wife, sister, housekeeper, whatever she was. Inside the house were Mrs Ripple, and visible behind her, Pearl of the black curly hair and shiny peacock-blue dress. Only today the dress was flame-pink and sleeveless and Mrs Ripple herself wore a flimsy garment with narrow straps which showed sunburnt shoulders and scrawny arms.

Philip didn't know why the sight of the woman with the dog caused him such a shock. He was staggered by her. His grasp on the topmost bar of the gate had tightened until the metal dug into his flesh. The weight of the package he carried suddenly reminded him of another marble object he had once lugged about on a warm day, Flora that he had carried to Arnham's house when he lived in Buckhurst Hill.

Arnham's woman came down the path towards him, the dog sniffing at his ankles. She didn't seem to recognise him. Her hawk-like face was strained, the eye sockets dark, the forehead deeply lined. She looked as if the heat had dried her out, actually physically depleted her. She passed him, staring trance-like ahead of her. Philip stared at her, he couldn't help it. He looked back and watched her go out of the gate and turn, blindly it seemed, up along the street.

Mrs Ripple said, 'Here you are then.' It was the mildest

greeting he had ever received from her. Pearl achieved a smile without parting her bright red greasy lips.

Mechanically he began opening the cardboard carton and easing out the slab on to the cushions of Mrs Ripple's settee. The dog was what had shocked him, he realised, the presence of the dog, the *kind* of dog. He wanted to ask Mrs Ripple who the woman was, yet he already knew who she was. He knew who she was and he knew who the dog was. They were Thiefie and Ebony.

'Well, I suppose that's an improvement,' Mrs Ripple was saying.

Pearl ran a red-nailed finger over the surface of the marble. 'At least you won't get soap and goodness knows what else trapped in the cracks. Imagine with that other one, the gunge that would have built up. I mean it doesn't bear thinking of.'

'They don't think of it, Pearl. They're men who design them, you see. We'd see some changes if it was women who had a say in it.'

Philip would have liked to tell her that in fact this particular series of vanity units had all been designed by woman. Once, that is, he would have liked to tell her. Now his mind had curiously blanked, emptied but for the presence in it of a small black Scottie dog that Senta had named Ebony and heard whimpering as its master died.

'Well, if you're happy with it,' he heard himself saying, 'I'll take it upstairs for you. The fitter will be along before the end of the week.'

'Have you noticed, Pearl, how it's always the same with these people? The beginning of the week is Wednesday morning but "before the end of the week" is late Friday afternoon.'

He scarcely heard her. He carried the marble slab up the staircase, very much aware of its weight, aware of it as a man three times his age might be. Inside the new bathroom he crossed to the window, now fussily cluttered with floral Austrian blinds, and gazed at the back of Arnham's house. The may tree, which when he first saw it had been festooned with blossoms, now bore a harvest of berries changing from green to russet colour. Beneath stood the figure of Cupid with his bow and quiver which had replaced Flora. But he noticed something else about that garden which struck him hollowly. No one had tended it for weeks. No one had mown the lawn or pulled out a weed or trimmed off a dead head. Rank grass grew six inches high with yellow and white flowering weeds among it.

The little black dog came running into the garden from round the side of the house. It disappeared into the tall grass as a wild animal disappears into the bush. Ebony, he thought, Ebony. Philip turned away and came out on to the landing. Sick though he felt, panic-stricken in some fearful unanalysable way, he had to know the truth. If necessary he would have to ask. In his present state of near-certainty which is still uncertainty, it would be unthinkable to leave here and drive home, to carry with him a doubt that would gnaw like a rat. He could feel in anticipation (through experience) the pain of it.

He didn't have to ask. He stood on the landing, holding on to the railing at the head of the stairs, listening to their voices. The door into the living room was open and he heard Mrs Ripple say, 'You know who that was?'

'Who what was?'

'The woman with the dog who came in to ask if I knew anyone who'd help her with the garden.'

'I didn't catch the name.'

'Myerson's her name. Myerson. Mark you, I don't like dogs in the house, I wouldn't have had it if it was anyone else, but I couldn't very well say anything in the circumstances. I'm surprised the name didn't ring a bell with you. It was her husband that was murdered — when would it have been? A month ago? Five weeks?'

'Murdered?' said Pearl. 'What was the name again?'

'Harold. Harold Myerson.'

'You may have mentioned it in your letter. I never read those things in the paper, I avoid those things. I may be a coward but I can't bear things like that.'

'He was murdered in Hainault Forest,' said Mrs Ripple. 'It was on a Sunday morning, a beautiful sunny morning. He was stabbed in the heart while he was out with that dog.'

18

She sat on the bed and he sat in the wicker chair. The window had been open but he had closed it out of fear. There was the room they were in and the looking-glass country, greenish, watery, clouded, a land of swamps, of that room reflected in the tilted mirror.

'I told you I killed him, Philip,' she said. 'I told you over and over I stabbed him with my glass dagger.'

He couldn't speak. It had been as much as he could do to articulate the words that demanded the truth from her. She was calmer and more reasonable, even gently amused, than he had ever known her.

'I see now that I must have killed the wrong man. But you did tell me over and over that Gerard Arnham lived there? You showed me the house. We drove past and you pointed to it and you said, that's where Gerard Arnham lives. I think you have to admit, Philip, that it was you who made the mistake, not me.'

She spoke as if his contention was only that she had picked the wrong victim. She might have been mildly reproving him for being late for an engagement. Philip had dropped his head into his hands. He sat there feeling the sweat form between his fingertips and the hot pulsing skin of his forehead. Her hand on his arm, the touch of her little child's hand, made him jump and flinch. It was like a lighted match brought close against bare flesh.

'It doesn't really matter, Philip,' he heard her say. He heard her voice soft and sweetly reasonable. 'It doesn't really matter who I killed. The point was to kill someone to prove my love for you. I mean – if you don't mind my saying this – it wasn't the old down-and-out, what's he called, Joley, that you killed, was it? You made a mistake there as well. But we did do it.' The sound she made was a soft rueful giggle. 'Next time,' she said, 'I expect we'd be better at it, we'd be more careful.'

He had jumped up and was on her before he realised what was happening. Her shoulders were in his hands, grasped with the nails digging in, and he was crashing her body up and down on the bed, pounding the frailness of her into the mattress, the flimsy ribcage, the bird's bones. She didn't fight him. She yielded to his violence, moaning a little. When he began to strike her she covered her face with her hands.

The sight of the ring he had given her, the silver and the milky stone, stopped him. That and her face, so feebly protected, cowering from his flailing hands seemed to paralyse him in mid-onslaught. He had been the man who hated violence, who couldn't imagine himself performing any brutish act. Even talking about it had offended him. Even thinking of it had seemed a source of corruption.

Upstairs the 'Great Waltz' from *Rosenkavalier* sent its sweet painful strains down through the ceiling. Disgusted with himself, he fell across the bed. He lay in a state of shock, unable to think, wanting to die.

Presently he was aware she had sat up. She was wiping her eyes with her fingers. Somehow his blows had cut her face, there was a trace of blood on one cheekbone. It was while she had been protecting her face with her hands that the moonstone ring had been pressed into the skin. Blood got on to her fingertip and she flinched when she saw it. She crouched on all-fours, looking into the mirror at the scratch on her face.

'I'm sorry I hit you,' he said. 'I went mad.'

'That's all right,' she said. 'It doesn't matter.'

'It does. I shouldn't have hit you.'

'You can hit me if you want. You can do what you like with me. I love you.'

He was stunned by her. His shock was so immense as

to have bludgeoned him into a kind of unconsciousness. He could only look helplessly at her and hear those words, uttered in an impossible context. Her face was soft with love, as if the features had begun to melt. The blood marred a silvery-white perfection, made her human. All too human.

"It was all true then?" he managed to say.

She nodded. She seemed surprised, but in a simple childlike way. 'Oh, yes, it was all true. Of course it was.'

'The part about following him and going up to him and saying you had something in your eye – that was true?' He could hardly say the words but he said them: 'And stabbing him – that was true?'

'I told you. Of course it was true. I didn't know you doubted me, Philip, I thought you trusted me.'

In a fever of fear and disbelief and panic, he had driven straight to her from Chigwell. He had neither returned to head office nor gone home, so it had been quite early when he arrived. And for once, for the first time perhaps, she had seen him arriving from the basement window. Her smile had died when she saw his face.

He had brought no wine, no food. It was the end of his world, or so he had felt when he pounded down the basement stairs. He would never eat or drink again. It was she who said after she had answered all his questions and confirmed it all, when he had no more words. 'Shall we have some wine? I should like to. Would you go out and get some, Philip?'

Out in the street he was a hunted person. It was a new feeling. On the way here he had been frightened but afraid only of what she might tell him, of what her looks and her words would confirm. Now he knew for sure, he felt pursued. Before the weekend he had reached a point at which he believed almost nothing she told him until it was confirmed by outside authority, he had nearly come to switch off belief when she began spinning a narrative. That authority had confirmed her part in the television serial and he had been happy, had been relieved. It was strange that now, when she recounted the most incredible things she had ever told him, he believed her utterly. There was no doubting any more.

He bought two bottles of cheap white wine. Even before he was back in her room he knew he couldn't face drinking any of it. He must keep his head clear. Oblivion was not for him, still less the sloppy euphoric fuzzy state they sometimes reached, when sex was slipped into like the dreams that come at dawn, as easily found and as dazedly yielded to. As he came back to the room, passing from the dusty heat of upstairs to the cool dimness below, the facts, the truth, slammed back at him once more, the reality that she had murdered in cold blood a defenceless stranger and he whispered to himself in incredulity, 'It can't be, it can't be . . .'

She began drinking the wine greedily. He carried his glassful with him out to the tap, poured it away, refilled the glass with water. In those smoky green glasses you couldn't tell whether the contents were wine or water. She put out her hand to him. 'Stay the night with me. Don't go home tonight.'

He looked at her in despair. He spoke his thoughts aloud. 'I don't think I could go home. I feel as if I couldn't leave this room, I couldn't see other people. I can only be with you. You've made it impossible for me to associate with others.'

This seemed to please her. He even had the momentary feeling that this had been her whole purpose, to set the two of them apart, to make them unfit for other company. He saw the madness in her face again, in the unfocused gaze, the sublime indifference to all that perplexes and horrifies humanity. It was Flora's face. That look had been on the marble features when he had seen her a lifetime ago lying in the flowerbed in Arnham's garden. This time he didn't try, as he had tried once before, to dispel from his own mind the notion of her madness. If she was mad she couldn't help herself. If she was mad she was helplessly unable to control what she did.

He took her in his arms. It was horrible, there was no pleasure in holding her like this. It was like holding some decaying drowned thing or a sack of garbage. He almost retched. And then pity came, for her and for himself, and he began to cry with his face on her shoulder and his lips pressed into her neck.

She stroked his hair. She whispered to him, 'Poor Philip, poor Philip, don't be sad, you mustn't be sad . . .'

He was alone in the house. He sat in the window of the living room, watching the light fade in the street. Glenallan Close, in a sunset like this one, bathed in pale red light, windless and basking, was as beautiful as it could ever be.

It had been a night and a day of almost continuous unrelieved suffering, incredible to look back on, beyond belief that two people had been able to bear it. Of course there had been no question of his going to work. After that sleepless night, those long crawling hours in which she had dozed and awakened by turns, had begged him to make love to her, once gone down on her knees to him with infinite pathos, and still he had failed – after all that he had gone up to the phone in the hall at eight in the morning and phoned Roy at home. He had no need to simulate a hoarse voice, a dry throat, an almost communicable weariness. All that was there already, as a result of those dreadful hours.

And with the coming of the sun it had begun again. No doors or windows had been opened the night before and the heat grew like an oven warming. Senta, who had slept till he came back, awoke and began crying. He wanted to hit her again then, to stop that meaningless pointless moaning. To keep himself from striking her he clutched his hands together. Violence that had been alien to him he was learning. He was learning that we are all capable of almost anything.

'You must stop,' he said. 'You must stop crying. We have to talk. We have to decide what to do.'

'What is there to do if you won't love me?'

Her face was sodden with weeping as if the skin had blotted up the tears. Wet strands of hair stuck to her face.

'Senta, you must tell me.' A thought struck him. 'Tell me the truth now. You have to tell me only the truth from now on.'

She nodded. He felt she was placating him, agreeing in order to avoid more trouble. Her eyes had become wary, greener and sharper, within their swollen lids.

'What did you mean when you said it wasn't the first time? You told me when you were talking about the police that this wasn't the first time. What did you mean?'

There was a pause while her eyes shifted, looked into the mirror, back at him. She spoke so innocently, in a way calculated to disarm.

'I mean I killed someone else once. I had this boy friend called Martin, Martin Hunt – I did tell you that. I did tell you there was someone before you. I thought he was the one. It was before I ever saw you. Long before we met. You don't mind, do you, Philip? You don't mind? If I'd known I'd never have gone near him, I'd never have spoken to him if I'd known I was going to meet you.'

He shook his head. It was a feeble ineffectual protest at something he didn't understand but which he knew was monstrous. 'What about him?'

Instead of replying, she said, creeping close to him but receiving no welcome, no warmth, 'You are going to protect me and save me and go on loving me, aren't you? Aren't you?'

It terrified him because he didn't know the answer. He didn't know what to say. He didn't know what he was more afraid of, the law and the power of it out there, or of her. It was important to him, as a man, to be afraid of neither. He forced himself to put his arms round her and hold her.

'I was jealous,' she said, her voice muffled. 'If you ever found another girl I'd kill her, Philip. I wouldn't harm you but I'd kill her.'

She had told him nothing but he lacked the heart to persist. He had held her in a mechanical way, his arm becoming a clamp strong enough to support another human being in its hinged angle. It was rather like the way in which he had carried Flora to Arnham's house. She felt as heavy and lifeless as stone.

Later he went out and bought food. He had made coffee and got her to drink some. They heard footsteps upstairs and the front door slam and when Philip looked out of the window, up at the pavement, he saw Rita and Jacopo going off towards the tube station with suitcases. In the afternoon Senta went upstairs and when she came back said she had taken two of Rita's sleeping tablets. Philip made sure there wasn't any wine in the room and as soon as she was asleep he left her. She would sleep for hours and he would come back in the night.

Someone had scored a deep scratch along the nearside doors of his car. It looked as if done with the rusty nail which the perpetrator had left on the bonnet. Joley wasn't outside nor in Caesarea Grove but bringing up the rear of the queue at the Mother Teresa food centre in Tyre Street. Philip nodded to him but didn't smile or wave. He was finding that deep shock and preoccupation with some huge and terrible event paralyses movement, turns the body in on itself, awfully concentrating the mind. He doubted whether he ought to be driving. He was no more fit to drive than if he had been drinking.

The house in Glenallan Close was empty but for

Hardy. The little dog made a great fuss of him, jumping up and licking his hands. Philip found sliced bread in the bread bin, coleslaw and ham sausage in the fridge, rejected all of it. Eating might be resumed one day when he no longer felt a blockage in his throat like a jammed trapdoor. He stood inside the living-room window, watching the aftermath of sunset, seeing the serene red-washed pearly sky as unreal, the backdrop of a different world from that in which such things happened. A deep longing filled him that it might not be true, he might have imagined or dreamt it, he might wake up.

The car slid into his vision, stopped outside the house. He thought, absurdly: the police. It was Arnham's Jaguar. Arnham and Christine got out of it, she with a bunch of flowers in one hand and a basket of what looked like raspberries in the other. Hardy heard Christine coming and ran out to the door.

She had caught the sun. There was a glow on her skin. 'We've been for a picnic,' she said. 'Gerard took the day off and we had this picnic in Epping Forest. It was ever so nice, like real country.'

A different world. He wondered if his face expressed the despair he felt. Arnham had a deep tan which made him look even more Italian or Greek. The white shirt he wore was open nearly to the waist, like a young man's, and he had jeans on. 'How are you, Philip? You've been in the wrong place today, I can tell you.'

From now on, he would always be in the wrong place. He said, not even trying to frame the words courteously, 'Where do you live now?'

'Still in Buckhurst Hill, but on the other side of the High Road. I didn't move far.'

Christine, who had fetched a vase full of water and was arranging her carnations in it, said in that innocent, charming, unthinking way of hers, 'Yes, Philip, I wanted so much to see Gerard's house. We were so near, really. I suppose I'm nosy but I do love to see a new home.

260

Gerard wouldn't take me there, he said it wasn't fit for me to see. He'd have to give it a good clean before I'd be allowed to set foot inside.'

Philip hesitated, then said coldly, 'I suppose the truth is you didn't want her to see you'd got rid of Flora.'

There was silence. Arnham went very red. The shot had gone accurately home. Philip hadn't actually believed this was the reason for Arnham's unwillingness to take Christine to his house but now he saw he had been right. Holding four or five of the carnations in one hand, holding them out very much in Flora's own attitude, Christine turned to look wonderingly at Arnham.

'Did you, Gerard? You didn't get rid of Flora really, did you?'

'I'm sorry,' Arnham said. 'I'm desperately sorry. I didn't want you to know. He's right when he says that's why I didn't want to take you home. I've got a small garden and you'd have been bound to ask. I'm sorry.'

'If you didn't like her I wish you'd said.' Philip wouldn't have imagined Christine could be so upset. 'I'd much rather you'd said and we could have taken her back again.'

'Christine, believe me, I did want her, I did like her. Please don't look like that.'

'Yes, I know I'm being very silly and very childish, but this has spoilt my day.'

'He sold her to some people in Chigwell.' Philip could never remember having been really vindictive before. It was a new, bitter flavour, sharp and satisfying in his mouth. 'Ask him if he didn't sell her to some people in Chigwell called Myerson.'

'I didn't sell her!'

'Gave her, then.'

'It wasn't like that. It was an accident. I went off to America, as you know, and I was there a month and they had the auction of the house and the contents while I was away. The statue shouldn't have been included, I left

261

instructions it shouldn't be sold, but there was a mix-up and it was sold.' Arnham was looking angrily at Philip 'I was aghast when I found out. I did my best to get it back and I did trace it to the dealer who had bought it Only by that time he had sold it to a buyer who paid cash.

'As a matter of fact, that was why I didn't get in touch with you, Christine. I may as well tell you the whole of it. I'd as soon your son wasn't hearing all this but since he's here . . .'

Once Philip would have left the room but now he didn't see why he should. He stood his ground.

'I wanted to see you,' Arnham said. 'I wanted to see you very much but I couldn't face telling you about Flora. I absolutely funked it. For a while I thought I'd be able to get her back, and when I couldn't and I'd moved into my new house and months had gone by, I thought I can't phone her now, it's too late, it's ridiculous. Apart from the fact that I felt I still couldn't explain about the statue. When I met your son in Baker Street that day I realised how much I'd - I'd missed you.' A look of brooding resentment was levelled at Philip. Arnham's heavy Latin face had taken on a purplish flush. 'I wanted to see you,' he said to Christine, his tone becoming reproachful. 'I wanted to get in touch and I did but I was worried all the time about the statue. I thought I'd have to tell you it had got broken or — or stolen.'

Philip gave a low unamused laugh. His mother had got up, lifted the vase of carnations and set it on the window-sill. She pulled at the flowers a bit, trying to make the arrangement symmetrical. She didn't speak. Hardy jumped off the chair he had been sitting on and trotted over to Arnham, his kind cheerful muzzle uplifted and twitching and his tail beginning to wag. Philip noted, as one might observe some fact confirmed beyond a doubt, Arnham's instinctive recoil. Then he put out a hand to touch Hardy's head, a sop, no doubt, to Christine.

She turned to face Arnham. Philip expected her to begin uttering reproaches, though this would have been very unlike her. But she only smiled and said, 'Well, that's over. I hope you feel it's cleared the air. Now I'll make us all some tea.'

'You're going to let me take you out to dinner, Christine?'

'I don't think so. It's rather late for that, I'm not used to eating so late and you've a long drive ahead of you. I'm afraid I didn't realise until today,' she said in a bright conversational way, 'what a very long drive it is.'

Philip left them and went upstairs. He had to return to Senta, yet there was nothing he wanted to do less. If anyone had told him two days before that there would come a time, and soon, when he wouldn't want to see her, when he would recoil from seeing her, he would have dismissed this with derision. Now he felt as he once had, very long ago, when a little child and his cat had become ill. He had loved the cat, which the Wardmans had acquired as a mature animal, a stray, had named Smoky for its black and grey brindled coat, and had transformed with care and good food into a beautiful sleek creature.

Smoky had slept on Philip's bed. He lay in Philip's lap in the evening while Philip did his homework. He was very much Philip's cat, petted and pampered and almost hourly caressed. Then, as he grew old, he became ill. Years and years had passed and Smoky was probably fourteen or fifteen. His teeth were bad and his breath smelt, his fur fell out and bald patches appeared on his coat, he stopped washing. And Philip lost his affection for him. He ceased to love him. He pretended to care still but it was a poor pretence. Awful though his guilt was, he came to avoid poor Smoky and his basket in the corner of the kitchen, and when his parents, fearful of telling him, at last made themselves suggest to him that

Smoky should out of kindness be put to sleep, he was relieved, a load was lifted from him.

Had he then loved the cat only for his beauty? Had he loved Senta only for her beauty? And what he thought of as the beauty of her mind, her self, her soul if you like? Now he knew that those areas of her being were not beautiful but ill, foul, sick, distorted. They were evil and they stank. Because of this, had he ceased to love her? It wasn't as simple as that. It wasn't simply that he flinched from her madness either, more that the person he had loved was imaginary, not the strange little wild animal with a twisted human brain that awaited him in Tarsus Street.

He opened his clothes cupboard and looked at Flora standing in the dimness within, her face framed between a pair of tweed trousers and the raincoat he had bought to replace the stolen one. The curious thing was that she no longer resembled Senta. Perhaps she never had and the likeness lay in his all too willing imagination. Her stone face looked blind and bland, the eyes empty of expression. She wasn't even a she but an it, a thing made of marble, perhaps not even modelled from the life, the work of an indifferent sculptor. He lifted her out, laid her on the bed. The idea came to him to replace her in the garden before he went out. There could be no reason not to do this now that he knew Arnham had parted from her long ago, now that Christine knew it all, now that Myerson who had owned her was dead. He carried her downstairs.

Gerard Arnham was leaving. The front door was open and Christine was down at the gate watching as he got into the Jaguar. Philip took Flora into the back garden and set her up in her old position beside the birdbath. Had she always looked so tawdry, so scruffy? The green stain which disfigured her bosom and the folds of her robe, the chip out of her ear, and new hitherto unnoticed damage, a may flower missing from the bouquet, changed her into a fitting ornament for a ruin. He turned away and, looking back, saw that a sparrow had come to perch on her shoulder.

In the kitchen Christine was drinking a second cup of tea.

'I called out to see if you wanted some, dear, but you weren't about. Poor Gerard was rather upset, wasn't he?'

Philip said, '*You* were pretty upset when he didn't come near you for months and months.'

'Was I?' She seemed puzzled, as if the effort of memory yielded nothing. 'I don't think he'll be back and I can't say I'm sorry. Audrey wouldn't have liked it.'

At any rate Philip *thought* she said Audrey. He had always thought she said Audrey, only perhaps he had never listened very closely. 'What has it got to do with her?'

'Not her, dear, *Aubrey*. My friend, Aubrey. You know who I mean, Tom's brother, Tom Pelham.'

The world floated a little, the floor floated. 'You mean, Senta's father?'

'No, Philip. He's Tom. This is his brother Aubrey Pelham, he's Darren's mother's brother and he's never been married, I met him for the first time at Fee's wedding. Philip dear, I'm sure I've never been secretive about this, I've never kept it dark, I always said I was going out with Aubrey, seeing a lot of Aubrey. You can't deny it, now can you?'

He couldn't deny it. He had been too occupied with his own affairs to pay it much attention. Audrey was the name he had heard, a woman's name. But it hadn't been for a woman that Christine had bought new clothes, bleached her hair, grown youthful.

'He wants to marry me, as a matter of fact. You – would you – would you mind if I married him?'

This was what he had wished for, longed for, a man into whose safe-keeping he could entrust her. How could the world be so full of things that were of paramount importance one day and meant less than nothing the next?

'Me? No, of course I wouldn't mind.'

'I just thought I'd ask. When your children are grown up I think you ought to ask them if they mind you getting married, though you don't expect them to ask you.'

'When is it going to be?'

'Oh, I don't know that, dear. I haven't told him yes yet. I thought it would be good for Cheryl if I married him.'

'Why good for Cheryl?'

'I told you, Philip, he's a social worker, he works with teenagers with problems like her.'

Philip thought, she's got it all worked out, she has arranged her life without me. And I always thought she was helpless, I thought she would need to lean on me for life. Suddenly he saw something else: that his mother was the kind of woman men would always want to marry, there would always be men anxious to marry her. Being married, that was what she was good at in her strange loving scatty way, and they could sense it.

It embarrassed him to do it, it wasn't like him, but just the same he put his arm round her and gave her a kiss. She looked up into his face and smiled.

'I may not be back for a while,' he said. 'I'm going to Senta's.'

She said vaguely, 'Have a good time, dear.' She was moving towards the phone in the hall, transparently waiting for him to leave so that, in private, she could transmit his permission and his reaction to Aubrey Pelham. He got into the car but didn't immediately start the engine. The unwillingness to rejoin Senta which he had felt while in the house was growing stronger. He was beginning to understand that a violent antipathy could be the reverse of which the obverse was passion. He saw her as evil, he saw her eyes looking at him, very green and glittering. The idea came to him of how it would be never to see her again, the relief, the peace. Somehow he knew that once he went back there he would be lost, but to write – why shouldn't he write and tell her it was all over, it had been a temporary insanity, bad for both of them?

He knew he couldn't. But he couldn't go straight back there either. His need was to put it off until long into the night. Darkness would make their reunion easier. There was a strange vision he had of shutting themselves up together, he and she, down in that basement room, admitting no one, never venturing out, keeping themselves safe. But it was a hateful prospect.

He drove slowly away from his mother's house. Going in the general direction of Tarsus Street, heading for it as if drawn by a magnet, he nevertheless knew the point must come when he left the destined route and digressed, at least for a little while. He couldn't face her now, immediately.

That point came when he would in the usual course of things have left the Edgware Road and turned into the back reaches of Kilburn. Instead he drove on. He was thinking of what Christine had said about Cheryl and he began to feel angry at this facile solution to her unknown trouble. A stepfather who was some sort of probation officer – that was to solve everything. Philip was remembering how once, before he had even met Senta, he had seen Cheryl down here, coming out of a shop in tears.

Except that it hadn't been a shop. Slowing to a stop, parking the car where he shouldn't have parked it, on a double yellow line, he got out and stared at the glittering place which, without doors or windows, revealed openly to the street its sparkling, strobe-lit interior, its ranked temptation bathed in flickering red and yellow. He had never been into such a place before, for he had never wanted to. At the seaside, occasionally in a pub, he had had a go and lost and been indifferent. Once, he remembered now, on a Channel crossing from Zeebrugge after a family holiday, his father had played a machine called Demon Dynamo. The name had stuck in his mind, it was so ridiculous.

There was a Demon Dynamo in here. There was a Space Stormer and a Hot Hurricane and an Apocalypse and a Gorilla Guerilla. He passed along the aisles, looking at the machines and at the faces of those who stood and played them, their expressions either still and enclosed or ardently concentrated. At a machine called Chariots of Fire a thin pale boy with a felt-head haircut succeeded in aligning a row of Olympic torches and the coins came cascading out. He looked very young but he must be over eighteen. Philip had read somewhere that these places were forbidden to under-eighteens, it was a new law, only recently passed. Did they think you magically became wise and mature with your eighteenth birthday?

The boy's face registered nothing. Philip was the son of a gambler so he didn't expect the boy to pocket his winnings and leave. He saw him move on to the Space Stormer.

Cheryl wasn't there but he knew now where he would find her.

19

At the café table she sat opposite him, bribed to be there by the five pounds he had promised her if she came with him and talked. For a while he was withholding it. He wondered when she had last washed her hair – washed herself, come to that. Her fingernails were dirty. When he looked at her right hand with a cheap silver ring loose on the middle finger, he could only imagine that hand eternally pulling away at the handle on a fruit machine, as mechanically as the hand that pumps equipment in a factory, but without that operator's indifference. Her face was lined, as only a young person's can be, with grooves and furrows that make it look not old but only very very tired.

He had found her at last in an amusement arcade in Tottenham Court Road, having searched in similar places the length of Oxford Street. There he watched her lose the last of her money and turn with what must have become an automatic reflex to try borrowing from the man at the next machine. Philip saw her take the refusal. The man didn't so much as look at her. He kept staring at the rows of fruit or whatever it was with the concentration of someone taking an eye test. The repeated shaking of his head he finally accompanied with a wave of his free hand in Cheryl's direction, a pushing away gesture. Scarlet and gold lights, both steady and flickering, the dark depths of the place illuminated with points and spots and glowing furnaces of light, gave to the arcade the look of a stage inferno.

It was difficult getting anything out of her because she was so obviously indifferent, now he had discovered this secret addiction of hers, as to what more he found out or what he thought. She spoke with a kind of bored reluctance. She had tasted her coffee and pushed it away, affectedly shuddering.

'He was dead. Nothing could bring me closer. It made me feel *like* him. I suppose you could say that. Or maybe it's in the blood, maybe I inherited it.'

'You can't inherit a thing like that.'

'How would you know? Are you a doctor?'

'How long have you been doing it? Ever since he died?' She nodded, making an ugly bored face, but she was restless, picking up the coffee spoon now, tapping the rim of the saucer with it. 'What got you into it in the first place?'

'I was walking by. I was thinking about Dad. Not any of you seemed to care about him dying the way I did. Not even Mum. I was walking by and thinking of him. I was thinking of a night we all came back from a holiday somewhere. We were on the ferry and he played the fruit machine and every time he won he gave me the money and let me have a go. The boat wasn't crowded and you were all somewhere eating and there was just Dad and me alone and it was night and stars were shining. I don't know how I remember that because it can't have been up on deck, can it? It was magic the way Dad kept winning and the money just rolling out. I was thinking of that and I thought, well, I'll go in and have a go – why not?'

'And you got hooked?' said Philip.

'I'm not *hooked*. It's not a drug.' For the first time there was animation in her face. She looked indignant. 'There was a guy in there just now said to me I was hooked. "You're an addict", he said like I was injecting something. I've never done that. I've never used smack. I've never even smoked. What's with people that they think you're hooked because you *like* something?'

'You steal for it, don't you? It's a habit you steal to keep on with.'

270

'I *like* it, Phil. Can't you understand? I like doing it more than anything in the world. You could call it a hobby. Like Darren is with his sport. You don't call him an addict. It's an *interest*, like you're supposed to have. People play snooker, don't they, and – and golf and cards and things, you don't say they're hooked.'

He said steadily, 'It isn't like those things. You can't stop.'

'I don't want to stop. Why should I? I'd be all right, I wouldn't have a problem, if only I'd got money. It's not having money that's my problem, not the machines.' She laid down the spoon. She pushed her hand across the table, turned it palm-upwards and stretched it out to him. 'You said you'd give me five pounds.'

He took the note out of his wallet and gave it to her. It was horrible. He didn't want to make a ceremony out of this, seeming to pass it over quickly as food to the starving, or at the end of a slow calculated cautionary process the way some people tease a dog with a biscuit, offering it and snatching it away. But as he produced the note, as casually as if he were repaying a loan, she grabbed it from him. She drew in her breath and compressed her lips. The note was held tight in her hand, not put away. She wouldn't keep it long enough to make that worth while.

When she had gone, was lost in there among the machines with their glittering improbable names, he went back to the car which he had left in a side street. It was a little after ten-thirty and dark. The interview with Cheryl had displaced the area of his anxieties. His mind was full of Cheryl and her desperate defence. He thought, she will be driven to steal again, she probably already is stealing, and she will be caught and she'll go to prison. The selfish self-preserving ego inside him said that might be the best possible thing that could happen to her. In prison they might give her treatment, they might help her. Her brother knew that this way she would be lost. I must do something, he thought, I must.

The postponement of his return to Senta he now saw must end. There was no putting it off. She would already be afraid, anxious, wondering what had happened to him. As he drove he began formulating ways of telling her they must part. If the police had discovered anything he would have been obliged to stay with her but, strangely, they knew nothing. It must be that no witness had come to them, no one had spoken to them of a girl with blood on her clothes or a girl in an empty train on a Sunday morning. It was because she was unconnected with Myerson, he thought. This was the murder of a stranger by a stranger, the kind that is the hardest to solve, the kind that has no reason behind it and no motive.

Am I then conniving at murder? Am I covering murder up? What good would it do to bring Myerson's killer to justice? Would it bring poor Myerson back? One of the reasons for apprehending a killer was to prevent such a person from killing again. He already knew that she had killed before. She had told him so obliquely enough, but she had told him. That had been the first use of a glass dagger.

The house in Tarsus Street lay in darkness. The shutters at the basement window were folded back but there was no light on inside. As he let himself into the hall he remembered the time when she had excluded him and his subsequent passion of unhappiness. How could he have felt like that then, so short a time ago, and feel like this now? If he hadn't told her that lie about killing John Crucifer, perhaps Myerson would still be alive. And he had told the lie solely to get back someone he no longer wanted.

He walked down the stairs with a slow heavy tread. He switched off the light and, in the darkness, let himself into the dark room. There was absolute silence but as he came near the bed he heard her sigh in her sleep. The way she was breathing and the depth of her sleep told him she had taken one of Rita's pills. Otherwise, at his approach, she would have woken. He took off his clothes and lay down beside her. It seemed the only thing to be done. For a long while, before sleep came, he lay there looking at the pale curve of her cheek against the brown cotton pillow. Strands of silver hair caught what light there was and gleamed in the dimness. She lay on her side with her little hands curled into fists and held under her chin. He lay apart from her for a while and then, tentatively, like a shy person who fears rejection, he laid his hand on her waist and drew her to him in the curve of his arm.

They were in her room and it was morning, early still, only a little after seven but broad daylight. The sun poured with rich abandon on to the shabbiness, the decay, through window panes filmed with dirt. Philip had made coffee. There was some milk left in a bottle but it had turned sour. Senta had wrapped herself in a couple of shawls, one tied round her waist, the other over her shoulders. The roots of her hair were showing red again. She was still in a sleeping pill trance, swimmy-eyed, her movements slow, but he could tell she already sensed the change in him. She was cowed by it and afraid. He sat at the foot of the bed and she at the head of it, leaning on the pillows. But now she crept towards him across the hillocks of the quilt and put out her hand timidly to take his. He felt like snatching his hand away but he didn't. He let it lie in hers, feeling a constriction in his throat.

To his own ears he sounded as if he had a bad cold. He tried to clear his throat. 'Senta,' he said, 'did you kill him with the second of the glass daggers?'

The question was so bizarre, the words themselves and their conjunction as well as the fact that he had actually seriously uttered them to someone he was supposed to love, to contemplate marrying, that he squeezed his eyes shut and pressed his fingers to his temples.

She was nodding her head. He knew what was going on in her mind. To his questions, to the facts and the danger, she was indifferent. She only wanted him to go on loving her. He said, trying to keep his voice steady and to remain cool, 'Then, don't you realise, the police will find you. It's a wonder they haven't by now. The glass daggers link the two deaths. Eventually, they'll find that link. They must have those details somewhere on their computer – why haven't they come to you?'

She looked at him and smiled. His hand was tightly enclosed by hers so she could smile. 'I want you to be jealous, Philip. I know it's not kind of me, but I do like it when you're jealous.'

Her interpretation of his questions made him see something new – that she was sliding away from normality. What hold she had on reality was loosening.

'I'm not jealous,' he said, trying to keep his patience. 'I know this Martin wasn't important to you. I'm worried for you, Senta, I'm worried about what's going to happen.'

'I love you,' she said and she held his hand in both hers kneading it painfully. 'I love you better than I love me, so why should I care what becomes of me?'

Strangely, horrifyingly, he knew it was true. She loved him like that and her face told him so. The words were unnecessary. He held her close to him in the bright dust-filled indifferent sunlight, pressed his hands on her back and his cheek against hers, his nerves unfeeling, his body restless to be gone. She nestled close to him and time passed, long moments that felt like hours until at last he had to say,

'I've got to go, Senta.'

She clung more closely. 'I can't take more time off,' he said. 'I've got to go to work now.'

He didn't tell her that first of all he was going to see Fee and Darren, to catch them before they left for work. He had to prise her off him, kissing her for comfort. The shawls spread over her, she curled foetus-like into the brown bedclothes. To exclude the harsh yellow light he pulled the shutters nearly closed and left the room quickly without looking back at her.

His brother-in-law presented a different and more attractive image at breakfast time than in those afternoon and evening hours when he was to be found sprawled in front of the screen. Newly shaven, he was the handsome bridegroom once again, a frown of concentration aging him as he studied, of all unlikely newspapers, the *Financial Times*. And Fee who had been bright and brisk, a hairdryer in one hand and plate of toast in the other, was astonished to see her brother, convinced he must have come because of some accident that had happened to their mother. Telling her everything was all right, Philip wondered at the use of this phrase which must always be meaningless.

He found himself postponing discussion of the true reason for his visit. Perhaps people often did that, he thought. Speak of the lesser anxiety first, the smaller care. Yet to place Cheryl in this category brought a rush of guilt. Fee was incredulous, then embarrassed. She lit a cigarette as if it was anything but addiction they were discussing.

'Fruit machines?' said Darren. '*Fruit machines?* I play fruit machines but no one calls me a junkie.'

'You're not addicted to them. You can control your need to play them and you can make yourself stop. Cheryl can't.'

Philip could tell that he was getting nowhere with these

two, who would have perfectly understood the perils, for instance, of alcoholism. It showed him how far Fee had grown away from him and how much nearer to Darren. Perhaps it was necessary and inevitable for the endurance of the marriage. The time had come and could be put off no longer. Darren had already got up from the table and was hunting for his car keys. Philip said,

'Who's Martin Hunt?'

'What?'

'Martin Hunt, Fee. I'm sure it's through you and Darren I've heard the name.'

She frowned, screwed up her nose at him in indignation or incredulity. 'You know who it is, you must know. What's wrong with your memory these days?'

'Is he – is he dead?'

'How should I know? I shouldn't think so. He's young. He's only twenty-four or twenty-five. Why would he be dead?'

'Who is he, Fee?'

'I don't know him,' she said. 'It was Rebecca I knew. Rebecca Neave that I was at school with. He was her boy friend. That's all I know, what I saw on telly and in the papers.'

It took him a little while to digest this, to understand the meaning of what she had said and to draw inferences. He wondered later if she had noticed how he had turned pale. He felt the blood drawn from his face and a goose-pimpling. It was something like faintness too. He held on to the back of one of Fee's dining chairs. Darren came up to Fee and said he was off and kissed her.

Fee had gone into the kitchen. She came back drying her hands on a piece of kitchen roll. 'Why did you want to know all that about Martin Hunt?'

He lied. Senta had taught him how and he could lie almost without a qualm. 'Someone told me he'd been killed in a car crash.'

Fee wasn't interested. 'I don't think so. We'd have

heard.' She disappeared again, came back wearing a cotton jacket. 'I've got to go to work, Phil. You coming? Oh, I nearly forgot. Mum phoned and told me Flora was back. I don't really know what she meant. I mean she just said Flora had come back as if she'd walked in of her own accord or something.'

They went downstairs, out into the street and the white sunlight. Philip didn't have to lie this time. 'I happened to find her. I thought Mum would like her back so I – I got her back.'

'Why didn't you say? Mum thinks it's a miracle. She thinks Flora just walked in and set herself up on that bit of concrete.'

'I'm sure she doesn't really,' Philip said abstractedly. 'Anyway I'll explain.'

Fee looked curiously at him as they parted. 'Did you come all the way over here at this hour just to ask me about a fellow you didn't even know you'd heard of?'

He was rehearsing some kind of explanation for Christine. It took his mind off more pressing concerns. It stopped him thinking about what he knew he must at some time confront. He would tell his mother that he had in fact known for a long time that Arnham no longer possessed Flora, that Flora was sold. He, Philip, had been advertising for her, had at last found her and brought her back as a surprise for Christine. The opportunity of giving a real performance of this farrago of inventions was denied him.

Cheryl had locked herself in her room. A white-faced Christine came up to Philip before he had even let himself into the house, before he had taken his key from the lock, came up to him and threw her arms round him. He held her shoulders, tried to speak calmly.

'What is it? What's wrong?'

'Oh, Phil, the police have been here. They brought Cheryl back and they searched the house.'

'What do you mean?'

He got her to sit down. She was shaking and he held her hand tightly. She spoke in a breathless gasping way. 'She was caught shoplifting. Only a bottle of perfume but she had, she had ...' Christine stopped, took a breath, began again, '... she had – other things in her bag. They took her to the police station and charged her or whatever it is they do and then they brought her home. There was a woman detective sergeant and a young man who was the constable.' Hysteria took hold of her and she broke into sobbing laughter. 'I thought it was so strange that way round, it seemed so funny in the midst of all that – that awfulness!'

He felt helpless. 'What's going to happen to her?'

'She has to come up in court tomorrow morning.' Christine said it calmly enough, coldly almost, until the sobs caught her again and she gave a cry of misery, clamping her hand over her mouth.

20

She was in her room with the door locked. Philip knocked at the door and rattled the handle. She told him to go away.

'Cheryl, I only want to say Mum and I will come to court with you.'

There was silence. He repeated what he had said.

'If you do that I won't go. I'll run away.'

'Aren't you being a bit stupid?'

'It's my business,' she said. 'It's nothing to do with you. I don't want you there hearing what they say.'

As he went downstairs he heard her unlock the bedroom door but she didn't come out. He wondered why the police had let her come home. Christine, seeming to read his thoughts, said, 'She can lock herself in, Phil, but we can't lock her in, can we?'

He shook his head. Christine had never told them what to do, constrained them, only left them to themselves and loved them. In Cheryl's case at any rate, that apparently hadn't been enough. He stood with Christine in the kitchen, drinking the tea she had made, and they heard Cheryl let herself out of the front door. For once she let herself out quietly. The door closed with a soft click. Christine made a whimpering sound. Philip knew that if he had said that he was going to Senta as usual, that he would be out all the evening and half the night, she wouldn't have protested. Now, letting Senta know he wasn't coming, no longer seemed of importance. Instead he felt how relieved he would be if this evening might be the start of a lifelong separation from her, if all that might become his past. But even as he caught at this hope he recalled her love for him.

'Do you think she'll come back?' Christine asked him.

For a moment he didn't know who she meant. 'Cheryl? I don't know. I hope so.'

He was out in the garden when the phone rang. It was dusk and he had taken Hardy as far as Lochleven Gardens and back, coming in the back way. Light from the kitchen window fell on the figure of Flora which cast a long black shadow on the grass. A stream of whitish-grey bird excrement had dried on one of her arms. Christine opened the window and called to him that Senta was on the phone.

'Why haven't you come?'

'I can't come tonight, Senta.' He told her about Cheryl, adding that he couldn't leave his mother. 'It's not possible to phone you, you know that,' he said as if he had tried.

'I love you. I don't want to be here without you. Philip, you're going to come and live here with me, aren't you? When are you going to come?'

He could hear Rita and Jacopo's music in the background. 'I don't know. We have to talk.'

There was terror in her voice. 'Why do we have to talk? Talk about what?'

'Senta, I'll come tomorrow. I'll see you tomorrow.' I'll tell you it's over, he thought, I'm leaving you. I'll never see you again after tomorrow.

When he had put the receiver back he began thinking of those people, women mostly, who lived with or loved someone they suspected of being a murderer. He was a man and he knew the woman he loved had done murder, but it came to the same thing. It astonished him that such people could ever consider giving the suspected person up to the police, 'shopping' them, but he was equally surprised that they could want to continue the association. Once, at a party, he had played a game where you had to say what a person would have to do to stop you loving or even liking them, wanting to know them. And he had said something silly, facetious, about being put off someone because they didn't clean their teeth often enough. He knew better now. His love for Senta had melted away when he knew she was responsible for Myerson's death.

Just before midnight Cheryl came back. Philip was sitting up waiting for her, hoping she would come. He had made Christine go to bed. He ran out into the hall when he heard her key in the lock and caught her crossing the hall.

'I only want to say I won't try to come to court with you if that's what you want.'

'The police are coming for me.' she said dully. 'They're coming in a car at nine-thirty.'

'You must tell them about the fruit machines.' As he spoke he felt what a stupid term it was, a frivolity in tragedy. 'You will tell them, won't you? They'll do something to help you.'

She didn't answer him. With a strange gesture, she pulled out the pocket linings of her jeans to show they were empty. She threw out of her jacket pockets a half-used tube of peppermints, a ten-pence piece. 'That's all I've got in the world. That's my lot. It'll be best if I go to prison, won't it?'

He didn't see her in the morning but went off to work before she was up. In the afternoon he phoned Christine to be told Cheryl had received a suspended sentence. If she committed another offence she would go to prison for six months. She was at home with Christine now and Fee had taken the afternoon off and was with them. He began preparing himself for the ordeal before him. Tomorrow it would all be over, he would have done it, he would have broken with Senta and a new phase of life, empty and cold, would stretch before him.

Would he ever be able to forget what she had done and that he had loved her? It might grow faint and vague but it would always be there. A man had lost his life because of her. Before that, someone else had died because of her. She would kill others as time went on. She was made that way, she was mad. For all the rest of his life he would be marked by it, he thought. Even if he never spoke to her again, never saw her, it would scar him.

Seeing her was something he was fully resolved on. After all, he had prepared the way. He had told her they had to talk and the fear in her voice showed him she went some way to guessing what he had to say. He would tell her all the truth, that he hated violence and violent death. Even talking or reading about these things was a horror to him. He would tell her how knowing what she had done had destroyed his love for her or, rather, that he now saw her as a different person, she wasn't the girl he had loved, that girl was illusory.

But how was he to handle her love for him?

Joley was among the men and women in the queue at the Mother Teresa Centre. Philip superstitiously noted his presence there. He had been saying to himself, as he approached Tarsus Street, that if he saw Joley he would go in and speak to Senta, if not, he would leave it and drive home. The old man with his barrow and his plastic carrier cushions constituted a sign which Joley reinforced himself by waving to Philip as he passed.

Philip parked the car. He sat at the wheel for a long time, thinking about her, remembering how he had used to rush up the steps and into the house, as often as not in too much of a hurry to lock the car behind him. And there had been the time when she took his keys away and he had thought of breaking in, so great was his misery and his longing for her. Why was it impossible to put his mind and his feelings back into that time? She was still the same girl really, she looked and sounded the same. Surely he could go into the house and down the basement stairs and into that room and take her in his arms and forget?

He started the car and turned round and drove home. He didn't know whether he was being weak or strong, purposeful or cowardly. Cheryl was out, Christine was out. He later came to know they were out together, had gone to Fee and Darren's with Aubrey Pelham. The phone began ringing at eight and he let it ring. It rang nine times between eight and nine. At nine o'clock he put the little dog on the lead and walked him two or three miles about the streets. Of course he imagined the phone ringing while he was out and he imagined her in the dirty sour-smelling hall at Tarsus Street, dialling, dialling. He thought of how it had been for him when she had expelled him from the house and he had tried to phone her.

The phone was ringing as he came in. He picked up the receiver. It was as if he suddenly understood he couldn't avoid answering the phone for the rest of his life. She was incoherent, sobbing into the phone, drawing breath to cry to him: 'I saw you in the street. I saw the car. You turned away and left me.'

'I know. I couldn't come in.'

'Why couldn't you? Why?'

'You know why, Senta. It's over. We can't see each other again. It's better never to see each other. You can go back to your life and I'll start mine again.'

She said in a small still voice, suddenly calm, 'I haven't any life except with you.'

'Look, we only knew each other for three months. It's nothing out of a lifetime. We'll forget each other.'

'I love you, Philip. You said you loved me. I must see you, you must come here.'

'It won't do any good. It won't make any difference.' He said goodnight to her and put the phone down.

It rang again almost immediately and he answered it.

He knew he would always answer it now. 'I must see you. I can't live without you.'

'What's the use of it, Senta?'

'Is it Martin Hunt? Is it because of him? Philip, I'm not making this up, this is for real, the uttermost absolute truth. I never slept with him, I only went out with him once. *He didn't want me, he wanted that girl.* He wanted her more than me.'

'It isn't that, Senta,' he said. 'It's nothing to do with that.'

As if he hadn't spoken she went on feverishly, 'That's why the police never came near me. Because they didn't know. They didn't know I even knew him. Isn't that proof? Isn't it?'

What sort of a woman was she that she thought a man would mind more about a sexual relationship than an act of murder?

'Senta,' he said, 'I won't end this without seeing you again, I won't do that. I promise. That would be cowardly. I promise I won't do it. I'll see you and we'll end it.'

'Philip, if I said I'd never done it, if I said I'd made it all up?'

'I know it's only the little things you tell lies about, Senta.'

She didn't phone again. He lay in bed sleepless for hours. Among other things, he missed her physical presence, but when he thought how he had made love to someone who had killed a man in cold blood, when he relived that, he had to get up and go to the bathroom to be sick. Suppose she killed herself? He suddenly thought how unsurprised he would have been had she suggested a suicide pact. That would have been like her. Dying together, going on hand-in-hand to some glorious afterlife, Ares and Aphrodite, immortals in white robes . . .

The fine weather came back next day. He woke up to early hot sunshine, a bright band of light across his pillow from the window where he had neglected to draw the curtains. A sparrow sat on Flora's outstretched hand. There was dew thick on the grass and the long densely blue shadows. It was a dream, he thought, all of it was a dream. Flora has always stood there, she was never removed to other owners, other gardens. Fee still lives here. I never met Senta. The murders didn't happen, I dreamed them. I dreamed Senta.

Downstairs the woman called Moorehead had arrived to have her hair permed. It was the first perm Christine had done for several weeks. The rotten egg smell, seeping everywhere and making breakfast impossible, evoked earlier times, the time before Senta. It helped to keep the illusion going. He made a pot of tea and gave a cup to Mrs Moorehead and Christine said what a treat it was for two old women to have a young man wait on them. Mrs Moorehead bristled up and Philip knew that when the perm was done and she was leaving she would tell Christine it was against her principles to tip the boss.

Cheryl came down. It was months since she had been up so early. She sat at the kitchen table drinking tea. Philip sensed that she wanted to catch him alone and borrow money from him. He escaped before she got the chance.

The car was going into the garage today to have the new radio put in. He left it there and was given a promise it would be ready by three. On the way back to Head Office he bought a newspaper. The evening paper had just come on to the streets and the front page headline told of a man charged with the murder of John Crucifer. Philip walked along reading the story. There was little to it but the basic facts. The alleged killer was Crucifer's own nephew, an unemployed welder, Trevor Crucifer, aged twenty-five.

It was extraordinary the feeling Philip had, as if he had finally and absolutely been exonerated. Someone else had killed the man and it was known. Officialdom and authority knew it. It was as if his own stupid ill-considered confession had never been made. It seemed to set him free of guilt as his own knowledge of his innocence never could. Suppose he were to open the paper and on an inside page find that Harold Myerson's true killer had also been found? That Senta's involvement was illusory and everything she had told him the result only of a series of coincidences and circumstantial parallels?

Roy sat in his office with the air conditioning turned off and the windows open. A letter had been passed to him from the managing director. It was from Mrs Ripple and listed seven separate faults she had found in her new bathroom.

'I'm without a car till three,' Philip said.

'Then you'd better take mine.'

Roy said the keys were in the pocket of his jacket which was hanging up in Lucy's room. As Philip went into the room the phone began to ring. Lucy wasn't there so he answered it. A voice asked if Mr Wardman was expected in that day.

'This is Philip Wardman speaking.'

'Oh, good morning, Mr Wardman. I'm a police officer. Detective Sergeant Gates, CID.'

They had offered to come to him at home or at work but Philip said, quite truthfully, that he had to go to Chigwell anyway. Gates had given him some idea of what it was about. He thought about it, turning it over and over in his mind, as he drove Roy's car through the lumbering congestion of London's eastern suburbs.

'We're making enquiries about a missing statue, Mr Wardman. Well, a stolen statue.'

Briefly he had been aghast, stricken silent. But Gates hadn't been hectoring or accusatory. He had spoken to Philip as to a potentially helpful witness, one of those who genuinely help the police in their enquiries. Philip

286

had several times been in the area – wasn't that a fact? The district of Chigwell Row, that is, from which the statue had disappeared. If they could come and talk to him or alternatively he could spare the time to come in and answer a few questions. . . .

At the wheel of Roy's car, the windows wide open, the sun shining, Philip told himself that was literally all they wanted, him to tell them if he had seen any suspicious persons in the neighbourhood. It occurred to him quite suddenly that Flora must be valuable, really valuable. That brought him a sense of chill. He thought of his job. But they didn't know, they *couldn't* know.

Gates had someone with him who introduced himself as a detective inspector. Philip thought this was rather a high-ranking officer to be deployed on an enquiry into the theft of a garden ornament. The inspector's name was Morris. He said, 'We've asked you to come here as the result of a rather interesting coincidence. I understand your young sister has been in a spot of trouble?'

Philip nodded. He was mystified. Why didn't they talk about Chigwell and Mrs Ripple's neighbourhood?

'I'm being very frank with you, Mr Wardman, perhaps franker than you've been led to believe we usually are. I don't personally care for secrets. A woman officer searched your home and saw a certain statue in the garden. She very intelligently made the connection between that statue and the one which was missing from Mrs Myerson's garden, having acquainted herself with the description of the missing one from the Metropolitan Police computer link.'

'Is she worth a lot then?' Philip managed to say.

'She?'

'Sorry. I meant the statue. Is it valuable?'

Gates said, 'Mrs Myerson's late husband paid £18 for

it at auction. I don't know if you call that valuable. Depends on your standards, I suppose.'

Philip had been going to say he didn't understand but he did now. It wasn't a question of Flora's value. They knew he had stolen her. The woman police sergeant had seen her when they brought Cheryl home, had identified her by that chip out of her ear and the green stain. The two officers were looking at him and he returned their gaze steadily. There was nothing for it. If he denied it they might accuse poor Cheryl. He couldn't understand why they hadn't accused Cheryl, come to that, in the circumstances, she seemed a natural choice.

'All right,' he said, 'I did take the statue. I stole it, if you like. But I did think, mistakenly as it happens, that I had some sort of right to it. Are you . . .' His strength wavered and he cleared his throat '. . . are you going to charge me with stealing it?'

'Is that your chief concern, Mr Wardman?' said Gates.

The question was incomprehensible. Philip rephrased what he had said. 'Am I going to be prosecuted?' Receiving no reply, he asked if they wanted him to make a statement.

It was strange the way they seemed to latch on to this as if they would never have thought of it for themselves, as if Philip had had a brilliant and original idea. A girl with a typewriter who might or might not have been a police officer herself took a statement from him. He told the truth which sounded untrue when expressed aloud. When he had finished he sat and looked at them, the two policeman and the girl who might or might not have been a policewoman, and waited for those words to be uttered which he had read in detective stories and heard on television: you are not obliged to say anything in answer to the charge . . .

Morris got up. He said, 'All right, Mr Wardman. Thank you very much. We needn't keep you any longer.'

'Is that all then?' Philip made himself say it in a firm calm voice.

'All for now, yes.'

'Are you going to prosecute me for taking the statue?'

There was some hesitation. Morris was gathering up papers from the desk. He looked up and said in a slow deliberate way, 'No, I don't think so. I don't think that will be necessary. That would be rather a waste of time and the public's money, don't you think?'

Philip didn't answer. It wasn't a question to which an answer was expected. He suddenly felt embarrassed, he felt foolish. Once he was outside relief came surging in to dispel the embarrassment. He would restore Flora to Mrs Myerson, he thought, it was the least he could do. If the police didn't come and collect her, he would bring her to Chigwell himself.

He drove to Mrs Ripple's and was conducted up to the bathroom where all the flaws in the list were pointed out to him to the accompaniment of a great deal of vituperative abuse and reiteration of what it had all cost. Pearl was nowhere to be seen, had perhaps gone home.

He drove back past Mrs Myerson's house. There was an estate agent's 'For Sale' board in the front garden. The Scottie dog Senta had named Ebony was asleep on the path in the shade. Philip had a sandwich in a pub in Chigwell and drove back to London when the traffic was at its lightest. He parked Roy's car and walked down to the garage to fetch his own.

Lucy said to him as he came into the office, 'A Mr Morris has been on the phone for you.'

For a moment Philip couldn't think who that was. Then he knew. The policeman was being discreet in not naming his function or his rank at Philip's place of work. But why had he phoned at all? Had they changed their minds?

'Did he leave a number?'

'He'll call back. I said you wouldn't be long.'

It was a lengthy fifteen minutes. Philip relived his earlier fears. If they were going to charge him he made up his mind to go and tell Roy immediately, get it over, face the worst. Then he knew he couldn't go on waiting like this. He looked up the police number in the phone directory and phoned Morris himself. It took a little while to locate him. Philip's mouth had grown dry and his heartbeat unpleasantly palpable.

When Philip told him who this was, Morris said, 'Have you got a girl friend, Mr Wardman?'

It was the last thing Philip expected. 'Why do you ask?' he said.

'Perhaps you know a girl with very long blonde hair – well, silver-blonde? A rather small girl, no more than five feet tall?'

'I haven't got a girl friend,' Philip said, unsure whether he spoke the truth.

21

His mind presented the explanation to him. It was like one of those puzzles in a newspaper. You look up the answer on the back page and when you read it, it is so clear and so obvious, you wonder how you could have failed to see it in the first place.

The police must have taken note of every event in Harold Myerson's recent past, spoken to every acquaintance he had, all his neighbours, noted every visitor to his house. Their interest would have been aroused by the theft of Flora and the description of the thief given to them by Myerson's next-door neighbour. One, or perhaps more than one, witness had described to them the small young girl with the long silver hair seen in the neighbourhood of Myerson's murder that Sunday morning, and later seen in a tube train. Might there be a connection between that girl and the thief of the statue? It was a long shot but the police did not neglect long shots.

Philip understood that if they had never seen Flora in his own garden, they would never have found him. They would never, except through him, have found Senta. It was he who had led them to Senta. He had led them to Senta by means of the statue she resembled.

All this passed through his mind while he was on his way to Tarsus Street. He hadn't waited, had said nothing to Roy. It was strange how the old longing for Senta had come back to him when he heard Morris describe her. He had no idea what he would say or do when he got there but he knew he had to go there and tell her and somehow help her. He couldn't deceive himself that the police wouldn't find her now.

The overcast sky had begun spilling out rain. First it came in separate isolated drops like large flat coins, then in a downpour such as falls in the tropics. But it didn't simply fall, it tore out of the sky and lashed in a splintered wall of water, a steel shutter of water dropped with a harsh clang. Instead of lightening as the rain was shed, the sky seemed to grow darker and all along his route lights were coming on in houses and office blocks. Cars had their lights on. The beams of his headlights made misty paths in the torrent.

Joley and an old woman with a dog in a basket on wheels were sitting together in the shelter of the church porch. The dog looked like one of those you sometimes see on sentimental birthday cards, peeping over the rim of the basket with its face between its paws. Joley waved. Philip thought suddenly, remembering it for some reason, that this was the day he and Senta had been due to start work on the upstairs flat. Last weekend they had decided, that sunny lovely happy weekend that seemed a thousand years away. On Friday evening they would go up to the flat and see what there was to do and he would help her with things she wanted done.

He had put the receiver down rather than answer any more of Detective Sergeant Morris's questions. He had replaced the receiver and cut off the policeman's voice. Morris would certainly have rung back immediately. When Lucy or Roy told him Philip had gone out he would know the phone call hadn't been accidentally cut off but deliberately terminated by Philip. He would know Philip was guilty or guilty by association or desperately anxious he shouldn't find out the identity of his girl friend. And that would make him waste no time in finding it out – her identity and her address. It would be easy. He had only to ask Christine. He had only to ask Fee. In their innocence they would give it to him at once.

Philip parked the car outside the house as near to the steps as he could get it. The nearside wheels were in a lake of water on which the rain drummed. The rain was a great grey roaring lashing curtain between him and the house. He remembered the rain that first night they had made love, the evening of Fee's wedding day, but it hadn't been like this, it had been mild compared to this. The house was only half-visible, for the rain made an obscuring wall, fog-like yet savage.

He threw open the car door, jumped out and slammed it behind him. Those seconds on the pavement and the steps before he was in the shelter of the porch were enough to soak him. He shook himself and stripped off his jacket. As soon as he was inside the hall he knew Rita and Jacopo were away. He could always tell, though he never really knew how. The house was rather dark. All houses would be dark due to the storm-induced twilight outside. He couldn't have said why he didn't switch the light on but he didn't.

There was no smell of joss stick coming up the basement stairs. There was no smell except the ingrained one you got used to when you habitually came to this house. He had rushed to get here but now he was here he hesitated outside her door. He had to brace himself for the sight of her. A long breath inhaled and expelled, his eyes squeezed closed and opened again, he let himself into the room. It was empty, she wasn't there.

But she had been there very recently. A candle was burning in a saucer on the low table in front of the mirror. It was a new candle, its tapering top burnt down only a little way. The shutters were closed, the room dark as night. She couldn't have gone out, not in this rain. He folded back the shutters. The rain streamed down the glass in a shaking sobbing waterfall.

Her green dress, a dress that might have been made of rain, water transmuted into silk, hung over the wicker chair. The high-heeled silver shoes stood side by side underneath. There were some sheets of paper with typing on them, clipped together and lying on the bed, that he thought might be her television script. He left the room and went up the stairs and hesitated at the top. She often went upstairs. It was a sort of parental home to her. He went up the next flight, came to the rooms he had glanced at that day she had had the bath in Rita's bathroom, the day on which she had come home in the morning and told him she had killed Arnham.

The rooms were just the same, the one which was full of bags of clothes and newspapers, the bedroom where Rita and Jacopo slept with its window covered by a pinned-up bedspread and foam underlay doing duty for a carpet on its floor. He opened the bathroom door. There was no one in there but as he came back on to the landing he heard a board creaking above his head. He thought, this was the day we were to begin up there. She has started without me, she has decided to make a start before I come. All that happened between us since then, all I said, all my horror and hatred have gone for nothing. He understood quite suddenly that all this time, since he began his drive here, since he parked the car and entered the house, he had been afraid of what she might have done, that she might have killed herself and he might find her dead.

He went to the foot of the stairs, the last flight. There he gradually became aware of the smell. It was a very strong appalling reek which leaked down those stairs. As he smelt it and felt it grow more powerful, as he was aware that it had been creeping down to him since first he set foot on this floor, he also knew that it was of something he had never smelt before. It was a new smell and one that, perhaps, few human beings are obliged to smell in the present day. The board above him creaked again. He went up the stairs, trying to breathe only through his mouth, shutting off his nose from sense.

The doors were all shut. He thought of nothing, he had ceased to think of how, once, they had planned to live up here. His movements were instinctive. He no longer heard the roar of the rain. He opened the door into the main room. The light was dim but it wasn't dark, for there were neither curtains nor shutters at the two dormer windows. This was the back of the house and through the streaming glass could be seen above rooftops a sky as grey and rough as granite. There was nothing in the room but an old armchair and on the floor between the half-open cupboard door and the left-hand window, something that looked like a stretcher or pallet, but which was in fact a door with a grey blanket laid on it.

Senta was standing beside it. She was wearing the clothes she had worn for her visit to Chigwell, the red cord top on which she said she had searched for blood-stains, the jeans, the running shoes. Her hair was tied up with a piece of red striped cloth. The smile she gave him transformed her. Her whole face became a smile, her whole body. She came to him with her arms out.

'I knew you'd come. I felt it. I thought, Philip will come to me, he didn't mean what he said, he *couldn't mean it*. Isn't it funny? I wasn't even afraid for more than a moment. I knew my love would be too strong for yours to stop.'

And it was, he thought, it was. It had returned in a cascade, like the rain. The pity and the tenderness he felt burned him, affecting the inside of his body with a painful burning sensation. There were tears at the back of his eyes. He put his arms round her and held her and she crushed herself against him as if she were trying to push her body inside his.

This time she was the first to move out of their embrace. She stepped back and looked at him very sweetly, her head a little on one side. He was aware, incongruously, that while holding her, while renewing his love for her, he had ceased to smell the smell. It returned now on a thick hot wave. The smell was one he associated with flies. She put out her hand and took his and said, 'Philip, my darling, you said you'd help me with something I have to do. Well, *we* have to do. It's something that has to be done before we can contemplate living up here actually.' She smiled. It was as mad a smile as he could ever imagine seeing on a woman's face, demonic and empty and split off from real things. 'I would have done it before, I know I *ought* to have done it before, but I'm not really physically strong enough to do things like that on my own.'

He had no thoughts. He could only stare and feel pain and feel her hand, small and hot, in his. There were all sorts of things he had to say, terrible things to tell her. All he could do was begin stupidly, 'You said Jacopo . . .'

'They're away till tomorrow. Anyway, it wouldn't do to let them know. We have to get this done before they come back, Philip.'

A butcher's shop left open and unattended for several long hot days, he thought. A shop full of rotting meat after everyone had died of the bomb or radiation sickness. She opened the cupboard door. He saw a kind of face. Like Flora's gleaming without life in the recesses of his own cupboard, but not like that, not like that at all. Something that had once been a girl and young, propped against the bare wall and still clothed in green velvet.

He made a sound of horror. He put both hands over his mouth. It seemed as if the whole inside of him rose up into his mouth and swelled there. The floor moved. He wasn't going to faint but he wasn't going to remain standing up either. His hands out like someone seeking water to swim in, he lowered himself till he crouched on the grey blanket pallet.

She hadn't noticed, it hadn't touched her. She was looking into the cupboard now as if what it contained was no more than a cumbersome or awkwardly shaped piece of furniture that somehow must be moved and disposed of. Apart from sight perhaps, her senses were shut off. He saw her reach into the cupboard and pick up from the floor a kitchen knife, its blade and handle blackened with old blood. She lied only about the little things, the minor details . . .

'You've got your car, haven't you, Philip? I thought we could carry it down on that thing you're sitting on and put it in my room till it gets dark and then we could . . .'

He screamed at her, 'Shut up, for Christ's sake, stop!'

She turned slowly, she turned mad pale watery eyes on him. 'What's the matter?'

They were the biggest things he had ever done, getting up off the floor, standing up, kicking that cupboard door shut. He put his arms round Senta and manhandled her out of that room. This was the next door to be shut. His nostrils, the entire inside of his head it seemed, his brain, were painted with that smell. There weren't enough doors in the world to shut it out. He dragged her to the top of the stairs, pulled her with him half-way down the stairs until they sprawled together on the treads. He held her shoulders, made a cage for her face with his hands. Her face was forced up against his, their mouths inches apart.

'Listen to me, Senta. I've given you away to the police. I didn't mean to but I have. They'll come here, they'll be here soon.'

Her lips parted, her eyes opened very wide. He was prepared for her to attack him with fists and teeth but she was still and limp, as if suspended from his hands.

'I'll get you away,' he said. 'I'll try to.' He hadn't meant to say this. 'That's what we'll use the car for. I'll get you away somewhere.'

'I don't want to go away,' she said. 'Where would I go? I don't want to be anywhere without you.'

She got up and he got up and they went downstairs. There was a new smell here, the old smell of sourness and mould. He thought, it is hours and hours since I spoke to Morris. She pushed open the door to the basement room. The candle had burnt itself out in a pool of wax. He folded back the shutters and saw that the rain had stopped. Water was running down the area wall and splashing against the kerb as cars passed. He turned back to her. At once he could see that only one thing concerned her, one thing was important to her.

'You do still love me, Philip?'

It might be a lie. He no longer knew. 'Yes,' he said.

'You won't leave me?'

'I won't leave you, Senta.'

He crouched on the bed beside her and turned his face away from its reflection in the mirror, its crumpled, frightened, damaged image. She crept across the mattress to him and he took her in his arms. She nestled up close to him and put her lips against his skin and he held her tight. He could hear cars going through the water up there and he heard one stop outside. The things we think of, he thought, the things we remember at terrible times. When he stole the statue he had thought, they wouldn't send a police car out for something like that.

But they would for this. They would for this.

TO FEAR A
PAINTED DEVIL

For
MARGARET AND CYRIL RABBS
with love

the sleeping and the dead
Are but as pictures: 'tis the eye of childhood
That fears a painted devil.

Macbeth

Prologue

He was nine. It was his first morning in England and he began to wonder if all English houses were like this one, large yet with small rooms, full of things that no one could use: armless statues, vases with lids to them, curtains as immoveably draped as one of his mother's evening gowns.

They had arrived the night before and he had passed through the hall wrapped in a blanket and carried in his father's arms. He remembered only the great front door, a heavy wooden door with a picture of a tree on it in coloured glass. They had left him to sleep as long as he would and someone had brought breakfast for him on a tray. Now as he descended the stairs, crossing the half-landing which a bronze soldier guarded with his lance, he saw the hall below him and his steps faltered.

It was a fine morning but the room looked as rooms do at twilight, dim and still. Instead of being papered the walls were hung with embroideries stretched on frames, and between them curtains that covered—what? Windows? Doors? It seemed to him that they covered things people were not supposed to see. There was a single mirror with a wooden frame and this frame, of carved and polished red wood, looked as if it had grown branches of its own, for strips of wood shaped into leaves and twigs twined across the glass.

Within this mirror he could see not himself but an open door reflected and beyond it the beginning of the garden.

The door stood wide and he went through it, seeking the garden where he knew the sun must be shining. Then he saw the picture. He stood quite still and he stared at it.

It was a painting of a lady in an old-fashioned dress of striped silk, bright blue and gold, with a little gold cap on her head. She was holding a silver plate and in the plate was the head of a man.

He knew it must be a very good painting because the artist had made it look so real. Nothing was left out, not even the blood in the plate and the white tube things in the man's neck where it had been cut from his body.

The lady wasn't looking at the thing in the plate but at him. She was smiling and there was a strange expression on her face, dreamy, triumphant, replete. He had never seen such a look in anyone's eyes before but suddenly he knew with an intuition that had in it something of an *a priori* knowledge, that grown-ups sometimes looked at each other like that and that they did so out of the sight of children.

He tore his eyes from the picture and put his hand up to his mouth to stop them hearing his scream. Then he rushed blindly away, making for the glass place that separated this room from the garden.

He stumbled at the step and put out his hand to save himself. It touched something cool and soft—but only for a moment. The coolness and softness were succeeded by a terrible burning pain that seemed to smite him exactly like the shock he had had from his mother's electric iron.

Away in the garden someone laughed. He screamed and screamed and screamed until he heard doors banging, feet flying, the women coming to him from the kitchen.

PART ONE

1

'PRUSSIC acid?' The chemist was startled. He had been a member of the Pharmaceutical Society for ten years and this was the first time anyone had made such a request to him. Not that he would grant it. He was a responsible citizen, almost—in his own estimation—a doctor. 'Cyanide of Potassium?' He looked severely at the small man in the suit that was too dark and too thick for a hot day. 'What d'you want that for?'

Edward Carnaby, for his part, was affronted. Mr. Waller was only a chemist, a pharmacist really, not a proper chemist who worked in a laboratory. Everyone knew that doctors poked their noses into one's affairs, trying to find out things that were no business of theirs, but not chemists. You asked for what you wanted—razor blades or shaving cream or a camera film—and the chemist gave it to you. He wrapped it up and you paid for it, When all was said and done Waller was only a shopkeeper.

'I want it for killing wasps. I've got a wasp nest on the wall of my house under the roof.'

He fidgeted uneasily under Waller's accusing gaze. The fan on the ceiling, instead of cooling the shop, was only blowing the hot air about.

'May I have your name, please?'

'What for? I don't have to have a prescription for it, do I?'

11

Waller ignored the sarcasm. Responsible professional men must not allow themselves to be ruffled by cheap cracks.

'What gave you the idea of cyanide?' As he spoke the curtain of coloured plastic strips that hung across the entrance to the dispensary parted and Linda Gaveston came out in her pink overall. Her appearance angered Edward, partly because she looked so cool, partly because he felt that a girl whose parents lived on Linchester had no business to be working as an assistant in a chemist's shop. She smiled at him vaguely. Edward snapped:

'If you must know, I read about it in a gardening book.'

Plausible, Waller thought.

'Rather an old-fashioned book, surely? These days we get rid of wasps by using a reliable vespicide.' He paused, allowing the unfamiliar word to sink in. 'One that is harmless to warm-blooded . . .'

'All right,' Edward interrupted him. He wasn't going to make a scene in front of one of those snooty Gavestons. 'Why didn't you say so before? I'll take it. What's it called?'

'Vesprid.' Waller shot him a last baleful look and turned round, but the girl—showing off, Edward thought—was already holding the tin towards him. 'Two and eleven.'

'Thanks,' Edward said shortly, taking the penny change.

'The instructions are enclosed.'

Linda Gaveston lifted her shoulders slightly and slipped between the waving strips in the way she had seen a night club girl insinuate herself through a bead curtain on television.

'There goes a nut,' she said to Waller when Edward had gone. 'He lives near us.'

'Really?' Like all the shopkeepers in Chantflower village Waller had a great respect for Linchester. Money flowed from it as from a spring of sweet water. 'Not quite what one has been led to expect.' He watched Edward get into his

12

salesman's car, its back seat full of cardboard boxes. 'It takes all sorts,' he said.

On that hot afternoon Freda Carnaby was the only Linchester housewife who was really working and she was not a wife at all. She was cleaning the windows in the single living room of Edward's chalet partly because she was houseproud and partly because it was a good excuse for watching the cars coming round The Circle. Linchester business men kept short hours and the man she was looking for might be early. He would wave, even perhaps stop and renew his promise to see her later, and he would notice afresh how efficient she was, how womanly. Moreover he would see that she could look smart and pretty not only in the evenings but also with a wash leather in her hand.

Considering who she was looking for it was ironic that the first car to appear was Tamsin Selby's. Even if you didn't see the number plate (SIN 1A) you would know it was Tamsin's Mini because, although it was new, its black body and white roof were already marked with raindrops and with dust, and the back seat was full of leaves and twigs, rubbish from the fields. Freda pursed her lips in happy disapproval. If you had money and you bought nice things (what that monogram of a number plate must have cost!) you ought to take care of them.

Dr. Greenleaf's car followed fast on her tail. It was time, Freda considered, that he bought a new one. A doctor, she had read in one of her magazines, was nowadays the most respected member of a community, and therefore had appearances to keep up. She smiled and bobbed her head. She thought the doctor's kindly grin meant he was grateful to her for being so healthy and not taking up his surgery time.

By the time Joan Smith-King arrived with her shooting

13

brake full of the Linchester children she had fetched from school, Freda had finished the window.

'All delivered in plain vans,' Joan said cheerfully. 'Den says I ought to have a C licence.'

'Can I go to tea with Peter?' Cheryl called. 'Can I, Auntie Free? Please.'

'If you're sure she's no trouble,' Freda said. Cheryl might be only a salesman's daughter, but she had nice manners. She, Freda, had seen to that. But going out to tea was a nuisance. Now Cheryl would come rushing in at seven just when Freda wanted to be relaxed and ready with coffee cups on the best traycloth, paper napkins and sherry in a decanter.

'Ghastly these wasps.' Joan looked up at the chalet roof where the wasps were dribbling out from under the eaves. 'Tamsin said Patrick got a nasty sting on his hand.'

'Did he?' Freda took her eyes from Joan's face and stared innocently at the hedge. 'Don't be late,' she said to Cheryl. Joan moved off, one hand on the wheel, the other pulling Jeremy off Peter, shoving her daughter Susan into Cheryl's lap. The baby in its carry-cot on the front seat began to cry. Freda went round the back and into the spotless kitchen.

She was re-doing her face from the little *cache* of cosmetics she kept in a drawer when she heard Edward's car draw up on the drive. The front door slammed.

'Free?'

She bustled into the lounge. Edward was already at the record-player, starting up The Hall of the Mountain King.

'You might have shut the gates,' she said from the window, but she didn't press the point. A wife could expect small services, not a sister. A sister was only a housekeeper, a nanny to Edward's motherless daughter. Still . . . she cheered up. A couple of years and she might have a child of her own.

14

'How long till tea?'

'Five thirty sharp,' said Freda. 'I'm sure I never keep you waiting for your meals, Ted.'

'Only it's car maintenance at seven.'

Edward went to a different class each night. French on Mondays and Thursdays, accountancy on Tuesdays, carpentry on Wednesdays, car maintenance on Fridays. Freda approved his industry. It was a way, she supposed, of forgetting the wife who had lived just long enough to put the curtains up in the new house and who had died before the first instalment was due on the mortgage.

'What are you going to do?'

She shrugged. He was her brother, but he was also her twin and as jealous of her time as a husband might be.

'Sometimes,' he said, 'I wonder if you haven't got a secret boy-friend who pops in when I'm out of the way.'

Had there been talk, gossip? Well, why not? Only a few days now and everyone would know. Edward would know. Funny, but it made her shiver to think of it.

He turned the record over and straightened up. Solveig's Song, music for a cold climate, soared into the stuffy room. The pure voice pleased Freda, reminding her of large uncluttered rooms she had so far seen only from the outside as she passed with her shopping baskets. On the whole, she thought, she would like to live there. She wouldn't be squeamish. He loves me, she thought, not thinking of Edward. A long shudder of pain and anxious happiness travelled down from her shoulders and along her thighs to her feet in their tight pointed shoes.

'I wouldn't like that, Free,' he said. 'You're best off here with me.'

'We shall have to see what time brings forth, shan't we?' she said, staring through the diamond panes at Linchester, at ten more houses that encircled a green plot. How nice, how stimulating it would be next year to see it all from a different angle. When she turned round Edward was beside her, flicking his fingers in front of her face to break up the myopic stare.

'Don't,' she said. Hurt, he sat down and opened his home-work book, *An Outline of Monetary Economics.* Freda went upstairs to lacquer her hair, straighten her stocking seams and spray a little more Fresh Mist under her arms.

Denholm Smith-King was used to performing small and, for that matter, large services for his wife. With five children he could hardly do otherwise. He was already at home when she arrived back, making what he called euphemistically 'a cup of tea'. In the Smith-King household this meant slicing and buttering a whole large loaf and carving up a couple of pound cakes.

'You're early,' she said.

'Not much doing.' He greeted Cheryl vaguely as if he was uncertain whether or not she was one of his own children. 'Things are a bit slack so I hied me to the bosom of my family.'

'Slack?' She found a tablecloth and spread it on what had once been a fine unblemished sheet of teak. 'I don't like the sound of that, Den. I'm always meaning to talk to you about the business. . . .'

'Did you find anyone to sit in with the mob tomorrow night?' he asked, adroitly changing the subject.

'Linda Gaveston said she'd come. I asked her when I was in Waller's.' Joan found the piece of pasteboard from the mêlée on the mantelpiece and read its message aloud: 'Tamsin and Patrick Selby At Home. Saturday, July 4th, eight p.m. Of course I know how affected Tamsin is, but At Home's going a bit far.'

16

'I reckon you can go as far as you like,' said Denholm, 'when you've got a private income and no kids.'

'It's only a birthday party. She's twenty-seven tomorrow.'

Denholm sat down heavily, a reluctant paterfamilias at the head of his table. 'Twenty-seven? I wouldn't have put her at a day over twenty.'

'Oh, don't be so silly, Den. They've been married for years.' She had been piqued by his admiration of another woman, but now she looked at him tenderly over their children's heads. 'Fancy being married for years to Patrick Selby!'

'I daresay it's all a matter of taste, old girl.'

'I don't know what it is,' Joan said, 'but he frightens me. I get the shivers every time I see him walking past here with that great German dog of his.' She wiped the baby's chin and sighed. 'It came in the garden again this morning. Tamsin was most apologetic. I'll grant her that. She's a nice enough girl in her way, only she always seems only half awake.'

'Pity they haven't got any kids,' Denholm said wistfully. Uncertain as to whether he was wishing children on to the Selbys from genuine regret for their childlessness or from motives of revenge, Joan gave him a sharp look.

'They're first cousins, you know.'

'Ah,' said Denholm, 'brought up together. One of those boy and girl things, was it?'

'I don't know,' said his wife. 'He's not likely to confide in anyone and she's far too much of the little girl lost.'

When tea was over the children drifted into the garden. Joan handed her husband a tea towel and began to wash up. Jeremy's scream made them both jump and before it had died away Denholm, who knew what it meant, was out on the

17

lawn brandishing the stick he kept in the storm porch for this purpose.

Only Cheryl had not backed away. The other children clung to Denholm as he advanced between the swing and the sandpit.

'Get out of it, you great brute!'

The Weimaraner looked at him courteously but with a kind of mild disdain. There was nothing savage about her but nothing endearing either. She was too autocratic, too highly-bred for that. Haunch-deep in marigolds, she was standing in the middle of Denholm's herbaceous border and now, as he shouted at her again, she flicked out a raspberry pink tongue and delicately snapped off a larkspur blossom.

Cheryl caught at Denholm's hand. 'She's a nice dog, really she is. She often comes to our house.'

Her words meant nothing to Denholm but he dropped the stick. Insensitive as he was, he could hardly beat the dog in the presence of the woman who had appeared so suddenly and so silently on the lawn next door.

'Queenie often comes to our house,' Cheryl said again.

Tamsin Selby had heard. A spasm of pain crossed her smooth brown face and was gone.

'I'm so dreadfully sorry.' She smiled without showing her teeth. 'Please don't be cross, Denholm. She's very gentle.'

Denholm grinned foolishly. The Selbys, both of them, always made him feel a fool. It was the contrast, perhaps, between their immaculate garden and his own cluttered playground; their pale hand-stitched clothes and what he called his 'togs'; their affluence and his need.

'It puts the wind up the youngsters,' he said gruffly.

'Come on, Queenie!' The long brown arm rose languidly in an elegant parabola. At once the dog leaped, clearing the hedge with two inches to spare. 'I hope we'll see you tomorrow, Denholm?'

'You can count on us. Never miss a good booze-up.' He was embarrassed and he went in quickly. But Cheryl lingered, staring over the hedge with curious intelligent eyes and wondering why the lady who was so unlike Auntie Free had fallen to her knees under the willow tree and flung her arms round the dog's creamy sable neck.

2

FIVE years before when Nottinghamshire people talked about Linchester they meant the Manor and the park. If they were county they remembered garden parties, if not, coach trips to a Palladian house where you paid half-a-crown to look at a lot of valuable but boring china while the children rolled down the ha-ha. But all that came to an end when old Marvell died. One day, it seemed, the Manor was there, the next there were just the bulldozers Henry Glide brought over from the city and a great cloud of dust floating above the trees, grey and pancake-shaped, as if someone had exploded a small atom bomb.

Nobody would live there, they said, forgetting that commuting was the fashion even in the provinces. Henry himself had his doubts and he had put up three chalet bungalows before he realised he might be on to a better thing if he forgot all about retired farmers and concentrated on Nottingham company directors. Fortunately, but by the merest chance, the three mistakes were almost hidden by a screen of elms. He nearly lost his head and built big houses with small gardens all over the estate, but he had a cautious look at the Marvell contract and saw that there was an embargo on too much tree-felling. His wife thought he was getting senile when he said he was only going to put up eight more houses, eight beautiful architect-designed houses around a broad green plot with a pond in the middle.

And that was what people meant now when they talked about Linchester. They meant The Green with the pond where swans glided between lily leaves as big as dinner plates; The Circle which was a smart name for the road that ran around The Green; the Cotswold farmhouse and the mock-Tudor lodge, the Greenleafs' place that might have been prefabricated in Hampstead Garden Suburb and flown complete into Nottinghamshire, the Selbys' glass box and Glide's own suntrap bungalow. They pointed from the tops of buses on the Nottingham road at the Gavestons' pocket-sized grange, the Gages' Queen Anne and the Smith-King place that had started off as a house and now was just a breeding box. They criticised the chalets, those poor relations and their occupants, the Staxtons, the Macdonalds and the Carnabys.

The two men in the British Railways lorry lived in Newark and they had never been to Linchester before. Now, on the calmest, most beautiful evening of the summer, they saw it at its best. Yet it was not the loveliness of the place that impressed them, the elegant sweep of The Circle, the stone pineapples on the pillars at the Manor gates, nor the trees, elms, oaks and sycamores, that gave each house its expensive privacy, but the houses themselves and their opulence.

Over-awed and at the same time suspicious, they drove between the pillars and into The Circle itself, looking for a house called Hallows.

The lorry rumbled along the road, making ruts in the melting tar and sending white spar chips flying, past the three mistakes, past Shalom, The Laurels, Linchester Lodge.

'That's the one I'd fancy,' said the driver, pointing to the Cotswold farmhouse with a hint of Swiss chalet in its jade-coloured balconies. 'If my pools come up.' His mate was silent, consumed with envy and with scorn.

'Keep your eyes open, Reg. It's gone knocking-off time.'

21

'Blimey,' said his mate, throwing his cigarette end into the Gavestons' rhododendrons, 'I haven't got X-ray eyes. It's half a mile up to them front doors, and what with the trees.'

'Now, I'd have them down. Keep out the light, they do. And I'd do something about that empty bit in the middle. You could put up a couple of nice bungalows where that pond is. Here we are. Hallows. I don't know what I brought you for. I could have done better on my tod.'

But he was glad of Reg's help when it came to unloading the parcel. It was heavy and, according to the label, fragile. Something like a door it was or a big mirror. He could just feel a frame thing through the corrugated cardboard.

They humped it up the drive between two rows of young willows until they came to the paved court in front of the house.

Hallows was beautiful—by most people's standards. Reg and the driver found it on the dull side compared with its ornate neighbours. This house was plain and rectangular, built of York stone and pale unpolished wood; there were no gables and no chimneys, no shutters and not a single pane of stained glass. The windows were huge, backed with white venetian blinds, and the front doors were swing affairs of glass set in steel.

'Are you looking for me?' The voice, delicate, vague, unmistakeably upper-class, came from above their heads. The driver looked up to a long undecorated balcony and saw a woman leaning over the rails.

'British Railways, lady.'

'Too dreadful! ' Tamsin Selby said. 'I'd forgotten all about it.'

It was true, she had. The delivery of this parcel had been planned in a sprightly, almost malicious mood, very different from her present one. But it had taken so long in coming, so much had happened. She disappeared through the balcony windows back into the bedroom.

'How the rich live,' Reg said to the driver. 'Forgotten, my foot!'

Tamsin came out to them breathlessly. At all costs it must be got in and, if possible, hidden, before Patrick came home. She tried to take it from them but the weight was too much for her. The men watched her efforts with a kind of triumph.

'Would you be terribly sweet,' Tamsin said, 'and carry it upstairs for me?'

'Now, look,' the driver began, 'it's heavy . . .'

She took two half-crowns from the bag she had snatched up in the hall.

'Can't leave it here, can we?' Reg was grinning reluctantly.

'So kind,' said Tamsin. She led the way and they followed her, carrying the parcel gingerly to avoid scraping the dove-grey hessian on the hall walls, the paint on the curled iron baluster rails.

'In here, I think.'

The room was too beautiful for them. Poverty, never admitted, scarcely felt before, scummed their hands with ineluctable dirt. They looked away from the velvet curtains, the dressing-table glass ringed with light bulbs, the half-open door that showed a glimpse of a shower cabinet and tiles hand-painted with fishes, and down at their own feet.

'Could you put it on one of the beds?'

They lowered it on to the nearer of the cream silk counterpanes, avoiding the bed by the window where the turned-back cover revealed a lemon lace nightgown folded between frilled nylon pillow and frilled nylon sheet.

'Thank you so much. It won't be in the way here.'

She didn't even bother to smooth the silk where a corner of the parcel had ruffled it, but signed her name quickly and hustled them out of the house. After they had gone she closed the spare bedroom door and sighed deeply. Patrick would be home any minute now and she had meant to use those spare moments checking on everything, making sure she looked her best.

She went into the bedroom with the balcony and looked at herself in the glass. That was all right, just the way Patrick liked her to look, the way he had liked her to look once . . . The sun—she had spent most of the day in the sun—had done wonders for her already brown skin and had faintly bleached her dark honey hair. No make-up. To have put on lipstick would have been to spoil the image she liked to create, the facsimile of a smooth teak-coloured mask, straight nose, carved lips, cheekbones that were arched polished planes.

Her hair hung quite straight on to her brown shoulders. Even for him she refused to cut it short and have it set. The dress—that was all right at any rate. Patrick hated bright colours and this one was black and white. Plain as it was, she knew there might be something too casual about it, too suggestive of a uniform for emancipated women. O God, she thought, making a face at her own image and wishing for the first time in her life that it could be transmuted into the reflection of a brisk blonde *hausfrau*.

Downstairs the table was already laid for dinner: two place mats of blue linen—he had made her give up using the big damask cloths—black Prinknash plates, a long basket of French bread, Riesling dewed from the refrigerator. Tamsin gasped aloud when she saw that she had forgotten to throw away the vaseful of grasses. She grabbed them, scattering brown seeds, and rushed to the kitchen. The dog now, had she fed the dog?

'Queenie!'

How many times in the past months had he scolded her

24

for failing to feed the dog on the dot of five? How many times had he snapped at her for wasting her days dreaming in the garden and the fields, learning country lore from Crispin Marvell, when she should have been at home keeping up with the Gages and the Gavestons.

But she must have done it and, in her panic, forgotten all about it. The plate of congealing horsemeat and biscuit meal was still on the floor, untouched by the dog. Flies buzzed over it and a single wasp crawled across a chunk of fat.

'Queenie!'

The bitch appeared silently from the garden door, sniffed at the food and looked enquiringly at Tamsin with mournful eyes. She is the only thing that we have together now, Tamsin thought, the only thing that we both love, Kreuznacht Konigin, that we both call Queenie. She dropped to her knees and in her loneliness she put her arms round Queenie's neck, feeling the suede-smooth skin against her own cheek. Queenie's tail flapped and she nuzzled against Tamsin's ear.

Of the two female creatures desirous of pleasing Patrick it was the dog who heard him first. She stiffened and the swinging lethargic tail began to wag excitedly, banging against the cooker door and making a noise like a gong.

'Master,' Tamsin said. 'Go, find him!'

The Weimaraner stretched her lean body, cocked her head and stood for a moment poised, much as her ancestors had done listening for the huntsman's command in the woods of Thuringia a century ago. The heavy garage door rumbled and fell with a faint clang. Queenie was away, across the patio, leaping for the iron gate that shut off the drive.

Tamsin followed, her heart pounding.

He came in slowly, not looking at her, silent, his attention given solely to the dog. When he had fondled Queenie, his hands drawing down the length of her body, he looked up and saw his wife.

Tamsin had so much to say, so many endearments remembered from the days when it was necessary to say nothing. No words came. She stood there, looking at him, her hands kneading the black and white stuff of her dress. Swinging the ignition key, Patrick pushed past her, shied at a wasp that dived against his face, and went into the house.

'She hasn't eaten her dinner,' were the first words that he spoke to her. He hated dirt, disorder, matter in the wrong place. 'It's all over flies.'

Tamsin picked up the plate and dropped the contents into the waste disposal unit. Meat juice rubbed off on to her fingers. Patrick looked pointedly at her hand, turned and went upstairs. She ran the tap, rinsed her fingers. It seemed an age since he had gone—the wine, would it get too warm? Ought she to put it back in the fridge? She waited, the sweat seeping into her dress. Presently she switched on the fan.

At last he came in wearing terylene slacks and a tee shirt of pale striped cotton, and he looked handsome if you admired men with ash-blond hair and freckles so dense that they looked like tan.

'I thought you'd like melon,' she said. 'It's canteloupe.'

Suspiciously Patrick skimmed away the melting golden sugar.

'Not honey, is it? You know I hate honey.'

'Of course it isn't.' She paused timidly. 'Darling,' she said.

He made his way silently through chicken salad, potato sticks, fruit salad (all good hygienic food from tins and packets and deep freezers), eating sparingly, absentmindedly. The fan whirred and Queenie lay beneath it, paws spread, tongue extended.

26

'I've got everything in for the party,' Tamsin said.

'Party?'

'Tomorrow. It's my birthday. You hadn't forgotten?'

'No, it slipped my mind, that's all.'

Had it also slipped his mind to get her a present?

'There's heaps to do,' she said brightly. 'The lights to put up, and we've got to move the furniture in the—' Now it was more than ever important to pick the right word, '—the lounge in case it rains. And—Oh, Patrick, could you do something about the wasps? I'm sure there's a nest somewhere.' She remembered belatedly and reached for his hand. The fingers lay inert in hers, the big red swelling showing at the base of his thumb. 'Too frightful for you. How's it been today?'

'The sting? Oh, all right. It's going down.'

'Could you possibly try to get rid of them? They'll ruin the party.'

He pushed away his plate and his half-finished glass of wine.

'Not tonight. I'm going out.'

She had begun to tremble and when she spoke her voice shook.

'There's so much to do. Please don't go, darling. I need you.'

Patrick laughed. She didn't look at him but sat staring at her plate, moving the viscous yellow juice about with her spoon.

'I *am* going out. I have to take the dog, don't I?'

'I'll take the dog.'

'Thank you very much,' he said icily. 'I can manage.' He touched the venetian blind and glanced at the faint patina of dust on his fingertips. 'If you're bored there are things here which could do with some attention.'

'Patrick.' Her face had paled and there were goose pimples on her arms. 'About what you said last night—you've got to change your mind. You've got to forget all about it ' With a great effort she pushed three words from stiff lips: 'I love you.'

She might not have spoken. He walked into the kitchen and took the leash from the broom cupboard.

'Queenie! '

From deep sleep the Weimaraner galvanised into impassioned life. Patrick fastened the steel clip to her collar and led her out through the french windows.

Tamsin sat among the ruins of her meal. Presently she began to cry silently, the tears splashing into the wine glass she held in her cupped hands. Her mouth was dry and she drank. I am drinking my own sorrow, she thought. Five minutes, ten minutes passed. Then she went to the front door and out into the willow avenue. The sky was clear, azure above, violet and apricot on the horizon, thronged with wheeling swallows.

She stopped at the end of the drive and leaned on the gate. Patrick hadn't gone far. She could see him standing with his back to her on The Green staring down at the waters of the pond. The dog had tried, unsuccessfully as always, to intimidate the three white swans. Now she had given up and was following a squirrel trail, pausing at the foot of each tree and peering up into the branches. Patrick was waiting for something, whiling away his time. For what?

As she watched him, a pale green Ford swung into view from behind the elms. That funny little salesman fellow from the chalets, she thought, on his way to his evening class. She hoped he'd pass on with a wave but he didn't. He stopped. Few men passed Tamsin Selby without a second glance.

28

'Hot enough for you?'

'I like it,' Tamsin said. What was his name? Only one chalet dweller was known to her by name. 'I love the sun.'

'Ah well, it suits you. I can see that.'

Conversation would have to be made. She opened the gate and went over to the car. He mistook her action and opened the door.

'Can I give you a lift? I'm going to the village.'

'No. No, thanks.' Tamsin almost laughed. 'I'm not going out. Just enjoying the evening.'

His face fell.

'As a matter of fact,' he said, stalling, trying to keep her with him long enough for the neighbours to see him talking to the beautiful Mrs. Selby, 'as a matter of fact I'm playing truant. Supposed to be doing a little job exterminating pests.'

'Pests?'

'Wasps. We've got a nest.'

'Have you? So have we.' She looked up. Patrick was still there. 'My husband—we want to get rid of them but we don't know how.'

'I've got some stuff. It's called Vesprid. I tell you what. When I've done mine I'll bring the tin round. There's bags of it, enough to kill all the wasps in Nottinghamshire.'

'But how kind!'

'I'll bring it round in the morning, shall I?'

Tamsin sighed. Now she would have to have this wretched man in the way while she was preparing for the party.

'Look, why don't you come to a little do I'm having, a few friends in for drinks at about eight?' He looked at her adoringly and his eyes reminded her of Queenie's. 'If you could come early we could do the wasps then. Bring a friend if you like.'

A party at Hallows! A party at the biggest house on Linchester! Putting on his maudlin widower's voice, he said: 'I haven't been to a party since I lost my wife.'

'Really?' A chord had been struck. 'His wife's dead,' Patrick had said, 'and that's why . . .' What had she done? 'I'm sorry but I don't think I know your name.'

'Carnaby. Edward Carnaby.'

He looked at her, smiling. She took her hand from the car door and pressed it against her breastbone, breathing like one who has run up a steep hill.

Trust Tamsin Selby to be talking to a man, Joan thought, as she came out of her gate, holding Cheryl by the hand.

'Wave to your Daddy.'

The child was more interested in the man and the dog on The Green. Telling herself that she had meant to go that way in any case, Joan followed her reluctantly.

Patrick had never been one to waste words on the weather or other people's health. His eyes, which had been fixed with a kind of calculating disgust on Edward Carnaby, now turned upon Joan, taking in the details of her limp cotton dress, her sunburned arms and the brown roots of her hair where the rinse was growing out.

'Isn't it *hot*?' She was uncomfortable in his presence and felt the remark had been foolish. In fact, it was no longer particularly hot. A faint breeze was stirring the waters of the pond, ruffling it to match the mackerel sky.

'I don't know why English people make a cult of grumbling about the weather,' he said. He looked very Teutonic as he spoke and she remembered someone had told her he had spent his childhood in Germany and America. She laughed awkwardly and made a grab for Cheryl's hand. He had made it so clear he didn't want to talk to her that she jumped and blushed when he called her back.

30

'How's business?'

'Business?' Of course he meant Denholm's business, the factory. 'All right, I suppose,' she said, and then because ever since before tea there had been a vague, half-formed worry nagging at her mind, 'Den says things have been a bit slack lately.'

'We can't all get Harwell contracts.' He touched the trunk of a great oak and with a small smile looked up into its branches. 'They don't grow on trees. It's a matter of work, my dear Joan, work and single-mindedness. Denholm will have to watch his step or I'll be taking him over one of these days.'

She said nothing. Malice quirked the corners of his thin mouth. She looked away from him and at the dog. Then she saw that he, too, was staring in the same direction.

'Expansion is life,' he said. 'Give it a few months and then we'll make things hum.'

Shivering a little, she drew back from him, feeling a sudden chill that seemed to come not from the scurrying wind but from the man himself.

'We're late, Cheryl. It's past your bedtime.'

'She can come with me,' said Patrick, his curious smile broadening. 'I'm going that way.'

The green Ford had moved away from the Hallows gate but Tamsin was still there, watching. As the man and child walked off towards the chalets, Joan suddenly thought she would go and speak to Tamsin, demand the explanation she knew Patrick would never give to her. But Tamsin, she saw, was in no mood for talking. Something or someone had upset her and she was retreating up the willow drive, her head bent and her hands clenched beneath her chin. Joan went home and put the children to bed. When she came downstairs Denholm was asleep. He looked so like Jeremy, his eyes lightly closed, his cheek pink and smooth against the bunched-up cushion, that she hadn't the heart to wake him.

Edward Carnaby kept on turning back and waving all the way down to the Manor gates. Tamsin stared after him, unable to smile in return. Her knees felt weak and she was afraid she might faint. When she reached the house she heard Queenie bark, a single staccato bark followed by a howl. The howls went on for a few seconds; then they stopped and all was silent. Tasmin knew what the howls meant. Patrick had tied up the dog to go into someone's house.

She went upstairs and into the balcony room. In the faint bloom on the dressing-table Patrick had written with a precise finger: Dust this. She fell on the bed and lay facedownwards.

Half an hour had passed when she heard the footsteps and at first she thought they were Patrick's. But whoever it was was coming alone. There was no accompanying tip-tap of dog's claws on stone. O God, she thought, I shall have to tell him. Otherwise Patrick might, there in front of everyone at the party.

The doors were unlocked. There was nothing to stop him coming in, but he didn't. He knocked with the prearranged signal. What would he do when he knew it all? There was still a chance she could persuade Patrick. She put her fingers in her ears, willing him to go. He knocked again and it seemed to her that he must hear through glass and wood, stone walls and thick carpets, the beating of her heart.

At last he went away.

'Damnation!' she heard him say from beneath her as if he were looking through the lounge window. The footsteps hurried away down the avenue and out through the footpath on to the Nottingham road. The gate swung, failed to catch and flapped against the post, bang, swing, bang. Tamsin went into the room where the men had put the parcel. She broke her nails untying the string but she was crying too much to notice.

3

THERE are perhaps few things more galling to one's *amour propre* than to act in a covert, clandestine way when no such discretion is necessary. Oliver Gage was a proud man and now, creeping round the Hallows paths, tapping signals on the glass doors, he felt that someone had made a fool of him.

'Damnation!' he said, this time under his breath.

She had obviously gone out with *him*. Pressure had been put on her. Well, so much the better if that meant she had been preparing the ground. He would make his intentions clear at the party.

He went out into The Circle and made the humiliating detour necessary before he could find his car that he had parked on the ride off the main road. When he entered Linchester for the second time that night it was by the Manor gates and he drove into his own garage drive with a sense of disgruntled virtue and the shame he always felt when he returned to his house. Oliver lived in one of the largest houses on Linchester but it was too small for him. He hated it already. Every Friday night when he came up from his four days in London the sight of the house, magnified perhaps in his mind during his absence, sickened him and reminded him afresh of his misfortunes. For, as Oliver grew older, the sizes of his houses diminished. This was not due to a reversal in his financial life. One of the executives of a national daily, his income now topped the seven thousand mark, but only about a third of this found its way into Oliver's pocket. The rest, never seen by him yet never forgotten, streamed away via an army of solicitors and bank managers and accountants into the laps of his two discarded wives.

When he had married Nancy—pretty, witty Nancy! —and built this, the smallest of his houses to date, he had forgotten for a few months the other pressures on his income. Was not love a Hercules, still climbing trees in the Hesperides? Now, a year later, he reflected that the gods were just and of his pleasant vices had made instruments to plague him.

He unlocked the door and dropped his keys on to the hall table between the Flamenco doll and the cherry heering bottle that Nancy by the addition of a shade stuck all over with hotel labels had converted into a lamp. In all his matrimonial career Oliver had never before given houseroom to such an object. He hated it but he felt that, in ensuring it was the first thing his eye fell on when he entered his home, Providence was meting out to him a stern exquisite justice.

Nancy's sewing machine could be heard faintly from the lounge. The querulous whine of the motor fanned his ill-temper into rage. He pushed open the reeded glass door and went in. The room was tightly sealed and stifling, the windows all closed and the curtains drawn back in the way he loathed, carelessly, with no attention to the proper arrangement of their folds. Those curtains had cost him thirty pounds.

His wife—to himself and to one other Oliver occasionally referred to her as his present wife—lifted her foot from the pedal which controlled the motor and pushed damp hair back from a face on which sweat shone. Shreds of cotton and pieces of coloured fluff clung to her dress and littered the

35

floor. There was even a piece of cotton dangling from her bracelet.

'My Christ, it's like an oven in here!' Oliver flung back the french windows and scowled at Bernice Greenleaf who was walking coolly about the garden next-door, snipping the dead blossoms off an opulent Zephirine Drouhin. When she waved to him he changed the scowl into a rigid smirk 'What in God's name are you doing?' he asked his wife.

She pulled a cobbled strip of black and red silk from under the needle. 'I'm making a dress for Tamsin's party.'

Oliver sat down heavily, catching his foot in one of the Numdah rugs. ('If we have wood block flooring and rugs, darling,' Nancy had said, 'we'll save pounds on carpeting.')

'This I cannot understand,' Oliver said. 'Did I or did I not give you a cheque for twenty pounds last Tuesday with express instructions to buy yourself a dress?'

'Well . . .'

'Did I or did I not? That's all I ask. It's a perfectly simple question.'

Nancy's babyish, *gamine* face puckered. A curly face, he had called it once, tenderly, lovingly, touching with a teasing finger the tip-tilted nose, the bunchy cheeks, the fluffy fair eyebrows.

'Well, darling, I had to have shoes, you see, and stockings. And there was the milk bill . . .' Her voice faltered. 'I saw this remnant and this pattern . . .' She held an envelope towards him diffidently. Oliver glowered at the coloured picture of three improbably tall women in cylindrical cotton frocks. 'It'll be all right, won't it?'

'It will be quite ghastly,' Oliver said coldly. 'I shall be covered with shame. I shall be mortified. Tamsin always looks wonderful.'

As soon as the words were out he regretted them. Now

36

was not the time. Nancy was going to cry. Her face swelled as if the skin itself was allergic to his anger.

'Tamsin has a private income.' The tears spouted. 'I only wanted to save you money. That's all I think about, saving your money.'

'Oh, don't cry! I'm sorry, Nancy.' She almost fell from her chair into his lap and he put his arms round her with the distaste that was part of his marital experience, the distaste that always came as love ebbed. Every bit of her was damp and clinging and unbearably hot.

'I do want to economise, darling. I keep thinking of all that money going out month after month to Jean and Shirley. And what with both the boys at Bembridge . . .' Oliver frowned. He disliked the reminder that he had been unable to afford to send the sons of his first marriage to Marlborough. 'And Shirley always so greedy, insisting on sending Jennifer to a private school when state education is so good these days.'

'You know nothing at all about state education,' Oliver said.

'Oh, darling, why did you have to marry such unattractive women? Any other women would have got married again. Two such disastrous—well, tragic marriages. I lie awake at night thinking about the inroads on our income.'

She was off on a well-worn track, the Friday night special. Oliver let her talk, reaching to the mantelpiece for a cigarette from the box.

'And I haven't got anything exciting for your dinner,' she finished on a note of near-triumph.

'We'll go out to eat, then.'

'You know we can't afford it. Besides I've got to finish this filthy dress.' She struggled from his lap back to the sewing machine.

'This,' said Oliver, 'is the end.' Nancy, already involved

37

once more in fitting a huge sleeve into a tiny armhole, ignored him. She was not to know that it was with these words that Oliver had terminated each of his previous marriages. For him, too, they sounded dreadfully like the mere echoes of happy finalities. Must Nancy be his till death parted them? More securely than any devout Catholic, any puritan idealist, he had thought himself until recently, bound to his wife. Hercules had climbed his last tree. Unless— unless things would work out and he could get a wife with money of her own, a beautiful, well-dowered wife . . .

He stepped across the rugs, those small and far from luxuriant oases in the big desert of polished floor, and poured himself a carefully-measured drink. Then he sat down and gazed at their reflections, his and Nancy's, in the glass on the opposite wall. Her remarks as to the unattractiveness of his former wives had seemed to denigrate his own taste and perhaps even his own personal appearance. But now, as he looked at himself, he felt their injustice. Anyone coming in, any stranger would, he thought bitterly, have taken Nancy for the cleaning woman doing a bit of overtime sewing, her hair separated into rough hanks, her face greasy with heat and effort. But as for him, with his smooth dark head, the sharply cut yet sensitive features, the long hands that held the blood-red glass . . . the truth of it was that he was wasted in these provincial, incongruous surroundings.

Nancy got up, shook her hair, and began to pull her dress over her head. She was simply going to try on the limp half-finished thing but Oliver was no fool and he could tell from the way she moved, slowly, coquettishly, that there was also intention to tempt him.

'If you must strip in the living room you might pull the curtains,' he said.

He got up and put his hand to the cords that worked the

pulley, first the french windows, then at the long Georgian sashes at the front of the house. The silk folds moved to meet each other but not before, through the strip of narrowing glass, he had seen walking past the gate, a tall fair man who rested a freckled hand on a dog's head, a man who was strolling home to a beautiful well-dowered wife . . .

With this glimpse there came into his mind a sudden passionate wish that this time things might for once go smoothly and to the advantage of Oliver Gage. He stood for a moment, thinking and planning, and then he realised that he had no wish to be here like this in the darkness with his wife, and he reached quickly for the light switch.

It was fully dark, outside as well as in, when Denholm awoke. He blinked, passed his hands across his face and stretched.

'Ah, well,' he said to his wife, 'up the wooden hill.'

She had meant to save it all for the morning, but the hours of sitting silently beside the sleeping man had told on her nerves. His expression became incredulous as she began to tell him of the meeting on The Green.

'He was pulling your leg,' he said.

'No, he wasn't. I wouldn't have believed him only I know you've been worried lately. You have been worried, haven't you?'

'Well, if you must know, things have been a bit dicey.' She listened as the bantering tone left his voice. 'Somebody's been building up a big stake in the company.' Only when he was talking business could Denholm shed facetiousness and become a man instead of a clown. 'It's been done through a nominee and we don't know who it is.'

'But, Den,' she cried, 'that must be Patrick!'

'He wouldn't be interested in us. Selbys are glass, nothing but glass and we're chemicals.'

'He would. I tell you, he is. He's got that contract and he means to expand, to take you over. And it does rest with him. The others are just—what do you call it?—sleeping partners.'

She would have to say it, put into words the grotesque fear that had been churning her thoughts the entire evening.

'D'you know what I think? I think it's all malice, just because you once hit that dog.'

The shot had gone home, but still he hesitated, the jovial man, the confident provider.

'You're a proper old worry-guts, aren't you?' His hand reached for hers and the fingers were cold and not quite steady. 'You don't understand business. Business men don't carry on that way.'

Did they? he wondered. Would they? His own holding in the firm had decreased precariously as his family had increased. How far could he trust the loyalty of those Smith-King uncles and cousins? Would they sell if they were sufficiently tempted?

'I understand people,' Joan said, 'and I understand you. You're not well, Den. The strain's too much for you. I wish you'd see Dr. Greenleaf.'

'I will,' Denholm promised. As he spoke he felt again the vague indefinable pains he had been experiencing lately, the continual malaise. 'I'll have a quiet natter to him tomorrow at the party.'

'I don't want to go.'

Denholm did. Even if it was cold and there wasn't enough to drink, even if they made him dance, it would be wonderful just to get away for one evening from baby-feeding at ten, from Susan who had to have a story and from Jeremy who never slept at all until eleven.

'But we've got a sitter,' he said and he sighed as from above he heard his son's voice calling for a drink of water.

40

Joan went to the door. 'You'll have to talk to Patrick. Oh, I wish we didn't have to go.' She went upstairs with the glass and came down again with the baby in her arms.

Trying to console her, Denholm said weakly, 'Cheer up, old girl. It'll be all right on the night.'

4

WHEN he had been married to Jean, when indeed he had been married to Shirley, he had always been able to pay a man to clean the car. Now he had to do it himself, to stand on the gravel like any twenty-five pound a week commuter, squelching a Woolworth sponge over a car that he was ashamed to be seen driving into the office underground car park. There was, however, one thing about this morning slopping to be thankful for. Since he was outside he had been able to catch the postman and take the letters himself. With a damp hand he felt the letter in his pocket, the letter that had just come from his second wife. There was no reason why Nancy should see it and have cause to moan at him because of its contents. Those begging letters were a continual thorn in his flesh. Why should his daughter go on holiday to Majorca when he could only manage Worthing? Such a wonderful chance for her, Oliver, but of course she, Shirley, couldn't afford the air fare or equip Jennifer with a suitable wardrobe for a seven-year-old in the Balearics. Fifty pounds or perhaps seventy would help. After all, Jennifer was his daughter as well as hers and she was his affectionately, Shirley.

He dropped the sponge into the bucket and bent down to polish the windscreen. Over the hedge he saw that his neighbour was opening his own garage doors, but although he liked the doctor he was in no mood for conversation that

42

morning. Resentment caught at his throat like heartburn. Greenleaf was wearing another new suit! Gossip had it that the doctor was awaiting delivery of another new car. Oliver could hardly bear it when he compared what he thought of as the doctor's miserable continental medical degree with his own Double First.

'Good morning.'

Greenleaf's car drew level with his own and Oliver was forced to look up into his neighbour's brown, aquiline face. It was a very un-English face, almost Oriental, with dark, close-set eyes, a large intelligent mouth and thick hair, crinkly like that of some ancient Assyrian.

'Oh, hallo,' Oliver said ungraciously. He stood up, making an effort to say something neighbourly, when Nancy came running down the path from the kitchen door. She stopped as she saw the doctor and smiled winningly.

'Off on your rounds? What a pity to have to work on a Saturday! I always tell Oliver he doesn't know his luck, having all these long week-ends.'

Oliver coughed. His other wives had learned that his coughs were pregnant with significance. In Nancy's case there had hardly been time to teach her, and now . . .

'I hope I'll see you tonight,' said the doctor as he began to move off.

'Oh, yes, tonight . . .' Nancy's face had taken on its former lines of displeasure. When Greenleaf was out of earshot she turned sharply to her husband. 'I thought you said you left Tamsin's present on the sideboard.'

Oliver had a nose for a scene. He picked up the bucket and started towards the house.

'I did.'

'You bought that for Tamsin?' She scuttled after him into the dining-room and picked up the scent bottle with

43

its cut-glass stopper. 'Nuit de Beltane? I never heard of such extravagance!'

Oliver could see from the open magazine on the table that she had already been checking the price.

'There you are.' Her finger stabbed at a coloured photograph of a similar bottle. 'Thirty-seven and six!' She slammed the magazine shut and threw it on the floor. 'You must be mad.'

'You can't go to a birthday party empty-handed,' Oliver said weakly. If only he knew for certain. There might, after all, be no point in bothering to keep Nancy sweet. He watched her remove the stopper, sniff the scent and dab a spot on her wrist. While she waved her wrist in front of her nose, inhaling crossly, he washed his hands and closed the back door.

'A box of chocolates would have done.' Nancy said. She lugged the sewing machine up on its rubber mat. 'I mean, it's fantastic spending thirty-seven and six on scent for Tamsin when I haven't even got a decent dress to go in.'

'Oh my God!'

'You don't seem to have a sense of proportion where money's concerned.'

'Keep the scent for God's sake and I'll get some chocolates in the village.'

Immediately she was in his arms. Oliver crushed the letter down more firmly in his pocket.

'Can I really, darling? You are an angel. Only you won't be able to get anything nice in the village. You'll have to nip into Nottingham.'

Disengaging himself, Oliver reflected on his wife's economies. Now there would be the petrol into Nottingham, at least twelve and six for chocolates and he'd still spent nearly two pounds on Nuit de Beltane.

Nancy began to sew. The dress had begun to look passable. At least he wouldn't be utterly disgraced.

'Can I come in?'

The voice was Edith Gaveston's. Quick as a flash Nancy ripped the silk from the machine, rolled up the dress and crammed it under a sofa cushion.

'Come in, Edith.'

'I see you've got into our country way of leaving all your doors unlocked.'

Edith, hot and unwholesome-looking in an aertex shirt and a tweed skirt, dropped on to the sofa. From the depths of her shopping basket she produced a wicker handbag embroidered with flowers.

'Now, I want the opinion of someone young and "with it".' Oliver who was forty-two scowled at her, but Nancy, still in her twenties, smiled encouragingly. 'This purse . . .' It was an absurd word, but Edith was too county, too much of a gentlewoman, to talk of handbags unless she meant a small suitcase. 'This purse, will it do for Tamsin's present? It's never been used.' She hesitated in some confusion. 'I mean, of course, it's absolutely new. As a matter of fact I brought it back from Majorca last year. Now, tell me frankly, will it do?'

'Well, she can't very well sling it back at you,' Oliver said rudely. 'Not in front of everyone.' The mention of Majorca reminded him of his second wife's demands. 'Excuse me.' He went outside to get the car.

'I'm sure it'll do beautifully,' Nancy gushed. 'What did Linda say?'

'She said it was square,' Edith said shortly. Her children's failure in achieving the sort of status their parents had wanted for them hurt her bitterly. Linda—Linda who had been at Heathfield—working for Mr. Waller; Roger, coming down from Oxford after a year and going to agricultural college! She would feed them, give them beds in her house, but with other people she preferred to forget their existence.

Nancy said with tactless intuition: 'I thought you weren't terribly keen on the Selbys. Patrick, I mean . . .'

'I've no quarrel with Tamsin. I hope I'm not a vindictive woman.'

'No, but after what Patrick—after him influencing Roger the way he did, I'm surprised you—well, you know what I mean.'

Nancy floundered. The Gavestons weren't really county any more. Their house was no bigger than the Gages'. But still—you'd only got to look at Edith to know her brother lived at Chantflower Grange. I suppose she's only going to the party to have a chance to hob-nob with Crispin Marvell, she thought.

'Patrick Selby behaved very badly, very wrongly,' Edith said. 'And it was just wanton mischief. He's perfectly happy and successful in *his* job.'

'I never quite knew . . .'

'He set out to get at my children. Quite deliberately, my dear. Roger was blissfully happy at The House.' Nancy looked puzzled, thinking vaguely of the Palace of Westminster. 'Christ Church, you know. Patrick Selby got talking to him when he was out with that dog of theirs and the upshot of it was Roger said his father wanted him to go into the business but he wasn't keen. He wanted to be a farmer. As if a boy of nineteen knows what he wants. Patrick said he'd been forced into business when all he wanted was to teach or some absurd thing. He advised Roger to—well, follow his own inclinations. Never mind about us, never mind about poor Paul with no-one to take over the reins at Gavestons, no heir.'

Nancy, greedy for gossip, made sympathetic noises.

'Then, of course, Roger had to say his sister wanted to earn her own living. Made up some stupid tale about our keeping her at home. The next thing was that impossible interfering man suggested she should work in a shop till she was old enough to take up nursing. I don't know why he did it, unless it was because he likes upsetting people. Paul had a great deal to say about it, I assure you. He had quite a stormy interview with Patrick.'

'But it was no good?'

'They do what they like these days.' She sighed and added despondently, 'But as to going tonight, one has one's neighbourhood, one cannot pick and choose these days.'

'Who else is coming?'

'The usual people. The Linchester crowd and Crispin of course. I think it's splendid of him to come so often considering how bitter he must feel.' Edith's sensible, pink-rimmed glasses bobbed on her nose. 'There was a clause in the Marvell contract, you know. No tree felling. Everyone's respected it except Patrick Selby. I know for a fact there were twenty exquisite ancient trees on that plot, and he's had them all down and planted nasty little willows.'

It was just like Oliver, Nancy thought, to come in and spoil it all.

'If you're looking for your cheque book,' she said innocently, 'it's on the record player. While you're about it you might collect my sandals.'

'Oh, are you going to the village?' Edith got up pointedly.

'I'm going into Nottingham.'

'Into *town*? How perfectly splendid. You can give me a lift.'

She picked up the wicker basket and they departed together.

Two fields and a remnant of woodland away Crispin

Marvell was sitting in his living room drinking rhubarb wine and writing his history of Chantefleur Abbey. Some days it was easy to concentrate. This was one of the others. He had spent the early part of the morning washing his china and ever since he had replaced the cups in the cabinet and the plates on the walls, he had been unable to keep his eyes from wandering to the glossy surfaces and the warm rich colours. It was almost annoying to reflect what he had been missing in delaying this particular bit of spring-cleaning, the months during which the glaze had been dimmed by winter bloom.

For a moment he mused over the twin olive-coloured plates, one decorated with a life-size apple in relief, the other with a peach; over the Chelsea clock with its tiny dial and opulent figurines of the sultan and his concubine. Marvell kept his correspondence behind this clock and it disturbed him to see the corner of Henry Glide's letter sticking out. He got up and pushed the envelope out of sight between the wall and the Circassian's gold-starred trousers. Then he dipped his pen in the ink-well and returned to Chantefleur.

'The original building had a clerestory of round-headed windows with matching windows in the aisle bays. Only by looking at the Cistercian abbeys now standing in France can we appreciate the effect of the . . .'

He stopped and sighed. Carried away by his own domestic art, he had almost written 'of the glaze on the apple'. It was hardly important. Tomorrow it might rain. He had already spent two years on the history of Chantefleur. Another few months scarcely mattered. In a way, on a wonderful morning like this one, nothing mattered. He gave the plate a last look, running his fingers across the cheek of the apple—the artist had been so faithful he had even pressed in a bruise, there on the underside—and went into the garden.

Marvell lived in an almshouse, or rather four almshouses all joined together in a terrace and converted by him into a long low bungalow. The walls were partly of white plaster, partly of rose-coloured brick, and the roof was of pantiles, old now and uneven but made by the hand of a craftsman.

He strolled round the back. Thanks to the bees that lived in three white hives in the orchard the fruit was forming well; they hadn't swarmed this year and he was keeping his fingers crossed. The day spent in carefully cutting out the queen cells had been well worth the sacrifice of half a chapter of Chantefleur. He sat down on the bench. Beyond the hedge in the meadows below Linchester they were cutting the hay. He could hear the baler, that and the sound of the bees. Otherwise all was still.

'All right for some people.'

Marvell turned his head and grinned. Max Greenleaf often came up about this time after his morning calls.

'Come and sit down.'

'It's good to get away from the wasps.' Greenleaf looked at the lichen on the bench, then down at his dark suit. He sat down gingerly.

'There were always a lot of wasps on Linchester,' Marvell said. 'I remember them in the old days. Thousands of damned wasps whenever Mamma gave a garden party.' Greenleaf looked at him suspiciously. An Austrian Jew, he could never escape his conviction that the English landed gentry and the Carinthian aristocracy came out of the same mould. Marvell called it his serfs to the wolves syndrome. 'The wasps are conservative, you see. They haven't got used to the idea that the old house has been gone five years and a lot of company directors' Georgian gone up in its place. They're still on the hunt for Mamma's brandy snaps. Come inside and have a drink.' He smiled at Greenleaf and said in a teasing voice, 'I opened a bottle of mead this morning.'

'I'd rather have a whisky and soda.'

Greenleaf followed him to the house, knocking his head as he always did on the plaque above the front door that said: 1722. Andreas Quercus Fecit. Marvell's reasons for living there were beyond his understanding. The countryside, the flowers, horticulture, agriculture, Marvell's own brand of viticulture, meant nothing to him. He had come to the village to share his brother-in-law's prosperous practice. If you asked him why he lived in Linchester he would answer that it was for the air or that he was obliged to live within a mile or two of his surgery. Modern conveniences, a house that differed inside not at all from a town house, diluted and almost banished those drawbacks. To invite those disadvantages, positively to court them in the form of cesspools, muddy lanes and insectivora as his host did, made Marvell a curio, an object of psychological speculation.

These mysteries of country life reminded him afresh of the cloud on his morning.

'I've just lost a patient,' he said. Marvell, pouring whisky, heard the Austrian accent coming through, a sign that the doctor was disturbed. 'Not my fault, but still . . .'

'What happened?' Marvell drew the curtains, excluding all but a narrow shaft of sunlight that ran across the black oak floor and up Andreas Quercus's squat wall.

'One of the men from Coffley mine. A wasp got on his sandwich and he ate the thing. So what does he do? He goes back to work and the next thing I'm called out because he's choking to death. Asphyxiated before I got there.'

'Could you have done anything?'

'If I'd got there soon enough. The throat closes with the swelling, you see.' Changing the subject, he said: 'You've been writing. How's it coming on?'

'Not so bad. I did my china this morning and it distracted me.' He unhooked the apple plate from the wall and handed it to the doctor. 'Nice?'

Greenleaf took it wonderingly in short thick fingers. 'What's the good of a thing like this? You can't put food on it, can you?' Without aesthetic sense, he probed everything for its use, its material function. This plate was quite useless. Distastefully he imagined eating from it the food he liked best, chopped herring, cucumbers in brine, cabbage salad with caraway seeds. Bits would get wedged under the apple leaves.

'It's purpose is purely decorative,' Marvel laughed. 'Which reminds me, will you be at Tamsin's party?'

'If I don't get called out.'

'She sent me a card. Rather grand. Tamsin always does these things well.' Marvell stretched himself full-length in the armchair. The movement was youthful and the light dim. Greenleaf was seldom deceived about people's ages. He put Marvell's at between forty-seven and fifty-two, but the fine lines which the sun showed up were no longer apparent, and the sprinkling of white hairs was lost in the fair. Probably still attractive to women, he reflected.

'One party after another,' he said, 'Must come expensive.'

'Tamsin has her own income, you know, from her grandmother. She and Patrick are first cousins so she was his grandmother too.'

'But she was the favourite?'

'I don't know about that. He had already inherited his father's business so I daresay old Mrs. Selby thought he didn't need any more.'

'You seem to know a lot about them.'

'I suppose I do. In a way I've been a sort of father confessor to Tamsin. Before they came here they had a flat in

Nottingham. Tamsin was lost in the country. When I gave that talk to the Linchester Residents' Association she bombarded me with questions and since then—well, I've become a kind of adopted uncle, Mrs. Beeton and antiquarian rolled into one.'

Greenleaf laughed. Marvell was the only man he knew who could do women's work without becoming old-womanish.

'You know, I don't think she ever really wanted that house. Tamsin loves old houses and old furniture. But Patrick insists on what are called, I believe, uncluttered lines.'

'Tell me, don't you *mind* coming to Linchester?' Always fascinated by other people's emotions, Greenleaf had sometimes wondered about Marvell's reactions to the new houses that had sprung up on his father's estate.

Marvell smiled and shrugged.

'Not really. I'm devoutly thankful I don't have to keep the old place up. Besides it amuses me when I go to parties. I play a sort of mental game trying to fix just where I am in relation to our house.' When Greenleaf looked puzzled he went on, 'What I mean is, when I'm at Tamsin's I always think to myself, the ha-ha came down here and here were the kitchen gardens.' Keeping a straight face he said, 'The Gages' house now, that's where the stables were. I'm not saying it's appropriate, mind.'

'You're scaring me. Makes me wonder about my own place.'

'Oh, you're all right. Father's library and a bit of the big staircase.'

'I don't believe a word of it,' the doctor said and added a little shyly, 'I'm glad you can make a game of the whole thing.'

52

'You mustn't think,' said Marvell, 'that every time I set foot on Linchester I'm wallowing in a kind of maudlin *recherche du temps perdu.*'

Greenleaf was not entirely convinced. He finished his whisky and remembered belatedly his excuse for the visit.

'And now,' he said, at ease on his own home ground, 'how's the hay fever?'

If the doctor had not perfectly understood Marvell's Proustian reference, he had at least an inkling of its meaning. On Edward Carnaby it would have been utterly lost. His French was still at an elementary stage.

Jo-jo monte. Il est fatigué. Bonne nuit, Jo-jo. Dors bien!

He looked up towards the ceiling and translated the passage into English. Funny stuff for a grown man, wasn't it? All about a kid of five having a bath and going to bed. Still, it was French. At this rate he'd be reading Simenon within the year.

Bonjour, Jo-jo. Quel beau matin! Regarde le ciel. Le soleil brille.

Edward thumbed through the dictionary, looking for *briller.*

'Ted!'

'What is it, dear?' It was funny, but lately he'd got into the habit of calling her dear. She had taken the place of his wife in all ways but one. Sex was lacking but freedom and security took its place. Life was freer with Free, he thought, pleased with his pun.

'If you and Cheryl want your lunch on time you'll have to do something about these wasps, Ted.' She marched in, brisk, neat, womanly, in a cotton frock and frilled apron. He noted with pleasure that she had said lunch and not dinner. Linchester was educating Freda.

'I'll do it right now. Get it over.' He closed the dictionary. *Briller*. To shine, to glow, emit a radiance. The verb perfectly expressed his own mental state. He was glowing with satisfaction and anticipation. *Edouard brille*, he said to himself, chuckling aloud. 'I've promised to pass the stuff on to some people.'

'What people?'

'The gorgeous Mrs. Selby, if you must know. I met her last night and she was all over me. Insisted I go to her party tonight.' Now you couldn't say things like that to a wife. 'She wouldn't take No for an answer,' he said.

Freda sat down.

'You're kidding. You don't know Tamsin.'

'Tamsin! That's all right, that is. Since when have you and her been so pally?'

'And what about me? Where do I come in?'

'Now, look, Free, I'm counting on you to sit in with Cheryl.'

The tears welled into her eyes. After all that had happened, all the love, the promises, the wonderful evenings. Of course it wasn't *his* fault. It was Tamsin's party. But to ask Edward!

'There's no need to get into a tiz. She said I could bring a friend. I don't know about Cheryl, though.'

'Mrs. Staxton'll sit,' Freda said eagerly. 'She's always offering.' Seeing his face still doubtful, his eyes already returning to the French primer, she burst out miserably, 'Ted, I want to go to the party! I've got a right. I've got more right than you.'

Hysteria in Freda was something new. He closed the book.

'What are you talking about?' She was his twin and he could feel the pull of her mind, almost read her thoughts. A terrible unease visited him and he thought of the previous night, the woman's eyes staring past him towards the pond,

54

her sudden unexplained coldness when he had said who he was.

'Freda!'

It all came out then and Edward listened, angry and afraid. The happy mood had gone sour on him.

5

STRINGS of little coloured bulbs festooned the willow trees. As soon as it grew dusk they would be switched on to glow red, orange, green and cold blue against the dark foliage of the oaks in the Millers' garden next door.

Tamsin had shut the food and drink in the dining room away from the wasps. Although she had only seen two throughout the whole day she closed the double windows to be on the safe side. The room was tidy, and apart from the food, bare. Functional, Patrick called it. Now, cleaned by him while Tamsin hovered helplessly in the background, it met even his exacting requirements.

'It is, after all, a *dining* room, not a glory hole,' he had remarked in a chill voice to the vacuum cleaner. To his wife he said nothing, but his look meant Please don't interfere with my arrangements. When the tools were put away and the dusters carefully washed, he had taken the dog to Sherwood Forest, smug, silent with his private joy.

It was too late now to bother with a show of loving obedience. Tamsin dressed, wishing she had something bright and gay, but all her clothes were subdued—to please Patrick. Then she went into the dining room and helped herself to whisky, pouring it straight into a tumbler almost as if it was the last drink she would ever have. Nobody had wished her a happy birthday yet but she had had plenty of cards. Defiantly she took them from the sideboard drawer and arranged them on top of the radiator. There were about a dozen of them, facetious ones showing dishevelled housewives amid piles of crocks; conventional ones (a family of Dartmoor ponies); one whose picture held a secret significance, whose message meant something special to her and to its sender. It was unsigned but Tamsin knew who had sent it. She screwed it up quickly for the sight of it with its cool presumption only deepened her misery.

'Many happy returns of the day, Tamsin,' she said shakily, raising her glass. She sighed and the cards fluttered. Somehow she would have liked to break the glass, hurl it absurdly against Patrick's white wall, because she had come to an end. A new life was beginning. The drink was a symbol of the old life and so was the dress she wore, silver-grey, clinging, expensive. She put the glass down carefully (her old habits died hard), looked at the cards and blinked to stop herself crying. For there should have been one more, bigger than the others, an austere costly card that said To My Wife.

Patrick was never late. He came back on the dot of seven in time to bath and shave and leave the bathroom tidy, and by then she had washed her glass, returning it to its place in the sideboard. She heard the bathroom door close and the key turn in the lock. Patrick was careful about propriety.

Tamsin remained in the dining room for some minutes, feeling an almost suicidal despair. In an hour or so her guests would begin to arrive and they would expect her to be gay because she was young and rich and beautiful and because it was her birthday. If she could get out of the house for a few minutes she might feel better. With Queenie at her heels she took her trug and went down to where the currants grew in what had been the Manor kitchen gardens. The dog lay down in the sun and Tamsin began stripping the bushes of their ripe white fruit.

'I will try to be gay,' she said to herself, or perhaps to the dog, 'for a little while.'

Edward and Freda came up to the front doors of Hallows at a quarter to eight and it was Edward who rang the bell. Freda, whose only reading matter was her weekly women's magazine, had sometimes encountered the cliché 'rooted to the spot' and that was how she felt standing on the swept white stones, immobile, stiff with terror, a sick bile stirring between her stomach and her throat.

No-one came to the door. Freda watched her brother enviously. Not for him the problem of what to do with one's sticky and suddenly over-large hands that twitched and fretted as if seeking some resting place; he had the Vesprid in its brown paper bag to hold.

'Better go round the back,' he said truculently.

It was monastically quiet. The creak of the wrought iron gate made Freda jump as Edward pushed it open. They walked round the side of the house and stopped when they came to the patio. The garden lay before them, waiting, expectant, but not as for a party. It was rather as if it had been prepared for the arrival of some photographer whose carefully angled shots would provide pictures for one of those very magazines. Freda had read a feature the previous week, *Ideal Homesteads in the New Britain*, and the illustrations had shown just such a garden, lawns ribbed in pale and dark green where the mower had crossed them, trees and shrubs whose leaves looked as if they had been individually dusted. At the other end of the patio someone had arranged tables and chairs, some of straw-coloured wicker, others of white-painted twisted metal. A small spark of pleasure and admiration broke across Freda's fear, only to be extinguished almost at once by the sound of water gurgling down a drainpipe behind her ankles. A sign of life, of habitation.

The garden, the house, looked, she thought, as if it hadn't been kept outside at all, as if it had been preserved up to this moment under glass. But she was unable to express this thought in words and instead said foolishly:

'There isn't anybody about. You must have got the wrong night.'

He scowled and she wondered again why he had come, what he was going to say or do. Was it simply kindness to her—for he was, as it were, her key to this house—Tamsin's fascination or something more?

'You won't say anything, will you? You won't say anything to show me up?'

'I told you,' he said. 'I want to see how the land lies, what sort of a mess you've got yourself into. I'm not promising anything, Free.'

Minutes passed, unchanging minutes in which the sleek garden swam before her eyes. Then something happened, something which caused the first crack to appear in Edward's insecure courage.

From behind the willows came a sound familiar to Freda, a long drawn-out bay. Queenie. Edward jerked convulsively and dropped the Vesprid with a clang—a clang like the crack of doom—as the dog bounded from a curtain of shrubs and stopped a yard from him. It was an ominous sound that came from her, a throb rather than an actual noise, and Edward seemed to grow smaller. He picked up the tin and held it in front of him, a ridiculous and wholly inadequate shield.

'Oh, Queenie!' Freda put out her hand. 'It's all right. It's me.'

The dog advanced, wriggling now, to lick the outstretched fingers, when the gate opened and a tall fair man entered the garden. He was wearing a green shirt over slacks and Edward at once felt that his own sports jacket (Harris tweed knocked down to eighty nine and eleven) was unsuitable, an anachronism.

'How do you do?'

He was carrying something that looked like a bottle wrapped in ancient yellowing newspaper, and a huge bunch of roses. The roses were perfect, each bud closed yet about to unfurl, and their stems had been shorn of thorns.

'I don't think we've met. My name's Marvell.'

'Pleased to meet you,' Edward said. He transferred the Vesprid to his left arm and shook hands. 'This is my sister, Miss Carnaby.'

'Where is everyone?'

'We don't know,' Freda said sullenly. 'Till you came we thought we'd got the wrong night.'

'Oh, no, this is Tamsin's birthday.' He pushed Queenie down, smiled suddenly and waved. 'There she is picking my currants, bless her! Will you excuse me?'

'Well!' Freda said. 'If those are county manners you can keep them.'

She watched him stride off down the path and then she saw Patrick's wife. Tamsin got to her feet like a silvery dryad arising from her natural habitat, ran up to Marvell and kissed him on the cheek. They came back together, Tamsin's face buried in roses.

'Josephine Bruce, that's the gorgeous dark red one,' Freda heard her say. 'Virgo, snow-white; Super Star—Oh, lovely, lovely vermilion! And the big peachy beauty—this one—is Peace. You see, Crispin, I *am* learning.'

She stepped on to the greyish-gold stones of the patio and dropped the roses on to a wicker table. The Weimaraner romped over to her and placed her paws on the table's plaited rim.

60

'And look, lovely mead! You are sweet to me, Crispin.'

'You look like one of those plushy calendars,' Marvell said laughing. 'The respectable kind you see in garages on the Motorway. All girl and dog and flowers and liquor, the good things of life.'

'*Wein, weib und gesang* as Patrick says.' Tamsin's voice was low and her face clouded.

Edward coughed.

'Excuse me,' he said.

'O God, I'm so sorry.' Marvell was crestfallen. 'Tamsin dear, I'm keeping you from your guests.'

Afterwards, looking back, Freda thought Tamsin honestly hadn't known who they were. And after all Edward's stupid airs! Tamsin's face had grown dull and almost ugly; her eyes, large and tawny, seemed to blank out. She stood looking at them still holding a rose against her paintless lips. At last she said:

'I know! The man who goes to evening classes.'

Freda wanted to go then, to slink back against the stone wall, slither between the house and the wattle fence and then run and run until she came to the chalets behind the elms. But Edward was holding her arm. He yanked her forward, exposing her to their gaze like a dealer with his single slave.

'This is my sister. You said I could bring someone.'

Tamsin's face hardened. It was exactly like one of those African art masks, Freda thought, the beautiful goddess one in the saloon bar of that roadhouse on the Southwell road. Freda knew she wasn't going to shake hands.

'Well, now you're here you must have a drink. Masses of drink in the dining room. Where's Patrick?' She looked up to the open windows on the first floor. 'Patrick!'

Edward thrust the Vesprid at her.

'A present? How very sweet of you.'

61

She pulled the tin out of the bag and giggled. Freda thought she was hysterical—or drunk.

'It's not exactly a present,' Edward said desperately. 'You said to bring it. You said to come early. We could do the wasps.'

'The wasps? Oh, but I've only seen one or two today. We won't worry about wasps.' She flung back the doors and Patrick must have been standing just within. He stepped out poised, smiling, smelling of bath salts. 'Here's my husband. Do go and check the lights, darling.' And she linked her arm into his, smiling brightly.

Freda could feel herself beginning to tremble. She knew her face had paled, then filled with burning blood. Her hand fumbled its way into Patrick's, gaining life and strength as she felt the faint special pressure and the familiar cold touch of his ring. As it came to Edward's turn her heart knocked, but the handshake passed off conventionally. Edward's spirit was broken and he gazed at Patrick dumbly, half-hypnotised.

'What's this?'

Patrick picked up the Vesprid and looked at the label.

Freda couldn't help admiring his aplomb, the coldly masterful way he shook off Tamsin's hand.

'Doesn't it look horrid on my birthday table?' Tamsin bundled the tin back into the paper and pushed it into Edward's arms. She took his fingers in her own and curled them round the parcel. 'There. You look after it, sweetie, or pop it in a safe place. We don't want it mingling with the drinks, do we?'

Then Marvell rescued them and took them into the dining room.

By the time Greenleaf and Bernice got to Hallows everyone had arrived. He had been called out to a man with renal colic and it was eight before he got back. Fortunately Bernice never nagged but waited for him patiently, smoking and playing patience in the morning room.

'I shall wear my alpaca packet,' Greenleaf said. 'So it makes me look like a bowls player? What do I care? I'm not a teenager.'

'No, darling,' said Bernice. 'You're a very handsome mature man. Who wants to be a teenager?'

'Not me, unless you can be one too.'

Well-contented with each other, they set off in a happy frame of mind. They took the short cut across The Green and paused to watch the swans. Greenleaf held his wife's hand.

'At last,' Denholm Smith-King said as they appeared in the patio. 'I was just saying to Joan, is there a doctor in the house?'

'Ha ha,' said Greenleaf mechanically. 'I hope no-one's going to need one. I've come to enjoy myself.' He waved to Tamsin who came from the record-player to greet him. 'Happy birthday. Nice of you to ask us.' He pointed to the now loaded table. 'What's all this?'

'My lovely presents. Look, chocs from Oliver and Nancy, this marvellous bag thing from Edith.' Tamsin held the gifts up in turn, pouting at the bag as she praised it. 'Sweet delicious *marrons glacés* from Joan, and Crispin brought me —what d'you think? Wine and roses. Wasn't that lovely?'

Marvell smiled from behind her, looking boyish. 'Thy shadow, Cynara,' he said. 'The night is thine. . . . '

'So kind! And Bernice . . . ' She unwrapped the tiny phial of scent Bernice had put into her hand. 'Nuit de Beltane! How gorgeous. And I've just been telling Nancy how lovely she smells. Imagine, she's wearing it herself. You're all so good to me.' She waved a long brown hand as if their munificence exhausted her, making her more languid than usual.

63

Greenleaf crammed himself into a small wicker armchair. From within the dining room the music had begun the Beguine.

'Your daughter not coming?' he said to Edith Gaveston. She sniffed. 'Much too square for Linda.'

'I suppose so.'

Tamsin had gone, swept away in the arms of Oliver Gage.

'If you've a minute,' said Denholm Smith-King,' I've been meaning to ask you for ages. It's about a lump I've got under my arm. . . .'

Greenleaf, preparing for a busman's holiday, took the drink Patrick held out to him, but Smith-King was temporarily diverted. He looked quickly about him as if to make sure that most of the others were dancing, and he touched Patrick's arm nervously.

'Oh, Pat old man. . . .'

'Not now, Denholm.' Patrick's smile was brief, mechanical, gone in a flash. 'I don't care to mix business with pleasure.'

'Later, then?'

Patrick glanced at the ashtray Smith-King was filling with stubs, opened the cigarette box insolently and let the lid fall almost instantly.

'I'm not surprised you've got a lump,' he said, 'but don't bore my guests, will you?'

'Funny chap,' Smith-King said and an uneasy flush seeped across his face. 'Doesn't care what he says.' The red faded as Patrick strolled away. 'Now about this said lump. . . .'

Greenleaf turned towards him and tried to look as if he was listening while keeping his thoughts and half an eye on the other guests.

Most of them were his patients except the Selbys and the Gavestons who were on Dr. Howard's private list, but he sized them up now from a psychological rather than a medical standpoint. As he sometimes said to Bernice, he had to know about human nature, it was part of his job.

The Carnabys now, they weren't enjoying themselves. They sat apart from the rest in a couple of deck chairs on the lawn and they weren't talking to each other. Freda had hidden her empty shandy glass under the seat; Carnaby, like a parent clutching his rejected child, sat dourly, holding what looked like a tin in one of Waller's paper wrappings.

Beyond them among the currant bushes Marvell was showing Joan and Nancy the ancient glories of the Manor kitchen gardens. Greenleaf knew little about women's fashions but Nancy's dress looked out of place to him, ill-fitting (she'll have to watch her weight, said the medical part of him, or her blood pressure will go soaring up in ten years' time). It contrasted badly with the expensive scent she wore, whiffs of which he had caught while they were standing together by Tamsin's birthday table. Why, incidentally, had Gage looked black as thunder when Bernice handed over their own phial of perfume?

He was dancing with Tamsin now and of the three couples on the floor they were the best matched. Clare and Walter Miller lumbered past him, resolutely fox-trotting out of time. Rather against her will Bernice had been coaxed into the stiff arms of old Paul Gaveston who, too conscious of the proprieties to hold her close, stared poker-faced over her shoulder, his embracing hand a good two inches from her back. Greenleaf smiled to himself. Gage was without such inhibitions. His smooth dusky cheek was pressed close to Tamsin's, his body fused with hers. They hardly moved but swayed slowly, almost indecently, on a square yard of floor. Well, well, thought Greenleaf. The music died away and broke suddenly into a mambo.

'The thing is,' Smith-King was saying, 'it's getting bigger. No getting away from it.'

'I'd better take a look at it,' Greenleaf said.

A fourth couple had joined the dancers. Greenleaf felt relieved. Patrick was a difficult fellow at the best of times but he could rise to an occasion. It was nice to see him rescuing the Carnaby girl and dancing with her as if he really wanted to.

'You will?' Smith-King half-rose. His movement seemed to sketch the shedding of garments.

'Not now,' Greenleaf said, alarmed. 'Come down to the surgery.'

The sun had quite gone now, even the last lingering rays, and dusk was coming to the garden. Tamsin had broken away from Gage and gone to switch on the fairy lights. But for the intervention of his wife who marched on to the patio exclaiming loudly about the gnats, Gage would have followed her.

'How I hate beastly insects,' Nancy grumbled. 'You'd think with all this D.D.T. and everything there just wouldn't be any more mosquitos.' She glared at Marvell. 'I feel itchy all over.'

As if at a signal Walter Miller and Edith Gaveston broke simultaneously into gnat-bite anecdotes. Joan Smith-King gravitated towards Greenleaf as people so often did with minor ailments even on social occasions, and stood in front of him scratching her arms. He got up at once to let her sit next to her husband but as he turned he saw that Denholm's chair was empty. Then he saw him standing in the now deserted dining room confronting Patrick. The indispensable cigarette was in his mouth. Greenleaf couldn't hear what he was saying, only Joan's heavy breathing loud and strained above the buzz of conversation. The cigarette trembled, adhering to Denholm's lip, and his hands moved in a gesture of hopelessness. Patrick laughed suddenly and turning away, strode into the garden as the lights came on.

Greenleaf, not sensitive to a so-called romantic atmosphere, was unmoved by the strings of coloured globes. But most of the women cried out automatically. Fairy lights were the thing; they indicated affluence, taste, organisation. With little yelps of delight Nancy ran up and down, pointing and exhorting the others to come and have a closer look.

'So glad you like them,' Tamsin said. 'We do.' Patrick coughed, dissociating himself. He was taking his duties to heart, Greenleaf thought, watching his hand enclose Freda Carnaby's in a tight grip.

'Now, have we all got drinks?' Tamsin reached for Marvell's empty glass. 'Crispin, your poor arms!'

'There are mosquitos at the bottom of your garden,' Marvell said, laughing. 'I meant to bring some citronella but I forgot.'

'Oh, but we've got some. I'll get it.'

'No, I'll go. You want to dance.'

Gage had already claimed her, his arm about her waist.

'I'll tell you where it is. It's in the spare bedroom bathroom. Top shelf of the cabinet.'

Joan Smith-King was giggling enviously.

'Oh, do you have two bathrooms? How grand!'

'Just through the spare room,' Tamsin said, ignoring her, 'You know the way.'

The expression in her eyes shocked Greenleaf. It was as if, he thought, she was playing some dangerous game.

'I'm being absurd,' he said to Bernice.

'Oh, no, darling, you're such a practical man. Why are you being absurd anyway?'

'Nothing,' Greenleaf said.

Marvell came back holding a bottle. He had already unstoppered it and was anointing his arms.

'Thank you so much,' he said to Tamsin, 'Madame Tussaud.'

Tamsin gabbled at him quickly.

'You found the stuff? Marvellous. No, sweetie, that isn't a pun. Come and dance.'

'I am for other than for dancing measures,' Marvell laughed. 'I've been in the chamber of horrors and I need a drink.' He helped himself from the sideboard. 'You might have warned me.'

'What *do* you mean, chamber of horrors?' Nancy was wide-eyed. The party was beginning to flag and she was eager for something to buoy it up and, if possible, prise Oliver away from Tamsin. 'Have you been seeing ghosts?'

'Something like that.'

'Tell, tell!'

Suddenly Tamsin whirled away from Oliver and throwing up her arms, seized Marvell to spin him away past the record player, past the birthday table, across the patio and out on to the lawn.

'Let's all go,' she cried. 'Come and see the skeleton in the cupboard!'

They began to file out into the hall, the women giggling expectantly. Marvell went first, his drink in his hand. Only Patrick hung back until Freda took his hand and whispered something to him. Even Smith-King, usually obtuse, noticed his unease.

'Lead on, Macduff!' he said.

6

I F I T had been earlier in the day or even if the lights had
been on it would have looked very different. But as it was—
day melting into night, the light half-gone and the air so still
that nothing moved, not even the net curtains at the open
windows—the effect was instant and, for a single foolish
moment, shocking.

Marvell pulled a face. The other men stared, Paul Gaveston making a noise that sounded like a snort. Smith-King
whistled, then broke into a hearty laugh.

The women expressed varying kinds of horror, squeals,
hands clamped to mouths, but only Freda sounded genuinely distressed. She was standing close to Greenleaf. He
heard her low gasp and felt her shudder.

'Definitely not my cup of tea,' Nancy said. 'Imagine forgetting it was there and then coming face to face with it
in the night on your way to the loo! '

Greenleaf was suddenly sickened. Of all the people in the
Selbys' spare room he was the only one who had ever seen
an actual head that had been severed from an actual body.
The first one he had encountered as a student, the second
had been the subject of a post-mortem conducted on a man
decapitated in a railway accident. Because of this and for
other reasons connected with his psychological make-up, he
was at the same time more and less affected by the picture
than were the other guests.

It was a large picture, an oil painting in a frame of scratched gilt, and it stood propped on the floor against the watered silk wallpaper. Greenleaf knew nothing at all about painting and the view many people take that all life—or all death—is a fit subject for art would have appalled him. Of brushwork, of colour, he was ignorant, but he knew a good deal about anatomy and a fair amount about sexual perversion. Therefore he was able to admire the artist for his accuracy—the hewn neck on the silver platter showed the correct vertebra and the jugular in its proper place—and deplore a mentality which thought sadism a suitable subject for entertainment. Greenleaf hated cruelty; all the suffering of all his ancestors in the ghettos of Eastern Europe was strong within him. He stuck out his thick underlip, took off his glasses and began polishing them on his alpaca jacket.

Thus he was unable to see for a moment the face of the man who stood near him on the other side of Freda Carnaby, the man whose house this was. But he heard the intake of breath and the faint smothered cry.

'But just look at the awful way she's staring at that ghastly head,' Nancy cried, clutching Oliver's hand. 'I think I ought to understand what it means, but I don't.'

'Perhaps it's just as well,' her husband said crisply.

'What is it, Tamsin? What's it supposed to be?'

Tamsin had drawn her finger across the thick painted surface, letting a nail rest at the pool of blood.

'Salome and John the Baptist,' Marvell said. He was quickly bored by displays of naiveté and he had gone to the window. Now he turned round, smiling. 'Of course she wouldn't have been dressed like that. The artist put her in contemporary clothes. Who painted it, Tamsin?'

'I just wouldn't know,' Tamsin shrugged. 'It was my grandmother's. I lived with her, you see, and I grew up with

70

it, so it doesn't affect me all that much any more. I used to love it when I was a little girl. Too dreadful of me! '

'You're never going to hang it on the wall?' Clare Miller asked.

'I might. I don't know yet. When my grandmother died two years ago she left all her furniture to a friend, a Mrs. Prynne. I happened to be visiting her a couple of months ago and of course I absolutely drooled over this thing. So she said she's send it to me for my birthday and here it is.'

'Rather you than I.'

Tamsin giggled.

'I might put it on the dining-room wall. D'you think it would go well with a grilled steak?'

They had all looked at the picture. Everyone had said something if only to exclaim with thrilled horror. Only Patrick had kept silent and Greenleaf, puzzled, turned now to look at him. Patrick's face was deathly white under the cloud of freckles. Somehow the freckles made him look worse, the pallor of his skin blotched with what looked like bruises. When at last he spoke his voice was loud and unsteady and the icy poise quite gone.

'All right,' he said, 'the joke's over. Excuse me.' He pushed at Edward Carnaby, shoving him aside with his shoulder and stripping the counterpane from one of the beds, flung it across the picture. But instead of catching on the topmost beading of the frame it slipped and fell to the floor. The effect of its falling, like the sweeping away of a curtain, exposed the picture with a sudden vividness. The gloating eyes, the parted lips and the plump bosom of Herod's niece arose before them in the gloom. She seemed to be watching with a dreadful satisfaction the slithering silk as it unveiled the trophy in the dish.

'You bitch! ' Patrick said.

71

There was a shocked silence. Then Tamsin stepped forward and looped the counterpane up. Salome was veiled.

'Oh, really! ' she said. 'It was just a joke, darling. You *are* rude.'

Smith-King moved uneasily.

'Getting late, Joanie,' he said. 'Beddy-byes.'

'It's not ten yet.' Tamsin caught Patrick's hand and leaning towards him, kissed him lightly on the cheek. He remained quite still, the colour returning to his face, but he didn't look at her. 'We haven't eaten yet. All that lovely food! '

'Ah, food.' Smith-King rubbed his hands together. It would be another story if a scene could be avoided and Patrick perhaps yet made amenable. 'Must keep body and soul together.'

'The wolf from the door?' Marvell said softly.

'That's the ticket.' He slapped Marvell on the back.

Patrick seemed to realise that his hand was still resting in Tamsin's. He snatched it away, marched out of the room and down the stairs, his dignity returning. With a defiant glance at Tamsin, Freda followed him.

'It's a lovely night,' Tamsin cried. 'Let's go into the garden and take the food with us.' Her eyes were very bright. She linked her arm into Oliver's and as an afterthought clasped Nancy's hand and swung it. 'Eat, drink and be merry for tomorrow we die! '

They went downstairs and Tamsin danced into the diningroom. Greenleaf thought they had seen the last of Patrick for that night, but he was on the patio, subdued, his face expressionless, arranging plates on the wicker tables. Freda Carnaby stood by him, sycophantic, adoring.

'Well! ' said Nancy Gage. She pulled her chair up alongside Greenleaf's. 'I thought Patrick made an exhibition of himself, didn't you? Immature I call it, making all that fuss about a picture.'

'It is the eye of childhood that fears a painted devil.' Marvell passed her a plate of smoked salmon rolled up in brown bread.

'Juvenile,' Nancy said. 'I mean, it's not as if it was a film. I don't mind admitting I've seen some horror films that have absolutely terrified me. I've wakened in the night bathed in perspiration, haven't I, Oliver?' Oliver was too far away to hear. He sat on the stone wall in gloomy conference with Tamsin.

Nancy, beckoning to him, raised the salmon roll blindly to her mouth.

'Look out!' Greenleaf said quickly. He knocked the roll out of her hand. 'A wasp,' he explained as she jumped. 'You were going to eat it.'

'Oh, no!' Nancy leapt to her feet and shook her skirt. 'I hate them. I'm terrified of them.'

'It's all right. It's gone.'

'No, it hasn't. Look, there's another one.' Nancy flapped her arms as a wasp winged past her face, circled her head and alighted on a fruit flan. 'Oliver, there's one in my hair!'

'What on earth's the matter?' Tamsin got up reluctantly and came between the tables. 'Oh, wasps. Too maddening.' She was taller than Nancy and she blew lightly on to the fair curls. 'It's gone, anyway.'

'You shouldn't have brought the food out,' Patrick said. 'You would do it.' Since he had been the first to do so, this Greenleaf thought, was hardly fair. 'I hate this damned inefficiency. Look, dozens of them!'

Everyone had pushed back their chairs, leaving their food half-eaten. The striped insects descended upon the tables making first for fruit and cream. They seemed to drop from the skies and they came quite slowly, wheeling first above the

73

food with a sluggish yet purposeful concentration like enemy aircraft engaged in a reconnaissance. Then, one by one, they dropped upon pastry and jelly, greedy for the sweet things. Their wings vibrated.

'Well, that's that,' Tamsin said. Her hand dived for a plate of petit fours but she withdrew it quickly with a little scream. 'Get off me, hateful wasp! Patrick, do something.' He was standing beside her but farther removed perhaps than he had ever been. Exasperated and bored, his hands in his pockets, he stared at the feasting insects. 'Get the food in!'

'It's a bit late for that,' Marvell said. 'They're all over the dining-room.' He looked roofwards. 'You've got a nest, you know.'

'That doesn't surprise me at all,' said Walter Miller who lived next door. 'I said to Clare only yesterday, you mark my words, I said, the Selbys have got a wasp nest in their roof.'

'What are we going to do about it?'

'Kill them.' Edward Carnaby had opened his mouth to no one except his sister since, on their arrival, Tamsin had snubbed him. Now his hour had come. 'Exterminate them,' he said. He pulled the tin of Vesprid from its bag and dumped it in the middle of the table where Nancy, Marvell and Greenleaf had been sitting. 'You should have let me do it before,' he said to Tamsin.

'Do it? Do what?' Tamsin looked at the Vesprid. 'What do you do, spray it on them?'

Edward seemed to be about to embark on a long technical explanation. He took a deep breath.

Walter Miller said quickly: 'You'll want a ladder. There's one in my garage.'

'Right,' said Edward. 'The first thing is to locate the nest. I'll need someone to give me a hand.' Marvell got up.

74

'No, Crispin, Patrick will go.' Tamsin touched her husband's arm. 'Come on, darling. You can't let your guests do all the work.'

For a moment he looked as if he could. He glanced mulishly from Marvell to his wife. Then, without speaking to or even looking at Edward, he started to walk towards the gate.

'Blood sports, Tamsin,' Marvell said. 'Your parties are unique.'

When Patrick and Edward came back carrying Miller's ladder the others had moved out on to the lawn. By now the patio was clouded with wasps. Droves of them gathered on the tables. The less fortunate late-comers zoomed enviously a yard above their fellows, fire-flies in the radiance from the fairy lights.

Edward propped the ladder against the house wall. Making sure his heroics were witnessed, he thrust a hand among the cakes and grabbed one swiftly. Then he unscrewed the cap on the Vesprid tin and poured a little liquid on to the pastry.

'You'd better nip up to the spare bedroom,' he said to Patrick importantly. 'I reckon the nest's just above the bathroom window.'

'What for?' Patrick had paled and Greenleaf thought he knew why.

'I shall want some more light, shan't I?' Edward was enjoying himself. 'And someone'll have to hand this to me.' He made as if to thrust the poisoned cake into his host's hand.

'*I* am going up the ladder,' Patrick said icily.

Edward began to argue. He was the expert, wasn't he? Hadn't he just dealt efficiently with a nest of his own?

'Oh, for heaven's sake!' Tamsin said. 'This is supposed to be my birthday party.'

In the end Edward went rebelliously indoors carrying his bait. Marvell stood at the bottom of the ladder, steadying it, and when a light appeared at the bathroom window, Patrick began to climb. From the lawn they watched him peer along the eaves, his face white and tense in the patch of light. Then he called out with the only flash of humour he had permitted himself that evening:

'I've found it. Apparently there's no-one at home.'

'I reckon they've all gone to a party,' Edward called. Delighted because someone on the lawn had laughed, he licked his lips and pushed the cake towards Patrick. 'Supper,' he said.

Greenleaf found himself standing close by Oliver Gage and he turned to him to make some comment on the proceedings, but something in the other man's expression stopped him. He was staring at the figure on the ladder and his narrow red lips were wet. Greenleaf saw that he was clenching and unclenching his hands.

'Oh, look! What's happening?' Suddenly Nancy clutched Greenleaf's arm and startled he looked roofwards.

Patrick had started violently, arching his back away from the ladder. He shouted something. Then they saw him wince, hunch his shoulders and cover his face with his free arm.

'He's been stung,' Greenleaf heard Gage say flatly, 'and serve him bloody well right.' He didn't move but Greenleaf hurried forward to join the others who had gathered at the foot of the ladder. Three wasps were encircling Patrick's head, wheeling about him and making apparently for his closed eyes. They saw him for a moment, fighting, both arms flailing, his blind face twisted. Then Edward disappeared and the light went out. Now Patrick was just a silhouette against the clear turquoise sky and to Greenleaf he looked like a marionette of crumpled black paper whose convulsively beating arms seemed jerked by unseen strings.

76

'Come down!' Marvell shouted.

'O God!' Patrick gave a sort of groan and collapsed against the rungs, swaying precariously.

Someone shouted: 'He's going to fall,' but Patrick didn't fall. He began to slide down, prone against the ladder, and his shoes caught on each rung as he descended, tap, tap, flap, until he fell into Marvell's arms.

'Are you all right?' Marvell and Greenleaf asked together and Marvell shied at the wasp that came spiralling down towards Patrick's head. 'They've gone. Are you all right?'

Patrick said nothing but shuddered and put up his hand to cover his cheek. Behind him Greenleaf heard Freda Carnaby whimpering like a puppy, but nobody else made a sound. In the rainbow glimmer they stood silent and peering like a crowd at a bullfight who have seen a hated matador come to grief. The hostility was almost tangible and there was no sound but the steady buzz of the wasps.

'Come along.' Greenleaf heard his own voice pealing like a bell. 'Let's get him into the house.' But Patrick shook off his arm and blundered into the dining room.

They gathered round him in the lounge, all except Marvell who had gone to the kitchen to make coffee. Patrick crouched in an armchair holding his handkerchief against his face. He had been stung in several places, under the left eye, on the left wrist and forearm and on the right arm in what Greenleaf called the cubital fossa.

'Lucky it wasn't a good deal worse,' Edward said peevishly.

Patrick's eye was already beginning to swell and close. He scowled at Edward and said rudely:

'Get lost!'

'Please don't quarrel.' No-one knew how Freda had insinuated herself into her position on the footstool at Patrick's knees, nor exactly when she had taken his hand. 'It's bad enough as it is.'

'Oh, really,' Tamsin said. 'Such a fuss! Excuse me, will you? It might be a good idea for my husband to get some air.'

For the second time that night Denholm Smith-King looked first at his watch, then at his wife. 'Well, we'll be getting along. You won't want us.'

Marvell had come in with the coffee things but Tamsin didn't argue. She lifted her cheek impatiently for Joan to kiss.

'Coffee, Nancy? Oliver?' She by-passed the Carnabys exactly as if they were pieces of furniture. Oliver rejected the cup coldly, sitting on the edge of his chair.

'Perhaps we'd better go too.' Nancy looked hopelessly from angry face to angry face. 'Have you got any bi-carb? It's wonderful for wasp stings. I remember when my sister . . .'

'Come *along*, Nancy,' Oliver said. He took Nancy's arm and pulled her roughly. It looked as if he was going to leave without another word, but he stopped at the door and took Tamsin's hand. Their eyes met, Tamsin's wary, his, unless Greenleaf was imagining things, full of pleading disappointment. Then when Nancy kissed her, he followed suit, touching her cheek with the sexless peck that was common politeness on Linchester.

When they had gone, taking the Gavestons with them, and the Willises and the Millers had departed by the garden gate, Greenleaf went over to Patrick. He examined his eye and asked him how he felt.

'Lousy.'

Greenleaf poured him a cup of coffee.

'Had I better send for Dr. Howard, Max?' Tamsin didn't

ook anxious or excited or uneasy any more. She just looked annoyed.

'I don't think so.' Howard, he knew for a fact, wasn't on the week-end rota. A substitute would come and—who could tell?—that substitute might be himself. 'There's not much you can do. Perhaps an anti-histamine. I'll go over home and fetch something.'

Bernice and Marvell went with him, but he came back alone. The Carnabys were still there. Tamsin had left the front doors open for him and as he crossed the hall he heard no voices. They were all sitting in silence, each apparently nursing private resentment. Freda had moved a little way away from Patrick and had helped herself to coffee.

As if taking her cue from his arrival, Tamsin said sharply: 'Isn't it time you went?' She spoke to Edward but she was looking at Freda. 'When you've quite finished, of course.'

'I'm sure I didn't mean to be *de trop*.' Edward blushed but he brought out his painfully acquired French defiantly. Freda lingered woodenly. Then Patrick gave her a little push, a sharp sadistic push that left a red mark on her arm.

'Run along, there's a good girl,' he said and she rose obediently, pulling her skirt down over her knees.

' 'Night,' Patrick said abruptly. He pushed past Edward, ignoring the muttered 'We know when we're not wanted.' At the door he said to Greenleaf, 'You'll come up?' and the doctor nodded.

When he entered the balcony room behind Tamsin, Patrick was already in bed and he lay with his arms outside the sheets, the stings covered by blue pyjama sleeves.

By now his face was almost unrecognisable. The cheek had swollen and closed the eye. He looked, Greenleaf thought, rather as if he had mumps.

79

Queenie was stretched beside him, her feet at the foot of the bed, her jowls within the palm of his hand.

'You'll be too hot with him there,' the doctor said.

'It's not a him, it's a bitch.' Tamsin put her hand on Queenie's collar and for a moment Patrick's good eye blazed. 'Oh, all right, but I shan't sleep. I feel like hell.'

Greenleaf opened the windows to the balcony. The air felt cool, almost insolently fresh and invigorating after the hot evening. There were no curtains here to sway and alarm a sleeper, only the white hygienic blinds.

'Do you want something to make you sleep?' Prudently Greenleaf had brought his bag back with him. But Tamsin moved over to the dressing-table with its long built-in counter of black glass and creamy wood textured like watered silk. She opened one of the drawers and felt inside.

'He's got these,' she said. 'He had bad insomnia last year and Dr. Howard gave them to him.'

Greenleaf took the bottle from her. Inside were six blue capsules. Sodium Amytal, two hundred milligrammes.

'He can have one.' He unscrewed the cap and rattled a capsule into the palm of his hand.

'One's no good,' Patrick said. He held his cheek to lessen the pain talking caused him, and Tamsin, white and fluttering against her own reflection in the black glass wardrobe doors, nodded earnestly. 'He always had to have two,' she said.

'One.' Greenleaf was taking no chances. He opened his bag and took out a phial. 'The anti-histamine will help you to sleep. You'll sleep like a log.'

Patrick took them all at once, drinking from the glass Tamsin held out to him. 'Thanks,' he said. Tamsin waited until the doctor had fastened his bag and replaced the capsules in the immaculately tidy drawer. Then she switched off the light and they went downstairs.

'Please don't say Thank you for a lovely party,' she said when she and Greenleaf were in the hall.

Greenleaf chuckled. 'I won't,' he said.

The swans had gone to bed long ago in the reeds on the edge of the pond. From the woods between Linchester and Marvell's house something cried out, a fox perhaps or just an owl. It could have been either for all Greenleaf knew. His short stocky body cast a long shadow in the moonlight as he crossed The Green to the house called Shalom. He was suddenly very tired.

Marvell, on the other hand, was wide awake. He walked home through the woods slowly, reaching out from time to time to touch the moist lichened tree trunks in the dark. There were sounds in the forest, strange crunching whispering sounds which would have alarmed the doctor. Marvell had known them since boyhood, the tread of the fox—this was only a few miles north of Quorn country—the soft movement of dry leaves as a grass snake shifted them. It was very dark but the darkness was not absolute. Each trunk was a grey signpost to him; leaves touched his face and although the air was sultry they were cold and clean against his cheek. As he came out into Long Lane he heard in the distance the cry of the nightjar and he sighed.

When he had let himself into the house he lit one of the oil lamps and went as he always did before going to bed from room to room to look at his treasures. The porcelain gleamed, catching up what little light there was. He held the lamp for a moment against the mezzotint of Rievaulx. It recalled to him his own work on another Cistercian abbey and, setting the lamp by the window, he sat down with his manuscript, not to write—it was too late for that—but to read what he had written that day.

Red and white by the window. The snowflake fronds of the

Russian Vine and beside it hanging like drops of crimson wax, Berberidopsis, blood-red, absurdly named. The moonlight and the lamplight met and something seemed to pierce his heart.

Moths seeing the light, came at once to the lattice and a coal-black one — Marvell recognised it as The Chimney Sweeper's Boy—fluttered in at the open casement. It was followed by a larger, greyish-white one, its wings hung with filaments, swansdown in miniature. For a second Marvell watched them seek the lamp. Then, fearful lest they burn their wings, he gathered them up, making a loose cage of his hands, and thrust them out of the window.

They spiralled away from yellow into silvery light. He looked and looked again. There was someone in the garden. A shape, itself moth-like, was moving in the orchard. He brushed the black and white wing dust from his hands and leaned out to see who was paying him a visit at midnight.

7

ON Sunday morning Greenleaf got up at eight, did some exercises which he told his patients confidently would reduce their waist measurements from thirty-four to twenty-nine, and had a bath. By nine he had looked at *The Observer* and taken a cup of coffee up to Bernice. Then he sat down to write to his two sons who were away at school.

It was unlikely that anyone would call him out today. He had done his Sunday stint on the Chantflower doctors' rota, the previous week-end, and he intended to have a lazy day. Bernice appeared at about ten and they had a leisurely breakfast, talking about the boys and about the new car which ought to arrive in time to fetch them home for the holidays. After a while they took their coffee into the garden. They were near enough to the house to hear the phone but when it rang Greenleaf let Bernice answer it, knowing it wouldn't be for him.

But instead of settling down to a good gossip Bernice came back quickly, looking puzzled. This was odd, for Bernice seldom hurried.

'It's Tamsin, darling,' she said. 'She wants you.'

'Me?'

'She's in a state, but she wouldn't tell me anything. All she said was I want Max.'

Greenleaf took the call on the morning room phone.

'Max? It's Tamsin.' For almost the first time since he had

met her Tamsin wasn't using her affected drawl. 'I know I shouldn't be ringing you about this but I can't get hold of Dr. Howard.' She paused and he heard her inhale as if on a cigarette. 'Max, I can't wake Patrick. He's awfully cold and I've shaken him but . . . he doesn't wake.'

'When was this?'

'Just now, this minute. I overslept and I've only just got up.'

'I'll be right over,' Greenleaf said.

She murmured, 'Too kind!' and he heard the receiver drop.

Taking up his bag, he went by the short cut, the diameter of The Circle across the grass. On the face of it it seemed obvious what had happened. In pain from his stings Patrick had taken an extra one of the capsules. I ought to have taken the damned things away with me, Greenleaf said to himself. But still, it wasn't for him to baby another man's patients. Howard had prescribed them, they were safe enough unless . . . Unless! Surely Patrick wouldn't have been fool enough to take *two* more? Greenleaf quickened his pace and broke into a trot. Patrick was a young man, apparently healthy, but still, three . . . And the anti-histamine. Suppose he had taken the whole bottleful?

She was waiting for him on the doorstep when he ran up the Hallows drive and she hadn't bothered to dress. Because she never made up her face and always wore her hair straight she hadn't the bleak unkempt look of most of the women who called him out in an emergency. She wore a simple expensive dressing-gown of candy-striped cotton, pink and white with a small spotless white bow at the neck, and there were silver chain sandals on her feet. She looked alarmed and because of her fear, very young.

'Oh, Max, I didn't know what to do.'

'Still asleep, is he?'

Greenleaf went upstairs quickly, talking to her over his shoulder.

'He's so white and still and—and heavy somehow.'

'All right. Don't come up. Make some coffee. Make it very strong and black.'

She went away to the kitchen and Greenleaf entered the bedroom. Patrick was lying on his back, his head at an odd angle. His face was still puffy and the arms which were stretched over the counterpane, faintly swollen and white, not red any more. Greenleaf knew that colour, the yellowish ivory of parchment, and that waxen texture.

He took one of the wrists and remembered what Tamsin had said about the heavy feeling. Then, having slipped one hand within the bedclothes, he lifted Patrick's eyelids and closed them again. He sighed deeply. Feeling Patrick's pulse and heart had been just a farce. He had known when he came into the room. The dead look so very dead, as if they have never been alive.

He went out to meet Tamsin. She was coming up the stairs with the dog behind her.

'Tamsin, come in here.' He opened the door to the room where last night they had looked at the picture. One of the beds had been slept in and the covers were thrown back. 'Would you like to sit down?'

'Can't you wake him either?'

'I'm afraid . . .' He was a friend and he put his arm about her shoulders. 'You must be prepared for a shock.' She looked up at him. He had never noticed how large her eyes were nor of what a curious shade of transparent amber. 'I'm very much afraid Patrick is dead.'

She neither cried nor cried out. There was no change of colour in the smooth brown skin. Resting back against the bed-head, she remained as still as if she too were dead. She seemed to be thinking. It was as if, Greenleaf thought, all her past life with Patrick was being re-lived momentarily within her brain. At last she shuddered and bowed her head.

'What was it?' He had to bend towards her to catch the words. 'The cause, I mean. What did he die of?'

'I don't know.'

'The wasp stings?'

Greenleaf shook his head.

'I don't want to trouble you now,' he said gently, 'but those capsules, the sodium amytal, where are they?'

Tamsin got up like a woman in a dream.

'In the drawer. I'll get them.'

He followed her back into the other bedroom. She looked at Patrick, still without crying, and Greenleaf expected her to kiss the pallid forehead. They usually did. When instead she turned away and went to the dressing table he drew the sheet up over Patrick's face.

'There are still five in the bottle,' she said, and held it out to him. Greenleaf was very surprised. He felt a creeping unease.

'I'll get on to Dr. Howard,' he said.

Howard was out playing golf. Mrs. Howard would ring the club and her husband would come straight over. When Greenleaf walked into the dining room Tamsin was kneeling on the floor with her arms round the neck of the Weimaraner. She was crying.

'Oh, Queenie! Oh, Queenie! '

The room was untouched since the night before. The drinks were still on the sideboard and out on the patio some of the food still remained: heat-curled bread, melting cream, a shrivelled sandwich on a doyley. On the birthday table Marvell's roses lay among the other gifts, pearled with Sunday's dew. Greenleaf poured some brandy into a glass and handed it to Tamsin.

'How long has he been dead?' she asked.

86

'A good while,' Greenleaf said. 'Hours. Perhaps ten or twelve hours. Of course you looked in on him before you went to bed?'

She had stopped crying. 'Oh, yes,' she said.

'It doesn't matter. I don't want to upset you.'

'That's all right, Max. I'd like to talk about it.'

'You didn't sleep in the same room?'

'Not when one of us was ill,' Tamsin said quickly. 'I thought if he was restless it would be better for me to go in the back. Restless!' She passed her hand across her brow. 'Too dreadful, Max!' She went on rather as if she were giving evidence, using clipped sentences. 'I tried to clear up the mess in the garden but I was too tired. Then I looked in on Patrick. It must have been about midnight. He was sleeping then. I know he was, he was breathing. Well, then I went to bed. I was terribly tired, Max, and I didn't wake up till eleven. I rushed into Patrick because I couldn't hear a sound. Queenie had come up on my bed during the night.' Her hand fumbled for the dog's neck and she pushed her fingers into the plushy fur. 'I couldn't wake him so I phoned Dr. Howard. You know the rest.'

Patrick had died, Greenleaf thought, as he had lived, precisely, tidily, without dirt or disorder. Not for him the sloppy squalor that attended so many death-beds. From mild discomfort he had slipped into sleep, from sleep into death.

'Tamsin,' he said slowly and kindly, 'have you got any other sleeping pills in the house? Have you got any of your own?'

'Oh, no. No, I know we haven't. Patrick just had those six left and I never need anything to make me sleep.' She added unnecessarily: 'I sleep like a log.'

'Had he a weak heart? Did you ever hear of any heart trouble?'

'I don't think so. We'd been married for seven years, you

87

know, but I've known Patrick since he was a little boy. I don't know if you knew we were cousins? His father and mine were brothers.'

'No serious illnesses?'

A petulant cloud crossed her face briefly. 'He was born in Germany,' she said. 'Then, when the war came, they lived in America. After they came back to this country they used to come and see us sometimes. Patrick was terribly spoiled, coddled really. They used to make him wrap up warm even in the summer and I had swimming lessons but they wouldn't let him. I always thought it was because they'd lived in California.' She paused, frowning. 'He was always all right when he was grown-up. The only time he went to Dr. Howard was when he couldn't sleep.'

'I think you will have to prepare yourself,' Greenleaf said, 'for the possibility of an inquest, or, at any rate, a post-mortem.'

She nodded earnestly.

'Oh, quite,' she said. 'I understand. That'll be absolutely all right.' She might have been agreeing to cancel an engagement, so matter-of-fact was her tone.

After that they sat in silence, waiting for Dr. Howard to come. The Weimaraner went upstairs and they heard her claws scraping, scraping at the closed door of the balcony room.

As things turned out, it never came to an inquest. Greenleaf stood in at the post-mortem because he was interested and because the Selbys had been friends of his. Patrick had died, like all the dead, of heart failure. The death certificate was signed and he was buried in Chantflower cemetery on the following Thursday.

Greenleaf and Bernice went to the funeral. They took Marvell with them in Bernice's car.

'Blessed are the dead,' said the Rector, a shade sardonically, 'which die in the Lord.' Since coming to Linchester Patrick had never been to church.

Patrick's parents were dead; Tamsin had been an orphan since she was four. They had both been only children. Consequently there were no relatives at the graveside. Apart from the Linchesterites, only three friends came to support the widow: the two other directors of Patrick's firm of glass manufacturers and old Mrs. Prynne.

Tamsin wore a black dress and a large hat of glossy black straw. Throughout the service she clung to Oliver Gage's arm. On her other side Nancy, sweating in the charcoal worsted she had bought for her February honeymoon, sat with a handkerchief ready. But she never had to hand it to Tamsin who sat rigid and dry-eyed.

It was only when the coffin was being lowered into the ground that a small disturbance occurred. Freda Carnaby tore herself from Mrs. Staxton's arm and, sobbing loudly, fell to her knees beside the dark cavity. As he said afterwards to Greenleaf, Marvell thought that like Hamlet she was going to leap into the grave. But nothing dramatic happened. Mrs. Staxton helped her to her feet and drew her away.

When it was all over Tamsin slung two suitcases into the back of the black and white Mini (SIN 1A) and with Queenie in the seat beside her, drove away to stay with Mrs. Prynne.

PART TWO

8

Two days later the weather broke with a noisy spectacular thunderstorm and a man died when a tree under which he was sheltering on Chantflower golf course was struck by lightning. The silly season had begun and this was national news. For the Linchester housewives kept indoors by continuous rain, it was for days the prime topic of conversation —until something more personal and sensational took over.

The young Macdonalds had taken their baby to Bournemouth; the Willises and the Millers, each couple finding in the other the perfect neighbours and friends, were cruising together in the Canaries. Tamsin was still away. With four empty houses on Linchester Nancy was bored to tears. When Oliver came home for the week-ends, tired and uneasy, he found his evening programmes mapped out for him.

Tonight the Greenleafs and Crispin Marvell were invited for coffee and drinks. Opening his sideboard, Oliver found that Nancy had laid in a stock of cheap Cyprus sherry and bottles of cocktails as variously coloured as the liquid that used to be displayed in the flagons of old-fashioned pharmacy windows. He cursed, clinging to the shreds of his pride and remembering the days that were gone.

The mantelpiece was decorated with postcards. Nancy had given pride of place to a peacock-blue panorama from Clare Miller, relegating two monochrome seascapes to a

93

spot behind a vase. He read Sheila Macdonald's happy scrawl irascibly. Tamsin was at the seaside too, but Tamsin had sent nothing . . .

From where he stood, desultorily watching the rain, he could hear Nancy chattering to Linda Gaveston in the kitchen. Occasionally something clearly audible if not comprehensible arose above the twittering.

'I said it was dead grotty' or 'How about that, doll?' conflicted inharmoniously with Nancy's 'You are awful, Linda.'

Oliver grunted and lit a cigarette. These visits of Linda's, ostensibly made to deliver Nancy's order of tablets of soap or a packet of Kleenex, always put him in a bad temper. They invariably led to petulance on Nancy's part, to dissatisfaction and a carping envy. It amazed Oliver that a village chemist like Waller could stock such an immense and catholic variety of luxury goods, all of which at some time or another seemed so desirable to his wife and at the same time so conducive to the saving of money. The latest in Thermos flasks, automatic tea-makers, thermostatically controlled electric blankets, shower cabinets, all these had in the year they had lived on Linchester, been recommended to Nancy and coveted by her.

'It would be such a saving in the long run,' she would say wistfully of some gimmick, using the suburban colloquialisms Oliver hated.

Moreover it was surprising that behind Waller's counter there stood concealed the most expensive ranges of cosmetics from Paris and New York, scent and creams which were apparently exclusive to him and not to be found in Nottingham or, for that matter, London. He was therefore pleasantly astonished when the door had closed on Linda to see Nancy come dancing into the room, contented, gay and in a strange way, gleeful.

94

'What's got into you?'

'Nothing.'

'For a poor house-bound, forsaken child bride,' he said, recalling earlier complaints, 'you're looking very gay.'

Indeed she appeared quite pretty again in the honeymoon skirt and a pink sweater, not a hand-knitted one for a change but a soft fluffy thing that drew Oliver's eyes and reminded him that his wife had, after all, an excellent figure. But his words, sharp and moody, had altered her expression from open calm to secretiveness.

'Linda told me something very peculiar.'

'Really?' he said. 'Surprise me.'

She pouted.

'Not if you're going to talk to me like that.' For a moment, a transient moment, she looked just as she had when he had first seen her dancing with the man she had been engaged to. It had been such fun stealing her from him, especially piquant because the fiancé had also been Shirley's cousin. 'Nasty Oliver! I shall save it all up till the Greenleafs get here.'

'I can see,' said Oliver in his best co-respondent's voice, 'I can see I shall have to be very nice to you.'

'Very, very nice,' said Nancy. She sat on the sofa beside him and giggled. 'You are awful! It must be the country air.' But she didn't say anything after that and presently Oliver forgot all about Linda Gaveston.

When Marvell rang the door-bell she didn't bother to tidy her hair or put on fresh make-up. There was something of a bacchante about her, exhibitionistic, crudely female. Suddenly Oliver felt old. Her naiveté embarrassed him. He went to dispense drinks from his own stock, leaving the bright mean bottles in the sideboard.

Greenleaf and Bernice had barely sat down when she said brightly:

'Has anyone heard from Tamsin?'

Nobody had. Oliver fancied that Marvell was looking at him quizzically.

'I don't suppose she feels like writing.' Bernice was always kind and forbearing. 'It's not as if we were any of us close friends.'

'What would she have to write about?' Greenleaf asked. 'She's not on holiday.' And he began to talk about his own holiday, planned for September this year, and to ask about the Gages'.

Holidays were a sore point with Oliver who hoped to do without one altogether. He need not have worried. Nancy was obviously not going to let the subject go as easily as that.

'Poor Tamsin,' she said loudly, drowning the doctor's voice. 'Fancy being a widow when you're only twenty-seven.'

'Dreadful,' said Bernice.

'And in such—well, awkward circumstances.'

'Awkward circumstances?' said Greenleaf, drawn unwillingly from his dreams of the Riviera.

'I don't mean money-wise.' Oliver winced but Nancy went on: 'The whole thing was so funny, Patrick dying like that. I expect you'll all think I've got a very suspicious mind but I can't help thinking it was . . .' She paused for effect and sipped her gin. 'Well, it was fishy, wasn't it?'

Greenleaf looked at the floor. The legs of his chair had caught in one of the Numdah rugs. He bent down and straightened it.

'I don't know if I ought to say this,' Nancy went on. 'I don't suppose it's common knowledge, but Patrick's father . . .' She lowered her voice. 'Patrick's father committed suicide. Took his own life.'

'Oh, dear,' said Bernice comfortably.

'I really don't know who it was told me,' Nancy said. She picked up the plate of canapés and handed it to Marvell. To his shame Oliver saw that only half a cocktail onion topped the salmon mayonnaise on each of them. 'Do have a savoury, won't you?'

Marvell refused. The plate hovered.

'Somebody told me about it. Now who was it?'

'It was me,' Oliver said sharply.

'Of course it was. And Tamsin told you. I can't imagine why.'

All childish innocence, she looked archly from face to face.

Marvell said: 'I'm afraid I'm being obtuse, but I can't quite see what Patrick's father's suicide has to do with his son dying of heart failure.'

'Oh, absolutely nothing. Nothing at all. You mustn't think I was insinuating anything about Patrick. It's just that it's one of the funny circumstances. On its own it would be nothing.'

Oliver emptied his glass and stood up. He could cheerfully have slapped Nancy's face. 'I think we're boring our guests,' he said, bracketing himself with his wife and trying to make his voice sound easy. 'Another drink, Max? Bernice?' Marvell's glass was still full. 'What about you, darling?'

'Oh, really!' Nancy burst out laughing. 'You don't have to be so discreet. We're all friends. Nothing's going to go beyond these four walls.'

Oliver felt himself losing control. These people *were* discreet. Would it, after all, ruin his career, damn him as a social creature, if in front of them he were to bawl at Nancy, strike her, push her out of the room?

He stared at her, pouring sherry absently until it topped over the glass and spilled on the tray.

'Damnation!' he said.

'Oh, your table!' Bernice was beside him, mopping with a tiny handkerchief.

'Linda Gaveston was here today,' Nancy said. 'She told me something very peculiar. No, I won't shut up, Oliver. I'm only repeating it because I'd be very interested in having an opinion from a medical man. You know that funny little man who's a commercial traveller? The one who lives in the chalets?'

'Carnaby,' said Marvell.

'That's right. Carnaby. The one who was so difficult at the party. Well, the day before Patrick died he came into Waller's shop and what d'you think he tried to buy?' She waited for the guesses that never came. 'Cyanide! That's what he tried to buy.'

Greenleaf stuck out his lower lip. They had only been in the house half an hour but he began to wonder how soon he could suggest to Bernice that it was time to leave. His drink tasted thin. For the first time since he had given up smoking as an example to his patients he longed for a cigarette.

'Waller wouldn't sell anyone cyanide,' he said at last.

'Ah, no,' said Nancy triumphantly, 'he didn't. But that's not the point, is it? He wanted cyanide and maybe he managed to get it . . .' She drew breath. 'Elsewhere,' she said with sinister emphasis. 'Now why did he want it?'

'Probably for killing wasps,' said Marvell. 'It's an old remedy for getting rid of wasps.'

Nancy looked disappointed.

'Linda overheard the conversation,' she said, 'and that's just what this fellow Carnaby said. He said he wanted it for wasps. Linda thought it was pretty thin.'

Thumping his fist on the table, Oliver made them all jump.

'Linda Gaveston is a stupid little trouble-maker,' he said furiously.

'I suppose that goes for me too?'

'I didn't say so,' said Oliver, too angry to care. 'But if the cap fits . . . I hate all this under-hand gossip. If you're trying to say Carnaby gave Patrick cyanide you'd better come straight out with it.' He drank some whisky too quickly and choked. 'On the other hand, perhaps you'd better not. I don't want to pay out whacking damages for slander.'

'It won't go any further. Anyway, it's my duty as a citizen to say what I think. Everyone knows Edward Carnaby had a terrific motive for getting Patrick out of the way.'

There was an appalled silence. Nancy had grown red in the face and her plump breasts rose and fell under the clinging pink wool.

'You're all crazy about Tamsin. I know that. But Patrick wasn't. He didn't care for her a bit. He was having an affair with that awful little Freda. Night after night he was round there while her brother was out at evening classes. He used to tie that great dog of theirs up to the gate. It was just a horrid sordid little intrigue.'

As much as Oliver, Greenleaf wanted to stop her. He was immeasurably grateful for Bernice's rich cleansing laughter.

'If it was just a little intrigue,' Bernice said lightly, 'it can't have been important, can it?'

Nancy allowed her hand to rest for a moment beneath Bernice's. Then she snatched it away.

'They're twins, aren't they? It means a lot, being twins. He wouldn't want to lose her. Patrick might have gone off with her.'

But the tension was broken. Marvell, who had taken a book from the fireside shelves and studied it as if it were a first edition, now relaxed and smiled. Oliver had moved over to the record player and the red glaze had left his face.

'Well, what does Max think?' Nancy asked.

How wise Bernice had been, laughing easily, refusing to catch his eye! Greenleaf didn't really want to do a Smith-King and flee at the scent of trouble. Besides Oliver had some good records, Bartok and the wonderful Donizetti he wanted to hear again.

'You know,' he said in a quiet gentle voice, 'it's amazing the way people expect the worst when a young person dies suddenly. They always want to make a mystery.' He wondered if Bernice and, for that matter Marvell, noticed how dismay was evoking his guttural accent. 'Real life isn't so sensational.'

'Fiction stranger than truth,' Marvell murmured.

'I can assure you Patrick didn't die of cyanide. You see, of all the poisons commonly used in cases of homicide cyanide is the most easily detected. The smell, for one thing . . .'

'Bitter almonds,' Nancy interposed.

Greenleaf smiled a smile he didn't feel.

'That among other things. Believe me, it's fantastic to talk of cyanide.' His hands moved expressively. 'No, please,' he said.

'Well, what do you really think, then?'

'I think you're a very pretty girl with a vivid imagination and Linda Gaveston watches too much television. I wonder if I might have some more of your excellent whisky, Oliver?'

Oliver took the glass gratefully. He looked as if he would gladly have given Greenleaf the whole bottle.

'Music,' he said, handing records to the discerning Marvell.

'May we have the Handel?' Marvell asked politely. Nancy made a face and flung herself back among the cushions.

The sound of the rain falling steadily had formed throughout the conversation a monotonous background chorus. Now, as they became silent, the music of The Faithful Shepherd Suite filled the room. Greenleaf listened to the orchestra and noted the repetition of each phrase with the appreciation of the scientist: but Marvell, with the ear of the artist *manqué*, felt the absurd skimped room transformed about him and, sighing within himself for something irrevocably lost, saw a green grove as in a Constable landscape and beneath the leaves a lover with the Pipes of Pan.

9

THE rain ceased as darkness fell and the sky cleared suddenly as if washed free of cloud. It was a night of bright white stars, so many stars that Greenleaf had to point out and admire—although he did not know their names—the strung lights of Charles's Wain and Jupiter riding in the south.

'Patines of bright gold,' said Marvell. 'Only they're not gold, they're platinum. Patines of bright platinum doesn't sound half so well, does it?'

'It's no good quoting at me,' said the doctor. 'You know I never read anything but the *B.M.J.*' He drew a deep breath, savouring the night air. 'Very nice,' he said inadequately. 'I'm glad I summoned up the energy to walk back with you.'

'It was a sticky evening, wasn't it?' Marvell went first, holding back brambles for Greenleaf to pass along the path.

'Silly little woman,' Greenleaf said, harshly for him. 'I hope Gage can stop her gossiping.'

'It could be awkward.' Marvell said no more until the path broadened and the doctor was walking abreast of him. Then suddenly, 'May I ask you something?' he said. 'I don't want to offend you.'

'You won't do that.'

'You're a doctor, but Patrick wasn't your patient.' Marvell spoke quietly. 'I asked you if I would offend you because I was thinking of medical etiquette. But—look, I'm not scandal-mongering like Nancy Gage—weren't you very surprised when Patrick died like that?'

Greenleaf said guardedly, 'I was surprised, yes.'

'Thunderstruck?'

'Like that poor fellow on the golf course? Well, no. You see a lot of strange things in my job. I thought at first Patrick had taken an overdose of sodium amytal. I'd given him an anti-histamine, two hundred milligrammes of Phenergan, and one would potentiate . . .' He stopped, loth to give these esoteric details to a layman. 'He had the sodium amytal and I advised him to take one.'

'You left the bottle with him?'

'Now, look.' Greenleaf had said he wouldn't be offended. 'Patrick wasn't a child. Howard had prescribed them. In any case, he didn't take any more. That was the first thing Glover looked for at the post-mortem.'

Marvell opened the orchard gate and Greenleaf stepped from the forest floor on to turf and the slippery leaves of wild daffodils. The petals of a wet rose brushed his face. In the darkness they felt like a woman's fingers drenched with scent.

'The first thing?' Marvell asked. 'You mean, you looked for other things? You suspected suicide or even murder?'

'No, no, no,' Greenleaf said impatiently. 'A man had died, a young, apparently healthy man. Glover had to find out what he died of. Patrick died of heart failure.'

'Everybody dies of heart failure.'

'Roughly, yes. But there were signs that the heart had been affected before. There was some slight damage.'

They had come to the back door. The kitchen smelt of herbs and wine. Greenleaf thought he could detect another less pleasant scent. Mildew. He had never seen mushrooms growing but Marvell's kitchen smelt like the plastic trays of

103

mushrooms Bernice bought at the village store. Marvell groped for the lamp and lit it.

'Well, go on,' he said.

'If you must know,' Greenleaf said, 'Glover made some enquiries at Patrick's old school. Tamsin didn't know anything and Patrick's parents were dead. He'd never complained to Howard about feeling ill. Only went to him once.'

'May I ask if you got anything from the school?'

'I don't know if you may,' Greenleaf said severely. 'I don't know why you want to know. But if there's going to be a lot of talk . . . Glover wrote to the headmaster and he got a letter back saying Patrick had had to be let off some of the games because he'd had rheumatic fever.'

'I see. So you checked with the doctor Patrick had when he was a child.'

'We couldn't do that.' Greenleaf smiled a small, bitter and very personal smile. 'Patrick was born in Germany. His mother was German and he lived there till he was four. Glover talked to Tamsin's Mrs. Prynne. She's one of these old women with a good memory. She remembered Patrick had had rheumatic fever when he was three—very early to have it, incidentally—and that the name of his doctor had been Goldstein.'

Marvell was embarrassed.

'But Dr. Goldstein had disappeared. A lot of people of his persuasion disappeared in Germany between 1939 and 1945.'

'Stopping for a quick drink?' Marvell asked.

Five minutes passed before he said anything more about Patrick Selby. Greenleaf felt that he had been stiff and pompous, the very prototype of the uppish medical man. To restore Marvell's ease he accepted a glass of carrot wine.

The brilliance of the white globe had increased until now only the corners of the parlour remained in shadow. A small wind had arisen, stirring the curtains and moving the trailing violet and white leaves of the Tradescantia that stood in a majolica pot on the window sill. It was rather cold.

Then Marvell said: 'I was curious about Patrick.' He sat down and warmed his hands at the lamp. Greenleaf wondered if Bernice, at home in Shalom, had turned on the central heating. 'Perhaps I have a suspicious mind. Patrick had a good many enemies, you know. Quite a lot of people must be glad he's dead.'

'And I have a logical mind,' said Greenleaf briskly. 'Nancy Gage says Carnaby tried to buy cyanide. Patrick Selby dies suddenly. Therefore, she reasons, Patrick died of cyanide. But we *know* Patrick didn't die of cyanide. He died a natural death. Can't you see that once your original premise falls to the ground there's no longer any reason to doubt that? No matter how much Carnaby hated him—if he did, which I doubt—no matter if he succeeded in buying a ton of cyanide, he didn't kill Patrick with it because Patrick didn't die of cyanide. Now, just because one person appears to have a thin motive and access—possible access—to means *that were never used at all*, you start reasoning that he was in fact murdered, that half a dozen people had motives and that one of them succeeded.' He drank the carrot wine. It was really quite pleasant, like sweet Bristol Cream. 'You're not being logical,' he said.

Marvell didn't reply. He began to wind the clock delicately as if he was being careful not to disturb the sultan and his slave whose fingers rested eternally on the silent zither. When he had put the key down he blew away a money spider that was creeping across the sultan's gondola-shaped shoe. Then he said:

'Why wasn't there an inquest?'

Greenleaf answered him triumphantly. 'Because there wasn't any need. Haven't I been telling you? And that wasn't up to Glover and Howard. That's a matter for the coroner.'

'No doubt he knows his own business.'

'You don't have inquests on people who die naturally.'
Greenleaf got up, stretching cold stiff legs, and changed the
subject. 'How's the hay fever?'

'I've run out of tablets.'

'Come down to the surgery sometime and I'll let you
have another prescription.'

But Marvell didn't come and Greenleaf saw nothing of
him for several days. Greenleaf began to think that he would
hear no more of Patrick's death—until surgery time on
Wednesday morning.

The first patient to come into the consulting room through
the green baize door was Denholm Smith-King. He was on
his way to his Nottingham factory and at last he had summoned the courage to let Greenleaf examine him.

'It's nothing,' the doctor said as Smith-King sat up on the
couch buttoning his shirt. 'Only a gland. It'll go down eventually.'

'Then I suppose I shall just have to lump it.' He laughed
at his own joke and Greenleaf joined in politely.

'I see you've cut down on the smoking.'

He was startled and showed it, but his eyes followed the
doctor's down to his own right forefinger and he grinned.

'Quite the detective in your own way, aren't you?' Greenleaf had only noticed that the sepia stains had paled to
yellow and this remark reminded him of things he wanted
to forget. 'Yes, I've cut it down,' Smith-King said and he
gave the doctor a heavy, though friendly buffet on the back.
'You quacks, you don't know the strains a business man has
to contend with. You don't know you're born,' but his
hearty laugh softened the words.

'Things going better, are they?'

106

'You bet,' said Smith-King.

He went off jauntily and Greenleaf rang the bell for the next patient. By ten he had seen a dozen people and he asked the last one, a woman with nettle rash, if there were any more to come.

'Just one, Doctor. A young lady.'

He put his finger on the buzzer but no-one came so he began to tidy up his desk. Evidently the young lady had got tired of waiting. Then, just as he was picking up his ignition key, the baize door was pushed feebly open and Freda Carnaby shuffled in wearily like an old woman.

He was shocked at the change in her. Impatience died as he offered her a chair and sat down himself. What had become of the bright bird-like creature with the practical starched cotton dresses and the impractical shoes? Even at the funeral she had still looked smart in trim shop-girl black. Now her hair looked as if it hadn't been washed for weeks, her eyes were bloodshot and puffy and there was a hysterical downward quirk at the corner of her mouth.

'What exactly is the trouble, Miss Carnaby?'

'I can't sleep. I haven't had a proper night's sleep since I don't know how long.' She felt in the pocket of the mock-suede jacket she wore over her crumpled print dress. The handkerchief she pulled out was crumpled too. She pressed it with pathetic gentility against her lips. 'You see, I've had a great personal loss.' The linen square brushed the corner of one eye. 'I was very fond of someone. A man.' She gulped. 'He died quite recently.'

'I'm sorry to hear that.' Greenleaf began to wonder what was coming.

'I don't know what to do.'

He had observed before that it is this particular phrase that triggers off the tears, the breakdown. It may be true, it may be felt, but it is only when it is actually uttered aloud that its full significance, the complete helpless disorientation it implies, brings home to the speaker the wretchedness of his or her plight.

'Now you mustn't say that,' he said, knowing his inadequacy. 'Time does heal, you know.' The healer passing the buck, he thought. 'I'll let you have something to make you sleep.' He drew out his prescription pad and began to write. 'Have you been away yet this year?'

'No and I'm not likely to.'

'I should try. Just a few days would help.'

'Help?' He had heard that hysterical note so often but not from her and he didn't like it. 'Help a—a broken heart? Oh, Doctor, I don't know what to do. I don't know what to do.' She dropped her head on to her folded arms and began to sob.

Greenleaf went to the sink and drew her a glass of water.

'I'd like to tell you about it.' She sipped and wiped her eyes. 'Can I tell you about it?'

He looked surreptitiously at his watch.

'If it would make you feel better.'

'It was Patrick Selby. You knew that, didn't you?' Greenleaf said nothing so she went on. 'I was very fond of him.' They never say 'love', he thought, always 'very fond of' or 'devoted to'. 'And he was very fond of me,' she said defiantly. He glanced momentarily at her tear-blotched face, the rough skin. When she said out of the blue, 'We were going to be married,' he jumped.

'I know what you're going to say. You're going to say he was already married. Tamsin didn't care for him. He was going to divorce her.'

'Miss Carnaby . . .'

But she rushed on, the words tumbling out.

'She was having an affair with that awful man Gage. Patrick knew all about it. She used to meet him in London

108

during the week. Patrick knew. She said she was going to see some old friend of her grandmother's, but half the time she was with that man.'

Sympathy fought with and finally conquered Greenleaf's distaste. Keeping his expression a kindly blank, he began to fold up the prescription.

Misinterpreting his look, she said defensively:

'I know what you're thinking. But I wasn't carrying on with Patrick. It wasn't like that. We never did anything wrong. We were going to be married. And Nancy Gage is going about all over Linchester saying Edward killed Patrick because . . . because . . .' Her sobs broke out afresh. Greenleaf watched her in despair. How was he to turn this weeping hysterical woman out into the street? How stem the tide of appalling revelation?

'And the terrible thing is I know he was killed. That's why I can't sleep. And I know who killed him.'

This was too much. He shook her slightly, wiped her eyes himself and held the glass to her lips.

'Miss Carnaby, you must get a grip on yourself. Patrick died a perfectly natural death. This is certain. I know it. You'll only do your brother and yourself a lot of harm if you go about saying things you can't substantiate.'

'Substantiate?' She stumbled over the word. 'I can *prove* it. You remember what it was like at that awful party. Well, Oliver Gage went back by himself when it was all over. I saw him from my bedroom window. It was bright moonlight and he went over by the pond. He was carrying something, a white packet. I don't know what it was, but, Doctor, suppose —suppose it killed Patrick!'

Then, he got her out of the surgery, bundled her into his own car and drove her back to Linchester.

Three letters plopped through the Gage letter box when

the post came at ten. Nancy was so sure they weren't for her that it was all of half an hour before she bothered to come down from the bathroom. Instead, her hair rolled up in curlers, wet and evil-smelling with home-perm fluid, she sat on the edge of the bath waiting for the cooking timer to ping and brooding about what the letters might contain.

Two bills, she thought bitterly, and probably a begging letter from Jean or Shirley. A saturated curler dripped on to her nose. By this time the whole of the first floor of the house smelt of ammonia and rotten eggs. She would have to use masses of that air freshener stuff before Oliver came home. Still, that was a whole two days and goodness knew how many hours away. Surely Oliver would scarcely notice the smell when he saw how wonderful her hair looked, and all for twenty-five bob.

The timer rang and she began unrolling excitedly. When the handbasin was filled with a soggy mess of curlers and mushy paper she put a towel round her shoulders, a mauve one with Hers embroidered on it in white; His, the other half of the wedding present, was scrupulously kept for Oliver—and went downstairs.

The first letter she picked up was from Jean. Nancy knew that before she saw the handwriting. Oliver's first wife was their only correspondent who saved old envelopes and stuck new address labels on them. The second was almost certainly the telephone bill. It might be as well to lose that one. Now, who could be writing to her from London?

She opened the last envelope and saw the letter heading, Oliver's newspaper, Fleet Street. It was *from* Oliver. She looked again at the envelope and at the slanted stamp. To her that meant a kiss. Did it mean that to Oliver or had it occurred by chance?

'My darling . . .' That was nice. It was also unfamiliar and unexpected. She read on. 'I am wondering if you have forgiven me for my unkindness to you at the week-end. I was sharp with you, even verging on the brutal . . .' How beautifully he wrote! But that was to be expected. It was, after all, his line. 'Can you understand, my sweet, that this was only because I hate to see you cheapening yourself? I felt that you were making yourself the butt of those men's wit and this hurt me more bitterly than I can tell you. So for my sake, darling Nancy, watch your words. This is Tamsin's business and she is nothing to us . . .' Nancy could hardly believe a letter would make her so happy. '. . . She is nothing to us. We each possess one world. Each hath one and is one.' Hath, she decided, must be typing error, but the thought was there. 'The merest suggestion that I might be . . .' Then there was a bit blanked out with x's '. . . associated with a scandal of this kind has caused me considerable disquiet. We were not close friends of the Selbys . . .'

There was a great deal more in the same vein. Nancy skipped some of it, the boring parts, and lingered over the astonishing endearments at the end. She was so ecstatically happy that, although she caught sight of her elated face in the hall mirror, she hardly noticed that her hair was hanging in rats' tails, dripping and perfectly straight.

Marvell was determined to get Greenleaf interested in the circumstances of Patrick's death and he thought it would do no harm to confront him with a list of unusual poisons. To this end he had been to the public library and spent an instructive afternoon reading Taylor. He was so carried away that he was too late for afternoon surgery—his ostensible mission, he decided, would be to collect another prescription—so he picked a bunch of acanthus for Bernice and walked up to Shalom.

'Beautiful,' Bernice said. Her husband touched the

111

brownish-pink flowers. 'What are they?' Diffidently he suggested: 'Lupins or something?'

'Acanthus,' said Marvell. 'The original model for the Corinthian capital.'

Bernice filled a white stone vase with water. 'You are a mine of information.'

'Let's say a disused quarry of rubble.' The words had a bitter sound but Marvell smiled as he watched her arrange the flowers. 'And the rubble, incidentally, is being shaken by explosions. I've been sneezing for the past three days and I've run out of those fascinating little blue pills.'

Bernice smiled. 'If this is going to turn into a consultation,' she said, 'you'd better go and have a drink with Max.'

She began on the washing up and Marvell followed Greenleaf into the sitting room. Greenleaf pushed open the glass doors to the garden and pulled up chairs in the path of the incoming cooler air. The sky directly above was a pure milky blue and in the west refulgent, brazen gold, but the long shadow of the cedar tree lapped the walls of the house. The room was a cool sanctuary.

'It might be worth finding out exactly what you're allergic to, have some tests done,' the doctor said. 'It need not be hay, you know. You can be allergic to practically anything.'

Marvell hadn't really wanted to talk about himself but now, as if to give colour to his excuse, a tickle began at the back of his nose and he was shaken by a vast sneeze. When he had recovered he said slyly:

'Well, I suppose it can't kill me.'

'It could lead to asthma,' Greenleaf said cheerfully. 'It does in sixty to eighty per cent of cases if it isn't checked.'

'I asked,' said Marvell, re-phrasing, 'if an allergy could kill you.'

'No, you didn't. And I know exactly what you're getting at,

112

but Patrick wasn't allergic to wasp stings. He had one a few days before he died and the effect was just normal.'

'All right,' Marvell said and he blew his nose. 'You remember what we were talking about the other night?'

'What you were talking about.'

'What I was talking about, then. Don't be so stiff-necked, Max.'

They had known each other for two or three years now and at first it had been Dr. Greenleaf, Mr. Marvell. Then, as intimacy grew, the use of their styles had seemed too formal and Greenleaf who hadn't been to a public school baulked at the bare surname. This was the first time Marvell had called his friend by his first name and Greenleaf felt the strange warmth of heart, the sense of being accepted, this usage brings. It made him weak where he had intended to be strong.

'Suppose,' Marvell went on, 'there was some substance, perfectly harmless under normal circumstances, but lethal if anyone took it when he'd been stung by a wasp.'

Reluctantly Greenleaf recalled what Freda Carnaby had told him about the white package carried by Oliver Gage.

'Suppose, suppose. There isn't such a substance.'

'Sure?'

'As sure as anyone can be.'

'I'm bored with Chantefleur Abbey, Max, and I've a mind to do a spot of detecting—with your help. It obviously needs a doctor.'

'You're crazy,' said Greenleaf unhappily. 'I'm going to give you a drink and write out that prescription.'

'I don't want a drink. I want to talk about Patrick.'

'Well?'

'Well, since I last saw you I've been swotting up forensic medicine . . .'

'In between the sneezes, I imagine.'

'In between the sneezes, as you say. As a matter of fact I've been reading Taylor's *Medical Jurisprudence*.'

'Fascinating, isn't it?' Greenleaf said, in spite of himself. He added quickly: 'It won't tell you a thing about wasp stings or rheumatic fever.'

'No, but it tells me a hell of a lot about poisons. A positive Borgias' Bible. Brucine and thallium, lead and gold. Did you know there are some gold salts called Purple of Cassius? But of course you did. Purple of Cassius! There's a name to conjure death with.'

'It didn't conjure Patrick Selby's death.'

'How do you *know*? I'll bet Glover didn't test for it.'

'No, and he didn't test for arsenic or hyoscine or the botulinus bacillus, for the simple reason that there wasn't the slightest indication in Patrick's appearance or the state of the room to suggest that he might remotely have taken any of them.'

'I have heard,' Marvell said, 'that a man can die from having air injected into a vein. Now there's a very entertaining novel by Dorothy Sayers . . .'

Unnatural Death.

'So you do read detective stories!' Marvell pounced on his words.

'Only on holiday.' Greenleaf smiled. 'But Patrick hadn't any hypodermic marks.'

'Well, well,' Marvell mocked. 'Max, you're a hypocrite. How do you know Patrick hadn't any hypodermic marks unless you looked for them? And if you looked for them you must have suspected at the least suicide.'

For a few moments Greenleaf didn't answer him. What Marvell said was near the truth. He had looked and found— nothing. But had he been in possession of certain facts of which he was now cognisant, would he have acted as he had? Wouldn't he instead have tried to dissuade Howard

114

and Glover from signing the death certificate? He had done nothing because Patrick had not been his patient, because it would have been unprofessional to poach on Howard's preserves, because, most of all, Patrick had seemed a reasonably happily married man leading a quiet normal life. Happily married? Now, of course, it sounded an absurd description of the mess he and Tamsin had made for themselves, but then . . . You had to make allowances for the uninhibited way people behaved at parties, Tamsin's close dancing with Gage, Patrick's flirtation with Freda Carnaby. The possibility of murder had never crossed his mind. Why, then, had he looked? Just to fill the time, he thought, almost convincing himself, just for something to do.

And yet, as he answered Marvell, he was fully aware that he was skirting round the question.

'I looked,' he said carefully, 'before Glover began his examination. At the time there seemed nothing to account for the death. It was afterwards that Glover found the heart damage. There were no punctures on Patrick's body apart from those made by wasps. And he didn't die from wasps' stings, unless you might say he had a certain amount of shock from the stings.'

'If by that you mean the shock affected his heart, wouldn't you have expected him to have a heart attack at once, even while he was on the ladder, not three or four hours later?'

The damage caused by the rheumatic fever had been slight. Patrick must have had it very mildly. But in the absence of Patrick's parents and Dr. Goldstein, who could tell? 'Yes, I would,' Greenleaf said unhappily.

'Max, you're coming round to my way of thinking. Look, leaving the cause of death for a moment, wasn't there something very—to use Nancy's word—fishy about that party?'

'You mean the picture?'

'I mean the picture. I went upstairs to get the citronella

and there was the picture. Now, it wasn't covered up. It was in a room in Patrick's house. But he didn't know it was there. Did you see his face when he saw it?'

Greenleaf frowned. 'It was a horrible thing,' he said.

'Oh, come. A bit bloodthirsty. By a pupil of Thornhill, I should say, and those old boys didn't pull their punches. But the point is, Patrick was terrified. He couldn't have been more upset if it had been a real head in a real pool of blood.'

'Some people are very squeamish,' said Greenleaf who was always coming across them.

'About real wounds and real blood, yes. But this was only a picture. Now, I'll tell you something. A couple of weeks before he died Patrick was in my house with Tamsin and I showed them some Dali drawings I've got. They're only prints but they're much more horrifying than Salome, but Patrick didn't turn a hair.'

'So he didn't like the picture? What's it got to do with his death? He didn't die from having his head chopped off.'

'Pity,' Marvell said cheerfully. 'If he had we'd only have two-thirds of our present problem. No longer How? but simply Why? and Who?'

He got up as Bernice came in to take him on a tour of the garden.

'I need the advice of someone with green fingers.' She raised her eyebrows at their serious faces. 'Max, you're tired. Are you all right?'

'I'm fine.' He watched them go, Bernice questioning, her companion stooping towards the border plants, his head raised, listening courteously. Then Bernice went up to the fence and he saw that Nancy Gage had come into the garden next door. She evidently had some news to impart, for she was talking excitedly with a kind of feverish desire for the sound of her own voice that women have who are left

116

too much alone. Greenleaf could only remember the last time she had looked like that, but today there was no Oliver to stop her.

His wife's voice floated back to him. 'Tamsin's home, Max.'

Was that all?

He had hardly reached the lawn and heard Bernice say, 'Should we go over?' when Nancy caught him.

'Don't look at my hair,' she said, attracting his attention to it by running her fingers through the strawy mass. 'Something went wrong with the works.'

'Did you say Tamsin was home?'

'We ought to go over, Max, and see if she's all right.'

'Oh, she's all right. Brown as a berry,' said Nancy, and she made a mock-gesture of self-reproach, protruding her teeth over her lower lip. 'There I go. Come back all I said. Oliver says I mustn't talk about the Selbys to anyone, not anyone at all because of you-know-what.'

Marvell tried to catch Greenleaf's eye and when the doctor refused to co-operate, said, 'And what are we supposed to know?'

'Oliver says I mustn't go about saying Patrick didn't die naturally because it wouldn't do him any good.' She giggled. 'Oliver, I mean, not Patrick. He wrote it in a letter so it must be important.'

'Very prudent,' said Marvell.

Greenleaf opened his mouth to say something, he hardly knew what, and closed it again as the telephone rang. When he came back to the garden Nancy had gone.

'Little boy with a big headache,' he called to Bernice. 'Boys shouldn't have headaches. I'm going to see what it's all about and I'll look in on Tamsin on my way back.'

He went to get the car and nearly ran over Edith Gaveston's dog as he was backing it out. After he had apologised

117

she picked up the Scottie and stuck her head through the car window.

'I like your new motor,' she said archaically. 'Only don't blood it on Fergus, will you?'

Fox-hunting metaphors were lost on the doctor. He made the engine rev faintly.

'I see the merry widow's back.' She pointed across The Green. At first Greenleaf saw only Henry Glide exercising his Boxer; then he noticed that the Hallows' windows had all been opened, flung wide in a way they never were when Patrick was alive. The Weimaraner was standing by the front doors, still as a statue carved from creamy marble.

'Poor girl,' he said.

'Tamsin? I thought you meant Queenie for a minute. Poor is hardly the word I'd choose. That house, the Selby business and a private income! In my opinion she's well rid of him.'

'Excuse me,' Greenleaf said. 'I must go. I have a call.' The car slid out on to the tarmac. The Scottie yapped and Edith bellowed:

'Let's hope she hasn't come back to another scandal. One's enough but two looks like . . .'

Her last words were lost in the sound of the engine but he thought she had said 'enemy action'. He had no idea what she was talking about but he didn't like it. I'm getting as bad as Marvell, he thought uneasily, compelling his eyes to the road. Then he made himself think about headaches and children and meningitis until he came to the house where the sick boy was.

10

THE dog Queenie traversed the lawn of Hallows, re-acquainting herself by scent with the home she had returned to after a fortnight's absence. She assured herself that the squirrels' dray still remained in the elm by the gate, that the Smith-Kings' cat had on several occasions crossed the wattle fence and come to the back door, and that a multitude of birds had descended upon the currants, leaving behind them famine and evidence that only a dog could find.

When she had visited the locked garage and peered through the window, whining a little by now, she knew that the man she sought was not on Hallows land. She went back to the house, her tail quite still, and found the woman—her woman as he had been her man—sitting in a bedroom singing and combing her hair as she sang. The dog Queenie placed her head in the silk lap and took a little comfort from the combings that fell upon her like thistledown.

At first Greenleaf thought that the singing came from the wireless. But then, as he came up to the front doors, he realised that this was no professional but a girl who sang for joy, vaguely, a little out of tune. He rang the bell and waited.

Tamsin was browner than he had ever seen her and he remembered someone saying that Mrs. Prynne lived at the seaside. She wore a bright pink dress of the shade his mother

119

used to call a wicked pink and on her arms black and white bangles.

'I came,' he said, very much taken aback, 'to see if there was anything I could do.'

'You could come in and have a drink with me,' she said and he had the impression she was deliberately crushing the gaiety from her voice. She had put on weight and she looked well. The harsh colour suited her. 'Dear Max.' She took both his hands. 'Always so kind.'

'I saw you were back,' he said as they came into the lounge. 'I've been to see a patient in the village and I thought I'd look in. How are you?'

'I'm fine.' She seemed to realise this was wrong. 'Well, what is it you people say? As well as can be expected. You've had awful weather, haven't you? It was lovely where I was. Hours and hours of sun. I've been on the beach every day.' She stretched her arms high above her head. 'Oh, Max!'

Greenleaf didn't know what to say. He looked about him at the room which Bernice used to say was like a set-piece in a furniture store or a picture in *House Beautiful*. Now it was a mess. Tamsin could scarcely have been home more than two hours but there were clothes on the sofa and on the floor, magazines and newspapers on the hearthrug. She had covered the stark mantelpiece with shells, conches, winkles, razor shells, and there was a trail of sand on the parquet floor.

'How's everyone? How's Bernice? If you've been thinking I neglected you, I didn't send a single postcard to anyone. How's Oliver? And Nancy? What have you all been doing?'

Talking, he thought, about your husband. Aloud he said:

'We've all been going on in the same way. No news. Crispin Marvell's with Bernice now giving her some tips about gardening.'

120

'Oh, Crispin.' There was scorn in her voice. 'Don't you think he rather overdoes this country thing of his?' She caught his astonished eye. 'Oh, I'm being mean, I know. But I just don't care about anyone any more—not you and Bernice, Max—I mean the others. The first thing I'm going to do is sell this place and go far far away.'

'It's a nice house,' he said for something to say.

'Nice?' Her voice trembled. 'It's like a great hothouse without any flowers.' He had never thought her mercenary and he was surprised when she said, 'I ought to get eight or nine thousand for it. Then there's the Selby business.'

'What exactly . . . ?'

'Oh, glass,' she said vaguely. 'Test tubes and things like that. It never did terribly well until recently. But a couple of months ago they got a marvellous contract making stuff for Harwell. The money's rolling in. I don't know whether to stay or sell out to the other directors. Really, Max, I'm quite a rich woman.'

There were such a lot of things he longed to ask her but could not. Where, for instance, if the business hadn't been doing well, had the money come from to buy Hallows? Why had Patrick's father committed suicide? What of Oliver Gage? And why, most of all, was she a widow of three weeks' standing, singing for joy when she returned to the house where Patrick had died? It struck him suddenly that in their conversation, so intimately concerned with him, resulting as it did, solely from his death, she had never once mentioned his name.

She took a shell from the mantelpiece and held it to her ear. 'The sound of the sea,' she said and shivered. 'The sound of freedom. I shall never marry again, Max, never.' Freedom, he thought, unaware he was quoting Madame Roland, what crimes are committed in your name!

'I must go,' he said.

121

'Just a minute, I've something to show you.'

She took his hand in her left one and he sensed at the back of his mind that there was an unfamiliar bareness something missing. But he forgot about it as they entered the dining room. The french windows were open and beyond them the wicker furniture on the patio was damp from many rains. This room, he remembered, had always been the most austere in the house, its walls painted white, its window hung with white blinds, so that it looked like a ward in a new hospital. But above the long sleek radiator there had once been a plaque of smoky blue pottery, a tiny island in an ocean of ice. It had been removed to lie rejected and dusty on the table, and in its place hung the picture that had frightened Patrick, dominating the room and emphasising its barrenness by contrast with its own crusted gilt, its blue and gold and bloody scarlet.

'The gardener was here when I got back,' Tamsin said. 'He helped me to hang it. Too absurd, but I thought he was going to be sick.' She smiled and stroked the mother-of-pearl conch. His gaze, withdrawn for a moment from Salome, followed the movement of her hand and he saw what he had sensed. Tamsin had discarded her wedding ring.

'She always seems to be looking at you,' Tamsin said, 'like the Mona Lisa.'

It was true. The painter had contrived that Salome's eyes should meet yours, no matter in what part of the room you were standing.

'Is it valuable?' he asked, thinking of the thousands rich men would pay for monstrosities.

'Oh, no. Mrs. Prynne said it's only worth about twenty pounds.'

She was still looking at the picture but with neither gloating nor horror. As he turned curiously to look at her he thought he saw in her eyes only the same pride of possession one of his sons might feel for a tape recorder or an electric guitar. One woman's meat, one man's poison . . .

'Patrick . . .' he tried to begin, but he could not speak the name aloud to her.

'What's the matter, darling? Not the little boy?'
'No, no, he'll be all right. I'm looking in again tomorrow.'
'You've been so long.'
Instead of sitting down Greenleaf began to pace the room. The circumstances of Patrick's death were beginning to worry him a lot. If in fact there were sufficient grounds to suspect homicide, wasn't it his duty as the first medical man to have seen Patrick's body, as one of those present at the post-mortem, to see justice done? And if he only suspected shouldn't he, as discreetly as possible, probe just enough to discover whether suspicion was well-founded? Some of the information he had was given in confidence and he couldn't tell Marvell about it. But there was one person he could tell, one from whom he had never felt it necessary to keep the secrets of the consulting room. He could tell his wife.

Bernice might well laugh away his fears and this, he had to confess, was what he wanted. She would tell him he was tired, that he needed his holiday.

The television was on, dancers in some grotesque ballet gyrating like demons. He touched the knob. 'D'you want this?' She shook her head. He switched it off and told her.

She didn't laugh but said thoughtfully:

'Tamsin and Oliver. Yes, I can believe that.'

'You can?'

'I couldn't help noticing the way they danced together at Tamsin's party. I never thought Tamsin and Patrick were very happy together. Except—except until a few days before he died. It was when I called on them collecting for the

123

Cancer Campaign. Tamsin kept calling Patrick darling—she was very sweet to him. I remember thinking how odd it was.'

'But apparently Patrick was in love with Freda Carnaby. Freda Carnaby after Tamsin?'

Bernice lit a cigarette and said shrewdly, 'Did you ever notice how very teutonic Patrick was? The first four years of his life must have influenced him a lot. Of course, his mother was German. He was an awfully *kinder, küche, kirche* sort of person, house-proud, passionately neat and tidy. But Tamsin's a sloppy girl. Not in her appearance, she's vain about that, but about the house. You could see it narked Patrick.'

Greenleaf's mind went back half an hour. Again he saw the untidy rooms, the shells dribbling sand.

'Now, Freda Carnaby, she'd be different again. Very brisk and practical—or she used to be. All the time they've been here I've never seen her in slacks or without stockings, Max. Time and time again I've noticed it, women who wear those tight little pointed shoes are mad keen on polishing and turning out rooms. Patrick was cruel, too, you know, Max, but I don't think cruelty would get very far with Tamsin. She's too vague and self-sufficient. But Freda Carnaby! There's a masochist if ever I saw one.'

'You may be right,' Greenleaf said. 'But forget the Carnabys for a minute. What about Gage? I can imagine he might want to marry Tamsin.' He grinned faintly. 'He has marriages like other people have colds in the head. But apparently Patrick was going to divorce Tamsin anyway. Would Gage want to'—He almost baulked at the word—'to *kill* him?'

Bernice said unexpectedly, 'He's rather a violent man.'

'Violent? Oliver Gage?'

'Nancy told me something when they first came here. I

didn't repeat it because I know how you hate that kind of thing. She was proud of it.'

'So?'

'Well, when Oliver first met her she was engaged to some relative of his second wife's. Apparently Oliver just set out to get her. It's a strange way of conducting one's life, isn't it? Oliver and the fiancé were playing billiards in Oliver's house and Nancy came in. Anyway, the fiancé said something to her she didn't like and she told him she'd finished with him and that she was going to marry Oliver. Just like that. Oliver and the fiancé had a violent quarrel and the upshot of it was Oliver hit him over the head with a billiard cue.'

Greenleaf smiled incredulously.

'It isn't really funny, Max. He knocked the fellow out cold.'

'Hitting someone over the head is a long way from poisoning a man in cold blood. Freda Carnaby says she saw him carrying a packet. A packet of what? Glover was very thorough in his tests.' He sighed. 'I've never been interested in toxicology. When I was a student I didn't care much for medical jurisprudence. But I always come back to that in the end. If Patrick was killed, what was he killed with?'

'One of those insecticides?' Bernice asked vaguely. 'You know, you read about them in the papers. I thought they weren't supposed to leave any trace.'

'Not in the body maybe. But there would have been signs. He would have been very sick. The sheets on the bed, Bernice, they weren't clean sheets. I don't mean they were dirty —just not fresh on.'

'Observant of you,' said Bernice. She reached for the cigarettes, caught her husband's eye and let her hand drop.

'Besides, why would Gage want to do away with Patrick? There's always divorce. Unless he couldn't afford two divorces. He'd have to pay the costs of both of them, remember.'

'On the other hand, Tamsin has her private income.'

Greenleaf banged his fist on the chair arm.

'Wherever I go I keep hearing about that private income. What does it amount to, I'd like to know. Hundreds? Thousands? A couple of hundred a year wouldn't make any difference to a man in Oliver's position. Killing Patrick would secure his money too and that might pay for Nancy's divorce. And Tamsin . . .'

Bernice stared.

'You don't mean you think Tamsin . . . ? Would a woman murder her own husband?'

'They do, occasionally.'

She got up and stood before him. He took her hand and held it lightly.

'Don't worry,' he said. 'Maybe I do need that holiday.'

'Oh, darling, I don't want you to get into this. I'm scared, Max. This can't be happening, not here on Linchester.'

Reading her thoughts, he said gently, 'Whatever we have said no-one can hear us.'

'But we have said it.'

'Sit down,' he said. 'Listen. There's something we've got to realise. If someone did kill Patrick, Tamsin must be in it too. She was in the house. I left her and she says she went to bed. You're not going to tell me someone got into the house without her knowing?'

'You said she was happy?'

'Now? Yes, she's happy now. I think she's glad Patrick's dead. After I told her he was dead she didn't cry, but she cried later. She put her arms round the dog and she cried. Bernice, I think she was crying from relief.'

'What will you do?'

'I don't know,' he said. 'Maybe, nothing. I can't go about

126

asking questions like a detective.' He stopped, listening. A key turned in the lock and he heard the boys come into the hall. And if those women talk, he thought, if Nancy goes about saying Carnaby killed Patrick with cyanide and Freda says Gage killed him with a mysterious white packet, I shall begin to lose my patients.

11

'ONE large jar of zinc and castor oil cream, half a dozen packets of disposable nappies, a dozen tins of strained food . . .' Mr. Waller reckoned up the purchases rapidly. 'Gone are the days of all that mashing and fiddling about with strainers, Mrs. Smith-King. I always say you young mothers don't know how lucky you are. A large tin of baby powder and the Virol.' He handed the things to Linda who wrapped each up efficiently and sealed it with sellotape. 'I'm afraid that comes to three pounds seven and tenpence. Say it quickly and it doesn't sound so bad, eh?'

Joan Smith-King gave him a new five pound note.

'It's terrible the way it goes,' she said. 'Still, you can't expect it to be cheap taking five children away on holiday.' She jerked Jeremy's hand from its exploration of Linda's carefully arranged display of bathing caps, each an improbably coloured wig of nylon hair on a rubber scalp. 'I can't tell you how relieved I am to be going at all. My husband's had a very worrying time lately with the business but now everything's panned out well and he'll be able to take a rest.'

'There you are, Mrs. Smith-King. Three pounds, seven and ten, and two and two is ten, and ten and a pound is five pounds. Sure you can manage? What can we do for you, Mr. Marvell?'

'Just a packet of labels, please,' said Marvell who was

128

next in the queue. 'I'm going to start extracting honey in a day or two.' He pocketed the envelope and they left the shop together. Outside Greenleaf's car was parked against the kerb and the doctor was emerging from the newsagent's with the local paper.

'Have you seen it?' Joan Smith-King asked him. 'On the property page. You have a look.'

Greenleaf did as he was told, struggling with the pages in the breeze. The display box among the agents' advertisements wasn't hard to find: Luxury, architect-designed modern house on the favoured Linchester estate at Chant-flower in the heart of rural Notts. yet only ten miles from city centre. Large lounge, dining room with patio, superb kitchen, three bedrooms, two bathrooms.

'She doesn't let the grass grow under her feet,' said Joan. 'I'll be glad to see the back of that dog, that Queenie thing. My children are scared stiff of dogs.' Jeremy listened, learning terror at his mother's knee. 'You might not believe it but Patrick Selby was all set to ruin Den's business just because he once hit that dog. I mean, really! Imagine trying to take away someone's livelihood just because he took a stick to an animal.'

Marvell said softly:

'The dog recovered from the bite, the man it was that died.'

'Now look, I didn't mean . . .' A deep flush spread unbecomingly across her lantern jaws. She stepped back. 'I'm sorry I can't give you a lift. I've got a car full of kids.'

'Come on,' Greenleaf said. He tossed the paper into the back of the car. Marvell got in beside him.

'Sorry,' he said. 'I can see you don't like my detective methods. But it's funny, nobody loved him. His wife was bored with him, he got in the way of his wife's lover—Oh, I've found out about that—his girl friend's brother was afraid of him. Even I was annoyed with him because he cut

129

down my father's trees. Edith disliked him because he played God with her children and now you have Smith-King. I wonder what he was up to there, Max. He told me he was trying to get a Stock Exchange quotation for his shares and expand a bit. Do you suppose he had his cold fishy eye on Smith-King's little lot?'

'I'm not listening.'

'Do you happen to know what Smith-King's line is?'

'Chemicals,' Greenleaf said.

'Drugs mainly. And you realise what that means. He must have access to all kinds of lethal stuff. Or there's Linda. She works for Waller and I don't suppose she's above "borrowing" a nip of something for her mother. And what about that Vesprid stuff?'

Bernice had suggested insecticides. Doubt stirred until Greenleaf remembered how he had answered her. 'You'll have to stop all this, you know,' he said, 'Nobody could have got into the house because Tamsin was there.'

'Not all the time. After you'd gone she went out.'

'What?' Greenleaf signalled right and turned into Long Lane. 'How do you know?'

'Because she came to see me,' Marvell said.

Greenleaf had intended to drop Marvell at the almshouse and drive straight home. But Marvell's statement had suddenly put a different complexion on things. He slammed the car doors and they went up to the house.

'She came,' Marvell said, 'to bring me the currants. You remember the currants? She picked them before the party and put them in a trug.'

'A what?'

'Sorry. I keep forgetting you're not a countryman. It's a kind of wooden basket, a gardener's basket. In all the fuss

I forgot them and Tamsin brought them up to me. It must have been all of midnight.'

Midnight, Greenleaf thought, and she walked through those woods alone. She came down here while Patrick—if not, as far as anyone then knew, dying—was at least ill and in pain. She came to bring a basket of currants! It was no good, he would never understand the habits of the English countryside. But Tamsin was accustomed to them. She had learnt in these two years as much from Marvell as she would have from a childhood spent among the fields and hedgerows.

'I was sitting at the window reading through my stuff and I saw her in the orchard.' Marvell knelt down to tie up a hollyhock that the wind had blown adrift from the porch wall. Greenleaf watched him smooth the stem and press back the torn green skin. 'She looked like a moth or a ghost in that dress. Patrick didn't like bright colours. She was carrying the trug and that straw handbag Edith Gaveston gave her for a birthday present. I was—well, somewhat surprised to see her.' He straightened up and stepped into the porch. Greenleaf fancied that he was embarrassed, for, as he lifted the can and began watering the pot plants that stood on the shelves, he kept his face turned away.

'She came all this way to give you some currants?'

Marvell didn't answer him. Instead he said:

'It means, of course, that anyone could have got into the house. Nobody around here bothers to lock their doors except you and Bernice. I walked back with her as far as her gate.' He stroked a long spear-shaped leaf and, wheeling round suddenly, said fiercely: 'My God, Max, don't you think I realise? If I'd gone in I might have been able to do something.'

'You couldn't know.'

'And Tamsin . . . ?'

'Thought he was asleep,' he said, voicing a confidence he didn't feel. 'Why did she really come?'

Marvell was touching with the tips of his fingers a dark green succulent plant on the borders of whose leaves tiny leaflets grew.

'The Pregnant Frau,' he said. 'You see, she grows her children all round the edges of her leaves and each one will grow into another plant. They remind me of the leaves in Jacobean embroidery. And this one . . .' He fingered the spear-shaped plant, '. . . is the Mother-in-law's Tongue. You see I keep a harem in my porch.'

'Why did she come?'

'That,' Marvell said, 'is something I can't really tell you.' Greenleaf looked at him, puzzled as to whether he meant he refused to tell him or was unable to do so. But Marvell said no more and presently the doctor left him.

He hadn't meant to go back to the village and into Waller's shop. He *meant* to turn off at the Manor gates, but something impelled him on down the hill, unease perhaps, or the knowledge that Tamsin had left Patrick alone on the night he died.

'I want a tin of Vesprid,' he said, cutting short Waller's obsequious greeting. Instead of calling for Linda, Waller got it down himself.

'I suppose I shall have to wear gloves and a mask,' Greenleaf said innocently.

'Absolutely harmless to warm-blooded . . .' Waller's voice trailed away. In this company, and only then, was his confidence shaken. A small voice within his heart told him that to Greenleaf, Howard and their partners, he could never be more than the village medicine man. 'At least . . . well, I don't have to tell *you*, Doctor.'

When he got home Greenleaf transferred some of the

132

liquid into a small bottle and wrapped it up. It was far-fetched, incredibly far-fetched, to imagine Edward Carnaby going back to Hallows after the party, to wonder if Freda's story of Gage and the white packet was a cover-up for her brother's own trip with a tin of insecticide. Or was it? He went back to the car, drove to the post office and sent the package away to be analysed.

12

THE Chantflower Rural Council dustmen hadn't bargained
on the extra load of rubbish that awaited them outside the
Hallows back door. They grumbled loudly, muttering about
slipped discs and no overtime. Queenie stood on the steps
and roared at them.

'Now, if you'll just take these over to Mrs. Greenleaf I'll
give you a shilling,' said Tamsin to Peter Smith-King. He
was only ten and he looked dubiously at the two suitcases.
'The money'll be useful for your holiday. Come on, they're
not really heavy and you can make two journeys. Tell her
they're for Oxfam.'

The little boy hesitated. Then he went home and fetched
his box barrow. He trundled the cases across the Green,
dawdling to throw a stone at the swans, and found Bernice
on the lawn giving coffee to Nancy Gage and Edith Gaveston.

'Can we have a peep?' Nancy asked. Without waiting for
permission she undid the clasps on the larger case. The lid
fell back to reveal, on top of a pile of clothes, a straw handbag embroidered with raffia.

'Oh, dear!' Nancy said.

Edith blushed.

'Of course, I could see she didn't like it,' she said. 'She
barely said two words to me when I gave it to her, but really!'

'There's such a thing as tact,' Nancy said happily.

Edith snatched the bag and opened it.

134

'She hasn't even bothered to take the tissue paper out.'

'Goodness,' Nancy giggled, 'I don't know what use she thinks a handbag is to a starving Asian.' And her eyes goggled as she imagined an emaciated peasant clutching Edith's present against her rags.

'The clothes will be useful though,' Bernice said pacifically.

Nancy stared in horrified wonder as the doctor's wife lifted from the case the slacks and tee-shirt Patrick had worn on the evening of his death. For all their careful laundering they suggested a shroud.

Nancy was on her knees now, unashamedly burrowing. 'Two suits, shoes, goodness knows how many shirts.' She unfastened the other case. 'All Patrick's clothes!'

'Now if it were Paul. . . .' Edith began to describe minutely exactly how she would dispose of her husband's effects in the event of his death. While she was talking Bernice quietly sealed the cases and re-filled the coffee pot.

Returning after a few moments, she was aware from Nancy's expression that the conversation had taken a different and more exciting turn. The two women under the cedar tree wore ghoulish lugubrious looks. As she approached she caught the words 'very unstable' and 'a most peculiar family altogether'.

How difficult it was to close one's ears to gossip, how impossible to reprimand friends! Bernice sat down again, listening but not participating.

'Of course I don't know the details,' Nancy was saying.

'Black, please, Bernice,' Edith said. 'Well, that Mrs. Selby—I mean Patrick's mother—it gets so confusing, doesn't it? That Mrs. Selby ran away with another man. We used to call it bolting when I was a girl.' She pronounced it 'gel', snapping her tongue wetly from the roof of her mouth. 'Apparently they'd always been most happily married,

married for years. Patrick was grown up when she went off. She must have been all of fifty, my dear, and the man was older. Anyway, she persuaded Patrick's father to divorce her and he did, but . . .'

'Yes?' Nancy's forlorn, ghoulish face would have deceived no-one. Her mouth was turned down but her bright eyes flickered.

'But on the day she got her decree Patrick's father gassed himself!'

'No!'

'My dear, it was a terrible scandal. And that wasn't all. Old Mrs. Selby, the grandmother—Tamsin's grandmother, too. Dreadful this in-breeding. Look what it does to dogs! She made a terrible scene at the inquest and shouted that her son would still be alive but for the divorce.'

Bernice moved her chair into the shade. 'You're romancing, Edith. You can't possibly know all this.'

'On the contrary. I know it for certain.' Edith drew herself up, the lady of the manor making her morning calls. 'It so happens I read the account of the inquest in *The Times*. It stuck in my mind and when Nancy mentioned the suicide it all came back to me. Selby, a glass factory. There's no doubt about it being the same one.'

'It's all very sad.' Bernice looked so repressive that Nancy jumped up, scattering biscuit crumbs.

'I must love you and leave you. Oh, Bernice, I nearly forgot to ask you. Have you got the name of that man who put up your summer house?'

'I can't remember. Max would know.'

Nancy waited for her to ask why. When she didn't she said proudly:

'We're going to have that extension done at last, but Oliver says Henry Glide's a bit too pricey. A sun loggia. . . .' She paused. 'And a pram park!'

'Nancy, you're not. . . .? How lovely! '

Nancy pulled in her waist and laughed.

'No, not yet,' she said, 'but Oliver says we can go in for a baby any time I like.'

Trying not to smile at the ludicrous phrase, Bernice found herself saying once more that it was lovely.

'He's been as nice as pie about it and he's all over me. He hasn't been so lovey-dovey for months. Aren't men the end?'

I really ought to thank Tamsin properly for the clothes, Bernice thought after they had both gone. But she felt reluctant to go. Hardly anyone had set eyes on Tamsin since her return. She had become like a sleeping beauty shut up in her glass castle, or like a lurking witch. Bernice couldn't make up her mind whether Tamsin was really bad or whether the gossip had created in her own fancy an unreal Tamsin, a false clever poisoner. Anyway, she must go and be polite.

As she hurried across The Green she encountered Peter sitting on his barrow.

'I went to collect my shilling,' he said, 'but I couldn't find *her*.' He picked up a flat stone and concentrated on sending it skimming across the water. 'The dog's there, though.'

He threw this piece of information out quite casually but Bernice remembered what Max had told her and detected a current of fear.

'I'm on my way over now,' she said. 'Come with me if you like.'

Queenie was indeed there so Tamsin must be too. As she put out her hand to the dog's soft mouth Bernice had a strange feeling that something ought to click. When Tamsin went out without the dog she always shut her in the kitchen. The Weimaraner had been bred as a sentinel as well as a hunter. What was it Max had said last night about Tamsin visiting Crispin Marvell? She stopped and pondered. Tamsin's voice from above broke into her reverie.

'Come on in. I was in the bath.'

Peter slunk past the dog.

'Go into the dining room. I won't be a minute.'

Bernice pushed open the double doors and Peter went in first. The dining room door was just ajar. Peter went obediently ahead but Bernice waited in the hall. The last thing she wanted was to stay and talk.

She expected Peter to sit down and wait for his wages but he didn't. He stopped and stared at something. She could see nothing inside the room but the child's figure in profile, still as a statue. Then he came out of the room again, backing from whatever it was like someone leaving the presence of royalty. He looked at her and she saw that his face was white but stoical.

'Ughugh,' he said.

At once she knew what he had seen. Surely nothing else Tamsin possessed could summon that squeamish pallor even in a child of ten. She closed the door firmly and turned round. A gasp escaped her before she could control it. Tamsin was behind her, awfully near, clean and gleaming as a wax doll in her pink and white dressing gown. Suddenly Bernice felt terribly frightened. Tamsin had come so silently, the child was silent and now all the doors were closed.

'What's the matter with him?'

If he had been her own child Bernice would have put her arms around him and pressed his grubby cheek against her face. But she could give him no physical comfort. He was too old to hug and too young for explanations.

She felt her voice quiver and jerk as she said, 'I think he saw that picture of yours'.

'Too uncanny,' said Tamsin. She looked at Peter as if

138

she were seeing not him but another child staring out through his eyes. 'Patrick was just about your age when he first saw it, but he wasn't tough like you. He ran away and then *it* happened. The fuss and bother—you can't imagine.'

Bernice was just going to ask what had happened when Peter said sullenly, 'Can I have my shilling?'

'Oh, of course you can. It's there, all ready for you on the table.'

The moment of revelation had passed. Tamsin evidently thought Bernice had come to give Peter moral support, for she opened the door to show them both out.

'I only came to thank you for the things.'

'So glad they're useful. And now I must chase you both away. I've got people coming to look over the house.'

Edith was the first person on Linchester to find out that Hallows was sold and she got it from the gardener the Gavestons shared with Tamsin. As soon as he had told her, over mid-morning tea in the utility room, she slipped out to pass the news on to Mrs. Glide. Henry, after all, ought to be pleased that his handiwork found favour in the sight of buyers. On her way back she met Marvell returning from the shops with his sparse groceries in a string bag.

'Only yesterday, it was,' she said, 'and they made an offer on the spot. These *noveaux riches*, they buy and sell houses like you or Paul might job in and out on the stock market.'

Marvell pursed his lips, listening gravely.

'Now when we were young a house *was* a house. One's grandfather had lived in it and in the fulness of time one's grandson would live in it too.' She ended with sublime insensitivity, 'It was *there*, like the Rock of Ages'.

He smiled, murmured something, his mind working furiously. So Tamsin was leaving soon, escaping . . . When

Edith had left him he walked slowly across The Green towards Shalom. He tried the front door and the back. Both were locked. The Greenleafs were townspeople, fearful of burglars, cautious people who yet declared their absence with fastened bolts and conspicuously closed windows. Marvell scribbled a note on the grocer's chit and left it on the back doorstep weighted down with a stone.

Greenleaf found it when he came in at one.

'Can you drop in this afternoon?' he read. 'I've something to tell you. C.M.'

He suppressed a sigh. Tamsin would soon be gone and with her departure surely the rumours would cease. In a fortnight's time he would be off on holiday and when he came back Nancy would be too preoccupied with plans for the baby, Freda too tranquillised by drugs to bother about the vanished Selbys. And yet, he thought as he began to eat the cold lunch Bernice had left him, Marvell might want him for something quite different. In the past he had often been summoned to give an emergency injection of piriton when Marvell was almost numbed and blinded by hay fever. Without a telephone, Marvell was obliged to call or leave a note. It was even possible that he wanted to show the doctor his manuscript, perhaps finished at last. 'I've something to tell you . . .' Patrick. He could only mean Patrick. Probably another undetectable poison theory. Well, it was a way of passing his free afternoon.

As he washed his plate and stuck it in the rack to drain, he thought with the small grain of superiority he allowed himself, that when people spoke of the rewards of a medical vocation they ignored this one: the pleasure of shooting the layman's theories down in flames.

On the wooden bench by the back door Marvell sat reading a recipe for ratafia. It was an old recipe, part of a

140

collection his mother had made while still chatelaine of Linchester, and it had been handed down to her, mother to daughter, from a long line of forbears. Brandy, peach kernels, sugar, honey, orange flower water . . . He had no peaches, nor the money to buy them. The recipe said five hundred kernels and, basking in the warm soft sunlight, he imagined with some delight the preliminary labour to the making of ratafia: the consumption of those five hundred ripe peaches.

Presently he got up and began to walk around the house, touching the bricks, themselves peach-coloured. When he came to the side wall where Henry Glide had discovered the fissure, the terrible sign that the whole building was beginning to subside, he closed his eyes and saw only a red mist filled with whirling objects. Then, because he refused to deny facts and deceive himself, he forced his fingers to seek the crack as a man fearful of cancer yet resolute, compels his hand to probe the swelling in his body.

He jumped when Greenleaf coughed behind him.

'Penny for your thoughts.'

'They're worth more than that,' Marvell said lightly. 'To be precise, a thousand pounds.'

Greenleaf looked at him inquiringly.

'That,' said Marvell, 'is the price Glide is prepared to pay me for this land.'

'You're selling? But this place—I thought you were so fond of it.' Greenleaf described with splayed fingers a wide arc that embraced the squat yet elegant house, the shaven lawn, the orchard and the hawthorn hedge over which honeysuckle climbed, a parasite more lovely than its prey. All this meant little to the doctor but by a terrific effort of empathy he had learned its value to his friend. Even he who could scarcely tell a lily from a rose, felt that here the air smelled more sweetly and the sun's heat was moderated to a mellow beneficence. 'The house. It's so old. It's quaint.' He added helplessly, 'People like that sort of thing. They'd want to buy it.'

Marvell shook his head. He was still holding the recipe book and slowly the thought formed in his mind: I will make some ratafia, just a very small quantity, to take away and to remind me. . . .

Aloud he said to Greenleaf: 'It's falling down. The council says it's not safe to live in. I've had Glide here to look at it and all he said was he'd give me a thousand for the land.'

'How long have you known?'

'Oh, about a month now. A thousand's good going, you know. When the Marvells had Andreas Quercus—he was really called Andrew Oakes or something—when they had him build this place for four old persons of the parish of Chantflower, they didn't care that you could only get to it down a muddy lane and the old persons were too grateful to care.'

With what he felt to be tremendous inadequacy, Greenleaf said: 'I'm sorry. Where will you live?' So many questions leapt to his mind, Have you any money? What will you live on? He couldn't dream of asking them. The proximity of Linchester made poverty a more than usually shameful thing.

'I suppose I can get a room somewhere. I can teach. I shall have my thousand pounds. You'd be surprised what a long time I can live on a thousand pounds.' He laughed dryly and Greenleaf, seeing him in the light of this new knowledge, noticed how gaunt he was. This, then, was why Marvell had sent for him, to unburden his soul. I wonder, he thought, if I could rake up a bit, just to tide him over and have the place made watertight. But Marvell's next words temporarily banished all thoughts of a loan.

'I saw Edith this morning,' he said, 'as I was coming back

from the village. She said Tamsin had sold the house. Some people came and made her an offer.'

'Then she'll soon be gone,' said Greenleaf, relieved.

'And since perhaps neither of us will ever see her again I think I can tell you why she came to see me on the night Patrick died.'

He could see her now as she had come up through the orchard, swinging her basket, all pale in the moonlight with her mist-coloured dress, and paler still when she came within the radiance of his lamp. To his fanciful imagination the currants had seemed like beads of white jade veined with crimson. For all her affected speech, the superlatives that came from her lips so often that they lost their meaning and their force, her face had always been a mask, a shield deliberately maintained to hide intellectual cunning or perhaps a chance trick of nature concealing only vacuity.

'I think she is really very clever,' he said to Greenleaf.

He had put his head out of the window and called to her, then gone into the garden and asked after Patrick.

'Oh, Patrick—he spoiled my lovely party. Maddening creature.'

'You shouldn't have come all this way alone. I would have come up tomorrow.'

'Crispin darling, how should I know what you do here in your enchanted cottage? You might have wanted to make your wine tonight at some special witching hour.'

'I'll walk back with you.'

But she had unlatched the door already and pulled him after her into the little damp kitchen. The scent of the night came in with her and as for a moment she stood beside him, very close with her face uplifted, he could smell the richer perfume she wore, Nuit de Beltane, exotic, alien to an

143

English garden. This essence with its hint of witchcraft enhanced the atmosphere of magic unreality.

'So we sat down,' he said, shaking his shoulders as if to shed a memory. 'We sat a long way from each other but the lamp was between us and you know what oil lamps are. They seem to enclose you in a little snug circle. For a while we talked the usual trivia. Then, quite suddenly, she began to talk about us.'

'You and herself?'

'Yes. She said what a lot we had in common, how we both loved country things. She said there had always been a kind of bond between us. Max, I felt very uneasy.'

'And then?'

'I want you to understand how curiously intimate the whole situation was, the darkness around us, the circle of light. After a while she got up and sat beside me on the footstool. She took my hand and said she supposed I realised she hadn't been happy with Patrick for a long time. She's got one of those thick skins that can't blush, but I felt the blush was there.'

'Everyone can blush,' said the doctor.

'Well, be that as it may, she went on to tell me she knew why I came to the house so often. I didn't say a word. It was horribly awkward. She kept hold of my hand and she said she'd only realised how I felt when I brought her the mead and the roses. Max, believe me, they were just presents for a pretty woman from a man who can't afford scent or jewellery.'

'I believe you.'

'Suddenly she said very abruptly: "Patrick's leaving me. He wants a divorce. In a year I'll be free, Crispin." It was a blunt proposal of marriage.' Marvell went on quickly: 'I don't want marriage. For one thing I can't afford it. Everybody thinks I'm comfortably off, but the fact is most of the

144

money my father got for Linchester went in death duties. What was left was divided between my brother, my sister and myself and my share went on buying the almshouses. The family had sold them long ago. But I couldn't tell Tamsin all that. I felt she might offer me her own money.'

'That mysterious private income,' Greenleaf said.

'Not mysterious. It amounts to about fifty thousand pounds—the capital, that is—but Tamsin can't touch that. It's invested in oil or something and she has the income for life. I believe it would pass to her children, if she ever had any children. So, you see, I couldn't talk about money to her. Instead I said I was too old for her. I'm fifty, Max. She has a lot of natural dignity, but I thought she was going to cry. I don't mind telling you, it was the most embarrassing experience of my life. I suppose I was weak. I said quite truthfully that she was the most beautiful and the most exciting woman I knew. Then I said, "Wait till the year is up. I'll come and see if you've changed your mind." But she only laughed. She got up and stood outside the lamplight and said quite coolly, "Patrick will probably name Oliver Gage. I've been having an affair with him. Did you know?" I realised she was telling me I'd be taking Gage's leavings.'

'And that was all?'

'That was all, or nearly all. I tipped the currants into a bowl and walked back with her, carrying the empty trug. All the way back she was utterly silent and at the gate I left her.'

'Did you see anyone?'

'No-one. It was all so extraordinary, like a dream. But the most extraordinary thing was when I saw her the day after Patrick died, the next day. I didn't want to go, Max, but I felt I should. She was as cold as ice. Not miserable, you understand; the impression she gave me was of happiness and freedom. She might never have come to see me the night before. Then, when she came back, I met her out with

145

Queenie in Long Lane. She waved to me and said hallo. I asked her how she was and she said fine. I'm selling up and leaving as soon as I can. It was as casual as if we'd never been more than acquaintances.'

'Peculiar,' Greenleaf said.

'I don't mind telling you,' Marvell said with a smile, 'it was a hell of a relief.'

PART THREE

13

T w o days later Marvell began extracting honey. Green-leaf's jar would be ready for him in the afternoon, he told the doctor, if he cared to come along and collect it. But at half-past three Greenleaf was still sitting in his deck-chair under the shade of the cedar tree. Bernice had gone out and he was half-asleep. Each time he nodded off, snatches of dreams crept upon him, bright pictures rather than actual episodes. But they were not pleasant images and they mirrored a subconscious of which he had been unaware. Worst of all was the hideous cameo of Tamsin's painting that spiralled and enlarged, twisted and distorted until the head on the plate became Patrick's. He jolted out of sleep to a shrill insistent ringing. Consciousness, reality, came back as with the familiar feel of the canvas, the cool springy grass, he sought tranquillity. Almost in the past days he had found peace of mind. Was it all there still below the surface, a whirlpool of fear and doubt and indecision? The ringing continued and he was suddenly aware that this was not a sound within his head, but the peal of a real bell, the tele-phone bell.

Reminding himself that he was supposed to be on call, he hastened into the morning room. It was Edward Carnaby.

'I thought I wasn't going to get you,' he said reproachfully. 'It's my Cheryl, my daughter. A wasp got her on the lip,

149

Doctor. Her and Freda, they were having a bit of a picnic on The Green and this wasp was on a piece of cake . . .'

'Her lip?' From Patrick, Greenleaf's thoughts travelled back to the dead miner. 'Not inside her mouth?'

'Well, sort of. Inside her lip. She's scared stiff. Mind you, Freda's had something to do with that. They're both sobbing their hearts out.'

'All right, I'll come.'

'I thought we'd seen the last of those wasps,' he said as he walked into the Carnaby lounge. Of course it was the only living room they had but it seemed strange to him to cover the entire centre of the carpet with what looked like a dismantled internal combustion engine spread on sheets of newspaper.

'You'll have to excuse the mess,' Carnaby said, blackening his fingers in his haste to remove obstacles from the doctor's path. 'I borrowed it from the class. I can't seem to . . .'

'Never mind all that!' Freda was on the sofa, squeezing the child in a vice-like hug against her fussy starched blouse. Greenleaf picked his way over to her, stepping gingerly across coils and wheels. He thought he had seldom seen anyone look so tense. Her mouth was set as if she was grinding her teeth and the tears poured down her cheeks. 'Tell me quickly, Doctor, is she going to die?'

Cheryl struggled and began to howl.

'Of course she isn't going to die,' Greenleaf said roughly while Carnaby fumbled at his feet with bits of metal.

'She is, she is! You're just saying that. You'll take her to the hospital and we'll never see her again.'

He was surprised at so much emotion for she had never seemed to care for the child. Patrick's death must have left a real wound into which a new-found maternal love might pour. Patrick, always back to Patrick . . . He looked quickly

150

at Carnaby, wondering when the report would come from the analyst, before saying sharply to Freda:

'If you can't control yourself, Miss Carnaby, you'd better go outside.'

She gulped.

'Let's have a look at it, Cheryl.' He prised Freda off her and gently eased the handkerchief from her mouth. The lower lip was bulging into a grotesque hillock and it reminded the doctor of pictures he had seen of duck-billed women. He wiped her eyes. 'You're going to have a funny face for a day or two.'

The child tried to smile. She edged away from her aunt and pushed tendrils of hair from her big characterful eyes, eyes that she must surely have inherited from her mother.

'Mr. Selby had wasp stings,' she said and darted a precocious glance at Freda. 'I heard Daddy talking about it when they got back from that party. I was awake. I never sleep when I have a sitter.' Her lip wobbled. 'It was that Mrs. Staxton. She said wasps were ever so dangerous and she was scared of them, so Daddy said he'd got some stuff and she could take the tin. And she did, she took it home with her and a jolly good thing, because wasps *are* dangerous.' Greenleaf sighed with silent relief. The analyst's report could hardly matter now. Cheryl's voice rose into fresh panic. 'Mr. Selby *died*. Aunty Free said I might die.'

Greenleaf felt in his pocket for a sixpence.

'There's an ice-cream man by The Green,' he said. 'You'll catch him if you hurry. You get a lolly.' Carnaby looked at him, a foolish smile curling his mouth uneasily as if at some inconsequential joke. 'It'll be good for your lip.'

Freda watched her go with tragic eyes. She evidently thought Greenleaf had got rid of Cheryl in order to impart confidential information as to her probable fate. She looked affronted when he said instead:

151

'Patrick Selby did *not* die of wasp stings. I thought you had more sense, Miss Carnaby. To talk of dying to a child of eight! What's the matter with you?'

'Everybody knows Patrick didn't die of heart failure,' she said stubbornly.

Greenleaf let it pass. Her bosom quivered. The fallen tears had left round transparent blotches on the thin blouse through which frilly fussy straps and bits of underclothes showed.

'He must have died of the stings,' she insisted, 'and he only had four.'

'Five, but it doesn't matter. Cheryl . . .'

'He didn't. He only had four I was sitting with him and I could see.'

Greenleaf said impatiently:

'I should give that a rest, Miss Carnaby.'

Carnaby who had remained silent, ineffectually picking up things that might be ratchets or gaskets, suddenly said rather aggressively, 'Well, it's a matter of accuracy, isn't it, Doctor? It so happens Selby had four stings. I was in the bathroom and I saw the wasps get him. Unless you're counting the one he had a couple of days before.'

'One on his face,' Freda said, 'two on his left arm and one inside his right arm. I thought Cheryl—well, it might have taken her the same way, mightn't it?' The sob that caught her throat came out ludicrously like a hiccup. 'She's all I've got now,' she said. 'Patrick—I could have given him children. He wanted children. I'll never get married now, never, never! '

Carnaby hustled the doctor out into the hall, kicking the door shut behind him. Recalling what Bernice had said, Greenleaf wondered whether Freda's renewed cries were caused by true grief or the possible damage to the paintwork. Then, as he stood, murmuring assurances to Carnaby, the penny dropped. Not the whole penny, but a fraction of it, a farthing perhaps.

'She'll be all right,' he said mechanically. 'There's nothing to worry about.' The worry was all his now.

Then he went, almost running.

Back at Shalom his deck-chair awaited him. He sat down, conscious that on his way round The Circle he had passed Sheila Macdonald and Paul Gaveston without even a smile or a wave. They had been shadows compared with the reality of his thoughts. Before his eyes he could again see Patrick's body in the bed at Hallows that Sunday morning, the thin freckled arms spread across the sheet, sleeves pushed back for coolness. And on the yellowish mottled skin red swellings. One sting on the face, two on the left arm, one on the right arm in the cubital fossa—and a fifth. There *had* been a fifth, about six inches below. Not the old sting; that had been just a scar, a purplish lump with a scab where Patrick had scratched it. The Carnabys could be wrong. Both wrong? They couldn't both be mistaken. Why should they lie? He, Greenleaf hadn't bothered to count the stings on the previous night and when he had visited Patrick in bed the blue cotton sleeves had covered both arms down to the wrists. Tamsin had been uninterested, the others embarrassed. But Carnaby had watched the wasps attack, he had been there in the line of fire, staring from the bathroom window, and Freda had sat at Patrick's feet, holding his hand. Of all the guests at the party they were in the best position to know. But at the same time he knew he wasn't wrong. *Five* stings, one on the face, two on the left arm . . .

'Hot enough for you?' It was a high-pitched irritating voice and Greenleaf didn't have to look up to know it was Nancy Gage.

'Hallo.'

'Oh, don't get up,' she said as he began to rise. 'I'll excuse

153

you. Much too hot to be polite. You men, I really pity you Always having to bob up and down like jack-in-the-boxes.'

'I'm afraid Bernice has taken the boys into Nottingham.'

'Never mind. Actually I came to see you. Don't get me a chair. I'll sit on the grass.' She did so quite gracefully, spreading her pink cotton skirts about her like an open parasol. The renewal of love, strained and contrived though that renewal might be, was gradually restoring her beauty. It was as if she was a wilting pink and gold rose into whose leaves and stems nourishment was climbing by a slow capillarity. 'What I really came for was the name of that man who put up your summer house. We're rather spreading our wings—I don't know if Bernice told you—having an extension to our humble domain, and Mr. Glide—well, he is a bit steep, isn't he?'

'He's in the phone book Swan's the name. J. B. Swan.'

'Lovely. What a wonderful memory! What do you think? As I was coming across The Green I met that funny little Carnaby girl with an enormous lump in her lip. I asked her what it was and she said a wasp sting. She was sucking one of those filthy lollies. I ask you, the last thing! I said, now you run straight home to Mummy—I forgot she hasn't got a Mummy, just an Auntie and what an Auntie! —and get her to put bi-carbonate of soda on it.'

'Not much use, I'm afraid.'

'Oh, you doctors and your anti-biotics. I'm a great believer in the old-fashioned remedies.' She spoke with a middle-aged complacency and Greenleaf thought he knew exactly what she would be like in fifteen years' time, stout, an encyclopaedia of outworn and inaccurate advice, the very prototype of an old wife spinning old wives' tales. 'If I've said it once I've said it a dozen times, Patrick would be alive today if Tamsin had only used bi-carb.' As an after-

154

thought she exclaimed in an advertising catch phrase, 'And so reasonably priced!'

Momentarily Greenleaf closed his eyes. He opened them suddenly as she went on:

'As soon as we got back from that ghastly party I said to Oliver, you pop straight back to Hallows with some bi-carb. He hung it out a bit. Waiting for you to go, I'm afraid. Aren't we crafty? Anyway, he trotted across with his little packet . . .' It was an absurd description of the movement of that graceful, saturnine man, but Greenleaf was too interested to notice. '. . . but Tamsin must have gone to bed. She'd forgotten to lock the back door because he tried it, but that Queenie was shut up in the kitchen and she wouldn't let him in. He went round the back and all the food was still out there and Tamsin had left her presents on the birthday table, the chocolates and that bag and Crispin's flowers. She must have been terribly upset to leave it all like that. He hung about for five minutes and then he came home.'

'I expect she was tired,' Greenleaf said, his thoughts racing. So that was the answer to what he had been calling in his mind the Great White Packet Mystery. Simply Oliver Gage taking bi-carbonate of soda to his mistress's husband. And probably, he thought vulgarly, hoping for a little love on the side. No wonder he waited for me to go.

What Marvell had said about anyone being able to get into Hallows while Tamsin was out had now been shown to be manifestly false. The dog Queenie would guard her master against all comers—against all except one. The feeble motives of Edith Gaveston and Denholm Smith-King evaporated like puddles in the sun. But Tamsin had a motive, or rather many motives which crystallised into a gigantic single drive against Patrick's life. Tamsin was rich now and free. Not to marry Gage whom she had evidently sent about

155

his business, but free to be herself in a glorious scente‹
bright-coloured muddle.

'You're so silent,' Nancy said. 'Are you all right? I'‹
tell you what I'll do. I haven't got a thing on hand thi‹
afternoon. I'll nip indoors and make the poor grass widowe‹
a nice cup of tea.'

Greenleaf hated tea. He thanked her, rested his hea‹
against the canvas and closed his eyes.

14

PATRICK had died too late. Greenleaf repeated the sentence to himself as he came up to the front door of Marvell's house. Patrick had died too late. Not from the point of view of Tamsin's happiness, but medically speaking. Marvell had suggested it at the time the rumours began and Greenleaf had shrugged it off. Now he realised that it was this fact which all the time had been nagging at his mind. Had he died soon after receiving the stings or even if he had had a heart attack on seeing the picture—for Greenleaf was beginning to believe that in Patrick's history it corresponded to the something nasty in the woodshed of Freudian psychology—there would have been no mystery. But Patrick had died hours later.

Why had there been a fifth sting? A wasp in the bedroom? It was possible. Patrick had been heavily sedated. You could probably have stuck a pin in him without waking him. But why should a fifth sting kill him when four had made him only uncomfortable? He banged on the almshouse door for the second time, but Marvell wasn't at home. At last he went round to the back and sat down on the bench.

He had come for his honey and, after much heart-searching, to offer his friend a loan. Talking it over with Bernice after she came back from Nottingham, he had thought he could raise a few hundreds, enough perhaps to have the house made habitable according to the standards of Chantflower Rural Council. It was an awkward mission even though he intended to be quite pompous about it, insisting for the sake of Marvell's pride on the money being repayed at the normal rate of interest—Marvell would have to put his back into the history of Chantefleur Abbey. I am a peasant, he thought, and he is an aristocrat (the serfs to the wolves syndrome again). He might hit me. All alone in the garden, he chuckled faintly to himself. He didn't think Marvell would do that.

Presently he got up and walked about, for he was nervous. He hadn't counted on having to wait. Perhaps Marvell would be away for hours and he would have screwed up his courage in vain.

He passed the kitchen window and looking inside, saw that the table was laden with jars of honey, clear and golden, not the sugary waxen stuff you bought in the shops. There would be a pot for them and a pot for the Gages and the Gavestons. Poor though he was, Marvell was a generous man. Last year the harvest had been poor but there had been a jar on almost every Linchester table. Not Patrick's though. Patrick recoiled from honey as if it were poison.

Greenleaf turned away and began to follow the path towards the orchard. Under the trees he stopped and sat down on the stump of a withered ancient apple Marvell had felled in the winter. Apple, plum and pear leaves made a dappled pattern on the turf as the sunlight filtered through gnarled branches. All about him he could hear the muted yet ominous hum of the bees that had been robbed of their treasure. Marvell, he guessed, had reimbursed them, giving them—as he put it—silver for their gold. He had once shown the doctor the tacky grey candy he made for them from boiled sugar. But, just the same, bewilderment over their loss made them angry.

There were three hives made of white painted wood and

this had surprised Greenleaf the first time he had seen them for he had expected the igloos of plaited straw you see in children's picture books. Beneath the entrance to each hive—a slit between the two lowest boards—was a wooden step or platform on to which the bees issued, trickling forth in a thin dark stream. There was a suggestion of liquid in their movement, measured yet turbulent, regular and purposeful. Marvell had told him something of their ordered social life, and because of this rather than from the interest of a naturalist, he approached the hive and knelt down before it.

At first the bees ignored him. He put his ear to the wall of the hive and listened. From inside there came the sound as of a busy city where thousand upon thousand of workers feed, love, breed and engage in industry. He could hear a soft roar, constant in volume, changing in pitch. There was warmth in it and richness and an immense controlled activity.

For a moment he had forgotten that these insects were not simply harvesters; they were armed. Then, as he eased himself into a sitting position, one of them appeared suddenly from a tree or perhaps from the roof of the hive. It skimmed his hair and sank on the windless air until it was in front of his eyes. He got up hastily and brushed at it and at the others which began to gather about it. How horrible, how treacherous Nature could be! You contemplated it with the eye of an aesthete or a sociologist, and just as you were beginning to see there might be something in it after all, it rose and struck you, attacked you . . . He gasped and ran, glad that there was no-one to see him. Two of the bees followed him, sailing on the hot fruit-scented air. He stripped off his jacket and flung it over his head. Panting with panic and with sudden revelation, he stumbled into Marvell's garden shed.

The bee-keeper's veiled hat and calico coat were suspended from the roof, taped gloves protruding from the sleeves. The clothes looked like a guy or a hanged man. When he had slammed the door between himself and his pursuers, he sat down on the garden roller, sweating. He knew now how Patrick Selby had died.

'But wouldn't he have swelled up?' Bernice asked. 'I thought the histamine made you swell up all over.'

'Yes, it does.' Greenleaf bent over the kitchen sink, washing tool-shed cobwebs from his hands. 'I gave him anti-histamine . . .'

'Why didn't it work, Max?'

'I expect it did, up to a point. Don't forget, Patrick wasn't allergic to wasp stings. But if he was allergic to *bee* stings, as I think he must have been, the histamine reaction would have been very strong. Two hundred milligrammes of anti-histamine wouldn't have gone anywhere. The only thing for people with that sort of allergy is an injection of adrenalin given as soon as possible. If they don't have it they die very quickly.' She shivered and he went on: 'Patrick didn't have that injection. He was heavily sedated, he couldn't call for help and if there was no-one near . . .' He shrugged. 'There would have been a lot of swelling but the swelling would gradually disappear. I didn't see him till ten or eleven hours after he died. His face was a bit puffy and I put it down to the wasp sting under the eye. By the time Glover got to work on him—well! '

'An accident?'

'To much of a coincidence. Four wasp stings and then you get stung by a bee in your own bedroom?'

'He must have known he was allergic to bee stings.'

'Not necessarily, although I think he did. He hated honey. Remember? He knew about it all right and someone else knew too.'

'You mean he told someone?'

'Bernice, I have to say this. At the moment I can only say it to you, but I may have to tell the police. People with this sort of allergy usually find out about it when they're children. They get stung, have the adrenalin, and afterwards they're careful never to get another. But others know about it, the people who were there at the time.' Turning his back on the window behind which Nature seemed to seethe, he looked at the manufactured, man-made things in the modern kitchen, and at civilised, corseted, powdered Bernice. 'Tamsin and Patrick weren't only husband and wife; they were cousins. They'd known each other since they were children. Even if he half-forgot it, never spoke of it, she might remember.

'So simple, wasn't it? Patrick has the wasp stings and he takes the sodium amytal to make him sleep heavily. When he's asleep she goes to the only place where she can be sure of getting hold of a bee, Marvell's orchard, and she takes with her a *straw* handbag.'

'I see. Straw for ventilation, you mean. The bee wouldn't suffocate. She found the bee before Crispin saw her. But why stay there, why make love to him?'

'I don't know. So it was a good excuse for coming? I tell you I don't know, Bernice. But when she got back Patrick was under heavy sedation. You could have stuck a pin in him.'

'Oh, Max, don't!'

'I'm going over to see her now.' He brushed away the warning hand Bernice rested on his arm. 'I have to,' he said.

She was loading cases into the big car, Patrick's car, when he came slowly between the silver-green crinolines of the willows. The car was standing in front of the double doors and Queenie was lying on the driving seat watching the flights of swifts that swooped across the garden, off-course from their hunting ground on The Green.

'I'm leaving tomorrow, Max,' she said. He took the biggest case from her and lifted it into the boot. 'Such a mad rush! I've sold my house and the solicitor's dealing with everything. Queenie and I—we don't know where we're going but we're going to drive and drive. All the furniture—they've bought that too. I shan't have anything but my clothes and the car—I've sold the Mini—and oh, Max! I shall have enough money to live on for the rest of my life.'

The mask had not slipped at all. Only her lips, russet against the egg-shell brown of her face, smiled and swelled the lineless cheeks.

'Leave Queenie,' she said, for Greenleaf, no lover of animals, was caressing the dog's neck to hide his embarrassment and his fear. 'She thinks she's a bird dog. Come into the house.'

He followed her into the dining-room. The picture had been taken down and was resting against the wall. Was she planning to take it with her or have it sent on? She must have seen him hesitate for she took his hand and drew him to a chair by the window. He sat down with his back to the painted thing.

'You don't like it, do you?'

Greenleaf, unable to smile, wrinkled his nose.

'Not much.'

'Patrick didn't like it either.' Her voice sounded like a little girl's, puzzled, naive. 'Really, too silly! He wasn't awfully mature, you know. I mean, people grow out of things like that, don't they? Like being frightened of the dark.'

'Not always.' In a moment he would have to begin questioning her. He had no idea how she would react. In films,

162

in plays, they confessed and either grew violent or threw themselves upon your mercy. His mission nauseated him.

She went on dreamily, apparently suspecting nothing:

'That picture, it used to hang in a room in my grand-mother's house in London. The garden room we called it because it opened into a sort of conservatory. Patrick made an awful fuss the first time he saw it—well, the only time really. My uncle and aunt had come home from America and they stayed a couple of nights with my grandmother. Patrick was terribly spoilt.' She swivelled round until her eyes seemed to meet the eyes of Salome. 'He was nine and I was seven. Grandmother thought he was wonderful.' Her laughter was dry and faintly bitter. 'She never had to live with him. But she was fair, my grandmother, fair at the end. She left her money to me. So sweet! '

If only she would tell him something significant, some-thing to make him feel justified in setting in motion the machinery that would send this sprite-like creature, this breathless waif of a woman, to a long incarceration. And yet . . . Tamsin in Holloway, Tamsin coarsened, roughened in speech and in manners. It was unthinkable.

'That was nice for you,' he said stupidly.

'I loved her, you know, but she was a bit mad. Patrick's father committing suicide, it sent her over the edge. It gave her a sort of pathological fear of divorce.'

This is it, he thought. He needed to hear and at the same time he wanted to stop her. Almost unconsciously he fumbled along the window sill.

'Did you want a cigarette, Max?'

Taking one from the silver box, he said, 'I've given it up,' and lit it with shaking fingers.

'What was I saying? Oh, yes, about Grandmother. She knew I wasn't getting on all that well with Patrick. Funny, she made the match and she wanted us to make a go

163

of it. Just because we were cousins she thought we'd be alike. How wrong she was! After she died we went along to hear the will read—like they do in books. Dramatic, I can't tell you! Patrick wasn't mentioned at all. I don't know if she thought he'd had enough from his father—that went on this house—or perhaps she resented it because he never went to see her. Anyway, she left all her money to me, the income, not the capital, on condition . . .'

She paused as the dog padded in and Greenleaf listened, cursing the diversion.

'On condition Patrick and I were never divorced! '

O God, he thought, how it all fits, a pattern, a puzzle like those things the boys used to have, when you have to make the ball bearings drop into the right slots.

'As if I wanted to be divorced,' she said. 'I can't support myself. They were too busy educating him to bother about me.'

But Patrick had been going to divorce her. She would have had nothing. Without money from her Oliver Gage would have been unable to marry her, for the costs of her divorce and Nancy's would have fallen on him. Like everyone else he must have been deceived about her income until she got cold feet and told him. He pictured her confessing to Gage; then, when he recoiled from her, running ashamed and wretched—for Tamsin, he was sure, was no nympho-maniac—to Marvell, her last resort. When Marvell refused her there was only one way out . . .

'Does anybody know?' he asked sharply, not bothering to conceal a curiosity she must take for impertinence.

'It was so humiliating,' she said, whispering now. 'Every-body thought I was quite well-off, independent. But if Patrick had divorced me I would have been—I would have been destitute.'

164

It was a sudden bare revelation of motive and it recalled him to the real business of his visit.

'Tamsin . . .' he began. The cigarette was making him feel a little dizzy, and to his eyes, focussing badly, the woman in the chair opposite was just a blur of brown and bright green. 'I came to tell you something very serious. About Patrick . . .'

'You mean Freda Carnaby? I know all about that. Please! They were the same kind of people, Max. They really suited each other. If Patrick could have made anyone happy it was Freda Carnaby. But you mustn't think I drove him to it. It was only because of that—Oliver and me . . . I was so lonely, Max.'

He was horrified that she should think him capable of repeating gossip to her and to stop her he blundered into the middle of it, forgetting his doctor's discretion.

'No, no. I meant Patrick's death. I don't think he died of heart failure.'

Was it possible that, immured here since her return, she had heard nothing of the gossip? She turned on him, quivering and he wondered if this was the beginning of the violence he expected.

'He must have,' she cried. 'Max, this isn't something that'll stop me going tomorrow, is it? He was so hateful to me when he was alive and now he's dead—I can feel him still in the house.'

So intense was her tone that Greenleaf half-turned towards the door.

'You see what I mean? Sometimes when I go upstairs I think to myself, suppose I see his writing in the dust on the dressing-table? That's what he used to do. I'm not much of a housewife, Max, and we couldn't keep a woman. They were all frightened of Queenie. When I hadn't cleaned

165

properly he used to write in the dust "Dust this" or "I do my job, you do yours". He *did*.'

Were some marriages really like that? Yes, it fitted with what he had known of Patrick's character. He could imagine a freckled finger with a close-trimmed nail moving deliberately across the black glass, crossing the t, dotting the i.

Although he knew her moods, how suddenly hysteria was liable to wistfulness or vague reminiscing, he was startled when she burst out in a ragged voice:

'I'm afraid to go in his room! He's dead but suppose—suppose the writing was there just the same?'

'Tamsin.' He must put an end to this. 'How many wasp stings did Patrick have?'

She was still tense, hunched in her chair, frightened of the dead man and the house he had built.

'Four. Does it matter? You said he didn't die of the stings.' The air in the room was pleasantly warm but she got up and closed the door. It was stupid to feel uneasy, to remember the frightened charwoman, the Smith-King children. She sat down again and he reflected that they were shut in now with the strong watchful dog and that all the neighbours were away on holiday.

'How many did he have when he came in from the garden?'

'Well, four. I told you. I didn't look.'

'And after—when he was dead?'

He stubbed out the cigarette and held his hands tightly together in his lap. His eyes were on her as she coaxed the Weimaraner to her chair, softly snapping her fingers and finally closing them over the pearled fawn snout.

'There, my Queenie, my beauty . . .' Dry brown cheek pressed against wet brown nose, two pairs of eyes looking at him.

'I think he was stung by a bee, Tamsin.'

At a word from her the dog would spring. For armour

166

he had only the long curtains that hung against the window blinds. Wrapped around him they would protect him for a moment, but the dog's teeth would rip that velvet and then . . . ?

'Stung by a *bee*?'

'Perhaps it was an accident. A bee could have got into the bedroom—'

'Oh, no.' She spoke firmly and decisively for her. 'It couldn't happen that way.' Her mouth was close to the dog's ear now. She whispered something, loosening her fingers from Queenie's dewlap. Greenleaf felt something knock within his chest like a hand beating suddenly against his ribs. But it was ridiculous, absurd, such things couldn't happen! The dog broke free. He braced himself, forgetting convention, pride, the courage a man is supposed to show, and covered his face as the chair skidded back across the polished floor.

15

FOR one of those seconds that take an age to live through he was caught up in fear and fettered to the chair. His eyes closed, he waited for the hot breath and the trickling saliva. Tamsin's voice came sweet and anticlimactic.

'Oh, Max, I'm awfully sorry. That floor! The furniture's always sliding about.'

I make a bad policeman, he thought, blinking and adjusting his chair back in its position by the window. But where was the dog and why wasn't he in the process of being mauled? Then he saw her, puffing and blowing under the sideboard in pursuit of—an earwig!

'You baby, Queenie. She'll hunt anything, even insects.' It was all right. The drama had been nothing but a domestic game with a pet. And Tamsin, he saw, had noticed only that he was startled by the sudden skidding of a chair. 'Talking of insects,' she said, 'it's funny about the bee. It's a coincidence, in a way. You see, that's what happened when Patrick first saw the picture. I'd never seen him before and I was watching from the garden. He ran into the conservatory and there was a bee on a geranium. He put out his hand and it stung him.'

The shock was subsiding now.

'What happened?' he asked rather shakily.

Tamsin shrugged and pulled Queenie out by the tail.

'Why, nothing happened. It made me laugh. Children are

cruel, aren't they? Grandmother and my aunt, they made a dreadful fuss. They put him to bed and the doctor came. I remember I said, "He must be an awful coward to have the doctor for a bee sting. I bet you wouldn't have got the doctor for me," and they sent me to my room. I told him about it when we were older but he wouldn't talk about it. He only said he didn't like bees and he couldn't stand honey.'

'Didn't it ever occur to you that he might be allergic to bee stings?'

'I didn't know you could be,' she said, her eyes wide with surprise.

He almost believed her. He wanted to believe her, to say, 'Yes, you can go. Be happy, Tamsin. Drive and drive—far away!'

Now more than ever it seemed likely that the bee had got there by chance. Hadn't he opened the window in the balcony room himself? Wasps stung when they were provoked; perhaps the same was true of bees and Patrick's killer, alighting on his exposed arm, had been alerted into venom by a twitch or a galvanic start from the sleeping man. If Tamsin were guilty she would clutch at the possibility of an accident and no law could touch her.

'I asked you about an accident,' he said. 'Could a bee have stung him by accident?'

'I suppose so.' Marvell is wrong, he thought. She isn't clever. She's stupid, sweetly stupid and vague. She lives a life of her own, a life of dreams sustained by unearned, unquestioned money. But dreams can change into nightmares . . .

Then she said something that entirely altered the picture he had made of her. She was not stupid, nor was she a murderess.

'Oh, but it couldn't!' Dreamy, vague children often do best in examinations, drawing solutions from their inner lives. 'I know it couldn't. Crispin told me something about bees once. They're different from wasps and when they sting they die. It's like a sort of hara-kiri, Max. They leave the sting behind and a bit of their own inside with it. Don't you think it's horrid for them, poor bees? The sting would still have been in Patrick's arm if it had been an accident. We'd have seen it! '

Unwittingly he had given her a loophole. A guilty woman would have wriggled through it. Tamsin, in her innocence, was confirming that her husband had been murdered.

'Max, you don't mean you think I . . . ?

'No, Tamsin, no.'

'I'm glad he's dead. I am. I tried everything I could to make him forgive me over Oliver and give that woman up. But he wouldn't. He said I'd given him the chance he'd been waiting for. Now he could divorce me and Freda's name wouldn't have to be brought into it at all. Oh, outwardly he was perfectly friendly to Oliver, but all the time he was having his flat in town watched. Oliver and Nancy must come to the party. Then, when he'd got everything lined up he was going to drop his bombshell.' She paused and drew a little sobbing breath, rubbing away the frown lines with her ringless fingers. 'He liked to make people suffer, Max. Even the Smith-Kings. Did you see how he was torturing Denholm at the party?' When Greenleaf said nothing she went on in a shaky voice that fell sometimes to a whisper, 'Oh, that awful party! The evening before, he went straight to Freda's house. I was desperate, I cried and cried for hours. Oliver came but I wouldn't let him in. All those weeks when we were at the flat he'd been hinting that he'd get Nancy to divorce him. My money would pay for that and keep us both. I had to tell him there wouldn't be any money. I did tell him at last, Max, I told him at the party.'

170

And Gage had sat beside her gloomily, Greenleaf remembered. There had been no close sensual dancing after that.

'He went on and on about it. He even tried to think of ways of upsetting the will. But d'you know something? I don't want to be married. I've had enough of marriage.' Her voice grew harsh and strident. 'But I'd have married anyone who would have supported me. Can you see me working in an office, Max, going home to a furnished room and cooking things on a gas ring? I'd even have married Crispin!'

'Marvell hasn't any money,' he said. 'His house is falling down and he won't get much for the land.'

She was thunderstruck. The mask slipped at last and her big golden eyes widened and blazed.

'But his books . . . ?'

'I don't believe he ever finishes them.'

To him it was the saddest of stories, that Marvell should have to leave the house he loved, that her nightmare of the room with the gas ring might become real to him. Because of this her ringing laughter was an affront. Peal upon peal of it rang through the room; hot laughter to burn and cleanse away all her old griefs. The Weimaraner squatted, alert, startled.

'What's so funny?'

She no longer cared what he might think or say.

'It's mad, it's ridiculous! He spent the night here, you know, the night Patrick died. He spent it with me. I was so scared when you made me sit on the bed in the back bedroom. I felt you must sense that—that I hadn't been alone. Oh, Max, Max, don't you see how crazy it is?' He stared, his hurt suspicion melting, for he saw that she was laughing at herself. 'I wanted to marry him for his money,' she said, 'and he wanted to marry me for mine, and the mad thing is we hadn't either of us got a bean!'

16

SHE walked with him to the gate. He shook hands with her and impulsively—because he was ashamed of the thoughts he had harboured—kissed her cheek.

'Can I go tomorrow? Will it be all right, Max?' She spoke to him as if he *were* a policeman or a Home Office official. In denying the possibility of accidental death she had declared, if not in words, that Patrick had been murdered. But Greenleaf knew she hadn't realised it yet. Sometime it would reach her, surfacing on to her mind through that rich, jumbled subconscious, and then perhaps it would register no more strongly than the memory of a sharp word or an unfriendly face. By then she might be driving away on the road that led—where? To another terse young company director who would be fascinated for a time by witchlike innocence? Greenleaf wondered as he drew his lips from her powderless cheek.

'Good-bye, Tamsin,' he said.

When he came to the Linchester Manor gates he looked back and waved. She stood in the twilight, one hand upraised, the other on the dog's neck. Then she turned, moving behind the willows, and he saw her no more.

He entered Marvell's garden by way of the orchard gate. The bees were still active and he gave the hives a wide berth.

It occurred to him that Marvell might still be out but if this were so he would wait—if necessary all night.

By now it was growing dark. A bat brushed his face and wheeled away. For a second he saw it silhouetted against the jade-coloured sky like a tiny pterodactyl. He came to the closed lattice and looked in. No lamps were lit but the china still showed dim gleams from the last of the light. At first he thought the room must be empty. The stillness about the whole place was uncanny. Nothing moved. Then he saw between the wing and the arm of a chair that had its back to the window a sliver of white sleeve and he knew Marvell must be sitting there.

He knocked at the back door. No footsteps, no sound of creaking or the movement of castors across the floor. The door wasn't locked. He unlatched it, passed the honey-laden table and walked into the living room. Marvell wasn't asleep. He lay back in his chair, his hands folded loosely in his lap, staring at the opposite wall. In the grate—the absurd pretty grate that shone like black silver—was a pile of charred paper. Greenleaf knew without having to ask that Marvell had been burning his manuscript.

'I came earlier,' he said. 'I had something to ask you. It doesn't matter now.'

Marvell smiled, stretched and sat up.

'I went to tell Glide he could have the land,' he said. 'You can take your honey, if you like. It's ready.'

Greenleaf would never eat honey again as long as he lived. He began to feel sick, but not afraid, not at all afraid. His eyes met Marvell's and because he couldn't bear to look into the light blue ones, steady, mocking, unfathomably sad, he took off his glasses and began polishing them against his lapel.

'You know, don't you? Yes, I see that you know.'

Hazily, myopically, Greenleaf felt for the chair and sat down on the edge of it. The wooden arms felt cold.

'Why?' he asked. His voice sounded terribly loud until he realised that they had been speaking in whispers. 'Why, Crispin?' And the Christian name, so long withheld, came naturally.

'Money? Yes, of course, money. It's the only real temptation, Max. Love, beauty, power, they are the obverse side of the coin that is money.'

From his dark corner Greenleaf said: 'She wouldn't have had any if Patrick had divorced her. That was the condition in the will.' The man's surprise was real but, unlike Tamsin, he didn't laugh. 'You didn't know?'

'No, I didn't know.'

'Then . . . ?'

'I wanted more. Can't you see, Max? That place, that glass palace. . . . With the money from that and his money and her money, what couldn't I have done here?' He spread his arms wide as if he would take the whole room, the whole house into his embrace. 'Tell me—I'm curious to know— what did she want from me?'

'Money.'

He sighed.

'I thought I would know love,' he said. 'But, of course, I do see. That kind of sale is a woman's privilege. May I tell you about it?'

Greenleaf nodded.

'Shall we have some light?'

'I'd rather not,' the doctor said.

'Yes, I suppose you would feel that way. I think that like Alice I had better begin at the beginning, go on till I get to the end, and then stop.'

What sort of a man was this that could talk of children's books on the edge of the abyss?

'As you like.'

'When Glide told me about the house I thought I had come to the end of my world. The bright day is done and we are for the dark.' He paused for a moment and rubbed his eyes. 'Max, I told you the truth and nothing but the truth, but I didn't tell you the whole truth. You know that?'

'You told me one lie.'

'Just one. We'll leave that for the moment. I said I'd begin at the beginning but I don't know where the beginning was. Perhaps it was last year when Tamsin was helping me extract the honey. She said Patrick didn't like it. He was afraid of bees and everything associated with them, but he'd only been stung once. That was when he was a little boy at their grandmother's house. He'd been frightened by a picture of a girl holding a man's head on a plate and he'd run into the conservatory. A bee stung him on his hand.'

'Yes, she told me.'

'Max, she didn't know why the doctor had been sent for. She thought it was because Patrick was a spoiled brat. She didn't know why the doctor had given him an injection, had stayed for hours. But at the time I was reading a book about allergies. I was interested because of that damned hay fever. When she'd gone I looked up bee stings and I found why the doctor had stayed and what kind of an injection Patrick had had. He must have been allergic to bee stings. I didn't say anything to Tamsin. I don't know why not. Perhaps, even then . . . I don't know, Max.'

'Some people grow up out of allergies,' Greenleaf said.

'I know that too. But if it didn't come off, who would know?'

'It did come off.'

Marvell went on as if he hadn't spoken.

'It wasn't premeditated. Or, if it was, the meditation only

took a few minutes. It began with the picture. I don't know
this part—I'm only guessing—but I think that when Tamsin
was offered the picture things were all right between her and
Patrick, as right as they ever were. Of course she knew he'd
hated it when he was a child but she thought he'd grown
out of that.'

'When it arrived,' Greenleaf said slowly, 'she must have
been trying to patch things up between them. He might think
she'd sent for it to annoy him, so she had it put in her room,
a room he never went into.'

'I saw it—and, Max, I told them about it in all innocence!'

'Tamsin was past caring then.'

He must be kind, not a policeman, not an inquisitor.

'Go on,' he said gently.

'It was only when Patrick reacted the way he did that I
remembered the bee sting. The temptation, Max! I was sick
with temptation. I don't know how I got down those stairs.'

'I remember,' Greenleaf said. 'I remember what you said.
Something about the eye of childhood fearing a painted
devil. I thought it was just another quotation.'

Marvell smiled a tight bitter smile.

'It is. Macbeth. It doesn't mean that in the text. It doesn't
mean that Macbeth was looking with a child's memory, but
only in a childish way. I suppose it was my subconscious that
gave it that meaning. I knew that Patrick feared it because
of what had happened when he *was* a child. Then the wasps
got him. Even then I couldn't see my opportunity. I wasn't
sure of Tamsin. I'd never made love to her. For all I knew I
was just an old pedagogue to her, a domestic science teacher.
At midnight she came into my orchard.'

'But she wasn't carrying that straw bag,' Greenleaf said
quickly. 'It wasn't at all her style. Besides, when Oliver Gage
came round with the bi-carb Tamsin was out but the bag
was on the birthday table.'

Marvell got up and, crossing to the window, opened the casement. 'My one lie,' he said. Greenleaf watched him drawing in great breaths of the dark blue air. 'Will you be in a draught?'

'It doesn't matter.'

'I felt—I felt suddenly as if I was going to faint.' From shock? From fear? Greenleaf wondered with dismay if for months now Marvell hadn't been getting enough to eat. 'I'll close it now.' He shifted with precise fingers the long wisps of Tradescantia. 'I'd like the lamp. You don't mind?' When Greenleaf shook his head, he said urgently, 'Darkness—darkness is a kind of poverty.'

When the lamp was lit Marvell put his hands round it. They had the opacity age brings and the thought came to Greenleaf that had his son's hands covered that incandescence the light would have seeped through them as through red panes.

'It all happened as I've told you,' Marvell went on, 'except that I didn't say no to Tamsin. I told her I'd walk back with her but that I'd left my jacket in the orchard. I went down to the shed to get my gloves and my veil and a little box with a mesh lid. Someone had once sent it to me with a queen bee in it.

'When we got to Hallows I went in with her. She'd told me you'd given Patrick a sedative and we both knew I was going to stay with her. We didn't say it but we knew. She didn't want to look at Patrick and she went to take a shower. While she was in the bathroom and I could hear the water running I went into Patrick's room. I still wasn't sure the sting wouldn't wake him. There was a big pincushion on the dressing-table. I took a pin and stuck it very lightly into him. He didn't stir.'

Greenleaf felt a deathly cold creep upon him, a chill that culminated in a tremendous galvanic shudder.

177

'Then I put the bee on his arm and I—I teased it, Max, till it stung him.' He slid his hands down the lamp until they lay flat and fan-spread on the table. 'I can't tell you how I hated doing it. I know it's sentimental, but the bees were my friends. They'd worked for me faithfully and every year I took their honey away from them, all their treasure. They'd fed me—sometimes I didn't have anything but bread and honey to eat for days on end. Now I was forcing one of them to kill itself for my sake. It plunged its sting into those disgusting freckles. . . . My God, Max, it was horrible to see it trying to fly and then keeling over. Horrible! '

Greenleaf started to speak. He checked himself and crouched in his chair. They were not on the same wavelength, a country G.P. and this naturalist who could kill a man and mourn the death of an insect.

Marvell smiled grimly. 'I had to stay after that. I had to stay and see she didn't go into that room. She hated Patrick but I don't think she would have stood by and let him die.' He stood up straight and in the half-dark he was young again. 'I made love to Tamsin under the eyes of Herod's niece.' His shoulders bowed as if to receive age like a cloak. 'At the time I thought it a pretty conceit. I should have remembered, Max, that they might both understand the desires of old men. I thought it was love.'

He sat on the table edge and swung his legs.

'I left at four. She was asleep and Patrick was dead. I checked. The dog came upstairs and I shut her in with Tamsin.

'Perhaps I was vain, Max, perhaps I thought I had a kind of *droit de seigneur*, perhaps I'm just old-fashioned. You see, I thought that still meant something to a woman, that she would have to marry me. When she made it plain she didn't want me, I felt—My God! She'd wanted me before, but I'm fifty and she's twenty-seven. I thought . . .'

'Crispin, I *do* see.' It was more horrible than Greenleaf had thought it could be. He hadn't anticipated this grubbing into the roots of another man's manhood. Please don't. I never wanted to. . . .'

'But it was only money, always money.' He laughed harshly but quite sanely into Greenleaf's face. 'It's all better now, all better. I am Antony still! '

'But why?' Greenleaf asked again. 'Why tell me so much?' He felt angry, but his anger was a tiny spark in the fire of his other emotions: amazement, pity and a kind of grief. 'You led me into this. You made me suspect.' He spread his hands, then gripped the chair arms.

Marvell said calmly: 'Naturally, I intended to get away with it at first.' His face was a gentle blank. He might have been describing to the doctor his methods of pruning a fruit tree. 'But when I knew that I had killed Patrick in vain, for nothing, I wanted—I suppose I wanted to salvage something from the waste. They say criminals are vain.' With a kind of wonder he said: 'I *am* a criminal. My God, I hadn't thought of it like that before. I don't think it was that sort of vanity. All the moves in the game, they seemed like a puzzle. I thought a doctor and only a doctor could solve it. That's why I picked on you, Max.'

He made a little half-sketched movement towards Greenleaf as if he was going to touch him. Then he withdrew his hand.

'I meant to try to get you interested. Then Nancy started it all off for me. I've always thought hatred was such an uncivilised thing, but I really hated Tamsin. When you suspected her I thought, to hell with Tamsin! ' He raised his eyebrows and he smiled. 'If it had come to it, perhaps. . . . I don't think I could have let her suffer for what I did.'

'Didn't you think what it would mean if I found out?'

Marvell moved to the fireplace and taking a match from the box on the mantelpiece struck it and dropped it among the charred sheets of the manuscript. A single spiring flame rose and illuminated his face.

'Mac,' he said, 'I had nothing to hope for. I've had a fine life, a good life. You know, I've always thought that was the true end of man, tilling the soil, husbanding the fruits of the soil, making wonderful things from a jar of honey, a basket of rose petals. In the evenings I wrote about the things of the past, I talked to people who remembered like me the days before taxes and death duties took away almost everything that made life for people like me a kind of—a kind of golden dream. Oh, I know it was a dream. I wasn't a particularly useful member of society but I wasn't a drag on society either. Just a drone watching the workers and waiting for the summer to end. My summer ended when Glide told me about this house. That's what I meant when I said the bright day was done and I was for the dark.' As the flame died he turned from the fireplace and clasping his hands behind his back looked down at Greenleaf.

'I don't know what to do,' the doctor said. It was the phrase of despair, the sentence desperate people used to him from the other side of the consulting room table.

Marvell said practically: 'There's only one thing you can do, isn't there? You can't be a party to a felony. You're not a priest hearing confession.'

'I wish,' Greenleaf said, a world of bitterness making his voice uneven, 'I wish I'd kept to it when I said I didn't want to hear.'

'I should have made you.'

'For God's sake!' He jumped up and they faced each other in the circle of yellow light. 'Stop playing God with me!'

180

'Max, it's all over. I'll have a wash, I'll put some things in a bag. Then we'll go to the police together.' As the doctor's face clouded he said quickly. 'You can stay with me if you like.'

'I'll wait for you.' Not here though. In the garden. 'I'm not a policeman.' How many times had he said that in the past weeks? Or had he in fact said it only to himself in a repetitive refrain that irritated his days and curled itself around his sleep?

Marvell hesitated. Something leaped into his eyes but all he said was: 'Max . . . forgive me?' Then when the doctor said nothing he picked up the lamp and carried it before him into the passage.

The garden was a paradise of sweet scents. At first Greenleaf was too bemused, too stunned for thought. He moved across the grass watching his own shadow going before him, black on the silvered grass. The great trees shivered and an owl flying high crossed the dappled face of the moon.

In the house behind him he could see the lamplight through a single window, the bathroom window. The rest of Marvell's home was as dark and as still as if Glide had already bought it, as if it was waiting with a kind of squat resignation the coming of the men with the bulldozers. A year would elapse perhaps, only six months if the weather held. Then another house would arise, the mock-Tudor phoenix of some Nottingham business man, on the ashes of the cottages Andreas Quercus had made when George I held court in London.

The light was still on. No shadow moved across it. I must leave him in peace, Greenleaf thought, for a few more minutes. He has lived alone, loving loneliness, and he may never be alone again.

Avoiding the orchard where the bees were, he walked in

a circle around the lawn until he came once more to the back door. He went in slowly, feeling his way in the dark. His fingers touched the uneven walls, crept across the plates, the framed lithographs. At the bathroom door he stopped and listened. No sound came. Suddenly as he stood, looking down at the strip of light between door and floor, he thought of another house, another bathroom where Tamsin had showered her slim brown body while her lover gave to Patrick the sting that was his own individual brand of death.

He paced the narrow passage, sickness churning his belly and rising into his throat. When he could stand it no more he called, 'Crispin!' The silence was driving him into a panic. 'Crispin, Crispin!' He banged on the heavy old door with hands so numb and nerveless that they seemed no part of his tense body.

In a film or a play he would have put his shoulder to that door and it would have yielded like cardboard, but he knew without trying how impossible it was for him to attempt to shift this two-inch thick chunk of oak. Instead he groped his way back, wondering what that noise was that pumped and throbbed in the darkness. When he reached the open air he realised that it was the beating of his own heart.

He had to make himself look through that lighted window, pulling his hands from his eyes as a man pulls back curtains on to an unwelcome day. The glass was old and twisted, the light poor but good enough to show him what he was afraid to see.

The bath was full of blood.

No, it couldn't be—not all blood. There must be water, gallons of water, but it looked like blood, thin, scarlet and immobile. Marvell's face rested above the water line—the blood line—and the withdrawing of life had also withdrawn age and the lines of age. So had the head looked in Salome's silver platter.

Greenleaf heard someone sob. He almost looked round. Then he knew that it was he who had sobbed. He took off his jacket, struggling with it as a man struggles with clothes in a dream, and wrapped it around his fist and his arm. The window broke noisily. Greenleaf unlatched the casement and squeezed in over the sill.

Marvell was dead but warm and limp. He lifted the slack arms and saw first the slashes on the wrists, then the cut-throat razor lying beneath the translucent red water. Greenleaf knew no history but there came to him as he held the dead hands the memory of a lecture by the professor of Forensic Medicine. The Romans, he had said, took death in this way, letting out life into warm water. What had Marvell said? 'I am Antony still' and 'Max, forgive me.'

Greenleaf touched nothing more although he would have liked to drain the bath and cover the body. He unlocked the door, carrying the lamp with him, and left Marvell in the darkness he had chosen.

Half-way across the living room he stopped and on an impulse unhooked from the wall the olive-coloured plate with the twig and the apple. As it slid into his pocket he felt with fingers that had palpated human scars the bruise on the underside of the glazed fruit.

The wood with its insinuating branches was not for him tonight. He blew out the lamp and went home by Long Lane.

On Linchester the houses were still lit, the Gages' noisy with gramophone music, the Gavestons' glowing, its windows crossed and re-crossed by moving shadows. As he came to Shalom a taxi passed him, women waved, and Walter Miller's face, brown as a conker, grinned at him from under a pink straw hat. Home to Linchester, home to autumn, home to the biggest sensation they had ever known. . . .

Bernice opened the door before he could get his key out.

'Darling, you're ill! What's happened?' she cried and she put her arms round him, holding him close.

'Give me a kiss,' he said, and when she had done so he lifted her arms from his neck and placed them gently at her sides. 'I'll tell you about it,' he said, 'but not now. Now I have to telephone.'

A DEMON IN MY VIEW

Ruth Rendell

In a gloomy cellar the figure of a woman leans against the wall. Palely beautiful, she makes no move when the man advances on her from the shadows, puts his hands around her neck and strangles her.

Arthur Johnson is prim, fifty and a bachelor. To the outside world he is the very picture of respectability. No one knows of the dark lusts that bind Arthur to the pale lady in the cellar.

Then, one day, the lady is gone and a new victim must be found . . .

'Absolutely unputdownable . . . it is stamped on every page with the firm mark of a distinguished storyteller at the very height of her powers' *Graham Lord, Sunday Express*

FROM DOON WITH DEATH

Ruth Rendell

'Britain's leading lady crime novelist' *Sunday Express*

Margaret Parsons and her husband had just moved back to the small village in which she had grown up. They lived an uneventful, anonymous life and had nothing to hide.

Why then is Margaret found horribly strangled in a wood? Why do her childhood friends deny even having known her? And who is the secret admirer who has been sending her books of poetry?

SOME LIE AND SOME DIE

Ruth Rendell

For a while the pop festival at 'Sundays' went well. The sun shone, the groups played and everyone – except a few angry neighbours – seemed to enjoy themselves.

Then the weather changed. And in a nearby quarry two lovers found a body that made even Inspector Wexford's stomach lurch.

Dawn Stonor had been a local girl – back from London on a flying visit that not even her mother could explain – and the only clue that Wexford had was her strange connection with the star of the festival . . .

'One of the best crime novelists writing today' *Sunday Express*

NO MORE DYING THEN

Ruth Rendell

The mysterious death of little Stella Rivers was still fresh in the minds of everyone who lived in Kingsmarkham. No one wanted a repetition of that harrowing time. So when a five-year-old boy vanished the whole police force moved feverishly into action.

Chief Inspector Wexford thinks he knows all the obvious places to search . . . and whom to suspect. But there are no clues whatsoever – none, that is, until the anonymous letters start arriving . . .

MURDER BEING ONCE DONE

Ruth Rendell

'DEATH ONLY IS REAL'
So read the grim epitaph on a family vault. Appropriate
enough, for it was here, amid the decay and desolation of
Kenbourne Vale Cemetery, that the girl's body was found.

Detective Chief Inspector Wexford was in London for a rest
but he soon found himself deeply involved in this baffling
case.

A SLEEPING LIFE

Ruth Rendell

Kingsmarkham was one of those close-knit communities where everyone knew everyone else's business; so when Rhoda Comfrey's body was found under a hedge, Chief Inspector Wexford felt sure the case would be a simple one.

But although the victim was a familiar face to the locals, there was absolutely no evidence that she existed – no address book, no driving licence – nothing but forty-two pounds and three keys. But when Wexford begins to tackle the case, it turns into a maddening labyrinth of blind alleys.

A JUDGEMENT IN STONE

Ruth Rendell

Eunice Parchman applied for the job of housekeeper to the Coverdale family on the same kind of impulse that made her buy a box of chocolates or smother her invalid father. *If* they had been less desperate for help in their country house, they might never have employed her. *If* they had treated her less kindly, she might never have hated them. *If* they had never discovered her terrible secret, she might not have murdered them.

'The best woman crime writer we have had since Sayers, Christie, Allingham and Marsh' *Edmund Crispin, Sunday Times*

'Ruth Rendell is at the very height of her powers. It will be an amazing achievement if she ever writes a better book' *Daily Express*

'This could become a classic among chillers' *H. R. F. Keating, The Times*